THE MASQUERADE
SECOND EDITION

By Mark Rein·Hagen, Ian Lemke, and Mike Tinney,
with Frank Branham and Geoffrey Fortier

Mind's Eye Theatre

Credits:

Design: Mark Rein•Hagen with Mike Tinney and Ian Lemke

Developement: Ian Lemke and Mike Tinney

Authors: Geoffrey Fortier, Frank Branham, Mark Rein•Hagen, Ian Lemke, and Mike Tinney

Word of Darkness created by: Mark Rein•Hagen

Editing: Brian Campbell

Art Direction: Richard Thomas

Interior Photography: J. Lank Hancock

Cover Design: Lawrence Snelly and Matt Milberger

Layout and Typesetting: Kathleen Ryan

Authors of The Masquerade, First Edition: Mark Rein•Hagen, William Spencer-Hale, Jason Strayer, Ian Lemke, Mike Tinney, Frank Branham, Geoffrey Fortier, Chris Cowart, Darren McKeeman, and Sandra L. West

Playtesters: Unfortuantely, the number of players who playtested The Masquerade, Second Edition are so many that we cannot mention them all by name, though we would like to thank each and every one of them for their insight and input. We would also like to thank the playesters of **The Apocalypse** whom we forgot to mention. We would like to offer our sincerest apologies for having forgotten them and out thanks to the Storytellers and players.

Models: (Brujah) Kirsten Huskeson, Allen Tower, Mark White (Gangrel) Kris Baesman, Lance Boggs, Wade Lee (Malkavian) Brian Black, Donna Howard, Matt Phillips (Nosferatu) Jennifer Hartshorn, Scott Leonard, Eddie Maise (Toreador) Kalina Mercer, Paul Mercer, Heidi Pritchett (Tremere) Shawn Carter, Maureen Kumpf, and Heather Pritchett

WHITE WOLF
GAME STUDIO

780 PARK NORTH BLVD.
SUITE 100
CLARKSTON, GA 30021
USA

Sanctioning Information

If you would like to run a Mind's Eye Theatre game at a convention or similar large venue and plan on charging for the event, you need to obtain sanctioning from us in advance. Our support materials are top-notch, and our costs are low. Recently, Night Owl Productions has become an official subsidiary of White Wolf Game Studio. Night Owl is the place to inquire concerning sanctioning for Live-Action games. They can be reached at:

Night Owl Productions
4598 Stonegate Industrial Blvd.
Stone Mountain, GA 30083

THE MASQUERADE
SECOND EDITION

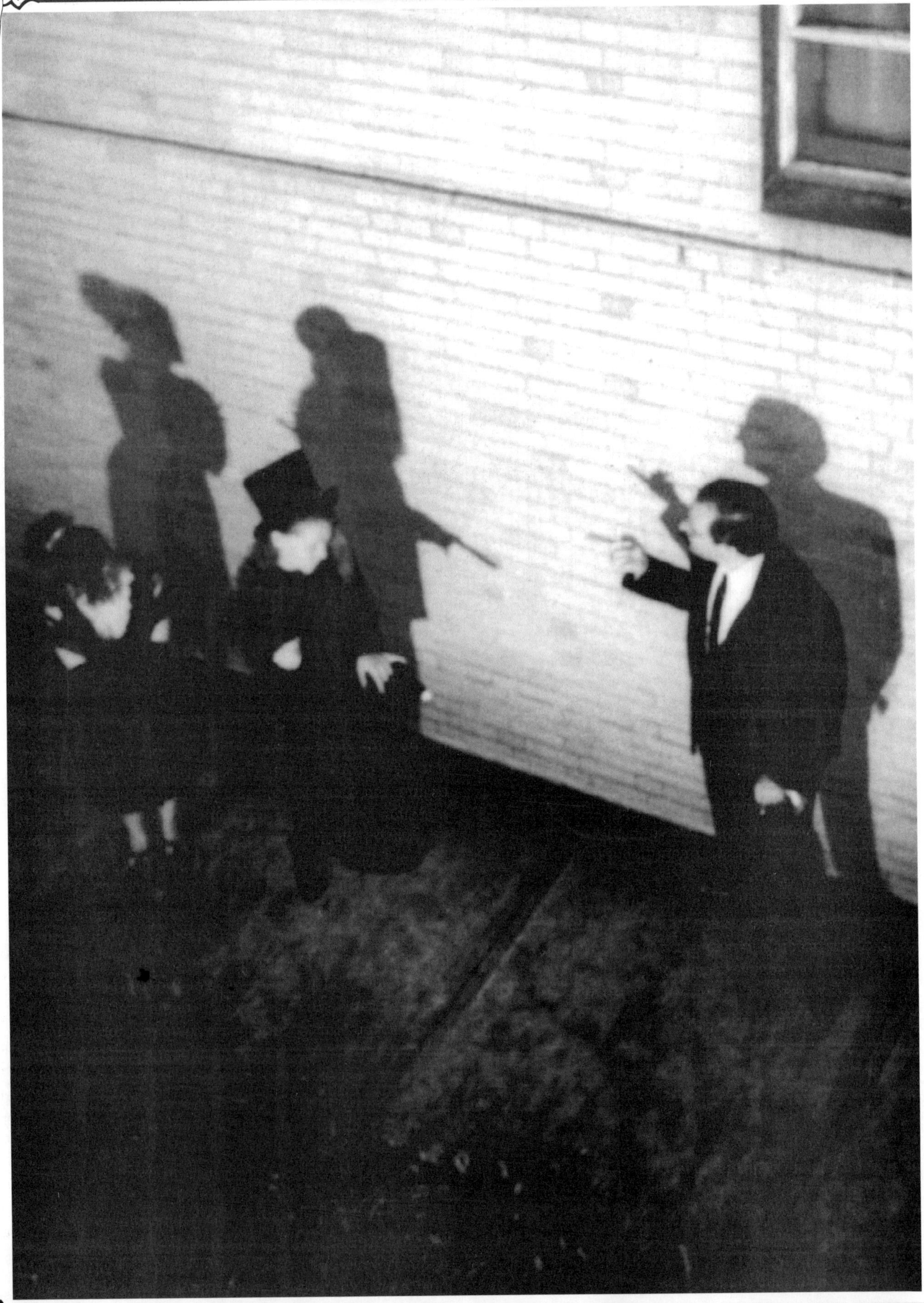

Prelude: Hammer and Anvil

Courtland frantically ran down the street. A thin sheet of bloodsweat matted his brow. He couldn't fathom how he got into this mess, but he knew he had to get out of it, and soon. His clan, the Ventrue, were already displeased with him for his frequently frivolous association with the Toreador. Ahh, yes, the Toreador. That's how he got into this mess... the Toreador, of course, and that mysterious Mr. Tippadeux who frequented their gatherings. Mr. Tippadeux, yes, it was all *his* fault.

Courtland's footsteps echoed through the Barrens. Hardly anyone was around so late, save for a bum down the street. He ducked into a nearby alley as he made a conscious effort to regain his composure. Then he heard the sultry voice of Mr. Tippadeux's companion. Her ashen trench coat blended into the grimy surface of the brick wall behind her.

"Hello again, Court-Land," Consuela purred. "Here for your next fix?" Courtland was furious with himself for getting into this situation, but he couldn't control his urges. Whatever these Setites were mixing with the vitæ they had given him, it was irresistible. His hands were trembling. *Keep it cool*, he thought to himself. *They don't have to know you need it this badly.*

"If you want your next fix, Court-Land, you'll have to do something for us first." Consuela's voice was absolutely captivating. Courtland seemed to be hanging on her every word.

"Now, Court-Land" Consuela whispered into his ear as her lips grazed him ever so teasingly, "You're going to help us with one of our problems. As you know, the Setites hold an auction once a month. It seems that the prince has taken offense to this and would like to see our business shut down."

Consuela reached out and took Courtland's hand. "She will no doubt send her Sheriff, Maddox," Consuela continued. She pressed another vial into Courtland's hand. "All you have to do is make certain Maddox gets the same habit you do. If you fail..." She closed her hand around his wrist like a vice. "Let's just say that there are worse things than not getting your fix." She drew him closer, kissed him gently on the forehead and then slowly drifted into the shadows.

Courtland was defeated. He knew that the Setites had him, body and soul. Now he would have no choice but to do their bidding and exist from one fix to the next. If the Ventrue elder ever found out, he'd be cast out for certain. The Harpies would be just as ruthless— one well-placed scandal could ruin him socially with the Toreador. The thought of losing his clan and his status made him ill, but he was trapped. He could do nothing more than comply with her bidding... for now.

"No," Courtland insisted. "It's over."

"On the contrary, my love, it's just beginning."

Courtland's eyes were drawn to the small vial of vitæ that dangled on a chain around Consuela's neck. "How badly do you want it?" Consuela asked. Her hand gently stroked Courtland's cheek. Courtland didn't answer; he didn't need to speak. The trembling of his hands and the fresh coat of bloodsweat covering his brow was the only answer Consuela needed. Courtland tried to mutter something, but he could not. As Consuela yanked the chain from her neck, he began to salivate. She gently tilted his head back and poured the rich vitæ down his throat.

The liquid felt like an icy fire. Hot and cold all at once, it sent spasms of pleasure throughout his body. Its fiery tendrils flowed through every inch of his body, and the Beast within him reveled. He opened his eyes to the now familiar glow of the world. His vision sharpened, his mind focused and euphoria spread throughout his body. He smiled.

He briefly entertained a faint hope. Could his addiction be cured? Hopefully, he might someday find a Kindred who could help him. That, however, would be a difficult task indeed. He had far more important matters to handle. After all, hadn't Consuela chosen *him?* As he licked the taste of dried blood from his teeth, the mere thought of her now filled his undead body with warmth. It felt good to belong to someone.

Courtland left the Barrens with a smile on his face, and his thoughts turned to the Sheriff. He had never much liked Maddox anyway. If anyone was deserving of this hell, it was certainly him. He quickened his pace. After all, Consuela was waiting.

Chapter One: Introduction

"No one commands me. No man. No god. No prince. What is a claim of age for ones who are immortal? What is a claim of power for ones who defy death? Call your damnable hunt. We shall see who I drag screaming to Hell with me."
— Günter Dorn, *Das Ungeheuer Darin*

This game is probably different from anything you've ever played. In some ways, it's not really a game at all. There is no board, there are no dice, and there is no set way of winning. **The Masquerade** is more concerned with stories than rules. In fact, this game has more in common with childhood games than with Trivial Pursuit or Monopoly. This game allows you to confront the Beast Within; it enables you to assume the role of a vampire.

If you have never played in a live game, be prepared for a departure from the realm of boardgames. Even if you've been playing tabletop roleplaying games for years, you will find that live gaming feels different. Rather than the game existing solely in your mind, it comes to life around you. The rush of adrenaline and the feel of "being" your character is much more intense. We have a name for this style of game. We call it **Mind's Eye Theatre**.

The Art of Storytelling

Before you become engrossed in the rules sections, remember that **The Masquerade** is a storytelling game. The story should always come first in your mind. If everyone involved in a dispute can agree on the outcome, ignore the rules. Rules are a safety net for when players can't decide what should happen in a situation.

Mankind has been telling stories since the time when cavemen sat around fires. Since that time, we have explored incredibly diverse types of media to tell out stories. Books, radio, television and even computer networks have carried our tales to others. Live-action roleplaying grew out of the roleplaying games of the seventies. Roleplaying games in the nineties no longer have an emphasis on looting strongholds for treasure and fighting so-called "monsters." Instead, they focus on telling stories in a unique way. Therefore, we call these diversions "storytelling games."

Storytelling games allow people to work together and weave a tale. This interactive type of storytelling is beginning to appear in other media as well. Various theater groups are experimenting with new types of interactive drama where audiences can be involved in the plays they watch. Cable companies are investing heavily to research networks supporting interactive television. We are changing not just the means by which we tell stories, but the methods as well.

The Live Gaming Paradigm

Tabletop roleplaying, however, still leaves most of the story under the control of one person. The Storyteller has to describe the entire world and any additional characters that the rest of the gaming group encounters. The Storyteller has total control of nearly everything in the world and creates most of the story, with the players contributing their parts.

Live gaming is starting to break the standard roleplaying mold. When a hundred or more people are telling a story at once, the Storyteller does not have to describe the entire world. The Storyteller creates ideas and goals and describes the world in terms of rules and descriptions to players. The players then act out their characters and create the story with small amounts of input from the Storyteller. Designing a live roleplaying story is not really like creating a traditional story. Rather, it is more like a chemistry experiment. You mix plot elements and see what happens. The story begins to take on a life of its own, with elements provided by all the players.

Another major shift that live gaming brings to the art of storytelling involves escaping the limitations of the medium. The game is no longer limited to words and imagination. Costuming, props and other visual cues can be an integral part of a live game. Instead of a Storyteller describing two people talking across the room, the players actually see them standing in the corner whispering. When you play a live game, you must keep in mind an old writer's adage: "Show, don't tell."

History of Live Roleplaying

Live roleplaying is actually not a new idea. Various groups have been experimenting with live games since the early 80's. Because many of these groups worked independently, three main traditions of live games have evolved. There are many variants to these three types of games. Innovative groups have run many new and unusual live gaming experiments at conventions over the last few years. These groups have only recently come together to exchange ideas.

Tabletop Variants: Many of the earliest live games appeared in Australia at various gaming conventions. Most of these games used simple revisions of tabletop rules or no rules at all, augmented by elaborate sound and dramatic techniques to make gaming more atmospheric. The method of telling the story is still the same one used in many roleplaying games. Descriptions of places and events still come from a single storyteller. Sometimes the players discover a story that has already taken place by investigating old documents and newspapers.

Live Fantasy Gaming: In the late eighties, several groups originated in different parts of the world to play live fantasy games. Many of these groups used systems involving foam weapons as part of their combat rules. One particularly interesting aspect of these games is that people were creating their own characters. Early efforts were very similar to the dungeon crawls of early tabletop roleplaying. However, some groups got large enough to populate entire fantasy villages once a month. Because of the combat system (swinging around padded weapons), many games of this variety take place outdoors.

Interactive Gaming: Other groups have merged the two traditions, creating short single-run games with elaborate characters. Instead of contact weapons rules, these games use ad-hoc rules for each story, covering skills, combat and magic. Unlike the early live experiments, stories happen during the game. Interactive games are currently very popular at North American gaming conventions, where large groups of roleplayers gather together.

Mind's Eye Theatre is almost a direct descendent of interactive gaming. **Mind's Eye Theatre** games share common rules so that storytellers can concentrate on creating the right "chemicals" for a good story.

Roleplaying

When you play **The Masquerade**, you take on the persona and role of a vampire. This is a character you invent and then roleplay over the course of a story and perhaps a chronicle (a series of connected stories). The life of your character is in your hands, for you decide what your character does and says. For the purposes of the game, you are your character. You decide what risks to accept or decline. Everything you say or do has an effect on the world.

During the game, you should always speak as your character. Unless you're speaking to a Narrator, whatever you say is what your character says. Because most of what a **Mind's Eye Theatre** player perceives will depend on the characters around him, the characters must be vivid and expressive. The characters direct the plot, but at the same time, the events of the game guide and develop the characters, helping them to weave the seamless tapestry of a story.

To an extent, you have a responsibility beyond simply portraying your character. Sometimes players need to consider the story as a whole, and often players will help make sure that other players enjoy the game. In the end, you should make sure that your actions do not completely ruin the story, for the story is as important as the characters.

Characters in **The Masquerade** are easy to create. It takes about 10 minutes to work out a basic personality and characteristics. However, it takes some effort to turn the collection of Traits and statistics into a living, breathing, working whole. You can create a character that's very different from yourself, but has enough of yourself in the character to make it seem three-dimensional. When Frankenstein created his monster, the task of sewing together the available parts was easy. Providing the final spark of life was difficult.

Cast

Most of the players of this game will create and roleplay characters. Players are members of the Cast, and their characters are central to the story. Being a Cast Member does not demand as much responsibility as being one of the people who helps run the game, but it does demand as much creativity and concentration.

As a Cast Member, you try to do things that allow your character to "succeed", achieving goals or helping others to do so in the context of the story. Making sure that your goals, strategies and schemes work to your advantage adds to the friction that builds the story.

Most Cast Members play protagonists, the "heroes" of the story who are free to do as they choose. Occasionally, you may find yourself playing the part of an antagonist. Antagonists are often essential characters to a particular story. They are characters who stand a good chance of being "defeated" during the course of a story. Usually antagonists may be required to perform certain actions to move the story along.

Narrators

Any story requires some people to become Narrators. These participants are the impartial judges who run the game. Narrators describe scenes and events that cannot be staged, adjudicate rules, and occasionally play the roles of antagonists. Generally, enlisting one Narrator for every twelve players is a good ratio. That ratio can be adjusted: it usually depends upon the how much experience your Troupe has.

As a Narrator, you must ensure that the rules are not broken, interpret rules when they are not fully understood, and keep the peace when rules are in dispute. Sometimes, you must arbitrate what happens in an unusual situation that is not covered by the rules. You have to coordinate with the Storyteller to make sure that the story moves along and that everyone is having fun. A Narrator cannot "win" a story and has no real goals. Her impartial position, however, places her in a unique position to watch a story unfold.

Narrators also take care of what happens when a character decides to interact with something in the game that is not a Cast Member. If a character needs to sneak past a security system or break someone out of a distant jail as part of a story, a Narrator will adjudicate whether or not he is successful. If a character has to go out to a distant alley to feed from a fresh victim, the Narrator will play that victim as an antagonist for a brief while.

Storyteller

The Storyteller is the ultimate authority and final judge in **The Masquerade**. The Storyteller creates the elements of the story that is told and is in charge of making sure that the story unfolds well. It is a demanding job, but it can be the most rewarding of all, for the Storyteller is a weaver of dreams.

As the Storyteller, it is your responsibility to set the wheels of the story in motion and make sure that they keep rolling. This does not mean that you dictate the course of the plot—that is the job of the Cast. You must make sure that the basis for a plot exists. You do not tell a story. Rather, you create the "chemicals" and elements of the plot and turn the cast loose to watch your ingredients mix. Most of your work happens before the game begins; after that, the Cast usually takes over.

During the game, however, you must be forever watchful and ready to create new elements to add to the mix to make sure that the story works out well. You have to make sure that everyone is involved in the story and in the game. If you do your "pre-game" job well, however, you will often spend most of your time as a Narrator.

You are also the ultimate arbiter of rules and a court of last resort. Other Narrators will handle many judgments for you, but sometimes a decision may have a serious impact on the story. At that point, your Narrators or Cast will appeal to you for judgment.

Rules

Although the main idea of this game is to roleplay and tell stories, **The Masquerade** still contains rules. They are needed to resolve what happens when a character does something that the player cannot do (like transforming into a bat and flying around) or does not want to do (like engaging in combat with another character). Rules are necessary to settle arguments— "Bang, bang, you're dead!" "No I'm not!"— and they add a vital dose of consistency to events in your world. Cast Members may resolve conflicts with each other by engaging in challenges, where they "bid" their Traits against each other.

This bidding can be performed (by experienced players) during normal conversation without a pause in actual roleplaying. Time outs are rarely necessary.

Winners and Losers

There is no real way to "win" a game when you play **The Masquerade.** Your character can do well or poorly, but there are no concrete conditions that grant the laurels of victory. Your character possesses motivations, ambitions and goals that help you decide what her aspirations are in a story. It is possible for everyone to "win."

Ultimately, the goal of **Mind's Eye Theatre** is to immerse yourself in the story and have fun doing it. If you have fun playing, then you certainly cannot consider yourself to have "lost" in a game.

Props

In order for others to visualize your character, you might choose to wear a costume and employ props. You must not use anything that can harm you or another Cast Member. Guns, fake guns, wooden stakes, foam stakes and water guns are strictly forbidden. The **Mind's Eye Theatre** system uses a bidding system in place of any actual physical combat. A player with a weapon might be tempted to hit someone with it or wave it about in a threatening manner. Actual physical danger is *never* an element in the game.

Cool costumes, jewelry, makeup and fangs are strongly encouraged. Some people get heavily into costuming when playing the game, and other players appreciate the effort involved in creating a very vampiric appearance. A Cast Member should bring whatever she needs to the **Mind's Eye Theatre** event to evoke the persona of her character.

Chronicle

Hopefully, you'll want to play this type of game more than once. Each time you play, you may choose to create new characters in a brand new story, or you can play the same character story after story, evening after evening. Your character can grow and change like a character in a novel instead of ending her saga after one brief encounter. **Mind's Eye Theatre** allows your character to develop and grow, gaining new allies, status, influence and power. There's also the possibility that your character might spiral down a twisted path of insanity, betrayal, fear and rage. Both possibilities are the stuff of legends.

What Has Changed

When we set out to create **Mind's Eye Theatre**, we envisioned people playing the game in small groups in their own homes. We thought that large games of 25 or more people playing **The Masquerade** would be fairly rare. **Mind's Eye Theatre** was intended as a different way to present the kinds of plots that occur in tabletop roleplaying.

We were wrong.

Many people are now playing in public places and at conventions, some of them in groups of over two hundred players. Rather than playing a small coterie of vampires, people are creating entire cities of vampires, from the prince and primogen down to the lowest neonate. Huge games have become more of the norm and not the exception. Players have given us plenty of feedback on the rules.

This second edition of **The Masquerade** is intended to help support really large games. Some of the changes you will find include:

• A new bidding system that speeds up challenges.

• A very detailed system of Status Traits. Status is now a very important part of the game. Holding an important position in vampiric society can now affect your social standing. Boons and Influences have also been rewritten to tie into this social structure.

• Disciplines have been rewritten to correspond more to the tabletop game for ease of conversion.

• Representing Humanity and Frenzy is now a part of the game. These systems depend on Beast Traits.

The World of Darkness

Your characters do not exist in a vacuum. Rather, they reside in a world that exists in our imaginations, a place known as the World of Darkness. It is the proverbial Hell in which your character lives and suffers. Your vampiric character lives to hunting and feed. Never again will she see the light of day.

The world is a Gothic-Punk nightmare, a frightening, surreal version of our own world. Here, soggy cardboard boxes are the humble shelters of the destitute, while nearby, towering spires of glass and steel claw toward heaven. It is a world of shocking contrasts.

Packs of street thugs prowl urban jungles. Bureaucratic sharks stalk the oceans of politics and business. Skulking in dark corners, ancient vampires vie for control of mortals and immortals. Omnipotent Methuselahs manipulate lesser vampires like pawns in a great game of chess. Lesser Kindred band together in secret societies to control those beneath them. At the bottom of the hierarchy, young anarchs band together in rough warrior gangs to steal the power of their oppressors.

The darkness is grimmer and the colors are more vivid. Cold, monochrome buildings are spattered with screaming graffiti. The corporate machine is huge and uncaring; spirits are crushed and people are forgotten. Some bodies end up in the streets— their blood adds a splash of crimson as it runs down city drains. The shocking brilliance of violence is more explosive when seen against the grim backdrop of urban decay.

There is no escape from the madness.

The Meaning of the Myth

To get into the feel of **The Masquerade**, you must be able to savor its mood. The game is stark and brooding, but with an underlying sensuality. The world of the Kindred is an erotic and provocative nightmare in which reason does not always play a role. The romance and mystique of the old gothics is set to the accompaniment of screaming guitars.

The romance is tinged with a layer of sadness. In **The Masquerade,** vampires are doomed from the moment they are Embraced. Although they are powerful beyond imagination, they are also cursed. No matter what they do, they remain monsters with a horrible unquenchable thirst for blood. They are hunted like animals. Stories in **The Masquerade** are unique because they often bear this element of tragedy. The traditional tragedy of classic theatre depicts a hero coming to a great and horrible demise. The hero's fate is clear from the very beginning. Because of who and what the hero is, he is damned from the moment the curtain rises, and the audience knows it. Characters in **The Masquerade** are doomed from the moment they receive their first Embrace...

Paradoxically, these tragically doomed characters have the potential to become heroes of uncommon valor. While their very nature is shunned, they do not have to be evil. They drink blood and are spawned from an ancient race, and thus possess the taint of evil. However, they are expected to be heroes and rise above their very nature. They certainly have nothing to lose.

Justice is only served if good overcomes evil. To "win" this game, a vampire must fight her dark side, restraining it with the bonds of human virtue. She must display courage and heroism and not fall prey to her own weaknesses. If she fails, the Beast Within takes over, and she will spiral into depths that even the Kindred find repulsive. Sometimes the tragedy of Final Death is a vampire's only hope of escape.

There is a slim possibility that a vampire may find a way to escape the curse and become mortal once again. Not all characters seek this, but some realize what they have become. Some seek Golconda, a state where their basic instincts do not control them. Golconda is even more difficult to survive than living with the curse of undeath, but it is still sought.

Characters spend much of their time combating evil. Instead of fighting monsters outside themselves, they combat what is inside. Some win. More often, they fail in a mad, screaming, terrible whirlwind of destruction.

The Becoming

The moment a human becomes a vampire is never forgotten, for the transformation is usually painful and traumatic. A mortal becomes a vampire when a Kindred drains all the blood from him and kills him. Just before the mortal dies, the vampire pierces his own skin and releases a small amount of his blood into the mortal's mouth. The potent vampiric blood rouses the poor soul, and he begins to drink hungrily from his sire's open wound. Some realize what is about to happen and find the willpower to resist. Some of them even die peacefully.

A newly made vampire takes on the lineage of his sire and is therefore of the same bloodline, or "clan". The bloodline affects which mystical powers, or "Disciplines", the character can have at the start of the game. Each clan also has a special weakness. Clans often work together to achieve a common end, although they often fight among each other.

For the next few years or decades, the childe (the young vampire) remains with his sire. His sire may choose to teach him nothing about vampiric society, rules or his own kind. He might be nurtured or abused, denied rights, or granted full freedom to learn more about his kind. Until he is released by his sire and presented to the prince of the city, he is not accepted into vampiric society.

Fledgling

The Beast is strong in you. Although you may regret what you are and the things you do, you cannot deny them or excise them from your soul. But resist you must, lest you slip away into complete degeneration and chaos.

It is difficult to be good, for so many of your urges drive you toward sin. If you falter, you will lose your essential humanity all the more quickly. If you do not strive to maintain some moral standard, the Beast will drive you to depths that you cannot imagine. You will cease to love or care about anything except the blood. When the Beast wins, the results are horrific.

The Hunger

Vampires must feed. It is not merely a need, but an all-consuming passion. The hunger for blood is not merely the instinct for survival, although blood is the only thing that can sustain a vampire. Vampires need the closeness of the feeding and the erotic sensation it gives them. They need the thrill of pursuing and capturing prey. Feeding brings the vampire closer to life and bestows the most powerful emotions a vampire can feel.

The blood does not need to be from a human, and the vampire does not need to kill his victim. However, the bloodlust often causes older vampires to lose control and drain all life from their victims. Some vampires forsake mortal lovers because of their fear of this happening.

Vampires can cover their feeding easily. Fangs leave only a small wound, which will disappear entirely if the vampire licks it. Some vampires can make their vessels forget the feeding, while some find mortals who live for the feeding.

Nature of the Beast

What does it mean to be a vampire? Kindred are not, despite their appearance, human. Vampires have an alien nature. They are an inhuman race. They are similar enough, however, for us to compare and contrast them to humanity. By comparing vampires to humans, it is possible to discover what their capabilities and limitations are. Vampires are not humans with fangs, they are monsters masquerading as humans. Just as a vampire stalks humans, a vampire lives in fear of the Beast within himself.

Welcome to the other side...

Chapter Two: Character

"Each person is many persons: a multitude made into one person; a corporate body; incorporated, a corporation… the unity of a person is as real, or unreal, as the unity or the corporation."
— N.O. Brown

Before you can begin to play **The Masquerade**, you must create a character. This character is the role you assume in the stories you and your friends tell. It's the person you enact, and you play that character throughout each game. Unlike make-believe, you don't just make up a character as you go along. Instead, you've got to create a character before you start playing. There's a certain amount of work involved— characters are created, not born. Character creation is a creative struggle, and even the most experienced roleplayers find it a challenge to build a compelling yet honest character.

This chapter describes how to create a unique character, starting with a general concept and translating that concept into values that can be used in the game. The process itself is very simple, but you should not hesitate to ask a Narrator (one of the "referees") any questions you might have.

Character creation is like cooking. You've got to gather the ingredients, stir them together and let the result bake for a while. You start by deciding what kind of character you want. Are you going to be a street-hardened punk or a rich and spoiled ex-debutante? Are you a college graduate, or were you tutored in life somewhere in the Appalachian Mountains? The background and personality of your character are the essential ingredients of his persona. From your basic concepts, you can work out the details.

Getting Started

• You can create a character at any age. Her culture and background is entirely up to you (with the approval of the Storyteller, of course). However, you start the game as a fairly young and inexperienced neonate, a newly-created vampire. You have only recently left the tutelage of your sire— the vampire who Embraced you. You know little of vampiric society or unlife, except what you've been told by your sire. In any case, you have been a vampire for 50 years or less. Your apparent age is the age when you "died."

• The Storyteller, the person who organizes the story, may restrict your character creation choices or offer you other choices besides those listed here. Many stories have special considerations that must be taken into account. There will often be certain roles that need to be filled in a story, and you may have to create a character to fill that need.

• **The Masquerade's** character creation process is designed as much to help you define your character as it is to provide you with a means to interact with the rules. The processes of creating the character and picking your strong and weak points are meant to help you sharpen the concept of your character.

• This game's character creation system is a selection system. By choosing Traits, qualities describing your character, from a series of lists, you build your character. It is best to list all the Traits and qualities you would like your character to have and then eliminate the ones that aren't essential to your character concept. You cannot have all the qualities you want; life isn't like that.

• It is your responsibility to create a character that suits the story. In this, you are guided by the Storyteller. If your character doesn't have a place in the story, you have to create a new character or create your own place.

Character Creation

"How often at this desk I sat into the depth of night and looked for you until over these books and papers you appeared to me, my melancholy friend."

— Goethe, *Faust*

The following is a breakdown of the character creation process.

Step One: Inspiration

Before you write a single thing, you need to find inspiration for the type of character you want to play. Once you're inspired, you need to develop a rough idea of who your character is.

This development involves choosing a concept, a clan and a personality (defined by choosing a Nature and Demeanor— see below). The better you relate these three aspects of your character, the more intricate and complete the end result will be. A character's Demeanor is often completely different from his concept, and the stereotypical image of a clan can be contradicted by choosing a contrasting Nature or Demeanor.

Though short lists are given in this chapter, complete descriptions of the clans, Natures and Demeanors can be found in Chapter Three.

Clan

Your choice of clan is arguably the most important element of your character. Your clan describes the essential lineage of your character. (Unless you are Caitiff, you are always of the same clan as your sire). The seven clans from which players may choose are all members of the vampire sect known as the Camarilla. There are other clans, but they exist either in their own sects or on the outskirts of Kindred society.

You do not necessarily need to choose a clan, for some younger Kindred are of such diluted blood that no single clan's characteristics are imprinted upon them. These Caitiff

Character Creation Process

- Step One: Inspiration — Who are you?
  — Choose your clan
  — Choose a Nature and Demeanor
- Step Two: Attributes —What are your basic capabilities?
  — Prioritize Attributes (seven primary, five secondary and three tertiary)
- Step Three: Advantages —What do you know?
  — Choose five Abilities
  — Choose three Disciplines
  — Choose three Influences
- Step Four: Last Touches— Fill in the details.
  — Assign Blood Traits
  — Assign Willpower Traits
  — Choose one Beast Trait
  — Assign one Status Trait ("Acknowledged")
  — Choose Negative Traits (if any)
- Step Five: Spark of Life — Narrative descriptions.

are increasingly common among the Kindred, but they are outcasts— accepted by none, scorned by all. If you wish to play such a character, simply list "Caitiff" as your clan.

Players choose or are assigned their clan. The Storyteller may desire a certain number of characters from each clan and may ensure that her quota is filled during the character creation process.

Nature and Demeanor

At this point, you should choose personality archetypes that suit your concept of the disposition and image of your character.

Your character's Nature is the most dominant aspect of her true personality. The Nature describes who your character really is on the inside, but your chosen Nature is not necessarily the only archetype that applies— people aren't one-dimensional.

You should also choose a Demeanor to describe the personality you pretend to possess. This is the role you play in the world, the facade you present. It should probably be different from the archetype you have chosen as your Nature, but whatever you choose is only your typical pose; people can change outward behavior as quickly as they change their mood. You may change your image at any time to suit different people and different situations. Demeanor has no practical effect on the rules; it is only intended to serve as a roleplaying tool.

Clans:

Complete clan descriptions can be found in Chapter Three.

• **Brujah** — Respecting no authority and acknowledging no leaders, the "rabble" consider themselves free.

Disciplines: Celerity, Potence, Presence

• **Gangrel** — Loners and rustics, the "outlanders" are the only Kindred who dare venture outside the city.

Disciplines: Animalism, Fortitude, Protean

• **Malkavian** — Commonly perceived to be insane, the "kooks" possess an uncanny vision and wisdom.

Disciplines: Auspex, Dominate, Obfuscate

• **Nosferatu** — Ostracized and misunderstood by others, the hideous "sewer rats" live out their sordid existence in hiding.

Disciplines: Animalism, Obfuscate, Potence

• **Toreador** — Known for their hedonistic ways, the "degenerates" prefer to think of themselves as artists.

Disciplines: Auspex, Celerity, Presence

• **Tremere** — Wizards of an ancient house, the "warlocks" work together to spread their influence and power.

Disciplines: Auspex, Dominate, Thaumaturgy (Path of Blood)

• **Ventrue** — Aristocrats of rarefied tastes and manners, the "blue bloods" are fiendishly cool and cunning.

Disciplines: Dominate, Fortitude, Presence

• **Caitiff** — Those with no clan: the outcasts and the dishonored.

Disciplines: Any (except Thaumaturgy)

Step Two: Attributes

Attributes are everything a character naturally, intrinsically is. Are you strong? Are you brave? Are you persuasive? Questions such as these are answered by the Attributes, the Traits that describe the basic, innate potential of your character.

The first step is to prioritize the different categories of Attributes, placing them in order of importance to your character. Are you more physical than you are social? Does your quick thinking surpass your physical strength?

Categories of Attributes:

• Physical Attributes describe the abilities of the body, such as power, quickness and endurance.

• Social Attributes describe your character's appearance and charisma— her ability to influence others.

• Mental Attributes represent your character's mental capacity and include such things as memory, perception, self-control and the ability to learn and think.

Nature and Demeanor:

Complete Nature and Demeanor descriptions can be found in Chapter Three.

• **Architect** — You seek to create something of lasting value, a legacy.

• **Bravo** — You are something of a bully; you like to be feared.

• **Caregiver** — You seek to nurture others.

• **Child** — You never really grew up, and you want someone to take care of you.

• **Conformist** — A follower at heart, you find it easy to adapt, adjust and comply.

• **Conniver** — There's always an easier way, one that usually involves someone else doing your work.

• **Deviant** — You're just not like everyone else.

• **Director** — You're accustomed to taking charge of a situation.

• **Fanatic** — You have a cause and it gives your life meaning.

• **Gallant** — You are as flamboyant as you are amoral.

• **Hedonist** — Life is meaningless, so enjoy it as long as it lasts.

• **Jester** — Always the clown, you can't take life, or death, seriously.

• **Judge** — You seek justice and reconciliation.

• **Loner** — You are forever alone, even in a crowd.

• **Martyr** — You need to be needed, and enjoy being morally superior.

• **Rebel** — No need for a cause; you rebel out of habit and passion.

• **Survivor** — You struggle to survive, no matter what the odds.

• **Traditionalist** — You prefer the orthodox and conservative ways.

The concept and clan of your character may suggest what your Attribute priorities should be, but feel free to pick any way you please. For now, think in the broadest of perspectives—you can get more specific after you understand the big picture.

After you've chosen the order of the three Attribute categories, you need to choose specific Traits from each category. The Traits are adjectives that describe your character's strengths and weaknesses, defining your character just as a character in a novel is defined. In your primary (strongest) Attribute category, you can choose seven Traits. In your secondary category, you can choose five. In your tertiary (weakest) category, you can choose only three. Thus, you receive a total of 15 Attribute Traits. You can take the same Trait more than once, if you wish, reflecting greater aptitude.

Attribute Traits:

Complete Attribute Trait descriptions can be found in Chapter Three.

- **Physical** — Athletic, Brawny, Dexterous, Enduring, Energetic, Ferocious, Graceful, Lithe, Nimble, Quick, Resilient, Robust, Rugged, Stalwart, Steady, Tenacious, Tireless, Tough, Vigorous, Wiry
- **Social** — Alluring, Beguiling, Charismatic, Charming, Commanding, Compassionate, Dignified, Diplomatic, Elegant, Eloquent, Empathetic, Expressive, Friendly, Genial, Gorgeous, Ingratiating, Intimidating, Magnetic, Persuasive, Seductive, Witty
- **Mental** — Alert, Attentive, Calm, Clever, Creative, Cunning, Dedicated, Determined, Discerning, Disciplined, Insightful, Intuitive, Knowledgeable, Observant, Patient, Rational, Reflective, Shrewd, Vigilant, Wily, Wise

The Rules Chapter describes how Traits function in the game. For now, you simply need to understand that these Traits reflect how competent your character is at different kinds of actions. The more Traits you have in one Attribute category, the more skillfully your character can perform actions involving that category.

Listed below are examples of Attribute Traits from which you can choose, separated into appropriate categories:

Step 3: Advantages

Advantages are the Traits that separate one character from another. They allow a player to take actions that would otherwise be impossible. There are three categories of advantages: Abilities, Disciplines and Influences.

Choosing Abilities

Abilities represent your training and knowledge beyond the outline provided by your Attributes. They are what you have learned and what you can do rather than what you are. Abilities let you perform specialized tasks that are only possible with training: picking locks, driving with skill or reading the Dead Sea Scrolls.

Choose five different Abilities from the list that follows.

Choosing Disciplines

Disciplines are vampiric powers—the supernatural abilities available to a vampire. Each vampire begins the game with three Disciplines, but a vampire may only choose the Disciplines that are typically possessed by his clan (see the clan lists, above). Each Discipline has two powers at the basic level. If the character has a Discipline, the first power listed must be chosen first. The character cannot advance to intermediate level powers in a given Discipline until all of the beginning powers of that Discipline have been learned. A

Abilities:

Complete Ability descriptions can be found in Chapter Three.

- **Animal Ken** — You have a rapport with animals and can train them.
- **Brawl** — You are skilled in unarmed combat.
- **Bureaucracy** — You understand the rules of government and organization.
- **Computer** — You can operate a computer.
- **Drive** — You can drive a car with skill.
- **Finance** — You can manage money.
- **Firearms** — You can handle guns and other ranged weapons.
- **Investigation** — You are a skilled detective.
- **Law** — You understand the legal system.
- **Leadership** — You understand the principles of command.
- **Linguistics** — You are fluent in at least one language.
- **Medicine** — You can heal people (you don't have to be a doctor).
- **Melee** — You are skilled in the use of many different hand-to-hand weapons.
- **Occult** — You know many of the ancient mysteries.
- **Performance** — You can act, dance, sing or play an instrument (maybe all of the above).
- **Repair** — You can fix nearly anything.
- **Science** — You understand the fundamentals of technology.
- **Scrounge** — You can drum up just about anything.
- **Security** — You can disarm security systems and pick locks.
- **Streetwise** — You understand street culture.
- **Subterfuge** — You know how to manipulate people.
- **Survival** — You can survive in the wilderness.

player may chose to work his way up to the intermediate level of a Discipline rather than choosing the basic levels of three different Disciplines. However, you must have your Storyteller's permission before selecting the advanced levels of any discipline. Only the basic level of each Discipline is shown here.

Choosing Influences

Influence reflects a character's control over mortal society. Influence is the source of most power and conflict in vampiric society and is the primary means of waging wars of intrigue. For instance, if you own a nightclub, that is reflected by an Influence Trait. If you are a wealthy stock market investor, that is also a function of Influence.

Disciplines:

Complete Discipline descriptions can be found in Chapter Three.

- **Animalism (Beast Within)** — You can arouse the Beast in others.
- **Auspex (Heightened Senses)** — Your senses are preternaturally sharp, even allowing you to pierce Obfuscate.
- **Celerity (Alacrity)** — You are supernaturally quick.
- **Dominate (Command)** — By gazing into another's eyes, you may give them commands.
- **Fortitude (Endurance)**— You are capable of resisting severe injury.
- **Obfuscate (Unseen Presence)** — You can remain obscure and unseen, even in crowds.
- **Potence (Prowess)** — You possess superhuman strength and vigor.
- **Presence (Dread Gaze)** — You may instill terror in others.
- **Protean (Wolf's Claws)**— You can sprout sharp talons from your fingers.
- **Thaumaturgy (Blood Mastery)** — You may control another via possession of the other's blood.

Influences:

Complete Influence descriptions can be found in Chapter Three.

- **Bureaucracy** — The organizers who really run City Hall.
- **Church** — The religious establishment.
- **Finance** — Big business, including the largest corporations.
- **Health** — The medical system, from clinics to research labs.
- **High Society** — Rich dilettantes, aristocracy and the art community.
- **Industry** — The factories and the unions.
- *Legal* — The court system: lawyers, judges, et al.
- **Media** — Newspapers, radio, TV and other forms of communication.
- **Military** — National Guard, Army, Navy, Marines, Air Force, Coast Guard.
- **Occult** — Cults and other mystical practitioners.
- **Police** — The cops.
- **Political** — Politicians of all stripes, from local to national.
- **Street** — Gangs, the homeless, small-time dealers— the guys in the know.
- **Transportation** — Trains, buses, ships, taxis and planes.
- **Underworld** — Organized crime: gambling, laundering, drugs and other rackets.
- **University** — The educational and scientific community.

You may choose three Influence Traits. Each represents a contact or holding in the area. You can take a single Influence Trait (such as High Society) more than once, indicating a greater degree of dominance. The only limitations on your Influence selection are those imposed by the background and identity of your character (but even seemingly weird Influences can be justified).

Step 4: Last Touches

The most important stage of character creation, in terms of character definition, is the application of last touches. These are the little details and flourishes that complete your character. During this stage, you may take Negative Traits— flaws in physique or personality. Negative Traits allow you to take additional (positive) Traits on a one-for-one basis. You also need to record your Blood Traits and Willpower Traits based on your generation. You must also choose your Beast Trait. Finally, you must be aware of your character's state of health.

Blood

Blood Traits work like other Traits, but they can only be used to heighten your physical power or heal yourself, and they can only be regained by feeding. Your Blood Pool indicates your maximum Blood Trait capacity, not necessarily the amount of blood you currently have in your system. Blood Traits are not assigned adjectives; each simply represents a volume of blood (about a vial's worth).

Beast Traits:

Full descriptions of Beast Traits may be found in Chapter Three.
- **Vigilante** — Witnessing needless death brings out your Beast.
- **Frustrated** — You crack easily under stress.
- **Item** — The sight of a particular object causes you to frenzy.
- **Blood** — You are unable to control your hunger when exposed to large quantities of blood.
- **Hunger** — You are unable to control your need for blood.
- **Lust** — You get carried away during feeding.
- **Phobia** — You have a terrible fear of something.
- **Sunlight** — The sight of sunlight causes you to enter a mindless panic.
- **Fire** — You are absolutely terrified of fire.

You start the game with three Blood Traits (unless you have lowered your generation by using Negative Traits). These Traits are either used as sustenance or as desperate situations arise. Chapter Three discusses the uses of Blood Traits.

Willpower

Willpower reflects your basic drive, self-confidence and tenacity. It is essential for controlling the actions and behavior of your character, especially in times of stress when predatory instincts emerge. You may choose only one Willpower Trait at this point in the game, although more can be gained by lowering your generation (see below).

Humanity

Beast Traits represent how close your character is to the Beast. The more Beast Traits you have, the more likely you will periodically lose control and enter into a state the Kindred call "frenzy". The more Beast Traits you possess, the less human you become. When a character accumulates five Beast Traits, she is completely overwhelmed by the Beast and becomes a mindless raving monster. At that point, the player must create a new character; her last one is now an uncontrollable monster.

Kindred must also start the game with a single Beast Trait. If you wish, you may take a second Beast Trait. This is worth the equivalent of two Negative Traits. However, remember that your character goes into a permanent frenzy upon receiving the fifth Beast Trait, so you would need only three more to lose your character.

Status Traits:

Admired, Adored, Cherished, Esteemed, Exalted, Famous, Faultless, Feared, Honorable, Influential, Just, Praised, Respected, Revered, Trustworthy, Well-Known

Status

One of the main aspects of your background is Status. Status is an indication of where your character stands in vampiric society, particularly within your city. You start with a single Status Trait, which represents the fact that you have been presented to the prince. Your existence has been recognized. If you are Caitiff, or choose to be an anarch, you have no initial Status Trait. This could be because you have never been presented to the prince, or you may have such a terrible reputation that any former Status has been lost. (Yes, you can acquire more than one Status Trait by taking on Negative Traits, but anarchs and Caitiff cannot gain Status this way.)

Your initial Status Trait is always the word "Acknowledged", representing the acknowledgment of your existence by the prince. Others can be chosen or earned as the story progresses.

You should be able to explain, in terms of your character's background, what your Status Traits represent. Just how are you Exalted? Why do others Cherish you?

Chapter Three describes all the uses of Status and indicates how more Traits can be gained.

Negative Traits

At this point, you may increase your character's power by selecting counterbalancing flaws. By taking a Negative Trait, you can, for example, add a new Trait to your Attributes or take another Ability. Negative Traits are Attributes that have a negative effect upon your character. They can be used against you in a challenge (a contest staged between you and other characters). Each Negative Trait is equal to one positive Trait; for each Negative Trait you take, you receive a positive Trait of your choice. You can take no more than five Negative Traits unless you have the Storyteller's permission. You can take whatever Negative Traits seem to fit your character; you need not take the full five, or any at all. However, it's fun to have at least one; ironically, Negative Traits make your vampire more human.

Each Negative Trait you take allows you to choose one of the following options:

• Take one additional positive Trait in any category of Attribute: Physical, Social or Mental. (The maximum number of Traits you can possess in a given category is listed in the "Generation Chart" in Chapter Three.)

• Take one extra Ability or Influence.

Optional: Your Storyteller may allow you other options for modifying your character. Possible options are:

• Lower your generation by one (from a base of 13th). It costs two Negative Traits to lower your generation by one level. All characters start at 13th generation unless generation is

Negative Traits:

Complete Negative Trait descriptions can be found under Attribute descriptions in Chapter Three.

• **Physical** — Clumsy, Cowardly, Decrepit, Delicate, Docile, Flabby, Lame, Lethargic, Puny, Sickly

• **Social** — Bestial, Callous, Condescending, Dull, Naive, Obnoxious, Paranoid, Repugnant, Shy, Tactless, Untrustworthy

• **Mental** — Forgetful, Gullible, Ignorant, Impatient, Oblivious, Predictable, Shortsighted, Submissive, Violent, Witless

lowered in this way. (Generation is your distance from Caine, the primordial First Vampire; having a lower generation places you "closer" to Caine and increases the potency of your blood.)

• Three Negative Traits allow the purchase of one new Basic Discipline (even one that is not a clan Discipline).

• One Negative Trait allows the purchase of a Status Trait (see above).

• You can take an extra Beast Trait or Derangement in lieu of two Negative Traits. That is, an extra Beast Trait or Derangement allows you to purchase two other positive Traits without acquiring the usual two Negative Traits. You can never take more than one extra Beast Trait or Derangement. Of course, Malkavians already have a Derangement, and a second must be taken to get two positive Traits. Malkavians begin with no more than two Derangement Traits, and vampires of other clans may begin with no more than one.

Generation

Unless a player buys down his generation with Negative Traits, his character will start at 13th generation. For every two Negative Traits spent in this fashion, the character can lower his generation by one. A character can NEVER buy his generation lower than 8th, unless he has the express permission of the Storyteller. More information on generation can be found in Chapter Three.

Health

Characters are considered to be at full health at the beginning of each story unless the Storyteller states otherwise. Of course, characters can be hurt or even destroyed during a story. There are four "levels" of health beneath Healthy: "Bruised," "Wounded", "Incapacitated", and "Torpor". Chapters Three and Four discuss these levels in full detail.

Derangements:

Complete descriptions of Derangements may be found in Chapter Three.

Amnesia, Crimson Rage, The Hunger, Immortal Terror, Intellectualization, Manic-Depression, Multiple Personalities, Obsession, Paranoia, Perfection, Power Madness, Regression, Undying Remorse, Vengeful

Generation Table

Generation	Blood Traits	Willpower Traits		Maximum Traits
		Starting	Max	
13th	3	1	3	10
12th	4	1	3	10
11th	5	2	4	11
10th	6	2	4	11
9th	8	3	5	13
8th	9	3	6	14
7th	11	4	7	16
6th	13	4	8	18
5th	16	5	9	20
4th	20	6	10	25
3rd	?	?	?	30

Step 5: Spark of Life

There are other aspects of a character that should be detailed. These flourishes are not necessarily important in terms of the game, but are vital with regard to roleplaying. In many cases, these "sparks" are provided for you, or at least suggested to you, by the Storyteller. Your character needs to be woven into the story, and these "sparks" allow the Storyteller to do just that.

Other Aspects

• **Background** — You need to create a background for your character, describing her life before the Embrace: what she did, how she lived and what was unique about her. This background may describe what your character did for a living, how she saw herself, and what others thought of her. Indeed, many Kindred find it difficult to abandon their concepts of themselves as humans and cling to the trappings of their former lives. Their pasts remain with them forever.

Regardless of when you were Embraced, whether in the days of Ancient Rome or in the modern age, you have spent 50 waking years or less as a vampire. All other years of undead existence are assumed to have been spent in torpor.

• **Secrets** — Each character has secrets of some sort, things that he doesn't want others to discover. One secret almost all Kindred possess is the location of a personal haven. The Storyteller is likely to give you a number of secrets that you need to protect over the course of the chronicle.

• **Motivations** — What is your purpose? What motivates you on a night-to-night basis? Is it hate, fear, lust, greed, jealousy or revenge? Describe your motivations in as much detail as possible; ask the Storyteller for help if you can't think of anything. Unless you are an experienced player, it's likely that the Storyteller will provide you with a motivation or two at the start of the chronicle.

• **Appearance** — You need to find the props and costume that will help others understand, or at least recognize, your character at a glance. You need to not only act like your character, but look like

him as well. Your character's appearance makes his Physical (and many Social) Traits visible to other characters.

• **Equipment** — Your character likely begins the game with equipment of one sort or another. Ask a Narrator for more details on your personal possessions and assets. If you want to spend money on equipment right away, feel free. You may buy weapons, clothing, homes, condos, cars... anything. Use an appropriate catalog for prices. (Be sure to get your Storyteller's approval if you wish to buy anything unusual or dangerous.)

• **Quirks** — By giving your character quirks (interesting personal details), you add a great deal of depth and interest to her. Write a few sentences on the back of your character sheet about the strange and interesting things that define your character. Examples of quirks include a twisted sense of humor, a gentleness toward animals, or a habit of grunting when answering yes to a question.

Advanced Character Creation

Sometimes the Storyteller may want players to create characters who are not typical starting characters. In such cases, additional Traits may be provided in many categories, and limits on Negative Traits may be raised. Rules for such "advanced" character creation are provided in Chapter Three. Ask your Storyteller for more details.

Sample Character Creation

Larry sits down and skims through a rulebook. Enthralled with the prospect of assuming the role of the undead (in his imagination, at least), he decides to create a character. Aileen, the Storyteller, lends a willing hand and guides Larry through the five-step process.

Step One: Inspiration

Larry thinks for a little while and decides he wants to play a rebellious, punkish vampire who doesn't take crap from anyone. However, he wants his character to be more than a savage brawler. He wants his character to have an image, to be charismatic in the eyes of other characters. His character will be a gang leader feared for his skill and power.

Larry decides his character was a child of the streets, raised on knuckle sandwiches and petty thievery. He tried to hold various inner-city jobs, but couldn't take orders well, so he never worked at one place for more than a couple of months. Of course, a man needs to eat, so Larry's character turned to crime, for which he had a natural aptitude.

Larry chooses the clan of Brujah, which he feels fits in best with his character concept.

Larry now thinks about an appropriate Demeanor and Nature. He decides that, even though his character constantly breaks the rules and rebels against authority, it's just part of the image he tries to portray. His overriding need is to impress and bedazzle those around him. The best way to do that, in his mind, is to act and look tough and rebellious. Larry chooses Rebel as his Demeanor and Gallant as his Nature.

Larry has a good grasp on who his character is. He names his character "Roark" and is ready to flesh the concept out.

Step Two: Attributes

Larry is now ready to pick Roark's Traits and starts by setting priorities. He considers the qualities Roark would need to survive on the streets. What qualities will prevent Roark from becoming just another worn-out, clichéd stereotype?

After pondering his choices, Larry decides that Roark has to be strong, hardy and quick. A gang leader needs to be tough. Larry also wants Roark to be attractive and charismatic. Thus, he makes Physical Attributes primary (with seven Traits), Social Attributes secondary (with five Traits) and Mental Attributes tertiary (with three Traits).

Thinking back to his original inspiration, Larry tries to describe his character the way an author would. He finally decides on Brawny, Nimble, Nimble (he chooses this Trait twice), Graceful, Tireless, Tenacious and Athletic as Physical Traits. For Social Traits, he chooses Intimidating, Intimidating, Alluring, Alluring and Charming. Last, he chooses Calm (a real departure from the punk image), Cunning and Wily for his three Mental Traits.

Roark has now progressed from a hazy shadow to a tangible character, but the job isn't finished yet. Now Larry has to decide what sort of powers and abilities Roark has.

Step Three: Advantages

Larry now picks five Abilities that his character would have picked up as a street criminal and gang leader. The street is Roark's home, battleground and playpen. Streetwise is Roark's first Ability. In his numerous rumbles, Roark has fought with everything from chains to two-by-fours, so Melee works well. Modern times being what they are, Firearms goes down next. Thinking of Roark's past,

Larry decides that Roark was once a car thief and learned to Drive well. Roark also dabbled in cat burglary, thus learning some of the finer points of Security.

Larry chooses three Disciplines from the five offered to all beginning Brujah. He decides a gang leader would need Celerity (Alacrity) and Potence (Prowess) to retain his position. Since Roark also has a strong Casanova side, he chooses the first level of Presence (Dread Gaze) as his third Discipline. He'll have to work on this one to build it up to the point that he can use it for attraction as well. So far, so good.

Influence is not terribly important to Roark, but he still has some. Larry decides that Roark is a secret partner in a lowlife downtown nightclub. He takes Underworld twice to reflect that. He also has a lot of contacts on the street and takes Street Influence as well.

Step Four: Last Touches

Larry is almost finished creating Roark and is itching to play, but there are some details left.

He makes note of the three Blood Traits with which he begins the game.

Larry marks down that he has one Willpower Trait.

For Humanity, one Trait really stands out—Frustrated has "Roark" written all over it. Larry almost looks forward to putting the Beast Trait into action.

Larry now looks over his character and decides that he wants to be as strong socially as he is physically. He also realizes that Roark never had an opportunity to hone his higher faculties. Larry therefore chooses two Negative Mental Traits—Ignorant and Shortsighted—so he can add two more positive Traits to any category he wants. He adds the two Social Traits of Commanding and Alluring (giving him a total of three Alluring Traits to use).

At this point, if Larry wants to lower Roark's generation, he can take more Negative Traits, two per generation drop. He can also buy more Disciplines at the cost of three Negative Traits per Basic Discipline. However, Larry decides Roark is flawed enough. He leaves him at 13th generation with only three Disciplines.

Step Five: Spark of Life

After noting Acknowledged as his single Status Trait, Larry jumps to his feet, his character card complete, and decides to work everything else out after he's been in Roark's shoes. Larry has to think like Roark so that he can learn how Roark smokes a cigarette, how he moves on the dance floor and how he sits in his chair. These little nuances of character that Larry can't write down on his character card are the details that will make Roark seem real. Ultimately, Roark will not be defined by a group of hastily scribbled words and numbers, but by Larry, who will, over the course of the game, think, move and act like his character.

This character creation process provides Larry with the empty veins and arteries of an inanimate vampire shell. Larry supplies the blood, the life. He's ready to begin the game.

Chapter Three: Characteristics

Caustic dripping grins the Reaper
Body count intensify getting weaker.
—Skinny Puppy, "First Aid"

There are seven clans in the Camarilla (the sect to which all characters are assumed to belong). According to legend, each of these is descended from an Antediluvian progenitor. Theoretically, each member of a clan can trace his roots back to a single Kindred. The origins of most clans have been lost in the mists of time. Some clan founders are little more than legend, and certainly none publicly walk the earth anymore... or so many would fervently hope.

Each member of a clan is of the same bloodline. All vampires of a given clan often possess the same powers, tendencies and appearances. In some cases, these similarities are invested with the Becoming. In other cases, vampires Embrace mortals who display the clan image or attitude. As members of the same clan tend toward certain similarities, others learn to expect certain actions from them, although individual personalities can still shine through.

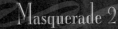

BRUJAH

"You are vexed and bitter, that is very good; if only you would get really angry for once, it would be even better."
—Goethe

Brujah is the most rebellious and antisocial of all clans. Its members forever search for the ultimate expression of their individuality. They are rebels. They tend to be stubborn, aggressive, ruthless, sensitive to slights and extremely vengeful. Brujah appear in a myriad of guises: punks, socialists, skinheads, beat poets, bikers, philosophers, rockers, goths, freaks and anarchists.

Members of the Brujah consider it their duty and right to challenge authority and the powers that claim it. Brujah possess a fierce hunger for freedom and refuse to serve as the puppets of others. They fearlessly sink into chaos in their pursuit of change and transformation. Many in the clan believe Kindred society would be completely corrupt if not for them.

Brujah are fanatical in their disparate beliefs. The only thing that unites the clan is its members' desire to overthrow the system. Many are bullheaded crusaders of the worst sort, fanatically devoted to their own causes and blind to any other shade of truth. Others are great intellectualists who desire to institute change through the superiority of their cause and ideals. Whatever their methodology, the Brujah are torn between the nobility of freedom and the anarchy that is the Beast.

While they lack organization, Brujah are not without common purpose. Diversity is their strength, but they always answer the call of their brethren in times of need. Regardless of past antagonism, when the call is made, the clan responds.

Other Kindred often afford the Brujah certain liberties because of their eccentricities and have learned to provide them leeway, for the Brujah are often seen as crazed destroyers.

Disciplines: Celerity, Potence, Presence

Advantage: Centuries of rebellion, sometimes in the face of insurmountable odds, have forged a powerful "us against them" attitude among the member of the Brujah clan. Brujah are quick to side with their own, even at the risk of personal danger. Prestation is neither requested nor offered for this aid. Refusing a brother aid is frowned upon and will result in the loss of a Status Trait and possibly even result in ostracism for the offender. Those who overuse or abuse this advantage will find themselves losing status. A Brujah who has lost all her Status Traits can no longer expect the aid of her former allies, who may ignore her at no risk.

The exception to this are the anarch Brujah, who have their own informal sort of status outside the Camarilla's social structure. These Brujah, although they have no recognized or official status, still willingly answer the call when help is needed.

Disadvantage: As a whole, the Brujah bloodline is cursed with an internalized rage and a hair trigger. While many spend their existence trying to come to grips with the destructive force within themselves, few if any have ever conquered it. Whenever a Brujah slips into a frenzy, she gives herself over entirely to it. All Brujah therefore begin with the Negative Mental Trait: Violent. The character receives no compensation for this Negative Trait. This Trait may not be bought off or lost by any means short of Golconda.

Organization: Among the Brujah, it would seem that might makes right. Any attempt to organize the clan would result in chaos because of the intrinsically rebellious nature of its members. Nonetheless, clan members are fiercely loyal to each other, especially when they rally behind a cause. Brujah meetings (known as Rants) are held frequently and often take place at concerts or raves. All vampires are invited to attend the Rants, but the violent nature of these gatherings usually deters all but the very brave or foolhardy.

Quote: *"Serve you? I'd rather swallow an Inquisitor's cross. The Brujah bow to no one!"*

Stereotypes:

• Gangrel — They truly have the warrior's spirit, but they are lethargic and complacent to the manipulation of tyrants. It is time to stop your flight and fight, Gangrel.

• Malkavian — One minute they're with us a hundred percent; the next, they're counting the holes in the ceiling tiles. I can't make head or tails of them.

• Nosferatu —They deserve better than the lot they've been given, but I'll be damned if the other clans of the Camarilla will given them half the chance we will.

• Toreador — Those effete bastards are so caught up with their trivial games they can't see the flames all around them.

• Tremere — They represent everything we despise. One of these days its going to come down to us or them.

• Ventrue — These blind hypocrites can and have sold the birth right of every free being in an attempt to secure themselves as a sort of outdated, pompous class of aristocrats.

Gangrel

"Nature never makes excellent things for mean or no uses."
—John Locke

The Gangrel are wanderers, rarely remaining in one place for any significant period of time. In this, they are very different from most Kindred, who usually find a haven and jealously guard it. There is no record of who the eldest in the Gangrel line is, and the clan has no established leaders. On the whole, Gangrel seem unconcerned with such things. They are known for being withdrawn, quiet and solemn. They certainly keep their cards close to their chests.

Clan Gangrel consists of survivors, vampires who are capable of making it on their own. They do not despise civilization or the society of their Kindred. They simply do not require it. They are known for their lack of concern about crossing the lands of the werewolves; indeed, it is said they have friends among them.

Gangrel always pick their progeny-to-be very carefully, seeking survivors who are capable of existing on their own. Once they Embrace these mortals, they abandon them, leaving their victims to make their own way through the world. Though they may watch their progeny from a distance, sires rarely interfere. When they feel the childer are ready, Gangrel sires present themselves and teach the childer the true ways of the line.

The Gangrel are very capable shapeshifters, which may explain their ability to cross wild areas unmolested. There are no reports of them being able to transform into anything other than wolves and bats, but there are tales of some Gangrel elders being able to achieve mist form. Perhaps because of this shapechanging power, Gangrel often have features distinctly resembling those of animals. Each time a Gangrel frenzies, she gains another animal feature.

If stories are to be believed, the Gypsies may be mortal descendants of the mysterious Antediluvian who stands at the head of the Gangrel line. They are under his protection, and any Kindred who harms or Embraces a Gypsy will answer to him (or her). Regardless of whether this is true or not, Kindred are loathe to harm Gypsies. Members of the Gangrel clan are expected, through long-standing clan tradition, to aid Gypsies whenever necessary. In turn, Gangrel have also been known to receive aid from Gypsies.

Certain members of Clan Gangrel have adopted much from Gypsy culture, including mannerisms, linguistic elements and even dress.

Disciplines: Animalism, Fortitude, Protean

Clan Advantage: Gangrel rarely allow themselves to be tied down to one place for long, except when they feel there is some task or goal they must accomplish before moving on. As a result, few princes enforce the laws of Presentation upon the nomadic Gangrel. This is not to say that they can not be told to leave by a prince, but they rarely worry about seeking out the prince of every domain where they wander.

Furthermore, when Gangrel deal with werewolves, they do not show a taint of the Wyrm because of early generation. Only Gangrel who have three or more Beast Traits will bear the scent of the Wyrm (see **The Apocalypse**). This is obviously of great advantage when dealing with the already unpredictable Garou, the werewolves with whom the Gangrel share the wild places in our world.

Clan Disadvantages: Each time the Beast (in the form of frenzy provoked by a Beast Trait) washes over a member of the Gangrel bloodline, it leaves a mark of its passing in its wake.

These marks take the form of animalistic features, like a hairy mane, pointed ears or slitted pupils. The player should record these on her character sheet and include them in her description. For every three of these features she possesses, the character must take either the Bestial or Repugnant Negative Social Trait. These traits can and probably will be taken multiple times as the Kindred becomes more and more animalistic.

Organization: The Gangrel do not really consider themselves a clan, at least in the sense that other clans do. They never have clan meetings and rarely attend Camarilla councils. Nonetheless, they do tend to enjoy one another's company, at least more than that of other vampires, and they can often be found together.

Quote: *"The city is not our home. It is simply where we are forced to reside. The outlands are where we belong. Our people have become ill and deranged because we have lived in this purgatory too long. We have grown dependent on the polluted blood of mortals."*

Stereotypes:

• Brujah — Their virtue is pure, but their vision is clouded with hate and pride.

• Malkavian — They are reservoirs of immense power, but they do not know how to tap their potential.

• Nosferatu — Kindred of strong spirit; we share much in common with them.

• Toreador — We hold them in contempt because they have earned nothing better. They must learn to serve instead of take.

• Tremere — Though they do not realize it, they are our enemies. They follow the path of greed and seek to destroy us all.

• Ventrue — Every sect must have leaders; each leader must serve the sect. These leaders are neither better nor worse than most.

MaLKAViaN

"Which one of you claims to be the craziest? Which one the biggest loony? Who runs these card games? Who's the bull goose loony here?"

—McMurphy, "One Flew Over the Cuckoo's Nest"

In each Kindred soul burns the corrupting breath of a ravenous Beast. The Beast scars each immortal differently, granting powers and weaknesses according to bloodline and ancestry. To those of Malkavian blood, the Beast has gifted wisdom, insight and madness. While the "weak-minded" erect barriers to protect their "sanity", Malkavians revel in the chaos of their reality.

Scoffing at the petty intrigues of other Kindred the way an adult scoffs at a child's infatuation with toys, Malkavians manipulate others to alleviate their boredom. They believe the insights they have distilled from madness prove that all other Kindred are insane.

Malkavians have no clan ordinances or requirements. They pay no dues and sign no contracts. As a Malkavian, you only have to be yourself... except, of course, on your unbirthday, when you're allowed to be anyone. Of course, if you choose just to be yourself, no one will chastise you. You are free of the bonds of sanity and the ennui of normalcy.

Malkavians have the privilege of running along the edge of the abyss, fiddling with the Devil and tempting fate and Kindred alike.

Welcome to the Greatest Show on Earth.

Disciplines: Auspex, Dominate, Obfuscate

Clan Advantage: A large number of Malkav's children cavort through their vampiric existence as carefree, if not careless, buffoons. At least, this is how the majority of Kindred perceive them. As a result, once per evening, any Malkavian may choose to ignore one of the following: any use of Status Traits in a Social Challenge, the loss of Status, or any of the other uses of Status. This benefit may only be evoked in a single situation and can only benefit the Malkavian personally. Any Status Traits risked in a challenge are neither lost, nor are they bid— they simply do not exist to the irreverent Malkavian.

Clan Disadvantage: While any Kindred can become insane during his existence, Malkavians begin that way. Upon character creation, one Derangement must be chosen to represent the madness their bloodline must bear (or enjoy, as the case may be). Furthermore, this Derangement is always active and should be continually played by the Malkavian. These Derangements can never be "bought off" or removed during the course of a chronicle. They are far too central an aspect of their personality.

Organization: Hierarchy? Organization? A scant few of us admit that these concepts exist, but why bother? In the end, only chaos is interesting.

Quote: *"We don't do quotes. Piece together your own jigsaw puzzle of meaningless words and dance around it in holy benediction. Meaning comes only from madness."*

Stereotypes:

• Brujah — Puffed up with self-importance. Only when they forget their tiresome quest for freedom will they truly be free.

• Gangrel — So close to the Beast, yet so far from wisdom.

• Nosferatu — These packrats hoard their scraps of gossip in their dirty sewers thinking these make them powerful.

• Toreador — Everything about their art reveals the meaninglessness of the universe. If they would only learn from their own art.

• Tremere — Always be on your worst behavior for these pompous fools.

• Ventrue — They are the most fun to play games with because they take everything so seriously.

NOSFERATU

"What a piece of work is man… and yet to me what is the quintessence of dust? Man delights not me."
— Shakespeare, *Hamlet*

The Nosferatu are the least human in appearance of all the clans. They look something like feral animals. Their smell and appearance are revolting— one could even say monstrous. Some have long bulbous ears, coarse-skinned skulls covered with tufts of hair or elongated faces covered with disgusting warts and lumps.

After a mortal has been Embraced by a Nosferatu, the poor individual undergoes an exceptionally painful period of transformation. Over several weeks, he slowly shifts from his mortal guise to his Nosferatu visage. In the beginning, the childe may revel in his newfound powers, but the pain and changes soon begin. It's likely that the psychological trauma is more painful than the physical torment.

Nosferatu only Embrace those mortals who are twisted in one way or another: emotionally, physically, spiritually or intellectually. They consider the Embrace too horrific to bestow on worthwhile human beings. By changing mortals into vampires, the sires hope to somehow redeem their childer. It's surprising how often this works. Underneath their grim exteriors, the Nosferatu are practical and mostly sane.

It is said that Nosferatu revel in being dirty and disgusting and do little to improve their appearance (not that there is much they can do). Indeed, they are cheerful amid their squalor, especially when others are forced to enter their realm. Nosferatu are known for being grumpy and lewd and cannot be trusted to maintain the standards of civilized society.

Though their power of Obfuscation enables Nosferatu to travel through mortal society, Nosferatu are not able to interact with it. They must therefore live apart. The habits that derive from such an existence extend even to their interactions with other vampires. Nosferatu avoid all contact, preferring their own solitary existence to the chaos of interacting with others.

Though they do not interact with other vampires, they do remain cognizant of the pulse of the city. Nosferatu often listen to the conversations of other vampires from hiding. They have even been known to sneak into a prince's haven to discover the elder's deepest secrets. If a vampire wants to know any information about the city or its immortal inhabitants, she need only speak with a Nosferatu.

The Nosferatu do stay in contact with one another and have developed a unique subculture among the Kindred. They play host to one another with the most elaborate politeness and gentility. They share their information among themselves, and as a result, they are probably the best informed of the Kindred.

Disciplines: Animalism, Obfuscate, Potence

Clan Advantage: The Nosferatu are the undisputed masters of the undercity. In any city where the Nosferatu have had a chance to set up shop, they will be able to enjoy several advantages by using the city's sewer system. First of all, a portion of the city's sewers are the sole property of the

Nosferatu clan; no others can access this area without a Nosferatu guide, the use of powerful Disciplines or as part of the story. Attempting to do so will result in the character either getting lost, alerting the Nosferatu or setting off any number of traps or precautions taken by the sewer's true masters. Furthermore, a Nosferatu standing near a sewer grate, manhole cover or the like may utilize it for the "Fair Escape" rule.

Clan Disadvantage: Because of their horrifying countenances, a Nosferatu may not initiate Social Challenges with others while her true visage is apparent. The exception to this is Social Challenges involving intimidation or threatening an opponent.

Organization: Nosferatu tend to look out for each other and mingle little with others. They are united in spirit, with an established network, but seldom have formal clan meetings of any sort.

Quote: *"I don't look for trouble, and if it comes, I hide. Damn right, pretty boy. You may call me chicken, but I've known a lot of Kindred over the years who got smart just a few seconds too late. It's not like we can't die. It's just that it don't come so easy now."*

Stereotypes:

• Brujah — Nice enough fellas, once you get past the crap.

• Gangrel — Good blokes; they know who they are.

• Malkavian — Creepy, ain't they? Don't even trust 'em.

• Toreador — Empty-headed whelps who should be spanked.

• Tremere — Shady characters, they're up to something.

• Ventrue — Too damn proper; something's stuck up their ass.

TOREADOR

"I will listen hard to your tuition,
And you will see it come to its fruition.
I'll be wrapped around your finger."
—The Police, "Wrapped Around Your Finger"

The members of this clan are known for their hedonistic tendencies, although that description is a misinterpretation of their true nature. They are indeed proud and regal Kindred, highly excitable and possessed of expensive tastes, but the word "hedonistic" is sometimes a bit extreme. Artists are always so misunderstood.

The Toreador are known to be the most sophisticated of the clans. They are concerned with beauty in a way no mortal can fathom. They use the rarefied senses and tastes given to them by the Embrace to become as consumed and impassioned as possible. For a Toreador, nothing matters as much as beauty, though in many cases, the search for beauty becomes a simple search for pleasure, and the Toreador indeed becomes little more than a seeker of pleasures.

Like all true artists, Toreador search for truth beyond an existence they fear to be meaningless. It is this struggle for truth, and ultimately salvation, that has inspired the clan with what it considers its mission: to protect the genius of the human race. Toreador are truly in love with the vigor and passion of mortals and never tire of marveling at mortal creations.

The clan as a whole considers itself a clan of conservators; its protectorate consists of the world's great artists. Toreador specifically seek out those whom they consider the most worthy and Embrace them, thus preserving their genius from the ravages of aging and death. Toreador constantly search for new talent and spend a great deal of time deciding who to preserve and who to leave to fate. Among the Toreador are some of the greatest musicians and artists who ever lived.

The greatest weakness of the Toreador is their sensitivity to beauty. They reflexively surround themselves with elegance and luxury so much that they sometimes turn into addicts of pleasure. Some of this lineage become concerned with nothing but their own continued pleasure— the reputation of the entire clan is sullied by the excesses of these few.

Disciplines: Auspex, Celerity, Presence

Clan Advantage: In their worldliness and continued dalliance with mortals, members of Clan Toreador inevitably collect a herd of fans, followers and hangers-on that can form a convenient and relatively safe source of vitæ. The character may harvest one Blood Trait per evening per level of Performance Ability she possesses. No challenges need to made, but the character must still take fifteen minutes per Blood Trait and must have access to her herd.

Clan Disadvantage: Toreador have a fine appreciation for artistic and natural beauty. This appreciation can reach epic proportions when it concerns truly captivating subjects. Any medium that the Storyteller decrees is sufficiently enthralling or the successful use of the Performance Ability at levels three or higher will entrance a Toreador for half an hour unless he spends a Willpower Trait. While in this state, the Toreador will ignore (but not be unaware of) her surroundings and avoid other responsibilities, even to the point of endangering himself. In this condition, any reasonably unobtrusive foe can surprise the distracted Toreador.

Organization: The members of this clan meet frequently, though these meetings are more social occasions than councils. In times of great urgency, Toreador become united and ferociously active, but they are typically too apathetic to be much of a force.

Quote: "*I remember my first love, a beautiful woman with a silver laugh. For ten years, we were constant companions, but in the end I had to let her go. She begged me to take her, but I could not. You may call me cruel, but in the end, I realized she was not a real artist, but an imitator. She was unworthy. I don't think I have ever recovered.*"

Stereotypes:

• Brujah — They have little respect for the accomplishments of civilization, but they do understand the virtue of change.

• Gangrel — We don't claim to understand them. Are they Kindred at all?

• Malkavian — Though chaos can be beautiful, it would be a difficult life.

• Nosferatu — These loathsome beasts ought to have been expelled from the Camarilla long ago. They hate all beauty and despise us for ours.

• Tremere — Honesty is not a word we associate with this clan, but we respect them for their dedication.

• Ventrue — The patricians of our kind, the Ventrue are the only ones with the refinement to appreciate art, though not as we do.

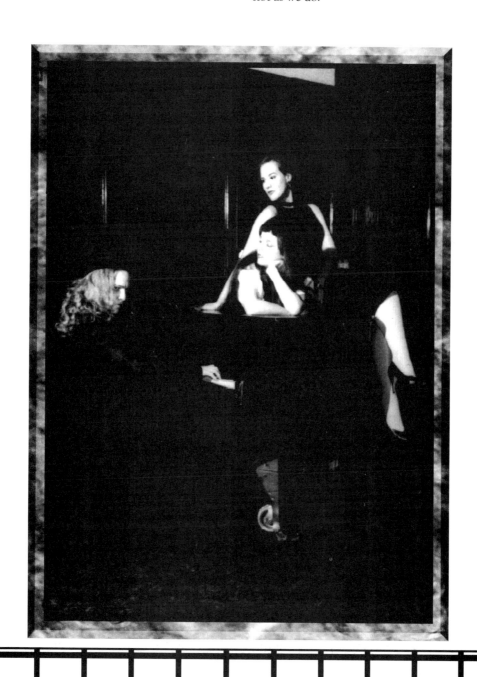

TREMERE

"No one has deceived the whole world, nor has the whole world ever deceived any man."
—Plato

The members of this clan are dedicated and extremely well-organized. Others, however, think of them as arcane and untrustworthy. They are aggressive, highly intellectual and manipulative and respect only those who struggle and persevere against all odds. The Tremere believe they must use the other clans in order to prosper.

Tremere are an odd lot indeed. They claim to have once been wizards who voluntarily gave up their "art" for the powers and eternal life of the vampire. They have never named a founder, and some claim they have none, having discovered and harnessed mystical powers to achieve their state. Many of the elder Kindred discount this claim, as they have met those made by the so-called "magicians" of Europe, who are almost uniformly deluded or schizophrenic.

The clan's link to the substance of blood apparently runs deep, as its members are rumored to be able to use blood in special ways to gain extraordinary powers. Some believe the oldest Tremere were actually practitioners of ancient magic. They also believe the knowledge of those practices has been passed down from generation to generation and is now viewed by young Tremere as natural and commonplace—certainly not magical.

The leaders of this clan are based in Vienna, although the clan has chantries on every continent of the world. A council of seven elders is said to control the entire clan. From that locus, they maintain a tightly ordered, highly hierarchical group and allow no one outside the lineage to view the clan's inner workings.

Young members of Clan Tremere are expected to obey their elders without question, but this is not as true as it once was. Tremere typically have immense love for and loyalty to their clan, largely because many are blood bound to the seven elders of the clan. Tremere come to love the clan because of the love they feel for their masters. Though there are some rebels and anarchs from the Tremere line, it is possible that they are merely adapting a pose for the sake of the clan, as part of their long-term schemes.

Disciplines: Auspex, Dominate, Thaumaturgy

Clan Advantage: Once they prove themselves to their superiors, lower ranking Tremere can expect training in both Disciplines and rituals. Many elders are paranoid of younger more aggressive Tremere and guard their knowledge jealously. However, most will reward loyal and effective clan members for their accomplishments. While they respect competent and powerful leaders, Tremere are highly competitive and will seize any opportunity to further their personal power as long as it does not jeopardize the clan as a whole.

Clan Disadvantage: The head of a chantry holds a Blood Trait of each member of that chantry. Furthermore, the Council of Seven in Vienna has access to another two Blood Traits, taken when the member was introduced as a childe. These Traits are used not only for punishment and control, but to help locate missing clan members, particularly those captured by any of Clan

Tremere's many enemies. Upon his presentation, a childe is also fed a Blood Trait from each of the seven elders, bringing him one third of the way to being bound to them. Furthermore, despite periods of internal strife, members of the clan form a tightly-knit group and usually cooperate with frightening efficiency against foes and obstacles.

Organization: Tremere are tightly organized and very hierarchical. Young members are expected to obey older ones without question, but that doesn't always happen anymore.

Quote: *"We must survive Gehenna and establish the tenets of our new world order once the horror is overcome. If we are to succeed, we must control the other clans. No more time can be wasted. If the other Kindred cannot be convinced to aid us, they must be forced to submit."*

Stereotypes:

• Brujah — Chaotic and savage, their disrespect and disunity will be their downfall.

• Gangrel — Noble Kindred, in their own way.

• Malkavian — So often they seem normal, but all members of their lineage carry their strange curse.

• Nosferatu — If they know what is best for them, they had best mind their own business, not ours.

• Toreador — Idle hedonists, but nonetheless, a compliment and a kind word go a long way towards bringing them under our sway.

• Ventrue — Too fractious to be truly effective; nonetheless, they are our chief rivals for control of the Camarilla.

Ventrue

"He must not flinch from being blamed for vices that are necessary for safeguarding the state."
—Machiavelli, *The Prince*

Culture, civilization, sophistication— the Ventrue are proudly dedicated to these tenets. After the Inquisition blazed across the world and scourged Kindred ancient and young, the Ventrue lead the way in uniting the clans of the Camarilla. The Camarilla is a vampiric society dedicated to a civilized, careful and secret existence within the mortal population, and based on the noble Six Traditions, laws that are just as important today as they were five hundred years ago. The Ventrue maintain the traditional structures that allow vampires to ignore the lesser concerns of safety and sustenance. Vampires are thus freed to attend to higher concerns and more sophisticated pursuits.

The Ventrue, in their own perspective, serve as the pillars of society through wise leadership and diplomatic politics. They seek to avoid brutish violence, preferring to settle disputes through genteel politics and enlightened debate. It is the clan's hope that by displaying its unity and strength, its courage and resolution, its foresight and knowledge, all vampires may follow its good example and join in a true utopia.

Ventrue consider the Masquerade to be the foundation of vampiric society and hence not to be trifled with. They feel that those who meddle with all that is sacred in the Camarilla should be rooted out and convinced of the sanctity and significance of the Masquerade. However, Ventrue realize that other Kindred should be treated gently, for they lack the clan's social wisdom. They hope that other vampires' transgressions arise from weak wills and simple minds, not from base meanness.

Ventrue assume (or take) great authority and great power. They feel they are responsible for Kindred society and seek to impose order upon it— their own order, regardless of what others want. As part of this order, young Ventrue are taught to respect their elders. Greater even than superiors, however, are the laws and traditions of vampiric society; all new Ventrue are expected to uphold and defend the Camarilla's laws. As lessers, they should be provided with examples of honorable sophistication. The childe of a Ventrue is the essence of nobility, with eternity as his dynasty.

Disciplines: Dominate, Fortitude, Presence

Clan Advantage: Clan Ventrue has always been intimately associated with wealth and resources. Whether this is the result of their exacting choice in progeny or by virtue of their bloodline is debatable. In either case, each Ventrue receives a free Finance Influence Trait. While this Trait can be expended or temporarily neutralized, it can not be destroyed or stripped from them. It cannot be permanently traded away, either.

Clan Disadvantage: The Ventrue maintain that they are an uncommon if not rarefied breed among the Kindred. It is perhaps quite fitting that their taste for vitae is similarly demanding. Upon Embrace, a Ventrue will instinctively become aware that only one type or source of blood will satisfy her hunger, such as "virgins", "children", "blond men" or "peasants".

Organization: Tradition is the greatest king. Ventrue favor age, experience and generation over youth and ability. They believe that the capable rise to the top as soon as they prove themselves. In all matters, the Ventrue embrace caution and debate all sides of a situation before acting. Of course, some situations require swift action, and such situations are usually recognized.

Much of Ventrue legislation and consideration occurs at regular weekly, monthly and yearly clan meetings. There the clan follows a firm agenda and rationally proposes new itineraries. In emergency situations, the eldest Ventrue of the city calls for an immediate meeting.

Quote: "Every jungle has its lion. It is natural and just that we rise to the top in this urban jungle, for we have been ordained to lead. The scepter of leadership is our birthright."

Stereotypes:

• Brujah — Mindless brutes who seek to ruin our society. It is our responsibility to stop them.

• Gangrel — These ferocious Kindred have little concern for the safety of society, but they at least have respect for it. They can be used.

• Malkavian — Selfish, regressed children who profane the noble with mockery and silliness. Humor them in order to use them.

• Nosferatu — Though they do their best, their repugnance prevents any possibility of true sophistication.

• Toreador — They are as flighty and capricious as art itself, but still dedicated to our great society.

• Tremere — While they too believe in organization and law, they play the game of manipulation with unbridled fanaticism. Beware.

Generation

Age is not the only measure of power among the Kindred. The potency of a Kindred's blood is of primary importance as well. All vampires are descended from Caine, the first and most powerful vampire. As the lifeblood of Caine is passed from sire to childe, the potency of that blood diminishes. Those who are the grandchilder of Caine possess much more potential power than those who are 13 generations removed.

Those at the bottom of this dark genealogical tree find themselves to be pale shadows of their distant ancestors. It's no wonder that these thin-blooded progeny often lust after the vitæ of their progenitors. Being a few generations away from Caine offers great power, but promises great danger.

Your generation indicates how many Attribute Traits you can have and dictates the number of Blood and Willpower Traits you possess. The "Generation Table" in Chapter Two indicates the maximum Attribute Traits, maximum Blood Traits, and starting and maximum Willpower Traits that different generations of vampires have. Starting characters are usually 13th generation, but can be of lower generation if Negative Traits are acquired to lower generation (see "Negative Traits" in Chapter Two). If your starting character is of lower generation, take the number of Blood Traits and Willpower Traits indicated on the chart. Note: Attribute Traits listed indicate the maximum you can have in your primary category— Physical, Social or Mental— starting at seven.

It's possible for characters to lower their generation after play begins. This is accomplished through diablerie or other unique means (see "Diablerie" in Chapter Five). If your generation does decrease during the game, your Blood Trait and Willpower Trait maximums are increased (though current levels do not automatically increase). Look on the chart to see what your new maximums are. Likewise, the maximum number of Attribute Traits (in the primary category), Abilities and Disciplines you may possess increases. However, your actual number of Attribute Traits, Abilities and Disciplines do not rise because you are now of lower generation. Attribute Traits, Abilities and Disciplines must still be acquired through normal life experiences (see "Experience" in Chapter Five).

Nature and Demeanor

Humans instinctively roleplay. Each moment of our lives is spent playing a role of some type or another. We are made up of many layers of personalities, some of which we create for the benefit of our peers.

Archetypes are a way of defining personalities. They describe the roles that are a collective characteristic of our identities, the personality types all people somehow share.

The psychologist Carl Jung invented the idea of archetypes as a way of describing any concept that resides in the collective unconscious of humanity. He believed that such complex symbols couldn't be rigidly categorized, but he did give names to some of the archetypes. Nonetheless, in order to incorporate the concept of archetypes into our system, a modified version of this idea is used to describe personalities (instead of concepts). Remember to take the following guidelines with a grain of salt.

Characters do not, in fact, fit into neat and tidy categories. Archetypes are molds for an infinite number of different personalities and should not be seen as absolute standards of personality. An archetype is a basic pattern or template. Each individual varies from that original in many ways. These personality archetypes are examples of the variety of human personalities. They are intended to guide, not restrict.

The key to the use of archetypes is the interaction between the character's Nature and Demeanor. Nature is the inner personality, the part the character does not usually reveal to others. Most people do not reveal their true, inner selves; they create a Demeanor instead. The Demeanor is a false front behind which the true self can be hidden. Demeanors may be as consistent as the character's eye color, or may change from minute to minute. Extraordinarily open, honest or simple-minded individuals have the same Demeanor and Nature.

Archetypes have a practical impact on the game, for characters can be manipulated according to their personalities. A character's Nature may be strong enough to pull him out of a frenzy if he is about to do something that goes against it. For example, a Bravo would be allowed a chance to stave off his frenzy if confronted by a lighter held by an anarch he had bullied in the past.

Nature also works like a Negative Trait. If you know someone's Nature, you may use it as a Negative Trait in any type of challenge. The Nature should have something to do with the challenge, so you could bid a Martyr Nature when trying to talk someone to going into a burning building to rescue a wounded Kindred. However, you could not use a Child Nature when trying to look at an aura.

The following is an in-depth account of the Natures and Demeanors listed in Chapter Two.

Architect

You believe in creating something of lasting value. You seek to leave a legacy of some kind for those who will come after you. You are the type of person who will seek to build a town, create a company or found an institution.

Bravo

You are a bully, a ruffian and a tough. You delight in tormenting the weak. You always demand to have things your way and do not tolerate those who cross you. Power and might are all you respect. You heed only those who can prove their power to you.

You see nothing wrong with forcing your will upon others. There is nothing you like better than to persecute, antagonize, heckle and intimidate those for whom you feel contempt. The emotions of kindness and pity are not completely foreign to you, but you do not show them often. While most Bravos despise the weak, others become their protectors.

Caregiver

You always try to help those who are around you, struggling to make a difference in the needs and sorrows of the unfortunate. People around you depend upon your stability and strength to keep them steady and centered. People come to you when they have problems.

Child

You are still immature in personality and temperament. You are a kid who never grew up. Though you can care for yourself, you prefer the security of being cared for by others. You often seek out someone to look out for you as a caretaker of sorts. Some see you as a spoiled brat, while others see you as an innocent cherub unspoiled by the evils of the world. This is a very common archetype for Kindred who were created when they were young. Such Kindred often mature mentally, but not emotionally.

Conformist

You are a follower. Taking charge is simply not your style. It is easy for you to adapt, attune, adjust, comply and reconcile yourself to a new situation in which you find yourself. You are attracted to the brightest star, the person whom you feel is best and will go the farthest. It is both difficult and distasteful for you to go against the flow. You hate inconsistency and instability, and know that by supporting a strong leader, you help prevent chaos from occurring. Any stable group needs some kind of Conformist.

Conniver

What is the sense of working hard when you can get something for nothing? Why work when, just by talking, you can get what you want? You are always trying to find the easy way out. You're on the fast track to success and wealth. Some people might call what you do swindling or even outright theft, but you know that you only do what everyone else does. You're just up front about it. Additionally, the swindling and plotting is a game, and you get great pleasure from outwitting someone. Connivers play many roles. You may be a thief, a swindler, a street waif, an entrepreneur, a con man or just a finagler.

Deviant

There are always people who simply do not fit in. You are a miscreant. Your beliefs, motivations and sense of propriety are the complete antithesis of the status quo. You are not so much an aimless rebel as an independent thinker who does not belong to vampiric society. You don't give a damn about other people's morality, but you do adhere to your own strange code of conduct. Deviants are typically irreverent, and some can have truly bizarre tastes and desires. You also dearly love to shock other people by striking out at their pointless codes and ethics.

Director

You despise chaos and disorder and tend to take control and organize things. You like to be in charge, live to organize and habitually strive to make things work smoothly. You trust your own judgment implicitly and tend to think of things in black-and-white terms.

Fanatic

You are consumed by a cause. It is the primary force in your life, for good or ill. You are driven to accomplish the directives of your self-appointed mission. Every ounce of sweat and passion you possess is directed toward it. Indeed, you may feel very guilty about spending time on anything else. You let nothing stand in your way— nothing that you cannot overcome, in any case. You and those around you may suffer, but your cause is everything. Before the game begins, make sure you define your cause and understand how it may affect your behavior.

Gallant

You are as flamboyant as you are amoral. Some see you as a rogue, a Don Juan, a rake, a paramour or just a lounge lizard. You see yourself as all these things. You're a consummate actor who loves to make as big a show of things as possible. Nothing attracts your attention more than an appreciative audience. You love people, and you love to impress them even more. Though you may indeed be a superior lover, you enjoy the chase almost as much as the kill. Gallants vary widely in temperament and ambition, holding little more in common than their love of attention.

Hedonist

There is no point to life, no meaning or direction. The best plan is to have as good a time as possible. Rome may burn, but you shall drink wine and sing songs. You are a bon vivant, a sensualist, a sybarite and a party animal. The words austerity, self-denial, self-discipline and asceticism have no place in your life. You prefer instant gratification. You don't mind a little hard work, as long as a good time awaits when the work is done. Most Hedonists have little self-control, for they so dearly love going to excess.

Jester

You are the fool, idiot, quipster, clown or comic, forever making fun of both yourself and others. You constantly seek the humor in any situation, and always strive to battle the tides of depression inside yourself. You hate sorrow and pain and constantly try to take other's minds off the dark side of life. Sometimes you will do nearly anything to forget that pain exists. Your particular brand of humor might not always impress your friends, but it makes you feel better. Some Jesters manage to escape pain and find true happiness, but most never find release. Most just stave off the pain a little longer.

Judge

As a facilitator, moderator, arbitrator, conciliator and peacemaker, you always seek to make things better. You pride yourself on your rationality, judgment and ability to deduce a reasonable explanation when given the facts. You constantly struggle to promote truth, but you understand how difficult it is to ascertain. You respect justice, for justice is the means by which truth can reign. You hate dissension and arguments and shy away from dogmatism. Judges often make good leaders, though a lack of vision can sometimes cause them to adhere to the status quo instead of searching for better options.

Loner

You are always alone, even in a crowd. You are the wanderer, hunter and lone wolf. Others might think of you as lonely, forsaken, isolated or remote. In truth, you prefer your own company to that of others for many different reasons. Perhaps you do not understand people, people dislike you, people like you too much, or you are simply lost in your own thoughts. Your reasons are your own. You prefer to walk alone, and you could care less about what others think or say about you.

Martyr

Many people possess the martyr instinct, but only a few act upon it. Even fewer people live the life of a martyr. You, however, are one of those few. Your desire for self-sacrifice may stem from a poor self-image, a lack of control or a profoundly developed sense of love. You are able to endure long-lasting and severe suffering because of your beliefs and ideals.

At the worst of times, a Martyr expects sympathy and attention because of his or her suffering, and may even feign or exaggerate pain or deprivation. In the best of times, a Martyr chooses to suffer injury or even Final Death rather than renounce religion, beliefs, principles, causes or friends.

Rebel

You are a malcontent, an iconoclastic and free-thinking creature. You are independent, free-willed and unwilling to join any particular cause or movement. You desire only the freedom to be yourself. You do not make a good follower and are not usually a very good leader. You tend to be deliberately insubordinate to authority, even to the point of stupidity.

Survivor

No matter what, you always manage to survive. You can endure, pull through, recover from, outlast or outlive nearly

any circumstance. When the going gets tough, you get going. You never say die and never give up. Nothing angers you as much as a person who does not struggle to make things better or who surrenders to the nameless forces of the universe. You utterly despise quitters.

Traditionalist

You are an orthodox, conservative and extremely traditional individual. What was good enough for you when you were young is good enough for you now. You almost never change. You oppose change for the sake of change. You may be seen by some as a miser, a reactionary or simply as an old fogy. You strive to always preserve the status quo.

Visionary

There are very few who look beyond the suffocating embrace of society and mundane thought to see something more. There are very few who are brave, strong or imaginative enough. Society treats such people with both respect and contempt, but it is the Visionary who perverts as well as guides society into the future.

You may be a spiritualist, shaman, New Ager, mystic, philosopher or inventor. Whatever you are, you are always looking for something more. You see beyond the bounds of conventional imagination and create new possibilities. Though you might have your head in the clouds and be of an impractical bent, you are filled with new ideas and perceptions.

Traits

Trait (trãt) n. A *distinctive feature, as of character*.
— American Heritage Dictionary

When a writer doesn't have the time or need to demonstrate what a character is like, descriptive words are used. These words must be carefully selected so that they reveal all the important features of the character's persona. These words are nearly always adjectives: "Vandalere was a *thin*, *frail* man — *weak* in body, but diabolically *cunning* in mind."

In **The Masquerade**, we use these adjectives in much the same way. Indeed, they are the basis of the game system. We call them Traits.

Traits have two primary purposes. The first and most important purpose is to enable you to describe your character concretely and thereby empower your roleplaying. The second is to enable you to interact with other characters in terms of the game system. The mechanics of **The Masquerade** revolve around the Trait system. Every challenge— confrontation between characters— is resolved using them.

The premise of this system is that a character who is described by a specific Trait tends to be pretty good at things that involve that Trait, and is certainly better than someone who doesn't have the Trait at all. For example, someone who is Brawny is a better arm wrestler than someone who isn't. Likewise, a marathon runner needs to be Tireless in order to finish a race still standing, and a child who is Persuasive has a good chance of convincing his mom that he didn't break a vase on the living room floor.

In theory, a player can choose any adjective and take it as a Trait. However, for a number of reasons, this is not suggested for any but the most expert. Many adjectives are unimportant, extraneous and impractical; there is no need for a Pyorrheal Trait, although it's possible that a vampire might get some form of gum disease. Still, the chances of that Trait being used in a bidding contest— the act of a challenge— are close to nil.

Anyway, allowing any adjective would play hell with the mechanics of the game. Players would have to carry around pocket dictionaries and flip pages every time some wisecracker bid "Vigesimal". If there are a set number of standard adjectives used as the Trait pool, everyone can be expected to know the meaning of every adjective and can know when each is applicable. For these reasons, **The Masquerade** has a list of Traits from which to choose.

If you decide to add more Traits to the list, here are some guidelines: keep the number of new Traits low, make sure all players understand them, and make sure that they don't duplicate existing Traits.

Attributes (Bidding Traits)

Creative players can think of ways to use nearly any Trait in nearly any challenge. Though this is most praiseworthy, players can sometimes go too far. To avoid this, the general rule on bidding Traits is very strict: you can only bid Traits from the category that best suits the nature of the challenge (i.e., Traits bid are from the same category— Physical, Mental or Social). Even then, however, not all Physical Traits (or Mental, or Social) are appropriate to all "Physical" (or "Mental", or "Social") challenges.

For example, beginners might think they can use all their Physical Traits in combat. This is incorrect. If your character is trying to kick someone, Resilient is not an appropriate Trait to bid as part of the attack. Likewise, if your character is trying to read an opponent's aura, Creative might not be an appropriate Trait.

For such an "inappropriate" Trait to be allowed, both parties must agree. When an opponent bids a Trait that you feel is extremely inappropriate, politely tell her that you're not going to allow its use. If she is insistent, reevaluate your grievance. If you still can't agree, appeal to any witnesses of the contest. Then, if there is still deadlock and no one is willing to compromise, seek out a Narrator to make a ruling. Appeals to a Narrator in these situations, however, should occur very, very rarely. Learn to handle confrontations on your own, quickly and socially.

To keep things simple, you can ignore the subtleties of Traits and, say, use any Physical Trait in any Physical Challenge. This approach is particularly useful when you have a number of novice players. Eventually you will go beyond this boring convention and only allow players to use Traits that are appropriate to the situation at hand. This method is more complicated, but it can be a lot more fun. Try it out.

Physical Traits

Athletic: You have conditioned your body so that it responds well in full-body movements, especially in competitive events.

Use: Sports, duels, running, acrobatics, grappling and Celerity.

Brawny: Bulky muscular strength.

Use: Punching, kicking, or grappling in combat when your goal is to inflict damage. Power lifting. All feats of strength.

Brutal: You are capable of taking nearly any action in order to survive.

Use: Fighting an obviously superior enemy.

Dexterous: General adroitness and skill involving the use of one's hands.

Use: Weapon-oriented combat (Melee or Firearms). Pickpocketing. Punching.

Enduring: A persistent sturdiness against physical opposition.

Use: When your survival is at stake, this is a good Trait to risk as a second, or successive, bid.

Energetic: A powerful force of spirit. A strong internal drive propels you and, in physical situations, you can draw on a deep reservoir of enthusiasm and zeal.

Use: Combat. Celerity.

Ferocious: Possession of brutal intensity and extreme physical determination.

Use: Any time that you intend to do serious harm. When in frenzy.

Graceful: Control and balance in the motion and use of the entire body.

Use: Combat defense. Whenever you might lose your balance (stepping on a banana peel, fighting on four-inch-thick rafters).

Lithe: Characterized by flexibility and suppleness.

Use: Acrobatics, gymnastics, dodging, dancing and Celerity.

Nimble: Light and skillful; able to make agile movements.

Use: Dodging, jumping, rolling, acrobatics. Hand-to-hand combat.

Quick: This Trait represents your speed and reactions.

Use: Defending against a surprise attack. Running, dodging, attacking. Celerity.

Resilient: This is strength of health. You are able to recover quickly from bodily harm.

Use: Resisting adverse environments. Defending against damage in an attack.

Robust: Resistant to physical harm and damage.

Use: Defending against damage in an attack. Endurance related actions that could take place over a period of time.

Rugged: You are hardy, rough and brutally healthy. You can shrug off wounds and pain to continue your struggles.

Use: When resisting damage, any challenge that you enter while injured. Earth Melding.

Stalwart: Physically strong and uncompromising against opposition.

Use: Resisting damage, or when standing your ground against overwhelming odds or a superior foe.

Steady: More than simply physically dependable, you are controlled, unfaltering and balanced. You have firm control over your efforts.

Use: Weapon attacks. Fighting in exotic locations. Piloting oil tankers.

Tenacious: Physically determined through force of will. You often prolong physical confrontations, even when it might not be wise to do so.

Use: Second or subsequent physical challenge.

Tireless: You have a runner's stamina — you are less taxed by physical efforts than ordinary people.

Use: Any endurance related challenge, second or subsequent physical challenge with the same foe or foes. Celerity.

Tough: A harsh, aggressive attitude and a reluctance ever to submit.

Use: Whenever you're wounded or winded.

Vigorous: This is a combination of energy, power, intensity and resistance to harm.

Use: Combat and athletic challenges when you're on the defensive.

Wiry: Tight, streamlined, muscular strength.

Use: Punching, kicking or grappling in combat. Acrobatic movements. Endurance lifting.

Negative Physical Traits

Clumsy: Lacking physical coordination, balance and grace. You are prone to stumbling and dropping objects.

Cowardly: In threatening situations, saving your own neck is all that is important. You might even flee when you have the upper hand, just out of habit.

Decrepit: You move and act as if you are old and infirm. You recover from physical damage slowly, are unable to apply full muscular strength, and tire easily.

Delicate: Frail and weak in structure; you are easily damaged by physical harm.

Docile: The opposite of the Ferocious and Tenacious Traits; you lack physical persistence and tend to submit rather than fight long battles.

Flabby: Your muscles are underdeveloped. You cannot apply your strength well against resistance.

Lame: You are disabled in one or more limbs. The handicap can be as obvious as a missing leg or as subtle as a dysfunctional arm.

Lethargic: Slow and drowsy. You suffer from a serious lack of energy or motivation.

Puny: You are weak and inferior in strength. This could mean diminutive size.

Sickly: Weak and feeble. Your body responds to physical stress as if it were in the throes of a debilitating illness.

Social Traits

Alluring: You have an attractive and appealing presence that inspires desire in others.

Use: Seduction. Convincing others.

Beguiling: This Trait represents the skill of deception and illusion. You can twist the perceptions of others and lead them to believe what suits you.

Use: Tricking others. Lying under duress.

Charismatic: This is a talent of inspiration and motivation, the sign of a strong leader.

Use: In a situation involving leadership or the achievement of leadership. Awe contests.

Charming: Your speech and actions make you appear attractive and appealing to others.

Use: Convincing. Persuading. Entrancement Challenges.

Commanding: Impressive delivery of orders and suggestions. This implies skill in the control and direction of others.

Use: When you are seen as a leader. Presence Challenges.

Compassionate: Deep feelings of care or pity for others.

Use: Defending the weak or downtrodden. Defeating major obstacles while pursuing an altruistic end.

Dignified: Something about your posture and body carriage appears honorable and aesthetically pleasing. You carry yourself well.

Use: Presence Challenges. Defending against Social Disciplines.

Diplomatic: You are tactful, careful and thoughtful in speech and deed. Few are displeased with what you say or do.

Use: Very important in intrigue. Leadership situations.

Elegant: You have a way about you that suggests refined tastefulness. Even though you don't need money to be elegant, you exude an air of richness and high society.

Use: High society or Toreador parties. Might be important in some clans for advancement. Defending against Social Disciplines.

Eloquent: This Trait signifies the ability to speak in an interesting and convincing manner.

Use: Convincing others. Swaying emotions. Public speaking.

Empathetic: You can identify and understand the emotions and moods of people with whom you come in contact.

Use: Gauging the feelings of others. Beast Within contests. Not useful in defense against Social Disciplines (might actually make it easier to use them on you).

Expressive: The ability to articulate thoughts in interesting, significant, meaningful ways. If you want someone to understand your meaning, this is the Trait to apply.

Use: Producing art, acting, performing.

Friendly: You fit in with all you meet. Even after a short conversation, most find it difficult to dislike you.

Use: Entrancement Challenges. Convincing others.

Genial: Cordial, kindly, warm and pleasant. You are pleasing to be around.

Use: Mingling at parties. Starting an Entrancement Challenge. Generally used in a second or later Social Challenge with someone.

Gorgeous: You are beautiful or handsome. You were born with a face and body that is good-looking to most people you meet.

Use: Modeling, posing. Beast Within Challenges. Entrancement Challenges.

Ingratiating: You know what to do to gain the favor of people who know you.

Use: Dealing with elders in a social situation. Entrancement Challenges. Defending against Social Disciplines.

Intimidating: A frightening or awesome presence that causes others to feel timid. This Trait is particularly useful when attempting to cow opponents.

Use: Dread Gaze and Majesty Challenges. Inspiring common fear. Ordering others.

Magnetic: People feel drawn to you; those around you are interested in your speech and actions.

Use: Presence Challenges. Beast Within Challenges. Seduction.

Persuasive: Your arguments and requests seem believable, convincing and correct. Very useful when someone else is undecided on an issue.

Use: Persuading or convincing others.

Seductive: You know how to entice and tempt. You can use your good looks and your body to get what you want from others.

Use: Subterfuge, Entrancement, Summoning and Seduction.

Witty: Cleverly humorous. Jokes and jests come easily to you, and you are perceived as a funny person when you want to be.

Use: At parties. Entertaining someone. Goading or insulting someone.

Negative Social Traits

Bestial: You have started to resemble the Beast of your vampiric nature. Maybe you have claw-like fingernails, heavy body hair or a feral glint in your eyes; however your Beast manifests, you definitely seem inhuman.

Callous: You are unfeeling, uncaring and insensitive to the suffering of others. Your heart is a frozen stone.

Condescending: You just can't help it; your contempt for others is impossible to hide.

Dull: Those with whom you speak usually find you boring and uninteresting. Conversing with you is a chore. You do not present yourself well to others.

Naive: You lack the air of worldliness, sophistication or maturity that most carry.

Obnoxious: You are annoying or unappealing in speech, action or appearance.

Repugnant: Your appearance disgusts everyone around you. Needless to say, you make a terrible first impression with strangers.

Shy: You are timid, bashful, reserved and socially hesitant.

Tactless: You are unable to do or say things that others find appropriate to the social situation.

Untrustworthy: You are rumored or perceived to be untrustworthy and unreliable (whether you are or not).

Mental Traits

Alert: You are mentally prepared for danger and can react quickly when it occurs.

Use: Preventing surprise attacks. Defending against Dominate Challenges.

Attentive: You pay attention to everyday occurrences around you. When something extraordinary happens, you are usually ready for it.

Use: Preventing surprise attacks. Seeing through Obfuscate when you don't expect it. Preventing Dominate.

Calm: You can withstand an extraordinary level of disturbance without becoming agitated or upset. You are a wellspring of self-control.

Use: Resisting frenzy or commands that provoke violence. Whenever a mental attack might upset you. Primarily for defense.

Clever: Quick-witted resourcefulness. You think well on your feet.

Use: Using a Mental Discipline against another.

Creative: Your ideas are original and imaginative. This implies an ability to produce unusual solutions to your difficulties. You can create artistic pieces. A requirement for any true artist.

Use: Defending against aura readings. Creating anything.

Cunning: Crafty and sly, you possess a great deal of ingenuity.

Use: Tricking others. Command Challenges.

Dedicated: You give yourself over totally to your beliefs. When one of your causes is at stake, you stop at nothing to succeed.

Use: Useful in any Mental Challenge when your beliefs are at stake. Defense against Forgetful Mind.

Determined: When it comes to mental endeavors, you are fully committed. Nothing can divert your intentions to succeed once you have made up your mind.

Use: Facedowns. Useful in a normal Mental Challenge.

Discerning: You are discriminating, and can pick out details, subtleties and idiosyncrasies. You have clarity of vision.

Use: Auspex-related challenges.

Disciplined: Your mind is structured and controlled. This rigidity gives you an edge in battles of will.

Use: Thaumaturgy contests. Facedowns. Useful in a Mental Discipline contest.

Insightful: The power of looking at a situation and gaining an understanding of it.

Use: Investigation (but not defense against it). Reading Auras. Using Heightened Senses. Seeing through Obfuscate when you expect it.

Intuitive: Knowledge and understanding somehow come to you without conscious reasoning, as if by instinct.

Use: Reading auras. Seeing through Obfuscate.

Knowledgeable: You know copious and detailed information about a wide variety of topics. This represents "book-learning".

Use: Forgetful Mind contests. Remembering information your character might know. Employing Thaumaturgy.

Observant: This Trait signifies depth of vision, the power to look at something and notice the important aspects of it.

Use: Heightened Senses. Picking up on subtitles that others might overlook.

Patient: You are tolerant, persevering and steadfast. You can wait out extended delays with composure.

Use: Facedowns or other mental battles after another Trait has been bid.

Rational: You believe in logic, reason, sanity and sobriety. Your ability to reduce concepts to a mathematical level helps you analyze the world.

Use: Defending against emotion-oriented mental attacks. Defending against an aura reading. Not used as an initial bid.

Reflective: Meditative self-recollection and deep thought. The Trait of the serious thinker, Reflective enables you to consider all aspects of a conundrum.

Use: Meditation. Remembering information. Defending against most Mental attacks.

Shrewd: You are astute and artful. You keep your wits about you and accomplish mental feats with efficiency and finesse.

Use: Defending against a Mental Discipline.

Vigilant: Alertly watchful. You have the disposition of a guard dog; your attention misses little. More appropriate for mental defense than for attack.

Use: Defending against investigation, Forgetful Mind and Command. Seeing through Obfuscate.

Wily: You are sly and full of guile. Because you are wily, you can trick and deceive easily.

Use: Tricking others. Lying under duress. Confusing mental situations.

Wise: This Trait represents an overall understanding of the workings of the world.

Use: Giving advice. Dispensing snippets of Zen. Defending against Dominate Challenges.

Negative Mental Traits

Forgetful: You have trouble remembering even important things.

Gullible: You are easily deceived, duped or fooled.

Ignorant: You are uneducated or misinformed, and never seem to know anything.

Impatient: This Trait means you are restless, anxious and generally intolerant of delays. You want everything to go your way— immediately.

Oblivious: Unaware and unmindful. You'd be lucky if you noticed an airplane flying through your living room.

Predictable: Because you lack originality or intelligence, even strangers can easily figure out what you intend to do next. Not a very good Trait for chess players.

Shortsighted: You lack foresight. You rarely look beyond the superficial; details of perception are usually lost on you.

Submissive: You have no backbone; you relent and surrender at any cost rather than stand up for yourself.

Violent: An extreme lack of self-control. You fly into rages at the slightest provocation, and frenzy is always close to the surface. This is a Mental Trait because it represents mental instability.

Witless: You lack the ability to process information quickly. In all seriousness, you are foolish and slow to act when threatened.

Abilities

"I can honestly say that I have learned a great deal from chess: how to be patient, how to bide my time, how to see the other man's point of view, how to persevere in uncompromising situations, how to learn from my failures."

—Fred Reinfeld, "The Complete Chessplayer"

While many complex actions in **Mind's Eye Theatre** can be easily and quickly executed with simple challenges, this is not always the case. Abilities are the skills, talents and knowledges used by characters.

An Ability allows a character to engage in, if not excel in, a particular type of activity. She would not normally be able to attempt the activity without it. Performing such a task often involves risking Traits. If the character is defeated in the challenge, she may choose to temporarily sacrifice a level in the appropriate Ability to call for a retest. While any Traits risked are still lost, it is possible to still win the challenge. An Ability lost in this manner is recovered at the beginning of the next session. If a character loses all her levels in an Ability in this manner, she may not use that Ability until at least one level is recovered.

Abilities can be chosen multiple times to represent a high degree of expertise in that skill or a broad number of fields, as is the case with Performance, Science and Linguistics.

Often, the use of Abilities is accompanied by a challenge of one sort or another. Some of these will be performed with a Narrator who will not only assign the relative difficulty of the challenge in Traits, but will actually perform the test with you. A Static Challenge is performed against a difficulty that is set by a Narrator. The Narrator can also interpret the amount of time required to attempt the skill, and may even ask the player to pretend she is performing the skill or drop out of play for the duration of the task.

Other Abilities can be used directly against another player, such as Subterfuge or Melee. These rarely need the assistance of a Narrator.

Animal Ken

Vampires are among the most efficient predators in the world. For humans, this is not always apparent, but animals seem instinctively aware of this and actively avoid the undead. A character who possesses Animal Ken, however, has practiced long and hard to regain (or simply never lost) the ability to interact and cooperate with natural animals. Given time and access to an animal, she may train it to perform simple tasks (i.e. fetch, guard, attack, etc.). When the command is given, the animal must make a Mental Challenge to successfully understand and carry out the order. The difficulty of the test will be based on the level of domestication of the animal as well as the complexity of the task required. The character may also attempt to calm an injured, attacking or frightened animal by defeating it in a Social Challenge.

Brawl

You are adept at using your body as a weapon. This includes any form or unarmed combat from dirty in-fighting to highly-stylized martial arts. The Brawl Ability may be used in coordination with claws, teeth and other types of such natural weaponry. In this manner, even a character who is stripped bare can still present himself as a formidable foe to an unwary opponent.

Bureaucracy

Each day, the world becomes more and more riddled by a staggering amount of complexity, paperwork and red tape. A Kindred knowledgeable in the ways of bureaucracy has the power to navigate this system and utilize it for her benefit. Bureaucracy can allow the character to appropriate licenses, use contractual agreements to her advantage and recover, alter or destroy files from organizations (in a pseudo-authorized manner, of course). Such actions can serve to ruin a rival or cover up an embarrassing breach of the Masquerade. Bureaucracy often requires a Mental or Social Challenge, depending on the type of roleplaying the character performs or as a Storyteller sees fit. Difficulty depends on such factors as security, accessibility of the information, or the cooperativeness of the target.

Computer

An information superhighway is being built, with electron asphalt, silicon off-ramps and fiber optic expressways. It's enough to make an elder Kindred's head spin. Some younger and more energetic members of the Damned have learned the secrets of this other world and can use them to their advantage. Kindred with this Ability can infiltrate systems, swap data, steal business and science secrets, and access records. A Mental Challenge is required to accomplish these and other similar acts. The difficulty is a function of system security and accessibility, equipment, time and rarity of information as assigned by a Storyteller. Failure can lead to investigation by natural and sometimes supernatural agencies that operate in the computer sphere.

Drive

The majority of adults have at least some familiarity with modern vehicles. A character with this skill is an adept driver capable of tailing and avoiding tails, avoiding collisions and using her vehicle as a weapon. These actions often require a Physical or Mental Challenge. Factors influencing difficulty could include vehicle type, road conditions and the sort of stunt desired. Furthermore, the Drive Ability can allow the character to move from one game scene to another quickly. A Storyteller can reduce any "out of game" travel time usually assigned for moving from scene to scene if the character has this Ability and access to a vehicle.

Finance

Money talks, and you are fluent in its language. You can follow money trails, perform and verify accounting tasks and understand such concepts as investment, buyouts and the like. These actions are a function of a Mental Challenge that depends on any precautions taken by the subject, the amount of money in question and the availability of information. In a chronicle, the level of Finance Ability a character has can determine his income. In general, $250 per level is a good rule of thumb, but this may vary widely from game to game. The final ruing is, of course, up to the Storyteller.

Firearms

Sometime during your existence, you have spent the time to familiarize yourself with a range of guns and similar projectile weapons. The most common use of this Ability is in combat, but a Storyteller can also allow you to attempt a Mental Challenge to perform other functions. You not only to understand how to operate firearms, but you can also care for them, repair them and possibly make minor alterations. A character without this Ability may still use a firearm, but cannot benefit from any other Ability-based advantages. Those without the Firearms Ability may also choose to use Mental Traits instead of Physical Traits during a challenge in which a firearm is involved.

Investigation

You possess the learned skills of a diligent investigator. This sort of attention to detail is most often found among private investigators, police officers, government agents and insurance claims personnel. In any case, you can often pick out or uncover details and clues that less wary individuals would overlook or ignore. With a Mental Challenge, you can tell if a person is carrying a concealed weapon or the like. When dealing with plots, you may also request a Mental Challenge with a Storyteller to see if any clues have been overlooked, piece together clues, or uncover information through formal investigation. Hunters often employ this Ability to track down their Kindred prey.

Law

Any judicial system, whether legal, civil or criminal, is based on layer after layer of confusing tradition, precedence and procedure. Your experiences with it, however, allow you to make the system work for you. You can use the Law Ability to write up binding contracts, defend clients, and know the rights of yourself and others. The difficulty of the Mental Challenges necessary to accomplish these tasks depends on factors like precedence, the severity of the crime, the legal complexity of the subject or the legal action desired.

Leadership

You have the gift of influencing and inspiring others. This is a function of confidence, bearing and a profound understanding of what motivates others. You may use this Ability to cause others to perform reasonable tasks for you. They must first be under your command or serving as your subordinates. Examples include: an elder and her clan, an officer and his soldiers, a CEO and his employees or a crime lord and her henchmen. These requests may not endanger the subject or violate the subject's Nature or Demeanor. Also, the subject must first be defeated in a Social Challenge.

Linguistics

You have received tutelage in one or more languages other than your native tongue. In their long lifetimes, some Kindred pick a multitude of languages, some long dead. This can be anything from ancient hieroglyphics to common national languages or complex dialects. The language known must be specified when the Linguistics Ability is chosen and may not be changed. Each level may be an individual language, or it may be assigned to the same language more than once to represent a particular fluency with that single language. This skill allows you and anyone who also knows the language to speak privately. Furthermore, you can translate written text in one of the languages you know. This may or may not require a Mental Challenge, depending upon the clarity of the text.

Medicine

This Ability represents an adeptness at treating the injuries, diseases and various ailments of living creatures. You can allow a living creature to recover a single Health Level per night with rest and a Mental Challenge. Collecting and properly storing blood requires this skill as well as the appropriate equipment. The difficulty of a challenge is influenced by the severity and nature of the damage, equipment at your disposal and any assistance or distractions. Other uses of this Ability include forensic information, diagnosis, pharmaceutical knowledge and determining the health and blood content of living creatures.

Melee

You possess a degree of training or experience with armed combat. Whether you acquired this experience on a medieval battlefield, in an urban slum or from formal training does not matter. You can use any weapon, from beer bottles and battle-axes to katanas and crossbows. A character without this Ability may not use any of the advantages of Abilities in armed combat, including retests.

Occult

There exists, on the fringe of mundane society, a wealth of arcane and alternative knowledge. Most of this offers enlightening insight into the nature of our mysterious universe. This Ability allows the character to tap and utilize this esoteric information. Examples of these uses include, but are not limited to: identifying the use and nature of visible magicks, rites and rituals; understanding basic fundaments of the occult; or having knowledge of cults, tomes and artifacts. Most uses of the Occult Ability require a Mental Challenge. The difficulty of this challenge can be subject to many factors, such as obscurity, amount of existing data and the character's individual scope of understanding (vampires know more about their own Disciplines, and so on). It is unheard of for members of Clan Tremere not to have least one level in Occult.

Performance

You have the gift to make your own original creations and/or express those creations to your peers. The genius of your creativity or the power with which you convey it is determined by a Social Challenge. A particularly sensitive type can even become entranced by the use of this skill. The Kindred must first be defeated in a Social Challenge. Your specialty should be declared when the skill is taken. Some examples include: painting, poetry, composing music or playing a single type of instrument. While not all Toreador actually create art, those who do tend to be truly gifted in their field.

Repair

You possess a working understanding of what makes things tick. With time, tools and parts you can fix or slightly alter most of the trappings of modern society. This knowledge also allows you to excel at sabotage. The Repair Ability is widespread among inventors, mechanics and handymen. Using this Ability usually calls for a Mental Challenge, the difficulty of which depends on such factors as the item's complexity, tools and parts available, extent of damage and time spent on the repairs.

Science

You have a degree of factual and practical expertise in a single field of the hard sciences. This knowledge will allow you to identify properties of your field, perform experiments, fabricate items, bring about results or access information a player could not normally utilize. A Mental Challenge is necessary for all but the most trivial uses of this skill. The difficulty depends on resources (equipment, data, etc.) available, complexity of the task and time. A field of study must be chosen when the Science Ability is taken. A few examples are Physics, Biology, Electronics and Chemistry. Other fields can be allowed at the Storyteller's discretion.

Scrounge

Scrounge allows the character to produce items through connections, wits and ingenuity. Many individuals who lack the wealth to purchase the things they desire or need develop this Ability instead. Many Nosferatu and poorer Brujah possess this Ability. Materials acquired with Scrounge aren't always brand new, are rarely exactly right and often require some time to acquire, but this Ability can sometimes work where finance or outright theft fail. A Mental or Social Challenge is necessary to use Scrounge. Some factors that influence the difficulty of the challenge include rarity and value of the item and local supply and demand.

Security

You have a degree of experience and knowledge of the variety of ways people defend and protect things. Not only can you counter existing security, such as locks, alarms and guards, but you can also determine the best way to secure items and areas. Other uses include breaking and entering, infiltration, safecracking and hot-wiring. Almost all applications of the Security Ability require a Mental Challenge determined by the complexity of the task, the thoroughness of the defenses, your equipment and the length of time required.

Streetwise

With this Ability, you have a feel for the street. You know its secrets, how to survive out there and how to utilize the network of personalities on the street. You can get information on events on the street, deal with gangs and the homeless and survive (if somewhat squalidly) without an apparent income. Some uses of Streetwise require a Social Challenge that is influenced by such things as composition of the local street community and the current environment on the street. A Nosferatu without at least a level of this Ability is an unusual creature, indeed.

Subterfuge

Subterfuge is an art of deception and intrigue that relies on a social backdrop to work. When participating in a social setting or conversation with a subject, you can attempt to draw information out of him through trickery and careful probing. This Ability is a favorite of the Kindred, whose taste for intrigue and politics is practically unequaled.

Information, such as one's name, nationality, Negative Traits, friends and enemies can be revealed by successfully using Subterfuge. The first requirement is that you get the target to say something dealing with the desired knowledge, such as entering a conversation about foreign culture to find out a character's nationality. If you can accomplish this, then you may propose your true question and initiate a Social Challenge. If you win, your target must forfeit the information. To use the Ability again, you must once again lure him into a conversation. Furthermore, Subterfuge may not reveal more than one Negative Trait per session, and it may be used to defend from others with Subterfuge. You could even slip false information that they would believe to be true if you defeat your opponent in the Social Challenge.

Conversely, the Subterfuge Ability may also be used to conceal information or lie without detection. This may not, however, be used to lie while under the influence of Command or other such Disciplines.

Survival

You have the knowledge and training to find food, water and shelter in a variety of wilderness settings. Each Mental or Physical Challenge allows the character to provide the basic necessities for herself or another living creature for one day. This Ability can also be used to track beings in a wilderness setting. The nature and difficulty is usually set by a Storyteller. Important factors in a Survival challenge are abundance or scarcity of resources, time of the year, equipment and the type of wilderness. Many Gangrel possessed this Ability in their days as mortals and find it useful even now when "living" off of the land.

Disciplines

In addition to immortality and regenerative abilities, all Kindred have access to the special gifts known as Disciplines. These powers, while strange and often wonderful, only serve to further alienate the Kindred from their mortal ties. Indeed, many Kindred, especially those with Advanced Disciplines, become drunk with their power and may even consider themselves to be deities when compared to their lessers.

According to legend, the earliest Kindred had access to the full spectrum of the following Disciplines, perhaps even more. After successive generations, their blood became thinner and their powers became more specific. It may be that only vampires with this particular quirk survived to our time. Whatever the case may be, the bloodlines or clans of today show a distinct definition in the Disciplines they possess. While any Kindred can learn and eventually master almost any Discipline, they will find their intrinsic or clan Disciplines the easiest to master.

To reflect this, characters may only begin the chronicle with Disciplines from their clan list (see the section on "Clans" for details). To learn out-of-clan Disciplines, a character must first locate a willing mentor who possesses the desired Discipline. Furthermore, the character must pay an increased experience point cost for these Disciplines (see the section on "Experience" for more details).

Kindred who have no clan (the Caitiff) are an exception to this rule. Because of their mixed heritage, they may begin with any three Disciplines, except Thaumaturgy. These Disciplines are considered their "clan" Disciplines from that point forward. Any other Disciplines are then considered out-of-clan and must be acquired and paid for as mentioned above.

When purchasing Disciplines, a character must first master the lower levels of a Discipline before moving on to more advanced levels. For example, before learning Rapidity, a character must possess Alacrity and Swiftness. In addition, some Disciplines, such as Thaumaturgy, have special limitations that must also be observed. These are listed along with the Discipline in question.

Regardless of the nature of the Discipline, it is suggested that a character actually learns the Discipline between sessions. This prevents the character from instantly gaining the most efficient or effective Discipline during actual play. Also it helps to realistically reflect the time it takes a Kindred to master her newly developing power.

Animalism

This collection of powers serves as a primal link between the Beast that lurks in the souls of all Kindred and the wild spirit of the natural order of things. While some might see the Kindred as unnatural and shunned by the world of the living, in truth, they occupy a very vital niche in the ecology of the World of Darkness. This Discipline represents, especially to the Gangrel, remaining in touch with and understanding the role Kindred play in nature's scheme.

Basic

Beast Within

Your affinity with the animalistic side of the Kindred gives you some power over it in others. In particular, you can draw upon a victim's bestial nature and force him to give in to this darker side.

This Discipline allows you to activate one of an opponent's Derangements (the victim chooses which one) if you can defeat him in a Social Challenge. You need not know any of your target's Derangements, but if you do, you need not risk one of your Social Traits when trying to activate that particular Derangement (knowing his Derangement takes the place of your Social Trait during your initial bid). If you should fail in the attempt to use Beast Within against a target, you may not try to use it again on her that evening. See the section on "Derangements" for the rules concerning active Derangements and recovering from Derangements.

The Beckoning

You can issue a compelling siren's song to nearby animals. Almost any type of animal that can be found in your current locale may be called, but you must declare what you are calling when you activate the Discipline.

Generally it costs one Social Trait to summon an animal, but a Narrator may issue a higher cost for larger, rarer or more unruly animals. As a rule, the summoned animal will arrive in ten to thirty minutes. The animal can be represented by a card that should usually be displayed prominently. Use the animal stats listed in Chapter Ten as a guide.

Intermediate

Song of Serenity

By reaching deep within the soul of an individual, you can tame his bestial nature, or at least quiet it for a while. This is useful not only in calming your allies, but also for robbing a foe of her spirit and energy.

The power requires a Social Challenge to successfully execute. If you win the test, Song of Serenity will bring a Kindred or Garou out of frenzy. Furthermore, if used against an individual who is not in frenzy, this Discipline will quench the fire in his soul, making him weak and malleable. In this state, he may not spend Willpower and gains the Negative Mental Traits: Submissive x 2. This use of the Discipline lasts for the remainder of evening or session. The Kindred may not use this Discipline on herself, and its effects are not cumulative.

Advanced

Embrace the Beast

This level of Animalism allows the user to tap the dark and brutal wellspring of power that lies in the souls of the Kindred, transforming her into a ferocious, unrestrained monster.

While under the influence of Embrace the Beast, the character is not affected by Dominate, Presence or Beast Within. Furthermore, for the duration of the power, the character gains the Physical Traits: Ferocious and Relentless. The Discipline is not without its drawbacks, however. The character may not initiate any Mental or Social Challenges (except for intimidation). Additionally, the character temporarily gains the Derangement: Crimson Rage. If she already has this Derangement, it becomes very active for the duration of the Discipline's use. It costs one Mental Trait to activate this Discipline. The Discipline comes to an end at either the end of the evening or session or upon completion of the character's first physical confrontation.

Auspex

Auspex encompasses the vast array of expanded sensory powers that some Kindred experience and can develop upon the Embrace. Most Kindred who are fortunate enough to possess this power find it exceptionally useful, not only for night-to-night survival, but also in allowing them to appreciate the beauty of their surroundings. The Toreador, in particular, delight in this last aspect.

Basic

Heightened Senses

You can vastly enhance one of your senses to provide access to a world of sensory input most people will never enjoy. Heightened Sense can be utilized by the character to spy on conversations, see in inky (but not complete) darkness, read letters by touch, identify an individual's scent or pick up tell-tale tastes. Any sense can be intensified by the Discipline, but only one sense can be magnified at any time.

A Storyteller may determine that a Mental Challenge is necessary for particularly difficult tasks. Additionally, if the character is bombarded by a large amount of sensory input while using this Discipline (i.e. loud music, bright light or an overpowering stench), she will totally lose the sense in question for fifteen minutes.

Aura Perception

Any sentient being possesses a halo of energy that surrounds him and shifts constantly with his mental and emotional state. A Kindred with this Discipline has honed her senses to such a degree that she can actually perceive and interpret these auras.

By winning a Static Mental Challenge, with a difficulty equal to number of Mental Traits the target has, you may demand that the target answer one of the following sort of questions honestly: "What is your Demeanor?", "Have you committed diablerie (within the last six months)?", "What is your current emotional state (brief summary)?", "Was the last thing you just said a lie?", or "What sort of creature are you?" (human, Kindred, Garou, mage, spirit, faerie, mummy, etc.). Additional uses of this Discipline will allow additional questions.

Intermediate

Spirit's Touch

This Discipline allows you to sense the residual energies and impressions that are left on an object when it is handled or touched. Specific information, such as the identity of the individual, her emotional and/or mental state and her perceptions, may be acquired by the use of the Discipline.

Various factors, such as brief contact, multiple handlers and the unusual nature of the handler or object, can dramatically affect the use of this Discipline. In some strange cases, no impressions may be present at all (at the direction of a Storyteller). Curiously enough, Kindred using Obfuscation powers leave no impressions. If the possessor of the object is nearby, the character may question him and he must answer honestly. Often, however, Spirit's Touch will require a Storyteller's assistance to use.

Telepathy

You have honed your preternatural senses to such a degree that you can actually receive and transmit thoughts. Be forewarned, though—many of the things buried within the minds of others are best left untouched. With effort, you can even force your way into stubborn minds, but a voluntary subject makes the task less difficult and less unpleasant for both parties.

Use of this Discipline upon a voluntary subject allows two (or more) characters to communicate privately. This communication is usually accomplished by note-passing or a quite side conversation that cannot be "overheard", except by Telepathy or similar powers. In order to accomplish this effect, other players are expected to ignore the note-passing or conversation. However, other characters with Telepathy will notice something unusual is going on and may attempt to win a Mental Challenge, against either player, to listen in on the conversation.

Telepathy can also be used to spy on a subject, access surface thoughts or discern the truth. If the user of the Discipline defeats her subject in a Mental Challenge, she may ask the victim one "yes or no" or short answer question about any subject or conversation the victim is currently engaged in. The subject must answer truthfully.

Individuals possessing active Derangements may bid them as Mental Traits when subjected to involuntary Telepathy. Each Derangement bid in this fashion requires the telepath to bid an additional Mental Trait, representing the difficulty of reading such a twisted mind. If the defender did opt to bid one or more of her active Derangements against the Telepath and wins the challenge, the aggressor has been infected with her madness. The aggressor must now either spend a Willpower Trait or actively play out one of the Derangements bid for thirty minutes. Unfortunately, the Telepath is now acutely aware of the defender's Derangement and may use it against her in the future.

Advanced

Psychic Projection

With a conscious mental exertion, you can safely sever the bound between your spirit and your body. In this state, your invisible spirit may travel noncorporeally through the physical world. Mundane barriers cannot hold you, but supernatural ones, such as pentagrams and wards, are another matter entirely. Individuals with highly advanced sensory powers (such as Heightened Senses, Telepathy and the like) may realize something is amiss, but must still win a Mental Challenge to perceive you.

Exercising Psychic Projection is not without its dangers. Your body is left helpless and inert during your sojourn. Furthermore, your ability to interact with the physical world is greatly diminished. You cannot, for example, stop or interfere with physical actions occurring around you. A Kindred can only use sensory Disciplines, such as Aura Perception, Heightened Senses (sight and sound only) and Telepathy. The only powers that may be used against you are those that affect the spirit or mind, and even then, the attacker must first be able to perceive your presence. If you wish to become visible and communicate with a single individual in the physical world, you may do so at a cost of one Mental Trait for every ten minutes.

Celerity

After the Embrace, many vampires benefit from a variety of amazing physical improvements. One of these is the Discipline of Celerity. This power reflects the Kindred's mastery of her form in the realm of speed and quickness.

When employed against a foe with an equivalent degree of Celerity, many of the advantages of this Discipline are negated. For example, an attacker with Swiftness would still get her bonus attack against a foe who also possessed Swiftness (as would the foe), but neither suffers from the Trait penalties. In any case, each combatant using Celerity still gets his total number of attacks. Also, a character using her Celerity to evoke a "Fair Escape" can be intercepted by a foe with an equal or greater degree of Celerity.

Basic

Alacrity

The character possesses a supernatural degree of speed and coordination that outstrips both normal mortals and her fellow Kindred.

If the character is aware of an upcoming physical threat, she may spend a Blood Trait to pre-empt the actions with a physical action of her own. Some examples of such threats include: melee attacks, falling objects, gunfire, oncoming cars or thrown objects. Examples of preemptive actions are: drawing a gun of your own, moving out of the path of a falling object, and so on. To pre-empt a foe using Alacrity, the character must have an greater degree of Celerity.

A character with Alacrity may utilize the "Fair Escape" rule against foes who do not have at least an equivalent degree of Celerity. This costs one Blood Trait to activate.

Swiftness

The character can move with a shocking degree of speed. To a character using Swiftness, slower foes and bystanders often appear to be standing still.

Swiftness allows the character to make a follow-up attack against a foe in physical combat. To do so, the player must declare she is activating Swiftness (an obvious breach of the Masquerade) before making a bid and expending a Blood Trait. The first challenge is then carried out as normal. Afterwards, if she is able, the character using Swiftness may instigate an immediate follow-up challenge. Foes that do not have or have not activated Swiftness may only defend themselves in this challenge. They may not harm the user of the Discipline in any way, nor may they use any Traits that they had bid in the prior challenge(s) in this follow-up challenge, even if they did not lose them.

A character with Swiftness may also expend a Blood Trait to cut in-game travel times in half.

Intermediate

Rapidity

With time and experience, you have outstripped the fledgling power of Swiftness. What was once merely dazzling speed is now a mind-numbing blur of motion. In a moment's notice, you can burst into a whirlwind of destruction, crippling, if not slaying, a slower opponent.

The character may make two extra challenges when employing Rapidity. Otherwise, the power is the same as Swiftness, including cost.

If used to cut travel time, the time is reduced to one-fourth.

Advanced

Fleetness

Your feats of speed defy ordinary logic. To the average observer, you almost disappear when your form explodes into motion. The roar of wind in your passing extinguishes small flames and causes loose clothes to whip about.

The character may take three extra challenges when employing Fleetness. Otherwise the power is the same as Swiftness, including cost.

If used to cut travel time, the time is reduced to one-eighth.

Dominate

One of the legendary power of vampires is their ability to control the thoughts and actions of others. This Discipline is partly responsible for this legend. Unlike its sister power, Presence, Dominate effects the conscious and sometimes unconscious mental facilities of a target.

To Dominate, a character must first establish eye contact with the target. Even so much as a brief meeting of the eyes is enough to fulfill this requirement. Players are expected to exercise a degree of honesty about this requirement. Any orders issued with Dominate must be verbal and clearly understandable by the target. Alternatively, a character using Dominate may issue the commands with Telepathy.

One major limitation of Dominate is that it is totally ineffective against Kindred of a lower generation than the user of the Discipline.

Basic

Command

This Discipline is a form of mind control exercised through the use of a piercing gaze and commanding voice. If you can catch the eyes of another player, you can attempt to exert your considerable mental control over her.

The character must first defeat her opponent in a Mental Challenge to employ this Discipline. After doing so, the user of the Discipline may issue a single simple command to her subject, such as "sleep", "stop", "freeze", "sit" or "leave". ("Silence!" is also acceptable.) The command cannot be blatantly suicidal or self-destructive, but it may drastically violate the subject's Nature or Demeanor. In any case, the effects of the command cannot last more than ten minutes.

Forgetful Mind

The character can use her mental powers to warp the conscious and unconscious memories of a victim. After defeating another character in a Mental Challenge, the character can add, alter or eliminate memories concerning a single event.

The extent of the information can be as limited as the color of someone's underwear or as encompassing as the entire experiences of a fifteen minute period of the subject's life.

Intermediate

Mesmerism

By staring into someone's eyes, you can insidiously creep into her mind and plant subtle suggestions that will direct and guide her behavior. These mental time bombs are hidden within the target's mind until a trigger event occurs.

Using this Discipline requires that you first defeat your subject in a Mental Challenge. Even if a suggestion is planted, your order will be ignored if it poses a clear threat to the target's life. You may only implant one suggestion in a given individual's mind at any one time. Furthermore, both the trigger and the suggestion must be concise and easily understandable. Some examples include:

Triggers:
- Upon seeing a particular person, item or place
  - Upon hearing a certain word or sound
  - At a precise time
  - After performing a specific action

Suggestions:
- Behave in a bizarre or inappropriate manner
- Deliver a brief spoken message
- Experience a single emotion
- Suddenly "recall" planted information

These details are subconsciously retained by the target until the trigger occurs and the suggestion is carried out. The target will not be able to explain why the action was performed. Once the suggestion is carried out, the Mesmerism is lifted.

Conditioning

Your powers of mental manipulation have reached such a level of prowess that you are now capable of completely reprogramming a target. The process involves a great deal of time and effort, but the results are astounding and practically irreversible. The end product is a fanatically loyal if somewhat dull servant. Your degree of control can even challenge the supposedly infallible power of the Blood Bond.

To begin the process, you must have complete access to the victim for the full duration of three consecutive evenings. During this time, you slowly erode the will of the subject, eventually replacing it with your own. To do so, you must defeat the subject in three consecutive Mental Challenges (one per night). Once this is accomplished, you must permanently expend a Mental Trait. If one of the challenges is unsuccessful, the entire process fails.

The degree of control that results is intense. Foremost among the effects is a permanent and automatic command, wherein even self-destructive orders will be carried out by the subject. Furthermore, the conditioned victim gains three Willpower Traits for the sole purpose of resisting control and manipulation that would cause her to perform actions that would be counterproductive to her master's wishes. If a previous Blood Bond exists, the Regnant and the Kindred who conditioned the subject must engage in a Mental Challenge (out of character) every time the two issue contradictory orders.

On the downside, the subject is little more than a pale automaton lacking free will, imagination and creativity. She is not without hope, however; this selfsame power can be used to restore the subject to normal, albeit at great risk.

Over the course of three nights, three Mental Challenges must be won by the reprogrammer. The difficulty of these challenges is variable and is set by a Storyteller, depending on such factors as the length of time and how intensely the subject was controlled. The subject's bonus Willpower Traits will come into play here to resist the would-be savior. If just one of these tests is failed by the reprogrammer, the subject's mind is permanently shattered, leaving her a vegetable. If successful, however, the reprogrammer only needs to expend a Willpower Trait to reaffirm the subject's identity and undo the effects of the Discipline.

Advanced

Possession

This Discipline allows the Kindred to forcibly inject her consciousness into another's body and suppress the existing will and personality. In doing so, the character usurps complete physical control of her host's body. However, the possessor's body is left completely inert and vulnerable while this Discipline is in use. Moreover, while in the foreign body, the invader will find herself subject to its physical limitations. The possessor may not use any of her physical Disciplines and may not use any of the host's mental or social Disciplines or faculties.

To execute Possession, the character must first touch her foe and then defeat her in a Mental Challenge. If successful, the original body falls over, apparently lifeless, and the character's consciousness immediately takes over the victim. The possessor may remain in the host's body until sunrise, when she must return to her own form. If her body has been destroyed, the Kindred will experience the Final Death. During the course of the Possession, the victim is totally unaware of her condition and surrounding.

Spiritually empty but physically viable bodies, such as the bodies of those Psychically Projecting or currently Possessing others, may not resist Possession. However, when the Projecting spirit tries to return to its body, the invader must succeed in a Mental Challenge to retain control.

Failing the Mental Challenge to possess the body is very disorienting. For a full minute, the character cannot control her body or concentrate. During this time, the character is very vulnerable to all manner of physical and mental attacks.

As a game effect, characters possessing the bodies of other characters should adopt the appropriate dress and trappings of the host body. Additionally, a name badge or label could be employed to signify the change.

Fortitude

All Kindred possess an amazing constitution, supplemented by gradual regeneration and an immunity to aging and most diseases. Kindred with Fortitude possess an even greater degree of toughness. Considering the numerous destructive forces a vampire can and probably will encounter in her long life, Fortitude can prove to be a tremendous asset.

Basic

Endurance

This level of Fortitude represents the character's ability to shrug off the effects of damage, including damage caused by fire or sunlight.

The character can ignore the side effects of being Wounded or Incapacitated. She is not out of play until she reaches Torpor or Final Death. This Discipline costs nothing to use and is automatically activated when needed.

Mettle

The Kindred's form has been hardened against the dangers and threats of the world. He gains an additional wound level, which is recorded on the character sheet. This wound level can be temporarily lost and healed back just like any other and is used as a second "Healthy".

Intermediate

Resilience

You are highly resistant to harm and injury from all sources, including the traditional banes of your breed— fire and sunlight. While excessive or persistent forces can still bring an end to your immortal existence, this does not come about easily.

Whenever the character suffers aggravated wounds, she may try to reduce them to ordinary wounds. This may only be attempted once per wound level taken. The character must spend an appropriate Physical Trait (Stalwart, Resilient, etc.) and win a Simple Test for each wound resisted. Therefore, if three aggravated wounds were suffered at once, the character could attempt to reduce each of them separately to ordinary wounds by spending three appropriate Traits and winning three Simple Tests.

Advanced

Aegis

The Kindred's ability to survive the hostile forces of the world has surpassed mere physical resilience. It takes a truly monumental and unrelenting force to destroy her. In the face of destruction, the character can call upon deep reserves of tenacity, enabling her to shrug off fatal injuries.

When the character suffers a result in a challenge that would destroy her, or if she encounters a lethal situation (such as direct exposure to sunlight), the player may permanently expend either three Physical or one Willpower Trait to avoid the character's destruction. In the case of direct exposure to sunlight, the character is unharmed for five minutes. The damage is not inflicted— its results are ignored. Indeed, those witnessing this Discipline often find it hard to believe that any creature could survive. Many will assume the character is destroyed unless given cause to believe otherwise.

Obfuscate

Kindred hide in the midst of teeming hordes of humanity. For those who are truly hideous, the gift of Obfuscation is priceless. Essentially, most of the powers of Obfuscate affect the minds of observers, preventing them from perceiving things as they truly are. As a result, surveillance devices, such as cameras, will still register the character normally. However, if a person employing such a device is relatively near the Obfuscating character, she will still be affected by the power and not be able to perceive the character. For example, a tourist with a video camera would not see a skulking Nosferatu at the base of the Washington monument through the camera's viewpiece. However, if he later watched the film at home, he would indeed notice the lurking figure that he somehow missed earlier.

Basic

Unseen Presence

This power allows you to remain obscured and unseen, even in crowds. You can walk about without being seen or heard, hovering about while listening to whispered conversations and escaping from dangerous situations.

While this Discipline is activated, other players must pretend not to see you; if you choose to spy upon others, they must continue normally, as if you are not there. To engage this power, you must cross both your arms in front of you, demonstrating your actions to everyone around you. As soon as you touch objects around you (other than walking around), talk to others or otherwise interact with your environment, you instantly become visible to everyone (uncross your arms).

If you are moving, a Kindred with Heightened Senses will detect something is amiss, but must defeat you in a Mental Challenge to actually pinpoint your location and see you. In any case, you cannot surprise an individual with Heightened Senses by using Unseen Presence.

You may attempt to evoke the "Fair Escape" rule with Unseen Presence by winning a Mental Challenge. If you win, you have slipped away unnoticed (watch out for characters with Heightened Senses, however). You cannot use this method of escape if you are currently involved in a challenge.

Mask of a Thousand Faces

This Discipline allows you to assume a new visage, a completely different appearance. Essentially, you adopt a very convincing disguise. You may be required to assume new props and clothes, change badges or utilize the appropriate hand sign to indicate your change in appearance. This Discipline is extremely valuable to the hideous Nosferatu.

Characters with Heightened Senses can sense something is amiss about your looks, but they must defeat you in a Mental Challenge to pierce the veil you project. This power affects minds and is useless against remote cameras and photographs (though a nearby viewer will still discount proof if the Obfuscating individual is in sight).

You possess one "instinctive" illusory disguise, which you can assume automatically while conscious. Other disguises may be temporarily adopted, but each one you use will cost one Mental Trait. While asleep, when in Torpor, or upon Final Death, you will return to your true appearance.

Intermediate

Cloak the Gathering

Not only can you mystically mask you own passing, but others can also benefit from your power. You may place those who you choose (if they are willing) under your mantle of Obfuscation, thereby rendering them invisible.

Individuals under the effect of this power must always remain within three paces of you to remain hidden. While Cloaked, you and your allies can still see each other. Each individual hidden by this Discipline must abide by the limitation listed under Unseen Presence or the Cloaked companion will immediately forfeit the Discipline's effect. If one member of the group becomes visible in this manner, the rest are unaffected. Furthermore, the newly revealed subject can no longer see her compatriots. If the user of the Discipline violates the limitations of Unseen Presence, all of the participants become visible.

After you disappear, you must expend a Mental Trait for each individual you wish to Cloak. Each individual Cloaked in this manner must cross her arms to indicate the use of Unseen Presence.

If a Kindred with Heightened Senses defeats one of the cloaked individuals, only that individual is perceived. However, if a perceptive Kindred challenges and defeats the Kindred projecting the Cloak, all of the subjects are revealed to the challenger. It is usually not readily apparent which Kindred in the gathering is employing this power.

Advanced

Soul Mask

What Mask of a Thousand Faces does to the body, Soul Mask accomplishes for the inner self. Kindred possessing Aura Perception and Telepathy often become smug in their ability to unearth others' deepest secrets and personalities. You, however, have the ability to render those powers impotent. Your true nature is inscrutable. This is not to say that your secrets cannot be fathomed, but it takes a very dedicated and decidedly nosy individual to do so.

A single Mental Trait must be expended for each piece of information about yourself you wish to alter. The types of information that can be masked are Nature, Demeanor, recent diablerie, emotional state, surface thoughts, type of creature and Derangements. Each of these "masks" must be recorded when the power is activated. The masks remain until sunrise or until you choose to change them (at additional cost).

Potence

Another distinctly physical Discipline that many Kindred benefit from is a supernaturally heightened degree of strength known as Potence. Those employing this gift find themselves able to perform incredible feats and inflict brutal amounts of damage. Unfortunately, like so many of the physical Disciplines, Potence easily marks the user as something more than human. As a result, exercising Vigor or Puissance is consider a breach of the Masquerade by many.

Basic

Prowess

You possess a degree of supernatural strength beyond that of the average Kindred. Even when you should be spent and exhausted, you can call upon the might that is your bloodright.

You may expend a single Blood Trait to recover all Physical Traits related to brute strength you have expended or lost this session. Potence may not be used to recover any other type of Physical Traits. Traits representing coordination, grace or speed are unaffected. The following Traits can be restored by Potence: Brawny, Wiry, Ferocious, Stalwart and Tough.

Might

You can redouble your efforts in any test of strength, often overcoming obstacles that would daunt a weaker or lesser Kindred.

If you should lose a challenge involving strength, you may call for a single immediate retest. Any Traits you lost remain lost, although you need not bid another Trait. You do, however, stand to win the object of the challenge should you win the second test. This Discipline can only be used once per challenge and cannot be recalled by an opponent's use of an Ability, but could be overcome by another Kindred using Might. Might may not be used in tests of coordination, grace or speed, only in tests that involve raw strength.

Intermediate

Vigor

Your physical strength has reached truly astonishing proportions. A display of this Potence immediately marks you as superhuman. In fact, use of Vigor in the company of mortals is considered to be a breach of the Masquerade. As a result, many Kindred refrain from using this level of strength unless in dire straits.

In practice, a character with Vigor gains the use of a fourth hand signal, which she may apply in Physical Challenges that are strength related. It cannot be employed in challenges of coordination, speed, grace or the like, although it may be employed in many combat challenges. This fourth hand signal is a clenched fist with thumb extended upward. It is called the "Bomb," and it interacts with the other symbols in a manner befitting its name: the Bomb defeats both or Rock and Paper, but in turn is defeated by Scissors (the fuse is cut). You must declare that you are able to use the "Bomb" before you can use it while resolving a test.

Advanced

Puissance

You possess monumental strength. What you consider casual exertion is sufficient force to deform metal and fracture stone. Your full strength will shatter the bones of the toughest mortal, rend plate steel and grind marble blocks into gravel. Even your fellow Kindred cannot survive the type of punishment you can inflict for long.

In hand-to-hand combat, you inflict an additional wound against your foes. Furthermore, you win all ties in Physical Challenges involving strength, regardless of who possess the most traits. Of course, if your opponent also has Puissance, the winner is determined normally.

Presence

Presence can be seen as sort of a supernatural magnitude of charisma, personality and appeal. Kindred possessing this Discipline are often seen as being magnetic or having an intangible quality that draws people to them. This perception is particularly common among mortals. While Dominate controls the logical and conscious mind, Presence appeals to the emotions of the subject.

Unlike Dominate, Presence can affect Kindred of lower generation.

Basic

Dread Gaze

You are able to project feelings of terror and fear upon others by looking into their eyes.

By defeating your target in a Social Challenge, you can cause her to run from you in a panic. The victim is unable to take any action against you or initiate a challenge. He must flee the area and may not stop until he is out of your presence. For the next hour, he will actively avoid you and will leave immediately should you appear. If somehow forced to remain in your presence, the individual will be extremely uncomfortable and must bid an additional Trait in any challenges against you. If you attack the victim, he may defend himself as normal.

Entrancement

This Discipline describes your ability to attract, sway and control others. Anyone you look upon can be ensnared by your seductive glamour. Even those who despise you and wish you harm can be rendered civil, if not docile.

You may attempt to Entrance an individual by engaging him in a Social Challenge. If you are successful, the target must speak to you politely and in a civil manner. Furthermore, he may not attack you while Entranced. The Entrancement is broken if you initiate an act of aggression against the subject or behave in an obviously insulting or crude manner towards them. Otherwise, the power lasts for one hour. If the user breaks the Entrancement by attacking the individual, she may not Entrance that individual again for the remainder of the night.

Intermediate

Summon

You may demand the immediate appearance of a person known to you. You can mentally summon your target to you, even across great distances, and the target cannot easily resist.

The standard method of employing this power is to select an out-of-game envoy to carry your summons. This should be someone who doesn't mind or who can take the time out perform this duty. The player utilizing the Summon Discipline declares to the envoy the number of Social Traits she wishes to devote to the power. Each Social Trait beyond the first allows a retest if the subject wins the Social Challenge or resists the power of the call. In the meantime, the summoner must remain in the same place so that the subject can find her if he loses the challenge. Any Social Traits invested in the call are considered lost, even if the subject relents.

There will often be quite a time lag when using this power. This is easy to understand when one considers the amount of time it will take to find the subject, engage in a challenge and respond. Players are therefore advised not to use this power frivolously.

Advanced

Majesty

You exude an aura of power and insurmountable might. Those around you find it difficult to think about, let alone act out, offenses against your person. You can expect to be treated with great respect, if not awe.

The effect of this Discipline extends about ten paces from you and immediately fades if you take offensive actions against anyone within range of your power. This effect is always active, at least while you are conscious, and takes no effort on your part. However, when in question, you should signify that you have Majesty by holding your arms out from your sides when you enter a room or other area.

Anyone attempting an offensive or aggressive action against you must first defeat you in a Social Challenge. The attacker may only continue if she is successful in the challenge. If she fails, she may not continue with the planned action and may not challenge your Majesty again that evening. Furthermore, unlike other powers, the subject may not spend a Willpower Trait to ignore Majesty's initial effects. Though Willpower may not be used to ignore the effects of Majesty, a Willpower Trait may be spent to challenge its effects at a later time. However, at least an hour must pass before the next attempt.

Protean

This Discipline allows a vampire to transform either her entire body or a part of her body into something nonhuman. The vampire can thus grow claws, turn into a bat or even become mist.

Basic

Wolf Claws

At will, you can instantly cause long, razor sharp claws to grow from your fingertips. The claws are obvious and may not easily be hidden. Using this power among mortals is easily a breach of the Masquerade.

When used in combat, Wolf's Claws cause aggravated damage.

Earth Meld

Eerily and effortlessly, you can sink into the protective bosom of the earth. This is an ideal way to flee such threats as fire and the sun, provided you can find and open patch of earth.

This can be used as a "Fair Escape". However, a Kindred using Earth Meld during combat as a defensive action will have to relent if he is attacked; he will fade into the ground at the end of the turn. The power will not work on any substance other than soil. Earth Meld leaves no trace of its use and only a few powers may be able to detect the hidden Kindred (Storyteller's discretion). This Discipline costs one Blood Trait to use, but the character may return to the surface at no cost.

Intermediate

Shadow of the Beast

You are capable of transforming into a wolf or bat. The process requires a full ten seconds and one Blood Trait. During this time, you may not engage in any other action, although you may make the transformation instantaneously with the expenditure of three Blood Traits.

The change only alters your body and normal clothes—weapons and other equipment do not change. Furthermore, certain Disciplines and Abilities may be impossible to use (for instance, bats cannot Drive). A Storyteller should be consulted in any questionable cases.

As a bat, you can navigate easily in darkness and utilize flight to escape most foes (as per the "Fair Escape" rules). You also gain the Traits: Quick x 3. However, you must avoid well-lit areas. Obviously, bats are difficult to attack in melee, so you are usually only vulnerable to ranged attacks.

As a wolf, you can pass as a normal animal to most individuals. You can communicate with other wolves (although this is different from understanding the Garou Tongue). You can possibly associate with Garou to a degree if they are not too hostile and you don't stink of the Wyrm too much. You gain the Traits: Ferocious, Tenacious and Cunning.

Advanced

Form of Mist

Through rigorous control of your physical form, you can slowly diffuse into a fine mist. This process requires intense concentration and one full minute. In this vaporous state, you can slip through any structure, provided it isn't airtight. You are also immune to physical injuries except for those caused by fire and sunlight. Movement in this form is slow, equivalent to walking, and strong winds will reduce this to a slow walk or even push you in an undesired direction.

It costs one Blood Trait to assume Mist Form and one to return to human form. While in Mist Form, the character may not use physical abilities or Disciplines. Obviously, being in such a state will also prevent certain other non-physical powers, like Command, Thaumaturgy, Wolf's Claws, rituals and so on.

Thaumaturgy

Perhaps the rarest of the Disciplines, Thaumaturgy is said to have been created by the Clan Tremere. Since it is almost exclusively found among Kindred of their bloodline, and because they are loathe to teach it to others, there may be a degree of truth to this rumor.

While characters may only start with the Path of Blood, it is the fundamental key to learning the other Paths mentioned below. See the section on other Paths for further details.

The Path of Blood

Basic

Blood Mastery

In possessing power over a portion of a subject's blood, you can, in turn, exercise power over him. You can declare the use of Blood Mastery before or even during a challenge, as long as you do so before a test is performed. To use Blood Mastery, you must possess a Blood Trait from the subject. Activating the Discipline destroys this Blood Trait. However, you automatically win that single test, and no retests allowed. If any Traits were bid by either party, they are not lost. This process often acts as a prerequisite to other Thaumaturgical rituals.

Inquisition of Captive Vitæ

You are able to ascertain certain bits of information by astutely examining the blood of an individual. You must have at least one Blood Trait to use this power, and the blood is destroyed in the process. Some types of information that may be gained are: clan, generation, creature type, diablerie (up to one year) and physical nature. The ritualist must win or tie a Simple Test for each question asked.

Intermediate

Theft of Vitæ

Through concentration, you can visibly coax blood from a container or target into your body. The source of the theft will be obvious, and one should expect an immediate attack if this is used on another Kindred. Against a visible receptacle, even one in the possession of another, the power is automatic. If the source of the blood is another creature or a hidden (but known) source, you must first win a Mental Challenge against the target. If you win, you may choose to expend a Mental Trait for each Blood Trait you want to siphon out of your target. Any Blood Traits above your maximum must be spent immediately or they are lost.

Once in your body, this blood is considered yours and cannot be used against the original owner in any other use of Thaumaturgy.

Potency of the Blood

You can manipulate the blood within you, distilling it and making it more potent, effectively lowering your generation. The more dramatic the alteration, the greater the price.

Each step from 13th to 10th — One Blood Trait

Each step from 10th to 8th — Two Blood Traits

Each step from 8th to 6th — Three Blood Traits

Each step from 6th to 5th — Four Blood Traits

5th to 4th (maximum reduction) — Five Blood Traits

These costs are cumulative. For example, it would take the prodigious sum of ten Blood Traits to lower a 10th generation vampire to 6th generation. While few Kindred can contain that much blood, there is nothing to say she couldn't have more blood externally present for the process. Kindred may only be under the effect of a single application of this Discipline at one time, and the effects fade at the next sunrise.

Advanced

Cauldron of Blood

With a touch, you can cause the very life-fluid inside a foe to boil and burn within her veins.

Unless the victim cannot resist, you must first win a Physical Challenge to establish a firm grip on the victim. Once this has been achieved, you spend a Willpower Trait to activate the Cauldron of Blood. At this point, you may choose to expend a variable number of Mental Traits. Each Mental Trait spent will destroy a single Blood Trait and inflict an ordinary wound. You may not inflict more wounds than the victim has Blood Traits. A human who loses two or more of her Blood Traits in this manner will die.

Other Paths

While the Path of Blood comes instinctively to the Tremere blood line, there are other less-easily mastered Paths available to a Kindred who displays an arcane bent or predisposition. Generally, none of the following Paths may be taken upon character creation. They may only be learned through experience and the instruction of a tutor of arcane text.

The first Path a character learns, the Path of Blood, is her primary Path. Subsequent Paths may not be raised above the character's mastery in her primary Path. In addition, the character, or her chantry, must seek out and uncover the knowledge required to study the Path. One method of doing this involves using the Occult Ability; other possibilities may form the basis for stories involving occultists or Clan Tremere in your chronicle. Knowledge must be found before it may be learned. Learning new Paths after the first requires time, patience and experience, just as any other Discipline.

Lure of Flame:

This Path allows the character to manipulate and create fire. Flames created by this path are unnatural, and they will not ignite objects until they are released by the magus.

Basic

Hand of Flame

The Kindred may instantly call forth a flaming wreath about her hands. If the Thaumaturgist defeats her foe in a Physical Challenge with the flaming appendage, she will inflict an aggravated wound instead of a normal one. Foes or objects hit with the Hand of Flame that are particularly flammable may ignite (Storyteller's discretion).

Flamebolt

By expending a Mental Trait, the Kindred may summon forth and hurl a fiery brand at range. This functions exactly like a ranged weapon except that the character uses her Occult Ability instead of Firearms. Mental Traits are used for any challenges involved. Other trivial (no test needed) uses of this power include lighting cigarettes and candles at range or destroying light cloth and paper items. More resilient items would require a Static Challenge.

Intermediate

Engulf

The Kindred can engulf a foe in a searing column of flames. The character must first win a challenge against the foe.

For the Thaumaturgist, this is a Mental Challenge using the Occult Ability (to master the fiery energies and place the flames accurately), while the defender must employ Physical Traits (to avoid the flames). To initiate the challenge, the attacker must expend a Willpower Trait. If the casting is successful, the subject combusts, suffering two aggravated wounds. For each challenge or every full five seconds (whichever is greater) that passes, the victim may attempt to win or tie a Simple Test to extinguish the flames. Failing or engaging in alternative actions results in another aggravated wound and continued burning. Success indicates that the flames are out and no further damage is inflicted.

Advanced

Firestorm

By will alone, the Kindred can summon up a firestorm that encompasses areas and can incinerate multiple foes.

To activate this Discipline, the character must expend a Willpower Trait and define the area she wishes to affect. This area may be no more than twenty feet in diameter. Animate targets in this area must win a Static Physical

Challenge (difficulty of six Traits) to leap to safety. If there is nowhere for a victim to escape (Narrator's discretion), he fails the test, or if he cannot or will not leave the area, he will suffer one aggravated wound.

Movement of the Mind: This path allows the character to move objects with the power of his mind.

Basic

Force Bolt

The character can focus her will into a tangible bolt of mental force that can send a foe reeling at range. Casting this effect requires the expenditure of a Willpower Trait. If the Thaumaturgist can defeat her opponent in a challenge (using her Mental Traits against the subject's Physical Traits), the subject is knocked down and stunned for fifteen seconds (counted aloud). During this time, the victim cannot not initiate any physical actions. She may use appropriate stamina-related Traits to avoid damage from further challenges. Opponents with Swiftness are only stunned for ten seconds. Rapidity reduces this to five seconds, and Kindred with Fleetness recover immediately. Treat this Discipline as ranged combat.

Manipulate

The Kindred can perform fine and delicate manipulation of items at range by concentrating intently upon them. Using Abilities in a challenge in this manner is somewhat difficult, however, and the character must risk two Traits instead of one on challenges of this manner. In general, the character may only manipulate objects that could be lifted in one hand by the average human. Furthermore, the speed of objects manipulated is equal to a casual walk. Range cannot exceed 100 feet.

Intermediate

Flight / Snare

The character can crudely lift and move large objects (no more then a few hundred pounds). If the caster uses this on himself, the character can "fly" for short distances and avoid falls. Against an opponent, this Discipline can hold foes at bay by holding them off the ground. This does not prevent the victim from firing a gun, calling for help or using her own Disciplines, however.

To successfully snare an opponent, the character must first defeat the subject in a challenge using his Mental Traits versus the subject's Physical Traits. This power is too awkward and clumsy to accurately drop objects on foes or hurl projectiles at an opponent.

If used to achieve flight, the power cost one Mental Trait per five minutes of use.

Advanced

Major Manipulation/Lifting/Control

With this power the character can lift great weights (up to an automobile) and immobilize or hurl foes away.

When used against an opponent, the character must first defeat him in a challenge (Mental Traits against the foe's Physical Traits). If the character chooses to immobilize her foe, the victim must remain absolutely motionless for as long as the attacker maintains complete concentration on the victim. While maintaining concentration, the attacker can take no other action.

Alternatively, after winning the challenge, a character may throw the opponent. The opponent will suffer one wound and must move (as an out-of-game action) to an area within 100 feet as directed by the character. Finally, objects thrown at or dropped on targets cause one (for man-sized objects) or two (for larger objects) wound levels if they hit their target. Once again, a challenge like the one mentioned above is necessary to hit a foe.

A Mental Trait must be spent to activate this power.

Weather Control:

This path allows the character to manipulate, change and otherwise command the weather.

Basic

Cloak of Fog

The Kindred can call up an obscuring fog that blankets the area. The fog bank can only appear out of doors and can cover an area of up to 100 feet across.

The Discipline costs one Mental Trait and fifteen minutes to activate. Within the fog, visibility (and thus ranged actions) are cut to five feet. Furthermore, any tests requiring sight require the character to risk two Traits instead of one. Heightened Senses and the like eliminate these penalties. At the Storyteller's option, fog may reduce the damage a vampire takes from sunlight.

Downpour

The Thaumaturgist can cause the skies to darken and moisture-laden clouds to bring rain. The rain is very heavy, but only affects a small area (about 100 feet) while surrounding areas are overcast and sullen.

This power costs a Mental Trait and fifteen minutes to activate. All those exposed to the torrential downpour must risk two Traits in any challenge dealing with physical actions and ranged actions are reduced to twenty feet. At the Storyteller's option, darkened rainstorm skies may reduce the damage taken by a vampire from sunlight.

Intermediate

Tempest

The vampire can alter the local weather patterns of large areas and call forth a variety of weather effects. By expending a Willpower Trait, the Kindred can summon the chosen type of weather form. The weather last for one hour, plus an additional hour for each Mental Trait the Kindred expends. The Storyteller may assign a higher cost or require a Static Mental Challenge for very unusual or unseasonal weather. Some examples of weather types the Kindred

can create are: thunderstorms, hailstorms, blizzards or clear skies. The game effects are similar to that of Cloak of Fog and Downpour, but the Tempest's effects are citywide.

Advanced

Call Lightning

By will alone, the Thaumaturgist bring forth devastating bolts of lightning from the heavens to smite his foes. This power only works out-of-doors in overcast, stormy or raining conditions and costs a Willpower Trait to activate. If the Kindred can defeat her foe in challenge with her Mental Traits and Survival Ability against the foe's Physical Traits, the attack succeeds and the victim suffers three aggravated wounds.

Rituals

Rituals are arcane formulas and incantations that, if properly and skillfully enacted, can bring about powerful magical effects. They are not, however, commonplace or easily mastered.

For each level (Basic, Intermediate or Advanced) of mastery in the character's primary Path, she can begin to study one of the following rituals of the same level. All rituals chosen in this manner are subject to Storyteller approval. Additional rituals may be learned with experience and instruction from a mentor who has mastered the ritual in question. The guidelines for uncovering and learning Paths also apply to rituals.

Basic

A Basic Ritual take 30 minutes to perform, unless an individual ritual description states otherwise.

Crimson Sentinel

This ritual allows the caster to inscribe a warding rune that will make it difficult or impossible for the subject to enter an area. The rune must be inscribed with one of the subject's Blood Traits and can affect an area up to fifteen paces across (a small room). The caster must also expend a number of Mental Traits when casting the ritual to set the difficulty. Once engaged, any time the subject attempts to enter the warded area, she must win a Static Challenge against this difficulty. If the rune is discovered and destroyed, the ritual is dispelled.

Defense of the Sacred Haven

This handy ritual can be used by a Kindred to protect a haven or chantry from of the oldest banes of her kind—sunlight. The ritual costs one Blood Trait to cast, but lasts as long as the structure is intact and the Kindred remains within. After it is cast, no sunlight can enter the haven by a window or door (as long as they remain closed). The ritual will affect a structure up to the size of a small house, but a Storyteller may rule that larger structures can be affected at a higher cost.

Deflection of the Wooden Doom

By performing this ritual within a circle of wood (of any sort), the caster can stave off the threat of staking to herself or another. The ritual costs one Mental Trait to enact, but it lasts until the character suffers a result that would leave her

staked. If this happens, the challenge is lost, the staking implement is destroyed and the enchantment is over. No wounds are inflicted to either party, and no Traits are lost. To represent the presence of this ritual, the player should record it on her character sheet, and a small wooden sliver (like a toothpick) should be carried on her person. Only one of these enchantments may be present on a subject at a given time.

Devil's Touch

The caster can place a temporary magical curse upon a mortal that causes others to view the subject with revulsion and disgust. The subject must bid at least two Traits on all Social Challenges while under of the effects of the ritual. A penny or similar coin must be slipped onto the victim by either skillful roleplaying or the Streetwise or Security Ability. The ritual ends when the coin is found and discarded, or at sunrise, whichever comes first.

Purity of Flesh

This ritual mystically purges impurities (mundane pollutants, poisons and drugs, but not diseases or magical effects) from a target by concentrating these impurities into the subject's blood. One Blood Trait from the subject is used to enact the ritual. Afterward, the blood is thoroughly putrid and useless. A Storyteller may require a Simple Test or challenge for particularly stubborn substances.

Engaging the Vessel of Transference

The caster can mystically prepare a vessel to act as a conduit, transferring blood contained within with that of anyone who comes in contact with it. For each Blood Trait placed within the container, it will enact a single transfer. No tests are made to accomplish this, and the victim will only notice a slight shivering sensation. Once all of the original blood has been transferred in this manner, the magic fades, but the blood collected remains. This ritual is often used to get blood samples or Blood Bond a subject. The ritual costs a Mental Trait to perform.

Ward Versus Ghouls

The caster can create an arcane sigil that will detrimentally affect any creature that contains both mortal and Kindred blood, such as a ghoul. The ward can be placed on an unbroken and immobile circle or loop. If a ghoul approaches the edge of this barrier (from within or without), she will feel very uncomfortable. If she should actually cross the barrier, the ghoul will suffer three aggravated wounds. Alternatively, the ward can be placed on a melee weapon. If this is the case, the weapon will inflict an aggravated wound (in addition to any normal damage) when used against a ghoul. Inscribing and enchanting the area requires a Trait of mortal blood, and the caster must permanently expend a Mental Trait. If the symbol is somehow discovered and destroyed, the ward's magic is destroyed. If the caster wishes, individual ghouls can be excluded from either version of the ward if they are present at the casting and donate a Blood Trait to attune the ward to ignore them.

Intermediate Rituals

Intermediate Rituals take an hour to perform, unless stated otherwise for an individual ritual.

Bone of Lies

The Thaumaturgist can enchant a mortal bone to ascertain if the holder is telling the truth or not. The bone must be at least 200 years old from a mortal who has never tasted of Kindred blood. This ritual takes one hour to perform, and the bone must be bathed in and absorb ten Blood Traits. Thereafter, each time someone bearing the bone lies, it will visibly darken. The bone may be used ten times before it is rendered useless.

Pavis of the Foul Presence

It is rumored that this ritual was created by the Tremere primarily to counter the power of their chief rivals in the Camarilla, the Ventrue. Indeed, it is almost never found outside the Tremere Clan. The ritual costs a Mental Trait to cast and lasts until its power is invoked or until sunrise, whichever comes first. When a Presence Discipline is used against the caster, a test is performed as normal, but if the ritual caster wins, the user of the Presence Discipline is instead affected by the Discipline. If the caster loses, the Presence power has no effect. In either case, the ritual is used and must be recast. Only one of these enchants may be present at one time. To represent the presence of this Discipline, the player must record it on her character sheet and wear (not necessarily visibly) a blue silken cord about her neck.

Ward Versus Lupines

This ritual performs exactly like the Ward Versus Ghouls except silver dust, not blood, is used to cast it. The ritual affects Lupines in all their forms.

Advanced

Advanced Rituals require 90 minutes to perform unless stated otherwise.

Night of the Red Heart

This ritual is performed in two sessions of one hour each. The first is cast just after sunset, and the other is performed just before sunrise. If enacted successfully, the target dies horribly upon rising of the morning sun. His heart boils and is consumed as if by the burning rays of the sun. The ritual requires three of the victim's Blood Traits and two fellow Thaumaturgists (though only one needs to know the ritual). The target of this ritual becomes immediately aware that she is the target of a ritual after the first part of the ritual is completed, although she may not be aware of the origin of the ritual. The target can only save her life by killing one of the Kindred performing the ritual or otherwise preventing the second ceremony. Both parts of the ritual must be cast in the same place and within the same city as the target. To invoke the final effect of the ritual, each caster must permanently expend a Mental Trait.

Nectar of the Bitter Rose

The mysteries of this ritual are held in strict secrecy by those able to cast it. The ritual's very existence is a threat few in the Camarilla would tolerate. During the course of this three-hour ritual, the life essence of a Kindred is drained and devoured by the participants. The victim must be present and somehow restrained throughout the entire process. The end result is a draught that may be shared by up to five Diabolists. Each drinker may benefit from the generation of the victim, if applicable, though only once per victim and ritual.

There are risks, however. Each Diabolists must engage in a Simple Test (no Traits are risked) against the victim. If the Diabolist wins or tie, she lowers her generation. If she should lose, the blood rejects her and she gains nothing from the ritual, nor may she ever benefit from the ritual in the future. At the very least, the victim of the ritual is utterly destroyed. His soul is consumed in the process. See the section on "Diablerie" in Chapter Five for further information.

Abandon the Fetters of Blood

Through this powerful and taxing arcane ordeal, a target can be freed from the legendary Blood Bond. To perform the ritual, all the blood from the subject and a single Blood Trait from her Regnant must be used to fuel the ritual. At the climax of the ritual, when the last of the target's blood leaves her body, she suffers the permanent loss of a Physical, Mental and Social Trait of her choosing as a result of the ordeal. The subject's blood is then returned and the Blood Bond is no more. The Regnant's blood is used during the course of the ritual.

Ward Versus Kindred

This ritual performs exactly like the Ward Versus Ghouls, except that Kindred blood is used to cast it and it affects vampires of all sorts.

Influence

Kindred have exerted their control over the mortal masses down through the ages. At first it might have been an easy way to draw vessels to them, make hunting easier and facilitating a more comfortable lifestyle. However, it is actually possible that this practice helped to form the first protocultures, spawning many of humanity's great civilizations. Others would argue just the opposite, that this garnering of power is just another manifestation of the Kindred's legendary hunger. In this instance, they are draining the life out of whole societies with their base and selfish manipulations. In any case, Influence is the mechanism by which Kindred control the daily affairs of the innumerable hordes of kine for their often inscrutable reasons.

Influence may take the form of contacts, allies or direct control of a mortal agency. In a practical sense, Influence can make almost any Kindred's life easier. It can be used to protect one's haven, hunting habits or illegal activities, not to mention the power it can levy against the foes of the Kindred. Although most of this sort of power has been hoarded by the paranoid ancient ones, there are plenty of opportunities for young and energetic Kindred to scheme and manipulate.

Characters may use Influence Traits directly by expending them to accomplish goals in a specific aspect of mortal society. Many Influences can perform similar functions, such as Street and Underworld, but generally one will be more efficient or easier at the function in question. The difficulty of a task is the number of Traits that must be expended to accomplish the task. This number is set by a Storyteller and can be subject to sudden change. The suggested guideline listed along with each area of Influence can change dramatically from chronicle to chronicle or even from session to session. Sometimes a Narrator will require a challenge of some sort to represent the uncertainty or added difficulty involved when exercising Influence. Some uses of Influence may not actually cost Influence to use, but rather require that the Kindred possesses a certain level of the Influence.

To use Influence directly, a player should contact a Narrator and explain what sort effect she wishes to cause. The Narrator will then decide the Trait cost, the time involved (real-time and game-time) and any tests concerning the Influence effect. Influence Traits used this way are considered temporarily expended. They are not recovered until the next session. The effects of using Influence can be brief and instantaneous or permanent and widespread, depending on the nature of the manipulation and the degree of power the character wields.

Sometimes players will want to perform actions that do not seem to fall under any single Influence group. Say a Toreador ancilla wants to open a premiere nightclub in the city. Obviously, she will need Finance, but High Society and Media might be useful to stimulate interest and bill the club as something really spectacular.

Furthermore, what if the area where she wants to put the club is not zoned for clubs? Bureaucracy could be useful to change this, not to mention in acquiring the proper licenses and permits. Therefore, in certain cases, a Storyteller may decide that two or more types of Influence are necessary to accomplish a goal. Not only is this more realistic, but it also encourages characters to interact to get the Influence they need.

Kindred can trade Influences with each other in a sort of undead live-action version of Monopoly. These trades may be permanent or temporary. In the case of permanent trades, the old owner erases the Trait from his sheet and turns over the Influence Card (if your chronicle uses these) to the new owner. The new owner then records her newly acquired Influence Trait on her character sheet. In some cases, a Kindred is merely doing a favor or loaning her Influence to another Kindred. In this case, the owner does not erase the Trait, but should make a note that it is no longer in her possession. The holder of the Influence Trait may use it immediately or hold onto to it until she feels she needs it. However, the original owner of the Influence Trait may not regain the Trait until it is expended by the current holder.

Obviously, an unwise Kindred can find his Influences tied up in the hands of others for a long time if he is not careful. For this reason, some chronicles may dictate that the Trait reverts to its original owner after a certain time. A good rule of thumb for this is one month. If sessions are scheduled less frequently than once a month, the Storyteller(s) should probably lengthen this time. Any exchange of Influence Traits requires the presence and assistance of a Narrator.

Sometimes characters may wish to try to counteract the Influence of other characters. In such cases, it generally costs one Trait per Trait being countered. An example would be if one Kindred was trying to get a story published in the newspaper as another was trying to squelch it.

Larger games sometimes require dedicated Narrators devoted solely to Influence. Storytellers running complex chronicles may also consider the advantages of using a system of recording the various expenditures and trading of Traits. In addition to making the use of Influence easier, this sort of system can actually help plotting and intrigue. Between games, Storytellers can use the log of Influence expenditure to see what characters are attempting to accomplish and write plots around these goals. In any game, the actions and manipulations of the various Kindred of a city can from an entire subplot. Many Kindred may wish to use their Influence Traits and other powers to monitor the action of their fellows and better carry out their own intrigues and agendas.

In practice, the use of Influence is never instantaneous and rarely expedient. While a character may be able to, say, condemn any building in the city, it will not be torn down that night. For sake of game flow, a Storyteller may allow trivial uses of Influence to only take half an hour. Major manipulations, on the other hand, can become the center of ongoing plots requiring several sessions to bring to fruition.

The guidelines below by no means limit to the number of Influence Traits that can be spent at one time or the degree of change a character may bring about. They are merely an advisory measure to help Storytellers adjudicate the costs of certain actions.

Bureaucracy

The organizational aspects of the local, state and even federal government fall within the character's sphere of control. She can bend and twist the tangle of rules and regulations that seem necessary to run our society as she sees fit. The character may have contacts or allies among government clerks, supervisors, utility workers, road crews, surveyors and numerous other civil servants.

Cost	Desired Effect
1	Trace utility bills*
2	Fake a birth certificate or driver's license
	Disconnect a small residence's utilities
	Close a small road or park
	Get public aid ($250)
3	Fake a death certificate, passport or green card
	Close a public school for a single day
	Turn a single utility on a block on or off
	Shut down a minor business on a violation
4	Initiate a phone tap
	Initiate a department-wide investigation
	Fake land deeds
5	Start, stop or alter a city-wide program or policy
	Shut down a big business on a violation
	Rezone areas
	Obliterate records of a person on a city and county level
6	Arrange a fixed audit of a person or business

Church

Even churches are not without politics and intrigue that an opportunistic Kindred may capitalize upon. Church Influence usually only applies to mainstream faiths, such as Christianity, Judaism, Buddhism and the Islamic faith. Sometimes other practices fall under the Occult Influence. Contacts and allies affected by Church Influence include: ministers, bishops, priests, activists, evangelists, witch-hunters, nuns and various church attendees and assistants.

(*) These effects can generally be accomplished without expending an influence trait.

Cost	Desired Effect
1	Earn money; learn about major transactions and financial events
	Raise capital ($1,000)
	Learn about general economic trends*
	Learn real motivations for many financial actions of others
2	Trace an unsecured small account
	Raise capital to purchase a small business (single, small store)
3	Purchase a large business (a few small branches or a single large store or service)
4	Manipulate local banking (delay deposits, some credit rating alterations)
	Ruin a small business
5	Control an aspect of citywide banking (shut off ATMs, arrange a bank "holiday")
	Ruin a large business
	Purchase a major company
6	Spark an economic trend
	Instigate widespread layoffs

Health

In our modern world, a myriad of organizations and resources exist to deal with every mortal ache and ill, at least in theory. The network of health agencies, hospitals, asylums and medical groups is subject to exploitation by a Kindred with Health Influence. Nurses, doctors, specialist, lab workers, therapists, counselors and pharmacists are just a few of the inhabitants of the health field.

Cost	Desired Effect
1	Access a person's health records*
	Utilize public functions of health centers at your leisure
	Fake vaccination records and the like
	Get a Blood Trait
2	Access to some medical research records
	Have minor lab work done
	Get a copy of coroner's report
3	Instigate minor quarantines
	Corrupt results of tests or inspections
	Alter medical records
4	Acquire a body
	Completely rewrite medical records
	Abuse grants for personal use ($250)
	Have minor medical research performed on a subject
	Institute large-scale quarantines
	Shut down businesses for "health code violations"
5	Have special research projects performed
	Have people institutionalized or released

Cost	Desired Effect
1	Identify most secular members of a given faith in the local area
	Pass as a minister *
	Peruse general church records (baptism, marriage, burial, etc.)
2	Identify higher church members
	Track regular congregation members
	Suspend lay members
3	Open or close a single church
	Dip into the collection plate ($250)
	Find the average church associated hunter
	Access to private information and archives of church
4	Discredit or suspend higher-level members
	Manipulate regional branches
5	Organize major protests
	Access ancient church lore and knowledge
6	Borrow or access church relics or sacred items
7	Utilize the resources of a Diocese

Finance

The world is bristling with trappings of money and those who make it. Kindred with the Finance Influence know the language of money and its haunts. They have a degree of access with banks, megacorporations and the truly rich denizens of the world. The character has a wide variety of servants to draw upon, such as CEOs, bankers, corporate yes-men, bank tellers, stock brokers and loan agents.

High Society

Above the head of the common masses exist an elite clique of mortals that by virtue of birth, possessions, talent or quirks of fate hold themselves above the great unwashed masses. High Society allows the character to direct and utilize the energies and actions of this exceptional mass of mortals. Among their ranks one can find dilettantes, the old rich, movie and rock stars, artists of all sorts, wannabes, fashion models and trendsetters.

Cost	Desired Effect
1	Learn what is trendy *
	Learn about concerts, shows or plays well before they are made public *
	Obtain "hard to get" tickets for shows
2	Track most celebrities and luminaries
	Be a local voice in the entertainment field
	"Borrow" $1,000 as idle cash from rich friends
3	Crush promising careers
	Hobnob well above your station *
4	Minor celebrity status
5	Get a brief appearance on MTV
	Ruin a new club, gallery, festival or other high society gathering

(*) These effects can generally be accomplished without expending an influence trait.

Industry

The dark world of the Gothic Punk milieu is built by pumping and grinding machinery and the toil of endless laborers. A character with the Industry Influence has her ashen fingers in this field. Industry is composed of union workers, foremen, engineers, contractors, construction workers and manual laborers.

Cost	Desired Effect
1	Learn about industrial projects and movements *
2	Have minor projects performed
	Arrange small accidents or sabotage
	Dip into union funds or embezzle petty cash for $500
3	Organize minor strikes
	Appropriate machinery for a short time
4	Close down a small plant
	Revitalize a small plant
5	Manipulate large local industry
6	Cut off production of a single resource in a small region

Legal

The Kindred presence is even present in the hallowed halls of justice and the courts, law schools, law firms and justice bureaus within them. Inhabiting these halls are lawyers, judges, bailiffs, clerks, DAs and attorneys.

Cost	Desired Effect
1	Get free representation for small cases
2	Avoid bail for some charges
	Have minor charges dropped
3	Manipulate legal procedures
	- small wills
	- minor contracts
	- court dates
	Access public or court funds for $250
	Get representation in most court cases
4	Issue subpoenas
	Tie up court cases
	Have most legal charges dropped
	Cancel or arrange parole
5	Close down all but the most serious investigations
	Have deportation proceedings held against someone

Media

The media serves as the eyes and ears of the world. While few in this day and age doubt that the news is not corrupted, many would be surprised at who closes these eyes and covers these ears from time to time. The media entity is composed of station directions, editors, reporters, anchormen, cameramen, photographers and radio personalities.

Cost	Desired Effect
1	Learn about breaking stories early *
	Submit small articles (within reason)
2	Suppress (but not stop) small articles or reports
	Get hold of investigative reporting information
3	Initiate news investigations and reports
	Get project funding and waste it, $250
	Access media production resources
	Ground stories and projects
4	Broadcast fake stories (local only)

Occult

Most people are curious about the supernatural world and the various groups and beliefs that make up the Occult world, but few consider it anything but a hoax, a diversion or a curiosity. They could not be farther from the truth. This Influence more than any other hits the Kindred close to home and could very well bring humanity to its senses about just who and what shares this world with them. Among the Occult community are cult leaders, alternative religious groups, charlatans, would-be occultist and New Agers.

Cost	Desired Effect
1	Contact and utilize common occult groups, practices
	Know some of the more visible occult figures *
2	Know and contact some of the more obscure occult figures *
	Access resources for most rituals and rites
3	Know the general vicinity of certain supernatural entities and possibly contact them (Kindred, Garou, mages, mummies, wraiths, etc.)
	Can access vital or very rare material components
	Milk impressionable wannabes for bucks ($250)
	Access occult tomes and writings (part of an alleged Book of Nod)
	Research a Basic Ritual
4	Research an Intermediate Ritual
5	Access minor magic items
	Unearth an Advanced Ritual
6	Research to find a new or unheard of ritual or rite from tomes or mentors

Police

"To defend and serve" is a popular motto among the chosen enforcers of the law of the land. But in these days, even those ignorant to the presence of the Kindred have reason to doubt the ability of the people who put their lives on the line daily on the common man's behalf. Perhaps they should wonder who they defend, who they serve and why. The Police Influence encompasses the likes of beat cops, desk jockeys, prison guards, special divisions (such as SWAT and homicide), detectives and various clerical positions.

Cost	Desired Effect
1	Learn about of police procedures *
	Police information and rumors
	Avoid traffic tickets
2	Have license plates checked
	Avoid minor violations (first conviction)
	Get "inside information"
3	Find bureau secrets
	Get copies of an investigation report
	Have police hassle, detain or harass someone
4	Access confiscated weapons or contraband
	Start an investigation
	Get money, either from evidence room or as an appropriation ($1,000)
	Have some serious charges dropped
5	Institute major investigations
	Arrange set ups
	Instigate bureau investigations
	Have officers fired
6	Paralyze departments for a time
	Have a major investigation closed down

Politics

It is said that imitation is the sincerest form of flattery. If this is so, the movers and shakers among the Kindred should be quite taken by the artful and cutthroat antics of their mortal counterparts in the field of politics. Some of these individuals include statesmen, pollsters, activists, party members, lobbyists, candidates and the politicians themselves.

Cost	Desired Effect
1	Minor lobbying
	Identify real platforms of politicians and parties *
	Be in the know *
2	Meet small time politicians
	Have a forewarning of processes, laws and the like
	Utilize a slush fund or fund raiser, $1,000
3	Sway or alter political projects (local parks, renovations, small construction)
4	Enact minor legislation
	Dash careers of minor politicians
5	Get your candidate in a minor office
	Enact more encompassing legislature
6	Block the passage of major bills
	Suspend major laws, temporarily
	Utilize state bureaus or subcommittees
7	Usurp county-wide politics
	Subvert, to a moderate degree, statewide powers
8	Call out a local division of the National Guard
	Declare a state of emergency in a region

Street

Disenchanted, disenfranchised and ignored by their "betters", an undercurrent of humanity has made its own culture and lifestyle to deal with the harsh lot life has dealt them. In the dark alleys and slums, one will find gang members, the homeless, street performers, petty criminals, prostitutes and the forgotten.

Cost	Desired Effect
1	Has an ear open for the word on the street
	Identify most gangs and know their turfs and habits
2	Can live without fear for the most part on the underside of society
	Has a contact or two in most aspects of street life
	Can access small-time contraband
3	Often gets insight on other areas of influence
	Can arrange some services from street people or gangs
	Can get pistols or uncommon melee weapons
4	Can mobilize groups of homeless
	Panhandle or hold a "collection" ($250)
	Respected among gangs, can have a word in almost all aspects of their operations
	Can get hold of a shotgun, rifle or SMG
5	Can control a single medium sized gang
	Arrange impressive protests by street people

Transportation

The world is in constant motion. It's apparent that prosperity is greatly based on the fact that people and productions fly, float or roll to and from every corner of the planet. Without the means to perform this monumental task, our "small" world quickly returns to a daunting orb with large, isolated stretches. The forces that keep this circulation in motion include: cab and bus drivers, pilots, air traffic controllers, travel firms, sea captains, conductors, border guards and untold others.

Cost	Desired Effect
1	A wizard at what goes where, when and why
	Can travel locally quickly and freely *
2	Can track an unwary target if they use non-personal transportation
	Arrange safe (or at least concealed) passage against mundane threats (sunlight, robbery, etc.)
3	Seriously hamper an individual's ability to travel
	Avoid most supernatural dangers when travelling (such as hunters and Garou)
4	Temporarily shut down one form of transportation (bus lines, ship, plane, train, etc.)
	Route money your way ($500)
5	Reroute major modes of travel
	Engage in smuggling with impunity
6	Extend control to nearby areas
7	Isolate small or remote regions for a short period

Underworld

Even in the most cosmopolitan of ages, society has found some needs and services too questionable or simply unacceptable. In every age, some organized effort has stepped in to provide for this demand regardless of the risks. Among this often ruthless and dangerous crowd are the likes of hitmen, Mafia, Yakuza, bookies, fencers and launderers.

(*) These effects can generally be accomplished without expending an influence trait.
(*) These effects can generally be accomplished without expending an influence trait.

Cost	Desired Effect	Cost	Desired Effect
1	Locate minor contraband (knives, small time drugs, petty gambling, scalped tickets, etc.)	1	Know layout and policy of local schools * Access to low level university resources Get records up to the high school level
2	Can get hold of pistols, serious drugs, stolen cars, etc. Can hire muscle to ruff someone up Fence minor loot Prove that crime pays (and score $1,000)	2	Know a contact or two with useful knowl edge or skills Minor access to facilities Fake high school records Obtain college records
3	Get hold of rifle, shotgun or SMG Arrange a minor "hit" Know someone in the Family	3	Faculty favors Cancel a class Fix grades Discredit a student
4	White-collar crime connections	4	Organize student protests and rallies Discredit faculty members Acquire money through a grant ($1,000)
5	Arrange gangland assassinations Get the service of a demolition man or firebug Supply local drug needs	5	Falsify an undergraduate degree
		6	Arrange major projects Alter curriculum institution-wide Free run of facilities

University

We live in an information age, and the quest for learning and knowledge begins in schools, colleges and universities. University Influence represents a certain degree of control and perhaps involvement in these institutions. Within this sphere of Influence, one will find the teachers, professors, deans, students of all ages and levels, Greek orders and many young and impressionable minds.

Blood

"Your blood is precious to me,
nor would I spill it in vain."
—Sinead O'Connor, "You Made Me the Thief of Your Heart"

Your Blood Traits can be used in number of ways. The most common way a character can regain Blood Traits is by feeding, but a Kindred can never imbibe more Traits than she has in her Blood Pool. Vampires of lower generation have much larger pools than those of higher generation, which is one of the greatest advantages of generation.

Using Blood Traits

Blood Traits aren't assigned adjectives as other Traits are. Each Blood Trait simply represents a volume of blood. Here is breakdown of the ways Blood Traits can be used in the game.

• One Blood Trait must be expended each night, upon the character's rise from sleep. This is simply the basic amount of nourishment the vampire requires to survive.

• Blood Traits can be used to heal Health Levels on a one-for-one basis. The wounds are healed instantly. Note, however, that injuries caused from fire and sunlight (aggravated wounds) require three Blood traits and a Willpower Trait to heal. You may also let other vampires drink your blood, thereby healing them. However, if a vampire is in torpor, only the blood of a vampire three generations lower can revive her.

• Blood is often used to fuel Disciplines, such as Celerity or the Path of Blood.

• Blood may be used to boost your Physical Traits during a physical challenge. Each Blood Trait spent adds one to your total Physical Traits for the duration of a single conflict.

Blood Traits used in this manner can be used just as if they were Physical Traits, including the ones used to bid. This lasts for the duration of the conflict, not the challenge. The difference is that a conflict may actually involve several challenges. Traits used may be held on to for up to five minutes after the last challenge in the conflict is completed, at which time all marked Traits are gone.

Each Trait used must be marked in some manner (crossed with an X).

Willpower

"Switch off the mind and let the heart decide…"
—Thomas Dolby, "Windpower"

Within each of us is the ability to do incredible things. In times of catastrophe, ordinary people have been known to perform extraordinary feats. If the circumstances are just right, an average person could lift an automobile to save a pinned pedestrian or run through a burning building to save a trapped child. A determined man can even fight death itself if he truly has the will to live. In **The Masquerade**, this ability to do the near impossible is governed by a Trait known as Willpower. Willpower gives a character the extra strength necessary to overcome obstacles and succeed where others would give up and fail.

Each character begins the game with a number of Willpower Traits. For vampires, the number of Traits depends on the character's generation. These Willpower Traits can be used for almost anything that the player deems important. A few examples of how Willpower can be used by vampires are listed below.

• Willpower can be used to negate the effects of frenzy (by using a Willpower Trait, the character gains a new tolerance of the situation that would ordinarily throw her into frenzy).

• Willpower allows a character to replenish all of her lost Traits in any one category: Physical, Social or Mental.

• Willpower allows a character to ignore the effects of any wounds, up to and including Incapacitation, for one challenge.

• A Willpower Trait can be expended to negate the effects of any one Mental or Social Challenge.

Once a Willpower Trait has been used, it is gone until the end of the story. At this time, the character regains all Willpower used during the course of the story. It is possible that a Narrator may choose to give a character a Willpower Trait during the course of a story as a reward for exceptional roleplaying. Such a reward would be given for playing a Nature appropriately, acting out a Derangement in an appropriate fashion or any other reason the Narrator deems suitable. This should not, however, be a common occurrence.

Beast Traits

The existence of a vampire is a rollercoaster of ups and downs. Some Kindred, however, live in a far more primitive world than others. These Kindred have succumbed to the bestial side of vampiric nature and often cannot control what they do. Beast Traits are a measure of how much a Kindred has given into her dark side—the Beast. Beast Traits affect several things:

–How often the Kindred goes into frenzy

Each Beast Trait has a description of a type of event that will send that character into a state of frenzy. Unless the character resists by spending a Willpower Trait, the character will automatically frenzy if that situation comes up. (See the section on "Frenzy" for more details on the effect this has on a character.)

–Waking up early

In games that begin at sunset, a player with Beast Traits may not join play for 15 minutes for each Beast Trait her character has. A character with three Beast Traits will have to start play at least 45 minutes after sunset.

Finally, upon receiving the fifth Beast Trait, the vampire goes into a state of permanent frenzy. The player has no control over the character and must surrender it to the

Storyteller and start anew. The Storyteller may allow the player to continue to play that character. The monster will usually be hunted down and extinguished.

Beast Traits come from the categories of Rage, Control and Terror to define the type of frenzy that each Trait causes. There are also two levels of Beast Traits: Subhuman and Monstrous. Subhuman Traits cause frenzies based on fairly uncommon events. Having a Subhuman Trait will tend to make you frenzy occasionally. The only worry you have is if another Kindred figures out what your Beast Trait is. Your weaknesses may then be exploited quite easily.

Monstrous Traits are evil. Once you pick up your first Monstrous Trait, be prepared to spiral straight down into a vampiric hell. You will barely be in control of yourself and will likely end up viewing the sunrise with only a stake through the heart for company. Princes have no love for crimes performed during a frenzy.

Rage

Subhuman Beast Traits

Vigilante — Frenzy whenever you encounter the death of a person (be it Kindred or kine). You are tormented by all the killing that vampires do, so much so that a death will send you into an uncontrollable rage. You will seek out and try to destroy the murderer. If you do not know the murderer, you will blame the nearest person and go after him.

Frustrated — Frenzy whenever beaten in a Mental Challenge. You will kill the next person who messes with your mind. If you lost a Static Challenge against a lock or alarm system, that object is history. That person over there looking at you funny is obviously trying to take control of your mind. Get him.

Item — Frenzy when encountering a particular item, like a stake. The stake wielder is asking for it. You may end up with some other item besides a stake, which the Storyteller must choose. Were you attacked by a psychotic with a pair of scissors when you were young? Or were you once shot 137 times with an Uzi?

Monstrous Beast Traits

Furious — Frenzy whenever someone crosses you in some way. Someone is not following your orders. Perhaps he has been telling the Harpies all about your little plan and now the word has spread all over town. Or maybe your rival has Blood-Bonded your favorite ghoul to herself. That makes you REALLY angry.

Violent — Frenzy whenever witnessing an act of violence. This is what happens to vigilantes who go overboard. If you see two Kindred fighting, you might beat up the one who is attacking (because he's just too violent). Beat up the other one (after all, he let himself be attacked). Attack the spectators (just because you're in the mood). Often this frenzy will continue until someone helps you stop, as you are only causing more violence (although it's really their fault!).

Bullied — Frenzy whenever beaten in a Social Challenge. Whoever won the Social Challenge deserves to get beaten up. The worst problem with this frenzy is that you cannot be talked down from a frenzy. (A Kindred will have to beat you in a Social Challenge to talk you down.) Even talking to someone in this frenzy is a sure way to make yourself the next target of their wrath.

Control

Subhuman Beast Traits

Blood— Frenzy whenever encountering a quantity of spilled blood. The smell of about a pint of blood when it is out in the open drives you wild. Start by lapping up the blood in front of everyone. Once the taste gets into your body, you need more blood until you are full. Even then, you may not stop.

Hunger — Frenzy whenever you are down to only a single Blood Trait. The Hunger starts to drive you, and you need the blood. Drink your first victim dry, then leave the dry husk as you pursue more blood. Feeding is all that matters. Covering up your killing is not part of being a "real" vampire.

Lust - Frenzy whenever encountering a willing victim to feed from. Feeding is like sex. When you find someone to feed from who is just as enthusiastic as you are, the drinking is more than just taking blood. You tend to get carried away and drink too much. Then you need to find more and more blood to help atone for your sins.

Monstrous Beast Traits

Blood Smell — Frenzy whenever encountering a crowd of people, animals or Kindred. This is similar to the Subhuman Beast Trait: Blood, but far more crippling. The smell of blood permeates throughout the city. You can smell the delicious blood inside of every human you pass. Here's a cruel trick: kidnap a Kindred with Blood Smell and drop him in a night club.

Desire — Frenzy whenever encountering whatever you most want. You want to be Prince? He's standing right over there. Take him out and the position is yours. Infatuated with the beautiful Toreador? Her "guardian" is approaching you now. This is a particularly nasty Trait to have.

Diablerie — Frenzy when encountering an incapacitated Kindred. This is not a very common situation, unlike most Monstrous Beast Traits. However, whenever you find a helpless Kindred, you have trouble resisting the easy way to lower your generation. Drink his blood, then his soul. Stock up on Willpower, or the Sheriff will be after you in no time.

Courage

Subhuman Beast Traits

Phobia — Frenzy when affected by a phobia. Perhaps you suffered from some phobia in your mortal life that grew into a terrible fear in your immortal life. Flee until you find some protection from whatever ails you. The Storyteller should choose the Phobia, but here are some examples:

• **Claustrophobia** — Closed, tight spaces turn your stomach. You can't breathe in constricted areas. (Never mind that you don't breathe.) This is one vampire who does not sleep in a coffin.

• **Agoraphobia** — You stick to the sewers or inside buildings. Things can swoop down on you in open areas. Besides, werewolves hate confined spaces, so you will panic and flee indoors as soon as possible.

• **Hydrophobia** — You are positive that those stories about running water are true. Go into a frenzy when immersed, or even forced to walk across water.

Sunlight — Frenzy whenever exposed to sunlight, a sun lamp, or UV radiation. Sunlight kills vampires, and so this is one of the few useful Beast Traits. However, sun lamps and black lights (which normally cause only a mild tingling to the skin) send you into a flight of terror. Avoid tanning salons and scope out your nightclubs carefully.

Fire — Frenzy whenever exposed to a quantity of flame. This is another potentially useful Trait, as fire is a great danger to vampires. Most vampires, however, will not freak out when they see a campfire, or when someone lights a cigarette. You will.

Monstrous Beast Traits

Pain — Frenzy whenever you take damage. Pain sends you running away screaming from whatever hurt you. The pain is so intense that you will forget to heal the wound with blood until you are calmed down. However, you will calm down 5-10 minutes after you get away from whatever hurt you.

Shame — Frenzy whenever beaten in a Physical Challenge. You are so unsure of yourself that any loss in a Physical Challenge will break your will. You will try to get away from the person who won the Physical Challenge. See what the Harpies say after you have a mental breakdown when failing to knock down a door.

Religion — Frenzy when confronted by a religious symbol. You've probably confronted someone with True Faith at some point. He messed with you so well that even a cross (or another appropriate religious artifact) will send you racing away. You can actually stand being around the object, but must enter a frenzy if you touch one, or have it presented before you.

Receiving Beast Traits

Kindred pick up Beast Traits when performing an act of violence or cruelty. It is up to a Narrator or the Storyteller to decide what warrants penalizing the player with a Beast Trait.

Generally a Narrator will have the player perform a Simple Test. If the player wins, she will not gain a Beast Trait. If she draws, she will gain a Subhuman Beast Trait. If the player loses the Simple Test, she will gain a Monstrous Beast Trait.

It also bears mentioning that a Kindred who performs a heinous action while under the effects of a frenzy is by no means exempt from gaining additional Beast Traits as a result of her actions— thus the downward spiral begins.

Here are some examples of particularly antisocial behavior:

• Committing Diablerie. This will almost always result in the Diabolist receiving a Beast Trait. The Narrator should have the player make two Simple Tests instead of one. Although the character will not receive more than one Beast Trait from this action, the chances of getting one increase drastically.

• Bringing about the destruction of another Kindred.

• Intentionally murdering a kine.

• Lying or scheming in some manner that causes a death.

• Torturing someone.

• Mass destruction.

The Storyteller should also choose which Trait to give to the offender. Awarding Beast Traits should not be done lightly, as only five are needed to sink a character. Once gained, a Beast Trait will scar your character permanently, as there is no way to lose them. If your character somehow manages to achieve the exalted state of Golconda, then your Beast Traits will be rendered temporarily ineffective. If you slip from the path, however, they will immediately be back to haunt you. When you fall, you fall hard.

A player can also choose to take a second Beast Trait at the start of the game. This is not advisable for beginning players, as the possibility of getting five Beast Traits becomes very real. The second Beast Trait taken in this way counts as two Negative Traits for the purpose of buying additional Traits, Abilities and Disciplines.

Chapter Four: Rules

My blood is running dry,
My skin is, my skin is growing thin
For every time you find yourself
You lose a little bit of me, from within.
— Indigo Girls

There are times when a player will want to have her character do something that can't be accomplished through simple roleplaying, such as attacking another person, picking a lock or even searching for a file in a computer system. When this happens, you need rules.

Rules are an imperative part of any game: they define what can and cannot be done. Without them, there would be no winners or losers— in effect, there would be no limits. Your limitations and parameters help to define who you are and give you a sense of accomplishment when you manage to triumph over others.

Still, the primary focus of this game is to tell a good story, and it's always best to try to defeat your opponents through roleplaying and manipulation rather than by direct confrontation. When confrontation does occur, rules are necessary to govern those situations.

Time

Time in **Mind's Eye Theatre** works as it does in real life. It moves forward inexorably, relentlessly. For the most part, everything is played out in real time, and players are expected to stay in character unless they have a rules question.

During the course of a story, it is assumed that a player is always "in character." A player should only rarely drop character when interacting with other players. Doing so ruins the atmosphere for everyone involved. Challenges may be talked through, but a player is always considered to be active in the game. If a player needs to take a break, he should inform a Narrator. That player should not interact with any of the other players while out of character.

The only other exception is when a Narrator calls for a "time out." This may be necessary to resolve a dispute or to change the scene if the story calls for it. When "Time Out!" is called, all players within hearing distance must stop whatever they are doing until the Narrator calls out the word "Resume." Time outs should be kept to a minimum, since they interrupt the flow of the story.

Challenges

During the course of most stories, there will come a time when two or more players will come into a conflict that cannot be resolved through roleplaying alone. This system allows for conflicts to be resolved simply and quickly, whether they're firefights or tests of will. This face-off is called a challenge. In most cases, a Narrator does not need to be present when a challenge is played.

Roleplaying does not necessarily have to end when a challenge begins. Experienced players can seamlessly integrate a challenge into their roleplaying so that outsiders don't know that anything unusual is going on. At the player's option, hand signals can be used to indicate when certain Traits and powers are being employed.

Lastly, in order for this system to work, players need to work together. Players need to educate each other on the rules and agree on what Traits can be used in a challenge. Compromise and cooperation are the bywords of the game.

The challenge system presented in this chapter is also part of the basic rules for the **Mind's Eye Theater** system. By combining **The Masquerade** with other games in the series, players can have vampires interact with werewolves, wraiths, mortals and other types of characters.

Using Traits

Before you can begin to learn how challenges work, you must first understand what defines a character's abilities. A character is created by choosing a number of adjectives that describe and define that person as an individual. These adjectives are called Traits and are fully described in Chapter Three. These Traits are used to declare a challenge against another character or against a static force represented by a Narrator.

Initial Bid

A challenge begins by a player "bidding" one of her Traits against her opponent. At the same time, she must declare what the conditions of the challenge are, i.e. firing a gun or attacking with a stake. The defender must then decide how she will respond. She can either relent immediately or bid one of her own Traits in response.

When players bid Traits against one another, they may only use Traits that could sensibly be used in that situation. Essentially, this means a player can usually only use Traits from the same category as her opponent's Traits. Most challenges are categorized as Physical, Social or Mental, and all Traits used in a challenge must be from the same category. Experienced players may offer each other more creative leeway, but that is strictly by mutual agreement.

If the defender relents, she automatically loses the challenge. For example, if she were being attacked, she would suffer a wound. If she matches the challenger's bid, the two immedi-

ately go to a test (described below). Those Traits bid are put at risk, as the loser of the test not only loses the challenge, but the Trait she bid as well.

For example, Vargoss, a mid-ranking Ventrue, is being attacked by Roxanne, a Brujah anarch. Roxanne begins her attack by bidding Ferocious. ("I Ferociously grab you by the lapels of your suit and headbutt you!" This is an appropriate Trait, since she's trying to gravely injure him.) Vargoss bids the Trait: Quick ("I try to Quickly jump out of the way and run for the door." He only wishes to escape so that he can warn the Sheriff of the anarch's attack.) The victory conditions have been established: if Roxanne wins, Vargoss is wounded; if Vargoss wins, he escapes (at least for now). The two now go to the test.

Testing

Once both parties involved in a challenge have bid a Trait, they immediately go to a test. The test itself is not what you may think— the outcome is random, but no cards or dice are used. The two players face off against one another by playing Rock-Paper-Scissors. It may sound a little silly, but it works.

If you lose the test, you lose the Trait you used. The Trait is lost for the duration of the story (this usually means the rest of the evening). Essentially, you've lost some of your self-confidence in your own capabilities. You can no longer use that Trait effectively, at least until you regain confidence in your Traits.

The test works like the moment in poker when the cards are turned over and the winner is declared. From the test, there may be one of two outcomes: either one player is the victor or the result is a tie.

In the case of a tie, the players must then reveal the number of Traits that they possess in the category used (Physical, Social or Mental). The player with the least number of Traits loses the test and therefore loses the challenge. Note that the number of Traits you've lost in previous challenges, or lost for any other reason, count towards this total. The trick to the declaration is that you may lie about the number of Traits you possess, but only by declaring less Traits than you actually have— you may never lie and say that you have more Traits than you actually do. This allows you to keep the actual number of Traits you possess a secret, although doing so may be risky. The challenger is always the first to declare his number of Traits. If both players declare the same number of Traits, then the challenge is a draw and both players lose the Trait(s) they bid.

Incidentally, certain advanced powers allow some characters to use gestures other than Rock, Paper and Scissors. Before they can use the gestures in a test, they must explain what they are and how they are used.

In continuing the example above, Roxanne and Vargoss now go to a test. They do Rock-Paper-Scissors. They both choose scissors, so they tie. They now compare Traits. Vargoss is a bit outclassed by the Brujah. Roxanne has seven Physical Traits, while Vargoss only has five. Vargoss loses and takes a wound. He thinks briefly about the ibuprofen in the top drawer of his desk.

Rock-Paper-Scissors

If you don't happen to know (or remember) what we mean by Rock-Paper-Scissors, here's the concept: you and another person face off and, on the count of three, show one of three hand gestures. "Rock" is just a basic fist. "Paper" is just a flat hand. "Scissors" is represented by sticking out two fingers. You then compare the two gestures to determine the winner. Rock crushes Scissors. Scissors cuts Paper. Paper covers Rock. Identical signs indicate a tie.

Adjudication

If you have question or argument about the rules or the conditions of a challenge, you need to find a Narrator to make a judgment. Try to remain in character while looking for a Narrator. Any interruption in the progress of the story should be avoided, so work problems out with other players if at all possible. If you don't know the exact correct application of a certain rule, it would be best to wing it rather than interrupt the flow of the story. Cooperation is the key to telling a good story.

Complications

There are a number of ways in which a challenge can be complicated. The above rules are enough to resolve most disputes, but the following rules help to add a few bells and whistles.

Negative Traits

Many characters have Negative Traits: these are Traits that can be used against a character by his opponent. During the initial bid of any challenge, after you have each bid one Trait, you can call out a Negative Trait that you believe your opponent possesses. If he does indeed possess the Negative Trait, your opponent is forced to bid an additional Trait, although you must still risk your one Trait as usual. If he does not possess that Negative Trait, *you* must risk an additional Trait. (Blood Traits cannot be used to substitute for Physical Traits in this instance.) You may integrate as many Negative Traits as you wish one by one during the initial bid phase of a challenge, as long as you can pay the price if you're wrong.

If your opponent does not have additional Traits to bid, then your Trait is not at risk during the challenge. Additionally if you guess more than one Negative Trait that your opponent cannot match, you gain that many additional Traits in the case of a tie or an overbid. The same works in reverse, favoring your opponent if you do not have additional Traits remaining to match incorrect Negative Trait guesses.

It can be risky to bid Negative Traits, but if you're sure about what you're doing, you can raise the stakes for your opponent, possibly even to the point where she relents rather than risking additional Traits. Just make sure that your sources of information are dependable.

For example, Lora is trying to seduce Sir James with Entrancement. She begins by bidding her Social Trait: Seductive. ("I Seductively demonstrate the aesthetics of my latest designer dress.") Sir James is far too Dignified to allow himself be taken in by Lora on a whim. ("I am Dignified, and care little for such frivolous things as fashion.") However, Lora suspects that Sir James is actually quite Shy and is unused to receiving such attention from a lady. ("Have you been too Shy to develop an appreciation for such things?") She is correct (Shy is one of Sir James' Negative Social Traits). Lora has just upped the stakes. If Sir James still wishes to resist her he must risk an additional Social Trait. However, things being what they are, Sir James decides that being Entranced by Lora might not be such a bad thing after all. He relents and receives some rather intriguing instruction from Lora.

Overbidding

Overbidding is the system by which elder vampires (who often have considerably more Traits than younger opponents) may prevail in a challenge, even if they lose the initial test. An elder vampire with 18 Social Traits should be able to crush a neonate with five. This system is designed to make that possible.

Once the test has been made, the loser has the option of calling for an "overbid." In order to call an overbid, you must also risk a new Trait; the original one has already been lost. At this point, the two players must reveal the number of Traits they possess, starting with the player who called for an overbid. If you have double the number of Traits as your opponent in the appropriate category, you may attempt another test. As with a tie, you may state a number of Traits less than the actual number you have and keep your true power secret. This can be dangerous, though, unless you are completely confident in your estimation of your opponent's abilities.

For example, Francisco is trying to Dominate Renauld into wearing a newpaper hat. They begin as usual with Francisco bidding Determined ("I am Determined to make you wear my mind control helmet!") and Renauld countering with Disciplined ("I am Disciplined at resisting obnoxious Malkavians."). They do a test— Francisco throws Paper and Renauld throws Scissors. Renauld wins. However, Francisco believes he can overbid this foolish Brujah. Francisco bids a second Mental Trait: Dedicated. ("I am a Dedicated researcher who must sacrifice your brain to the demon in my paper hat!") They now compare Traits. Francisco has 12 Mental Traits, while Renauld has only six. Another Test is performed. Francisco throws Scissors and Renauld throws rock. Francisco loses his second Trait as well as the challenge. Renauld puts on Francisco's rather fetching newspaper hat, embarassing himself in front of several Ventrue nearby.

Static Challenges

Sometimes you may have to undergo a challenge against a Narrator rather than against another player, such as when you are trying to pick a lock or summon an animal. In such circumstances, you merely bid the Trait that would be appropriate, then immediately perform a test against the Narrator. Before the test is made, the Narrator decides the difficulty of the task that you are attempting. The test proceeds exactly as it would if you were testing against another character. Of course, you may overbid in a static action, but beware, because the Narrator can overbid as well.

Sometimes Narrators may leave notes on objects, such as books and doors. These notes indicate the type of challenge that must be won for something to occur (such as understanding a book, opening a door or identifying an artifact). With experience, you may learn how difficult it is to open a locked door. However, difficulty ratings can be as different as lock types.

Simple Tests

Simple Tests are used to determine if you can do something successfully when there is no real opposition. Simple Tests are used often used when determining the extent of a Discipline's effect. Most Simple Tests do not require you to risk or bid Traits, although some may.

When a Simple Test is called, a test (rock-paper-scissors) is done against the Narrator. In most cases, the player succeeds on a win or a tie, although in some cases, it may be necessary for him to win.

Health

A character in The **Masquerade** has five Health Levels; these represent the amount of injury the character has suffered. These levels are Healthy, Bruised, Wounded, Incapacitated and Torpor. If a Healthy character loses a combat challenge, she becomes Bruised. If she loses two, she becomes Wounded, and so on.

• **Bruised** — When a character is Bruised, she is only slightly injured, having perhaps suffered a few scrapes and bruises, but little more until she is healed. In order to enter a new challenge, she must risk an additional Trait. Thus, to even have a chance in a challenge, a Bruised character must bid at least two Traits.

• **Wounded** — When a character is Wounded, she is badly hurt. She might be bleeding freely from open wounds, and may even have broken bones. She must bid two Traits to have a chance in a challenge. In addition, she will always lose during a test on a tie, even if she has more Traits than her opponent. If she has less Traits, her opponent gets a free additional test.

• **Incapacitated** — When a character is Incapacitated, she is completely out of play for at least ten minutes. After ten minutes has passed, the character is still immobile and may not enter into challenges until she has healed at least one Health Level. She is at the mercy of other characters. She is only capable of whispering and is barely aware of her surroundings while incapacitated.

• **Torpor** — When a character is in Torpor, she is in a deathlike state. She is effectively out of play until revived by another character. She is completely at the mercy of other characters and the environment around her. Vampires who are in Torpor can only be revived by the blood of another Vampire at least three generations lower than herself. The Storyteller may, of course, allow other exceptional circumstances to rouse a vampire from this state.

Healing

Vampires require blood in order to heal wounds. Blood Traits must be expended to restore Health Levels on a one-for-one basis. More information on Blood Traits can be found in Chapter Three.

Aggravated Wounds

Vampires cannot heal aggravated wounds with blood alone. Aggravated wounds are caused by exposure to sunlight, fire and the claws or teeth of a vampire or werewolf. Such wounds require the expenditure of three Blood Traits and a Willpower Trait to heal. Additionally, only one such wound may be healed per night. This represents the gradual regenerative properties a vampire possesses. Extreme injuries, such as broken or severed limbs, can be healed completely, but they require blood and time to heal.

The Mob Scene

During the course of many stories, you are inevitably going to be drawn into a challenge in which several people want to be involved. Multi-party challenges can be confusing, but if you follow these simple guidelines, you shouldn't have much difficulty. These rules are most useful in combat challenges, but they can be used with nearly any sort of group challenge.

The first thing you need to do is decide who is challenging whom. This is usually obvious, but when it's not, you need a quick way to work things out. Simply have everyone involved count to three at the same time. On three, each player points at the individual he is challenging.

The first challenge that must be resolved involves the person who has the most people pointing at him. Determine what the appropriate category of Traits would be— Physical, Social or Mental. Each player pointing at the defender must bid one appropriate Trait. This group must also choose a leader. The attacking group cannot exceed five people— there is a limit to the number of individuals who can attack a single person at one time. The defender must then bid as many Traits

as there are people opposing him. If he does not have enough Traits to do so, he automatically loses the challenge. If he does have enough Traits, a test is performed between the defender and the chosen leader of the attackers. The rest of the challenge continues as normal, although any comparison of Traits or overbidding may only be done by the group leader.

If the defender wins the test, he is unharmed, but he can choose to affect only one member of the attacking group. Usually, as in the case of a combat, this would mean inflicting one wound. Additionally, all Traits bid by the attackers are lost. If the attackers win, they may inflict one wound, and the defender loses all the Traits he had risked.

After the first challenge is concluded, go on to the next one. Continue the process until each character who has declared an action has been the target of a challenge or has donated Traits.

Order of Challenges

Some people question exactly what a player can respond with when he has been challenged. Typically, if someone initiates a Physical Challenge, the defender can only respond with Physical Traits, unless he possesses a Discipline or some other ability that is considered to be always active. He cannot respond with the use of a Discipline or another ability until after the first challenge has been completed. Some Disciplines are the exception to this rule. Such Disciplines will specify this contingency in their description. Social and Mental Challenges work the same way.

Chapter Five: Systems

*Garlic Pills — The advantages of garlic without the embar-
rassing side effects!*
— Radio Advertisement

This chapter discusses some of the additional rules and complications that sometimes come into play in **The Masquerade**. It also describes a multitude of different systems for resolving character interactions. However, this chapter is more a set of permutations than a set of rules. There is *nothing* contained in the next several pages that you *need* to know, only things that you might *want* to know. These complications can add more depth and detail to your game.

Combat

The basic challenge system used in **The Masquerade** has already been presented in Chapter Four. This section contains a few basic modifications to the combat system and elaboration on it.

Combat is the usual intent behind Physical Challenges. Essentially, combat involves two characters in physical conflict. The players agree what the outcome of the challenge will be, each player bids an appropriate Trait, and a test is resolved, determining the victor. The following rules allow for variances to those basic rules, such as situations using surprise or weapons.

The agreed outcome of a Physical Challenge usually involves the loser being injured. This is not, however, the only result possible. For instance, you could say that you want to wrest a weapon from your opponent's hands or that you're trying to trip him. The result can be nearly anything the two parties agree upon, whether that's simply raking someone with claws or dramatically throwing someone through a window. The results of a combat challenge may also be different for both participants. (For example, a frenzied Brujah may wish to attack a Toreador who affronted her, while the Toreador may simply want to escape).

Surprise

If a player does not respond within three seconds of the declaration of a Physical Challenge, the player is considered surprised: he is not fully prepared for what's coming. Sometimes a player is busy with another activity, doesn't hear a challenge or is playing a character who just isn't prepared for the attack (such as when the character is led into an ambush). It is considered highly improper to sneak around whispering challenges to try to get an element of surprise.

Surprise simply means that the outcome of the first challenge in a fight can only harm the surprised defender, not the challenger. For instance, if the defender did not respond in time to an attack, but still won the challenge, the challenger would not be injured. Furthermore, if the challenger loses the test by risking another Trait, she may call for a second challenge since she was operating from the benefit of surprise. With the second challenge, play continues as usual and winners and losers of a challenge are determined as normal.

Surprise is only in effect for the first challenge of a conflict; all further challenges are resolved normally, as explained below.

Weapons

No real weapons are ever allowed in **Mind's Eye Theatre** games, for obvious reasons. Even nonfunctional props are forbidden if they can be mistaken for weapons. This system does not use props of any kind, nor are players required (or allowed) to strike one another. Weapons are purely an abstraction in this game. Weapon cards, which display the facts and statistics of a particular weapon, can be used instead. The damage a weapon inflicts is limited only by mutual agreement, although it is generally assumed that an injury incurred from a blow reduces the target by a Health Level.

A weapon gives its wielder extra Traits. Sometimes this advantage is offset by a disadvantage in terms of a Negative Trait. Each weapon has one to three extra Traits; these may be used in any challenge in which the weapon is employed. These Traits *cannot* be used in place of your Traits when placing your initial bid. Instead, they add to your total when comparing Traits, such as in case of a tie during a test or an overbid. In addition, some weapons have special abilities that can be employed.

Disadvantages are weaknesses inherent to the weapon. These can be used by the wielder's opponent in precisely the same way as Negative Traits. The weapon's Negative Traits can only be used against the wielder of that weapon. Negative Traits for a weapon must be appropriate to the situation. For instance, if you are firing a gun and your opponent wants to apply the gun's Negative Trait: Loud against you, that Negative Trait could be ignored if you have taken the time to find some means of silencing the weapon.

If a Negative Trait of your weapon is named by your opponent, and that Trait applies to the situation, you suffer a one Trait penalty (i.e., you are required to risk an additional Trait). If your opponent calls out a Negative Trait of your weapon that doesn't apply to the situation, your opponent suffers a one Trait penalty in the challenge.

Statistics for weapons are written on cards and carried along with your character card. Weapon cards specify the capacities of each weapon. Weapon cards allow other players to see that you actually possess a weapon— when you have a weapon card in your hand, you are considered to be holding the weapon. Each weapon has a concealability rating. If the weapon is not concealable, you must have that card on display at all times. You cannot, for example, pull a rifle out of your pocket. Instead, you would must carry that card in hand at all times or, optionally, you could pin the card to your shirt, indicating that the rifle is slung over your shoulder.

Some weapons have special abilities, such as causing extra wound levels of damage or affecting more than one target.

Bidding Traits with Weapons

During a normal hand-to-hand fight, you bid your Physical Traits against your opponent's Physical Traits. However, if you're using the Firearms Ability, you can use Mental Traits instead. If your opponent is also using a Firearm, he will bid Mental Traits as well. If your opponent is not using a Firearm and is merely trying to dodge, then the attacker uses Mental Traits to attack, while the defender uses her Physical Traits to dodge. This is one of the few instances when Traits from different attributes will be used against one another.

Weapon Examples

- **Knife** — This easily-concealed weapon is very common.

Bonus Traits: 2

Negative Traits: Short

Concealability: Pocket

- **Club** — This can be anything from a chair leg to a tree limb.

Bonus Traits: 2

Negative Traits: Clumsy

Concealability: Jacket

- **Wooden Stake** — Though not the most powerful weapon, if it transfixes a vampire's heart, the victim is immobilized (see below).

Bonus Traits: 2

Negative Traits: Clumsy

Concealability: Jacket

- **Broken Bottle** — A good example of a weapon made from scratch.

Bonus Traits: 1

Negative Traits: Fragile

- **Sword** — This long-edged blade is nearly impossible to conceal.

Bonus Traits: 3

Negative Traits: Heavy

Concealability: Trench Coat

- **Pistol** — This covers nearly any sort of handgun.

Bonus Traits: 2

Negative Traits: Loud

Concealability: Pocket

- **Rifle** — Impossible to conceal

Bonus Traits: 3

Negative Traits: Loud

Concealability: None

- **Shotgun** — This powerful weapon fires a spray of pellets, making targets easy to hit and ballistics checks nearly impossible.

Bonus Traits: 3

Negative Traits: Loud

Concealability: Trench Coat

Special Ability: A shotgun may affect up to three targets if they are standing immediately next to each other and are further than ten feet from the person firing the shotgun. This is resolved with a single challenge against a group. The Traits are risked against the entire group. Up to three separate tests are performed (one test for each target). In this fashion, it is possible to simultaneously wound up to three opponents in a single challenge. The Trait risked by the attacker is used against all three opponents. If any of the three opponents win, the attacker loses that Trait. However, that Trait still applies to all three tests within that group challenge. Thus, a character can challenge up to three opponents while only risking one Trait with this weapon. Also, a shotgun can cause two wound levels to a single target standing within five feet.

- **Submachine Gun** — Though difficult to conceal, this weapon is very powerful.

Bonus Traits: 3

Negative Traits: Loud

Concealability: Jacket

Special Ability: a submachine gun may affect up to five targets if they're standing immediately next to each other and are further than ten feet from the person firing the submachine gun. This is resolved with a single challenge against a group (as described under the section on shotguns).

Stake through the Heart

The bane of all vampires is the dreaded wooden stake. Although all Kindred must live in fear of this threat, placing a stake into the heart of a conscious opponent is a difficult task at best.

A stake through the heart will completely immobilize a vampire. However, in order to do this, a character must first win a Physical Challenge against the vampire. He must then win two Simple Tests in order to successfully impale the vampire's heart. Even if one or both of the Simple Tests fail, the vampire only suffers a wound from the stake, yet is not immobilized.

Ranged Combat

Many weapons allow you to stand at a distance from a target and engage him in combat. In such situations, you still go over to the target (after shouting "Bang!") and engage in a challenge.

If you have surprised your opponent, even if you lose the first test, you have the option of calling for a second test. Once the second challenge is called, play continues as normal. Your target is considered surprised for the first attack, and if he has no ranged weapon with which to return fire, he is considered "surprised" for as long as you can attack him without facing resistance (that is, if he wins on a challenge, you don't take damage).

If your target is aware of you before you make your initial ranged attack and has a ranged weapon of his own, he is not considered surprised for your first attack. He may shoot back right away, and your challenges are resolved as stated below.

After your first shot is fired (the first challenge is resolved), your target may attempt to return fire (assuming he is armed). The loser of a firefight challenge loses a Health Level.

If the defender is unarmed, he may declare his victory condition as escape (providing he is not cornered). If the defender wins the challenge, the attacker is still unharmed, but his target, the defender, has escaped from view and must be searched out if the attacker decides to press the attack. In instances such as this, a new challenge cannot be made for at least five minutes.

Cover

Fighting with hand-to-hand weapons— clubs, knives or swords— requires that combatants be within reach of each other. Fighting with ranged weapons allows combatants to stand apart; participants can therefore "dive for cover." When you resolve each ranged combat challenge, you can present one Trait of cover to add to your total number of Traits. These cover Traits may not be used for bidding, but they do add to your total if Traits are compared. This cover can take the form of whatever obstacles are around and within reach of you (you don't actually dive for them). A Narrator might be required to tell you what cover is around, but if combatants know the area, they can agree upon what cover is available. In some instances, there may be no cover around, leaving a combatant in the open with only his own defensive Traits.

If cover is extensive— a brick wall, perhaps— it may be worth more than one Trait for one challenger. The number of Traits available for cover is left for challengers to agree upon, or for a Narrator to decree. Hiding behind a car, for example, might be worth two cover Traits, while hiding behind a thin wall might only count as one. If one combatant goes completely under cover— he cannot be seen at all and is thoroughly protected— he is considered impossible to hit. The attacker must change his position to get another clear shot.

Frenzy

Vampires, like mortals, are creatures of instinct. However, the instincts of a vampire are those of a hunter, not a gatherer. Vampires are the ultimate predators. They stand at the apex of the food chain. They are highly developed killing machines— the harbingers of death.

The predator nature of vampires is called the Beast by the Kindred. Even the most sedate and civilized vampire can turn into a ravaging, mindless animal with enough provocation. While in this frenzy of emotion, a vampire can often not tell friend from foe, control his desire for blood, or preserve the Masquerade.

Most Kindred struggle against the Beast. Those who give into its seduction of emotion eventually end up breaking the rules of vampiric society. Often they become outcasts if their crimes are not terrible enough; otherwise, they are sometimes hunted down and destroyed. Once a vampire has given herself to the Beast, it becomes easier and easier to be lured into a frenzy. The state of frenzy begins an almost inevitable downward spiral towards constantly raging bestiality.

The state of frenzy is handled in a **The Masquerade** through Beast Traits. Each Beast Trait has a description of a situation or situations that cause a vampire to enter a frenzy. The rule is simple: when that event happens, the character frenzies. The only way to avoid going into frenzy is by spending a Willpower Trait. Using a Willpower Trait will stave off the frenzy for about 10 minutes. During that time, the character should try to get away from whatever is calling out to the Beast within her.

While in a frenzy, a vampire is capable of nearly anything. However, the general trend of behavior of a frenzy is described by the type of Beast Trait that caused it. There are three types of frenzies:

Rage Frenzy— Such a frenzy causes the vampire to go into a terribly destructive rant. The Kindred will often try to destroy everything nearby. He will start with whatever sent him into the frenzy, followed by everything else in the immediate vicinity. His anger is swift and impossible to control.

Control Frenzy— These types of frenzies are usually associated with feeding. the Kindred will often begin to drink blood in huge quantities, going from victim to victim with no subtlety or attempt to maintain the Masquerade. The Kindred will tear through walls and even her friends to get at more blood until completely sated. Even then, she may still try to drink.

Terror Frenzy— These frenzies are caused by the few things that vampires fear. Fire or sunlight are two examples of stimuli that will cause a vampire to frantically run away from a source of fear. The vampire will be dangerous to approach until she is completely away from the flame or sunlight after a few minutes of calming down. Many well-intentioned Kindred have met their demise by trying to stop a vampire in a frenzy.

Frenzies do have one advantage. While in this state of blind emotion, you can ignore all damage, until your Health Level reduces you to Torpor or Final Death. Unfortunately, you may not heal yourself with blood while you are in a frenzy. While frenzied, you may not attempt any Social Challenges, and he need not risk any Social Traits if anyone tries to conduct a Social Challenge against him. Reasoning with someone who is screaming for blood can be somewhat awkward, to say the least.

When roleplaying a frenzy, remember not to do anything dangerous. Don't actually run during a Terror Frenzy or physically attack someone during a Rage Frenzy. This may sound like a silly warning, but this is one of the times where you are most likely to forget this prime rule of live roleplaying. Here are some ideas for roleplaying the different frenzies without freaking out people who aren't in the game.

When in a Rage Frenzy, narrow your eyes and walk slowly but purposefully. Growl when you speak, but not to the point of screaming. Breathe heavily and snort a bit. Stride toward your object, and challenge anything or anyone who crosses your path in combat. When something stops moving, change the object of your rage.

When under the influence of a Control Frenzy, lock your eyes on what you desire and never remove them. Lick your lips and completely ignore anything else. If anything tries to stop you, bash it (using a Physical Challenge, of course), or convince it to go away. Use a stream of words like "I want," "Mine!" or "I *will* have him!"

Rules Summary for Frenzy

Action	Rule
Starting a Frenzy	None. Event in a Beast Trait happens
Stopping a Frenzy	Spend a Willpower Trait before the frenzy
	OR Spend Willpower Trait and win a Static Mental Challenge against four Traits
	OR go against Nature and win Static Mental Challenge against four Traits
	OR burn out 10 minutes after the problem goes away
	OR have someone talk you down by winning a Social Challenge against twice the number of Beast Traits you possess
Special	While in a frenzy, you are not affected by Social Challenges
	You may ignore all damage until torpor.

When you have become the victim of a Terror Frenzy, widen your eyes, making sure to look at the object of your terror. Stutter. Back away from the object of your fear. Listen to people only when they stand between you and IT.

Ending a Frenzy

Before entering a frenzy, you may stave it off for 10 minutes by spending a Willpower Trait. If you are already in a frenzy, you can try to end the frenzy at any time by spending a Willpower Trait. You must then win a Static Mental Challenge against a difficulty of four Traits. The Willpower Trait is lost even if you fail the test. If the frenzy is about to cause you to do something which is completely against your Nature, you may try ONCE to end the frenzy without needing to spend a Willpower Trait. You must still win the Static Challenge, however.

You also get a free Static Challenge after whatever has caused you to frenzy goes away. Otherwise, the frenzy will burn itself out 5-10 minutes after the cause of the frenzy goes away. For a Rage or Terror Frenzy, this is when you are away from the object. For a Control Frenzy, this is when you have fed fully from a target, or have sated yourself.

You can also try to talk someone out of a frenzy by winning a Social Challenge against her. This is considered to be a Static Challenge with a difficulty equal to twice the number of Beast Traits the frenzied character possesses. (For instance, four Social Traits must be risked to calm down someone with two Beast Traits.) Remember that when trying to perform a Social Challenge against a frenzied vampire, she does not risk any Social Traits. That applies here as well—you are trying to reason with her Bestial nature. Failing the Social Challenge often draws the frenzied vampire's attention to you. It is hardly surprising that Kindred do not always trust each other.

Diablerie

Some vampires seek to become more powerful by draining the very essence of their elders. A particularly voracious Kindred can quickly come to rival the power of a Methuselah if he can pursue this dangerous course of Diablerie for very long. Their goal, however, is made exceedingly difficult by the elders, who have made the drinking of another Kindred's essence the most heinous crime one of the Damned can commit.

Diablerie is also very easy to follow, as the Kindred's aura will be marked. In **Masquerade**, a Diabolist's aura is tainted by black threads that remain for three months after the diablerie was committed. Any vampire who uses the Discipline of Aura Perception will recognize these bands and know the transgression of the Diabolist. Someone who kills his elders is almost sure to end his existence as the target of a Blood Hunt. If the prince declares a Blood Hunt on a criminal, any recognized Kindred may hunt the criminal down and destroy him. Doing so will immediately gain the favor of the prince.

The advantages of committing diablerie, however, are enough to tempt many Kindred into preying upon their own kind. Upon successfully draining a Kindred of lower generation, the Kindred gains some of the power of that extinguished vampire. The Diabolist lowers her generation by one, bringing her closer to Caine, increasing her resistance to control from more powerful Kindred, and increasing her Blood Pool. The Diabolist also gains two experience points if she can survive to the end of the evening on top of any which would normally be gained. The Diabolist also immediately receives a Beast Trait for the callous act. (See the section on "Frenzy" for a full list of Beast Traits.)

The actual process of Diablerie is called Amaranth by the elders. The Amaranth is a legendary undying flower, a treasure beyond price. According to legend, one was usually sent to an elder a week before such an attack.

Rules Summary for Diablerie

Action	Challenge
Stage 1: Drain Blood	Automatic one Trait/action
Stage 2: Drain Health	Physical Challenge against victim; Diabolist cannot defend Physically
Stage 3: Drinking Soul	Physical Challenge against victim (who has three additional Traits)
Stop drinking after Stage 2	Mental Static Challenge against difficulty of three Traits

For players choosing to risk Amaranth, additional rules follow. First, the target must be somehow incapacitated through combat or Disciplines. He must then be drained of Blood Traits at a rate of one Trait per action. Once the target of Diablerie is drained of Blood Traits, a lone vampire must drain her of Health Levels until the victim is in Torpor. Each Health Level drained in this way requires a separate Physical Test. The victim of diablerie may bid any remaining appropriate stamina-related Physical Traits to defend herself. However, if she wins a test, the Diabolist is not harmed, but merely delayed another round. Once the Kindred has begun to drain Health Levels, he is incapable of any other physical action. If another Kindred attacks him or tries to pull him away from his feeding, the Diabolist may not bid any Physical Traits to the challenge. His attention is fully consumed by the act of Amaranth. Thus, he will lose automatically unless some if his friends are standing nearby to aid him.

When the second part of Amaranth begins, both the Diabolist and the target collapse and are completely unaware of the world outside them. No Mental or Social Challenges may be directed against either of them.

The final part of Amaranth requires one last test for the Diabolist to free his target's essence from her body. This is a Physical Challenge. The target begins the challenge three Traits up on the Diabolist, so there will always be a test. The Diabolist may keep trying to finish the Amaranth until he can no longer match the three Physical Traits. If he can no longer challenge, he will lose a Health Level (from exhaustion) and drop away from the target.

No vampire may assist the Diabolist. However, one Kindred may drain away the Blood and Health Levels of someone to allow another to complete the final stage of Amaranth. The seduction of the last feeding, however, is very strong. To stop before fully extinguishing a vampire, a Kindred must spend a Willpower Trait and win a Mental Static Challenge against a difficulty of three Traits.

Golconda

One theme of **The Masquerade** is the Hero's Journey. Often a character will seek to explore the darkness in herself and the world around her in an attempt to overcome the curse she must endure. There is an elusive, mythical state many Kindred seek, one in which the horrors of the Beast are defeated and humanity is restored. The goal of this quest is known to many as Golconda.

There are several beliefs concerning what happens when a character approaches the end of this quest. Some believe that a Kindred who has attained Golconda may become mortal once again. Others say that such enlightened Kindred will attain a state in which she will no longer feel the urge to frenzy, the lust to feed or the desire to sin.

Golconda is a state of being wherein the character has managed to control her frenzies and can restrain the Beast. This blessed state is not easy to attain, but for many vampires, it is the only goal worth having. It must not be misunderstood, for it is not a reconnection to one's mortality. In fact, it's quite the opposite. Golconda is an acceptance and mastery of one's Bestial nature. It is the final acceptance of one's curse and the subsequent gaining of power over it.

Basic to Golconda is the act of remorse. This is not necessarily any sort of religious repentance, but rather a personal and immediate realization of the sins one has committed. The character must repeatedly perform acts of penance, such as donating to charities, aiding those in need, or, in some cases, even punishing herself. The worse the sin, the greater the act of atonement.

The Storyteller should allow characters to reach Golconda very rarely. This is usually only if the character undergoes a truly impressive process of trying to make things right and experiences profound remorse for what she is and what she has become. As the Storyteller, ask yourself whether a character truly feels remorse— whether she feels compassion or not. The player must also demonstrate truly exceptional roleplaying. How well has the player roleplayed through the whole process of grief and regret? Golconda should never be easily found. In most cases, it should occur only at the end of a chronicle. A new chronicle could begin later on with the same character, but with an entirely different concept and motif.

It should take many game sessions to complete the process. More than one character can attempt to reach Golconda, but it is normally something only a few can attain.

In some ways, Golconda can be seen as a movement among the Kindred, but if it is a movement, it does not have much organization. Some who have reached Golconda are very evangelistic and seek to encourage others to follow the same path. They wish to teach all Kindred of the peace that Golconda brings. Some of them even travel from city to city speaking about Golconda, encouraging those who are interested to learn more. They do not reveal the secrets of Golconda, however, for each supplicant must learn of it on his own. Hints are sometimes available, but understanding must come from the supplicant.

There is said to be an Antediluvian who has reached Golconda and supports those who spread word of it. This ancient's role in the Jyhad is supposedly to thwart those who would destroy all Kindred. Only the Inconnu would know anything of this creature. Of course, critics of the Golconda movement decry the whole thing as a minor intrigue in the greater Jyhad. Perhaps the truth will never be known.

Quest

There aren't absolute rules for determining when a character reaches Golconda, for this is something that must come about as a part of roleplaying. Golconda is a very elusive state of being— it is subtle and intangible. Thus, it is the Storyteller's responsibility to set the conditions under which the change can occur.

Golconda is a quest, not so much a "scavenger hunt" as a spiritual and mental journey into one's self. The quest for Golconda can take one to the astral plane or into the chaos of one's own mind. The roleplaying involved can become extremely powerful and should only be attempted after the character has been developed over a number of stories. The player must have a firm grasp of who and what the character is. Golconda is about the transformation of a personality; the character must have a complete and detailed personality for the process to be memorable.

The quest for Golconda often begins with the character's search for the nature of vampiric existence. In the first chapters of your story, you need to build a desire for Golconda and increase it's allure. Characters should slowly realize what it is all about.

The second stage of the story is the search for an elder who can tell the character more about Golconda. This being could only be one of the enigmatic members of the Inconnu, a group of ancient vampires (usually of the fourth or fifth generation). The mentor would have to be convinced to aid a character who wished to reach Golconda. The mentor may require that the supplicant completes different "tasks" to prove her dedication.

The character must prove that she does indeed feel remorse for past actions. Tasks demanded of her are likely to require her to make up for past actions, to right past wrongs, or even to go back to families of past victims and aid them. The roleplaying involved dredges up everything that has happened throughout the chronicle, making the player relive it. Hopefully, this catharsis will bring the player into even greater contact with her character.

When the mentor is finally convinced that the character has proven himself, he initiates the final stage of the quest— the ritual. This expansive ceremony can last several weeks or several months and involves many quests into the dreams of the supplicant. The dreams are said to be provoked by draughts of blood from one's closest companions, who travel with the supplicant through the world of dreams.

The mentor must oversee the ritual, and it often takes place at his or her haven. No one truly knows what occurs in this ritual, for only those who have successfully attained Golconda have lived through it... and they aren't talking.

Benefits

A vampire who reaches Golconda is at peace with himself. He no longer exists in a life filled with horror and self-pity. He has finally mastered the Beast Within by accepting that the Beast is a part of him.

There is only one major benefit to attaining Golconda in **Masquerade**. A vampire who reaches Golconda will no longer frenzy. He is no longer at the mercy of the Beast.

A lesser benefit of this is the fact that the character does not need to drink blood as often. The character only loses one Blood Trait per week, rather than one Blood Trait per day. Even if the vampire has reached the age where the need for even more potent blood arises, the desire is more subdued.

Blood Bond

It is possible to create a Blood Bond with another vampire, thereby making him your servant, and in some ways, your lover. Instilling the Blood Bond is referred to as having "Regnancy" over another. The one who holds it over the Bound vampire is known as the Regnant. The one who is held in Regnancy is commonly known as the Thrall. It's usually the elders who are Regnants and neonates who are Thralls, but not always. An essential strategy of the Jyhad is to hold many in Blood Bond, for it gives you retainers whom you can trust. Many Kindred are suspicious of each other, for they can never be sure which Kindred are really the Thralls of ancients.

Creation of the Bond

The Blood Bond is created by the exchange of blood between two vampires. The Thrall must drink the Regnant's blood three different times on three different occasions (on different nights). It can be any amount of blood, but this can be a sip, or even a taste if the Regnant is of ancient blood. Unlike the limitations of the many Disciplines, it is possible for weaker blood to hold Regnancy over more potent blood. Thus, a 10th-generation vampire can hold Regnancy over a ninth-generation vampire.

As more blood is consumed, the Bond is reinforced. Most Regnants have their Thralls drink of their blood several times a year just to make sure the Bond remains potent. Many Regnants are fearful that if the Bond is broken, the Thrall will seek vengeance. This is perhaps why so many Thralls are treated fairly well by their Regnant— after all, any Bond can fail. Hate can weaken the power of the Bond.

Once a vampire has been Blood Bound, he cannot be Bound again by another. He is thus "safe" from other Blood Bonds if he is already Bound. However, he can be Bound to a number of different vampires if he drinks of their blood at the same time, such as if it is mixed in a chalice before it is consumed. In fact, one of the most severe punishments of the Camarilla is to be forced to drink the blood of all the Kindred attending a Conclave. Usually the feelings produced by such widespread Bonding are more diffuse than normal, but they are no less powerful. The attachment is for the group and not any one individual. For instance, this diffusion of attachment is desired by the Tremere of their neonates, and this is why the clan often Bonds them to the seven elders.

All characters are already on their way to being Blood Bound, for their sires have already given them at least one taste of blood. Thus, if a character partakes of her sire's blood two more times, she is held in Regnancy. In some cases, the character may already be held in Regnancy by the sire.

Power of the Bond

Blood Bond is primarily an emotional power. Thralls view the vampires to whom they are Bound as central figures in their unlives. They are invariably obsessed with them. Though a Thrall may despise his Regnant, he will do nearly anything to aid him. The Thrall will do nothing to harm his Regnant and will even attempt to protect him against enemies. Although the Thrall usually understands on an intellectual level what is happening to him, he is unable to do anything about it.

Experiencing the Blood Bond is like falling in love. Once it happens, a vampire is caught in its grip until he somehow breaks free. He may know he is in love, and hate what it makes him do, but that understanding does not stop him from being in love, nor does it prevent him from doing the stupid things that people in love sometimes do. When roleplaying Blood Bond, use the "love" metaphor to understand just how deeply and completely your character is obsessed with his Regnant. A compassionate Regnant may, to some measure, feel this "love" in return.

Blood Bonds sometimes (but not always) give the Regnant insight into the moods and feelings of the Thrall. A Regnant may even know his Thrall's location from moment to moment if the bond has been maintained long enough. Sometimes the Regnant can intuitively find the Thrall simply by following his hunches.

Just because the Thrall is under the Regnant's influence does not mean the Thrall is helpless. Willpower Traits may be expended to resist the power of the Blood Bond. Depending on the circumstances, a single Willpower Trait eliminates the effects of the Bond for a single scene or conversation. However, if the Thrall wants to actively attack his Regnant, one Willpower Trait must be spent per challenge.

If a character's Regnant asks him to do a "favor," he does so if it is at all possible. However, if it requires him to risk his life, he does not need to do it. Requests in line with the Thrall's Nature and Demeanor are almost always fulfilled, while ones outside Nature and Demeanor are at least considered. If there is an emergency and the Regnant is attacked, the Thrall's first instinct is to go to aid her. Self-sacrifice is not unknown, especially if the Bond has been reinforced over the years. If the Thrall is treated well, the Bond is reinforced and grows stronger. If the Thrall is humiliated and degraded, the hate that develops diminishes the Bond's influence.

It is possible to break a Blood Bond, but it can be difficult. It requires not only a massive expenditure of Willpower over a long period time, but also necessitates that the character completely avoid his Regnant. If a Thrall does not see his Regnant for some time, the Bond may eventually die (after many decades or centuries). Some types of Natures, such as Child and Fanatic, may never escape the Blood Bond, while others, such as Conniver and Loner, may do so more easily. The breaking of a character's Blood Bond cannot be achieved through experience points or successful challenges. It must be roleplayed.

It is whispered that the vampires of the Sabbat know of ways to break the Bond, but it is said one must pledge fealty to them before they will teach it. Those who fiercely resent their bondage and retain some freedom to act independently may flee to the Sabbat.

Status

Status is the central focus of many Kindred's existence. It represents the amount of power and social prestige a character has within vampire society. Those of lower status are expected to give respect to those of higher status. As one's status increases, one is granted more rights and powers within the hierarchy of the Camarilla. Within a city, the prince typically (though not always) has the most status. Neonates generally have little status, while anarchs and most Caitiff have no status. In-between are the power-hungry ancillæ and elders who continually jockey for position in hopes of increasing their status.

One may wonder why vampires harbor so much concern over social standing. The answer is complicated, but beyond all other reasons, strict codes of status are essential to the survival of vampiric society. Kindred society is very similar to the feudal system of the Middle Ages: a prince rules over a group of elders, who in turn preside over a larger group of vampires. When a childe is sired, she is taught to show respect for her elders. She is also expected to learn the Six Traditions. (These are, grossly simplified: preserving the masquerade, respecting domain, obtaining permission before siring childer, being responsible for one's childer, receiving acceptance from a prince and not destroying other Kindred.) Without this respect, vampiric society would soon degenerate into a chaotic skirmish of position for domain, and the Masquerade would be broken. Thus, it is the sire's responsibility to teach her childe respect before presenting her to the prince.

There are several positions or stations Kindred may hold that give the holder great sway over the status of other Kindred. These posts are greatly sought and jealously guarded by those who hold them. Many of these positions are only attainable by powerful elders, but a few may be held by ancillæ or possibly even a precocious neonate.

Gaining and Losing Status

Once "accepted" by the prince, a neonate acquires a single Status Trait. This initial Trait is usually "Acknowledged". During the course of a chronicle, the character may gain or lose Status. In small games, the Storyteller is generally

the one responsible for awarding or taking away Status. However, larger games will usually allow the Status system of Camarilla society to blossom fully. As such, Status gains and losses are governed by other Kindred in the game and only monitored (and occasionally arbitrated) by the Storyteller.

Status may be gained by helping to preserve the Masquerade, doing favors for the prince or an elder or saving an elder's unlife. It may also be gained by overthrowing the holder of a station and assuming her mantle, granting it in return for a boon, or defeating a Sabbat menace in the city. The possibilities are endless; the point is to get your fellow Kindred to view you as more than just another Lick. Note that you may never gain more that one Trait of Status per story. There are only two exceptions to this rule: if the prince awards or sanctions an additional Trait, or if the Status Trait(s) are conferred when a Kindred assumes a station within Kindred society.

Status can be lost for a multitude of reasons, such as making an enemy of one who is your elder, ignoring a boon owed to another Kindred, or refusing to recognize another Kindred's Status. It can also be lost as a result of breaking the Masquerade, committing diablerie or breaking any of the Six Traditions. Obviously, if you plan to commit such acts, it would be best to ensure that no one is around to report your actions.

Using Status

A player usually starts out with one Status Trait. This represents the fact that he has been presented to the prince and accepted by the Kindred of the city.

There are essentially two types of Status: permanent and temporary. Permanent Status is recorded on your character sheet. It is your actual standing in Kindred society. No matter how much Temporary Status is lost, it has no effect on Permanent Status. Both Temporary and Permanent Status may be lost over the course of a story, although Temporary Status is usually lost more often. A Permanent Status loss or gain is permanently added or removed from your character sheet. Temporary Status losses or gains are added or removed for the duration of the story. Temporary Status Traits may be represented by Status Cards to easily keep track of them.

Status Traits may be used in any applicable Social Challenge and may be added to your Social Traits in a Social Challenge (if Traits must be compared). A character may choose to ignore the Status Traits of another character. By doing so, this character risks losing one or more of her own Status Traits permanently if word of the offense spreads to the Harpies. In a situation in which less influential people are offended, Status loss may only be temporary, or may not occur at all.

It would seem that anarchs and Caitiff have an advantage in this case, seeing as they have no Status to lose. (Some anarch groups, however, have their own form of Status.) However, having no Status usually hurts more than it helps. Anarchs are almost never granted favors by elders (they are untrustworthy and have no Status to back their deals). Anarchs are rarely given the benefit of the doubt, and are much more likely to be victims of an elder's wrath (it is much easier to pick on characters who have no political backing). Also, by not having Status, anarchs and Caitiff are considered outside of the Camarilla's protection and are thus extremely vulnerable in times of crisis.

Although paying "lip service" to your elders has its price, the benefits are almost always worthwhile— receiving protection, gaining the benefit of the doubt and getting favors granted. Therefore, as a general rule, it is considered prudent to possess and preserve at least one Status Trait.

The following are some examples of the uses of Status:

• Temporary Status may be used to add to your Social Traits during an applicable Social Challenge.

• Status is a measure of a character's credibility. In any situation where there is an open debate between Kindred (one Kindred's word against the other), Status is used as the determining factor. The same is true in the case of accusing another of a crime in which there is no concrete evidence. In all such cases, the character with the most Status is the one whose word is accepted.

• Temporary Status may be given to another to show your favor, though the individual to which you give the Status must return it immediately upon the asking. However, this Trait may be expended as a Temporary Trait by the bearer and is then gone for the duration of the story. This is the only way a character's Temporary Status can raise above her Permanent Status rating. Loaned Status can be used exactly as your own. Only one Trait of Status may be given to any one person in this fashion.

• You must posses at least one Trait of Status (your own or one borrowed from someone else) in order to petition the prince for any reason, such as when gaining feeding grounds or accusing someone of a crime.

• Anyone of higher Status may remove Permanent Status from those lower than themselves at a cost of one Permanent Status Trait per Trait removed. Temporary Status may be removed in the same fashion.

• You may grant Permanent Status to another of your own clan if they have less than half of your permanent Status. The cost for such a boon is one Temporary Status Trait, and the boon must be made publicly, such as during a meeting of the primogen or another such gathering.

• A clan may remove one Status Trait from its elder by expending a group total of Permanent Status Traits equal to the elder's Permanent Status. The Primogen may also lower the prince's Permanent Status in the same fashion.

• Remember, you may only gain one Status Trait per story, but may lose more than one Trait. Again, there are two exceptions to this: Status granted or sanctioned by the prince, and Status received for assuming a station.

Stations

There are seven stations which may be held by a Kindred. Each grants Status within a city. Of course, there may be more than this, but these are some of the most common, found in cities throughout the world. Certain responsibilities and powers are inherent to each of these stations. Kindred who hold these positions tend to guard them jealously for the powers they convey. All powers conferred by a station are lost if a character is removed from a station or relinquishes it.

The following is list of these seven stations and an outline of their powers and responsibilities:

The Prince — This is generally, although not always, the most powerful elder of a city. He is above all other Kindred in the city.

• The prince of a city automatically gains three additional Status Traits: Exalted, Well-Known and Famous. These Traits may never be lost permanently while the character remains prince.

• The prince may remove one Permanent Status Trait from someone at a cost of one Temporary Status Trait per Trait removed.

• The prince may grant Permanent Status Traits to any Kindred at a cost of one Temporary Trait for each trait awarded. The prince may also break the rule of only gaining one Status trait per story, allowing a character to gain more than one Trait. If a Prince wishes to confer more than three Permanent Status Traits upon another Kindred (in a single session), the fourth and subsequent Status Traits will cost the Prince Permanent Status instead of Temporary Traits. Note that it does not cost the prince Temporary Status to award a Kindred the first Status Trait when she is first Presented. The Trait: Acknowledged is automatically conferred as long as the prince chooses to recognize the neonate.

Seneschal — The Seneschal stands in for the prince whenever he is busy elsewhere, as well as serving as an advisor to the prince. This position has become increasingly rare. Few princes are willing to place that much trust in any one individual.

• The Seneschal gains the following two additional Status Traits: Cherished and Esteemed. These Traits cannot be permanently lost while the character remains Seneschal.

• The Seneschal may act in the prince's stead when the prince is out of the city. He is therefore entitled to all of the powers of the prince, though they may be reversed or revoked at any time by the Prince.

Primogen — Primogen members generally act as advisors to the prince, as well as representing their clan's interests. There is generally one primogen representative for each clan represented in the city. Some cities are even run by the primogen rather than a single prince.

• Primogen members each receive the additional Social Trait: Revered when they join the primogen. This Trait cannot be permanently lost for as long as then character remains on the primogen.

A primogen member may grant or remove Permanent Status Traits to or from any member of their clan at a cost of one Temporary Status for each Trait granted or removed.

Harpies— The Harpies are the rumormongers of the Kindred. The leader of the Harpies is selected by a majority vote of the primogen. This group serves primarily as the arbitrators of disputes involving boons and scandals. The office may be revoked by a majority vote of the Primogen at any time.

• The leader of the Harpies receives the additional Social Trait: Influential upon attaining the position. This Trait cannot be permanently lost as long as the character remains the leader.

• The Harpy automatically gets one Temporary Status Trait from each member of the primogen. These Traits may be used however the Harpy desires, even used against the owner. These Status Traits are given over to show the primogen's support of the Harpy.

• The Harpy may remove one Permanent Status Trait from a Kindred who has backed out of a boon or is part of a major scandal. There is no cost for this, although there must be a grain of truth to the scandal.

Evidence of some sort must be presented at a gathering of Kindred, at which time the Status Trait is removed.

• The Harpy may restore Status he has removed at a cost of one Temporary Trait per Trait restored.

• The leader of the Harpies may sponsor lesser Harpies by giving another Kindred a Status trait of his own. Lesser Harpies may remove Temporary Status just as the head Harpy removes Permanent Status, although their leader may choose to make such loss permanent.

Whips — Whips are the servants of the primogen. Each primogen member has the option of choosing at least one Whip. They act as intermediaries between the primogen member and the rest of the clan. They are also responsible for organizing a clan's Status.

• Whips have the same powers as the Primogen, although they do not gain an additional Status Trait.

Sheriff — The Sheriff is the enforcer of the prince and the primogen. He ensures that the Traditions are followed as well as enforcing any edicts of the prince.

• The Sheriff gains the additional Social Trait: Feared when he attains the position. This Trait cannot be permanently lost while he remains Sheriff.

• The Sheriff may demand that any Kindred within the city accompany him for questioning or judgment. Failure to do so causes the offender to lose one Permanent Status Trait.

• The Sheriff is immune to the powers of the Keeper of Elysium.

Keeper of Elysium — The Keeper of Elysium is responsible for ensuring that peace is maintained within the Elysium. He is also responsible for punishing those who have broken the Masquerade. The Keeper often works closely with the Sheriff in the performance of his duties, although at times, the two can be rivals.

• The Keeper of Elysium gains the additional Status Trait: Honorable upon attaining the office. This Trait may not be permanently lost as long as the character remains the Keeper.

• The Keeper may immediately remove one Permanent Status Trait from any Kindred he catches breaking the Masquerade. If he does not witness it himself, sufficient evidence must be brought forth. This removal is at no cost to the Keeper.

Prestation

Prestation is the art of cutting a deal. It is an invaluable resource for those who know how to use it. Consequently, those ignorant of its applications should beware. Shady deals and clandestine agreements between Kindred are at the core of vampiric politics. A vampire inevitably finds herself in a compromising situation and looks to her peers or elders for help. The object of Prestation is to arrange to have as many Kindred as possible indebted to you while simultaneously ensuring that they get no opportunity to repay you (otherwise, you would have no leverage). After all, when another Kindred owes you, you have power over her.

When striking a deal with another Kindred, it should be made clear who's doing the favor and who's receiving it. Except in cases of mutual favors, there should always be a bestower and a receiver. The receiver is considered to owe a boon to her bestower. This boon must be categorized as a trivial, minor, major, blood or life boon. The boon is then assigned an appropriate amount of Status Traits that the receiver must give to the bestower. It is possible that other arrangements may be made as well, such as giving Influence rather than Status. The agreement must be amenable to all Kindred involved in the deal. The bestower may continue to use the Boon Traits just as he would any other loaned Status Traits. However, the loss of Boon Traits is only temporary. The bestower's Boon Traits are restored at the beginning of the next story. At that time, the Boon Traits may be used again as usual. The primary difference between Boon Traits and usual loaned Traits is that the original owner of the Traits may not request their return, as is usual with such Traits. They may only be returned once the boon has been settled.

The only way for a receiver to rid herself permanently of a boon is to repay or ignore the favor. However, by ignoring a favor, the receiver not only certainly costs the Kindred Status, but also risks the ire of the bestower. If the bestower is a minor Kindred, a Status Trait may only be temporarily lost by the receiver who ignores a boon (the Status Trait returns with the next story). However, if the bestower has considerable social influence, word may spread of the receiver's offense, causing the permanent loss of a Status Trait, especially if word gets to the Harpies. Furthermore, when a major, blood or life boon is disregarded by the receiver (regardless of the bestower's standing), the receiver will lose Status. Breaking boons is considered a major social *faux pas* among vampires. The receiver who does so often finds herself on the wrong end of a stake.

When a deal is cut (a favor is arranged), both parties should agree on the nature of the favor, the number of Traits assigned to it, and any other stipulations or additions. There is usually one stipulation often required by a Kindred who bestows a boon: "You may not take any physical action against me for the duration of this boon." In terms of the story, the receiver may seek to eliminate the bestower rather than repay the favor, but the bestower can use the legal terms of their agreement as protection from harm.

It is usually a good idea to clarify agreements in writing and to have both parties sign the document to assure its validity. As a convenient means to keep track of prestation, we have printed cards upon which you can record your boons.

Paying back a favor— getting yourself out of debt— is usually an event arranged through roleplaying. You may make your services available to a person to whom you're indebted, may conveniently "be around" when your bestower is in trouble, or can set your bestower up, tricking him into a situation where your help is required. Essentially, a boon can be eliminated by returning an equivalent favor. However, if a bestower is ever in sufficient trouble, you might pay off your debt by returning only a small favor. Everything depends on your skill at bartering. To set some standard, a favor is as valuable as the Traits associated with it. Thus, a minor boon (two Traits) and a major boon (three Traits) are fair compensation for a life boon (five Traits).

Trivial boons are one-time favors, such as providing protection for someone for the evening, using one of your Disciplines to aid another, or supporting another's political move.

Minor boons can last more than one evening and usually entail the bestower going out of her way to do something for the receiver, such as allowing safe passage through a hostile city, revealing crucial information to the receiver, or disposing of some threat to the receiver.

Major boons usually entail a great expenditure of time or resources on the bestower's part. The effects of the favor usually last for many game sessions. An example of such a boon would be teaching the receiver a new Discipline or ritual or purchasing a nightclub to serve as the receiver's haven.

Blood boons occur when the bestower places herself in a potentially life-threatening situation in order to help the receiver (thus the name "blood boon"). The bestower is willing to shed her blood for the receiver.

Life boons involve the bestower actively risking her immortal life for the receiver so that the receiver may live.

Experience

Humans learn from experience. As sentient beings, we collate the information that is presented to us in our daily lives and hopefully become better people for our experience. Some of us do, while some of us ignore our lessons and must repeat the same mistakes again. During our life, we learn from the mistakes of yesterday and prepare for the challenges of tomorrow.

Experience in **The Masquerade** is represented by giving each character one to three experience points at the end of each story. The number of points awarded is based on how well the character performed during the course of the story and how active the player was in the game. The Narrator will decide how many points each player receives upon completion of the game. Most players will receive one point— this is standard. Exceptional roleplayers, those who played an exceptionally memorable part, will receive two. Three points will be awarded to those characters who portrayed acts of incredible insight and courage, making the game more memorable for the Narrator and other players. On a normal night, each player will receive one experience point.

Some basic guidelines for awarding experience follow. If you are a Narrator, you might want to adjust awards to suit your needs, but be careful. Awarding too many experience points can make the characters in the game too powerful and make your task as Narrator very difficult in future chronicles. It can also "spoil" the players and make them overconfident, which can make them difficult to deal with.

Awarding Experience

Awarding experience points requires a delicate balance between satisfying the players and maintaining the balance of the game. If you follow the guidelines below, you probably won't get into too much trouble, but feel free to experiment.

• **Automatic** — Each character receives one experience point per game. This represents the acquisition of common everyday knowledge.

• **Roleplaying** — Narrators should encourage roleplaying. The best way to do this is by rewarding it. This point should be automatically awarded to players who have all of their Traits left at the end of the night. These players obviously roleplayed well, and didn't have to spend any Traits in challenges. The best roleplayer in the cast usually receives this bonus.

• **Leadership** — You should award one point to players who played a major part in the story. They got involved, and their efforts propelled the plot. The player who was the most involved in advancing the plot usually receives this award. It should be noted that if more than one of the players were integral in the progression of the story, then each of the players who showed such leadership could be awarded this point.

Using Experience

After experience points have been awarded, they may be spent to purchase new Abilities, Traits and Disciplines, improving upon the character and giving the player a sense of satisfaction as he watches his character grow and improve. The following chart list the cost of improving Traits, Abilities and Disciplines

•**New Attribute Trait**— One experience point per Trait.

•**New Ability**— One experience point per Ability Trait.

•**New Discipline**— Three experience points for Basic Disciplines, six for Intermediate Disciplines, and nine for Advanced Disciplines. It costs an additional point to learn a Discipline outside of your clan.

•**New Willpower**— Three experience per Trait.

•**Buy off Negative Trait**— Two experience points per Trait.

Only one Ability, Trait or Discipline should be gained per session.

Chapter Six: Story Staging

I'll show you my home town, and it's down.
Yeah, so close you can tell by the smell,
so close you can hear them yell,
they throw the best damn parties at the rim of hell.
— D.A.D., "Rim of Hell"

Swirling lights. Vibrant sounds. Cold shadows in the corners. A tattered diary. A vial of vitæ. Strange markings on the wall. The experience of it all.

Storytelling is more than simply voice and action. The effects that create your playing environment also make your story come to life. When you're running a story, you don't want your players to merely *imagine* they're playing in a Gothic-Punk setting. You want them to *feel* they're there.

Setting the stage is, thankfully, relatively simple. It requires some effort and imagination, but with a little practice, you'll be whipping up Methuselah dens in no time. To help you get started, we've provided some hints and ideas. Ultimately, though, creating an environment is limited only by your imagination. Take the advice we provide and run with it.

Setting and Environment

More than anything else, the setting of a story has impact on a story's feel. Setting should therefore be taken into careful consideration when deciding on your story's mood (which is discussed later). The location you choose must fit the needs of your game as well as the atmosphere you have in mind.

Finding Locations

"Ray, you're scaring the straights."

—Bill Murray, "Ghostbusters II"

The first practical step in planning a game is finding a good place to play. Where you play the game is influenced by the specific needs of your story. Factors like the number of players involved, theme, mood and nature of the plot all have an influence on the type of location you choose.

The scale of the game is your first consideration. Make certain you have enough room for all the players to move about. Multiple rooms or areas are helpful. The best layout usually involves a central meeting room that all the players can congregate in and multiple smaller sites for secret meetings.

Although we assume you will be using your home as the location of your games, this may not be the case. If you are highly selective and cautious and your players are very experienced, there are a number of other sites you can use. Possibilities include college campuses, dorm lounges, museums, night clubs, coffee houses, conventions, parks, shopping malls, office buildings or warehouses.

Obviously, extreme care must be taken when using these sites. You must ensure that all of the players are courteous and unobtrusive when playing in a public place. No "mundanes" should ever realize a game is being played, and players need to understand that the session is over if anyone finds out about the game and is disturbed by what you're doing.

Some sites are more conducive to a certain types of stories. You may find a particular location is your favorite, but even then, you should keep your mind open to change. A change of locale, even if for only one scene, can help revive a dying Chronicle.

Most locations (or "sets") can be decorated to convey a specific mood. You must seek out sites that cater to the style of your game and nature of its plot. For best results, the setting should have a basis in reality. In other words, if it's a high energy social atmosphere you seek, stage your story in a nightclub. If you're looking for a calm and intellectual setting, perhaps a museum or art gallery is appropriate. When choosing a location, look for an area that establishes the mood and atmosphere you're after:

• **Party** — Raves, nightclubs, fraternity parties or anyplace where loud noises blend into the background.

• **Anarchy** — Raves, warehouses, parking lots; places that draw as little attention as possible.

• **Political Intrigue** — Hotels, coffee houses, conference halls, museums, shopping malls or your home. This style of game can be played just about anywhere, as it's typically low-key.

Don't even try to play **The Masquerade** outside your home if you don't think you can stay on top of everything. If things get out of hand, you have only yourself to blame. The responsibility for safety is always yours. If you have even one immature or uninhibited player, you should not try using new sites at all.

Set Dressing

With many of the above setting suggestions, you are unable to do much, if any, decorating. However, many of the locales (such as nightclubs, museums and amusement parks) that you cannot decorate already have the proper feel for your story. Other places, specifically your own home, probably need special modifications to create the proper mood and feel.

Decorating your home can be a simple process. Dark drapes (or sheets over the windows), indirect lighting and certain standing props can help turn your home into a nightclub or the audience chamber of a prince. When decorating your home or apartment, consider the type of story you're telling. Mood and feel are essential. They must be conveyed to the best of your ability. A dark tablecloth and candelabra can change a dining room into the prince's office. Avoid going with all black— it absorbs light. Dark red and violet mixed with black give the illusion of a dark setting without the problems that total darkness can create.

Talk with your friends. They may have access to a variety of unusual items to help decorate your home. Try to keep a central area open to allow players some freedom of movement. Clutter should be avoided (unless it's a specific component of the story). When decorating small meeting areas, try to contrast them to the main area. If the main area (say, your basement) is a nightclub and a secondary area (your dining room) is the prince's chambers, you probably want a contrast between the way the two are decorated. Even if players are only going up a flight of stairs, they should feel as though they're stepping into a different world (and many times, they will be).

Changing Scenes

Sometimes it's necessary to use one area for different settings within the same story. For example, let's say that for the first portion of the story, you're using your living room as the den of an anarch gang. Later in the story, the same room is used as a Tremere altar. You need to prepare for and execute a scene change without interrupting the story.

First of all, you need to arrange the decorations for the second scene ahead of time. You may even want to rearrange existing furniture for the second scene. All props and decorations for the second scene should be ready to go, discreetly tucked away before the game begins. These secondary "set dressings" can be place in an unused room off to the side, or put in a corner with a dark cloth draped over them. Any place that is easily accessible and inconspicuous is best.

Next, you should plan when a scene change occurs and why. In the above situation, the cue for a scene change occurs when the anarch characters (for whatever reason) decide to leave their hangout and travel to the Tremere altar (perhaps that's where a friend is being held prisoner). "Travel time" is the best way to justify a pause in the game while you make the scene change. A second location, which could represent a car or some other type of vehicle, should be ready ahead of time to represent the journey.

The actual set change should be performed quickly and efficiently. Lengthy set changes leave players bored. When your scene is changed, give it a last once-over, making sure everything is in place. A scene change should be just that. When the players enter the room again, they should have the distinct feeling that they're entering a new place. Your new decorations don't even need to be overly complicated. A quick shift of the couch or table, switching or removing a throw rug, draping a love seat, and moving or removing chairs all help to change the feel of a room without necessitating major alterations. Changing the lighting and music can also make a big difference in a set's feel.

Ambiance and Mood

"It's showtime!"

—Beetlejuice

Establishing the right feel for a scene is governed by setting and environment. However, ambiance and mood are established and maintained by effects that are imposed upon the environment. Effects like music and lighting are often the finishing touches for completing a scene.

Music

Music can be an integral part of establishing the mood of a story. It lends a hand in creating drama and, when appropriate, tension. When planning your story be certain to select music that complements your intended mood. Also make sure you have a variety of music on hand in case the mood changes. Here are some examples of mood and appropriate music. You can doubtlessly think of many others:

- **Dance Club** — high energy music / techno
- **Punk** — rock / progressive music / classic punk
- **Exclusive, Sophisticated** — classical music / jazz
- **Mysterious** — New Age music / tribal music

How you play your music is almost as important as what you choose to play. Your music should never be obtrusive or overpowering. You want to avoid forcing your players to overcome the music in order to interact with each other. Subtlety is lost that way. If possible, hide your speakers (unless they're a part of the scene). The best quality sound comes from small speakers positioned above the ground. You may also want to keep your stereo control off limits to players. Ultimately, your music should be heard, not "seen."

Audio Effects

Above and beyond music, certain sounds and effects can enhance an evening. Horror and sound effect CDs, found in any music store, are a good place to start. A good FX CD can provide a variety of sound effects to simulate many different events, like tires screeching, gunshots or barking dogs. Proper timing of these sounds is critical. If you're able to pre-mix a tape of effects, you can play them at appropriate moments in the story. Preparation is the key. Have your effects cued up ahead of time so that, with the mere touch of a button, the scream of a Lupine's victim can be heard by all. Preparation makes for more drama than having to delay the game while you set up the right sound.

Lighting FX

What good tale of vampires would be complete without appropriately eerie lighting? Unlike music, lighting doesn't merely lend a hand toward setting the mood, it establishes it. Players walking into a room immediately notice dim lights and the flickering shadows they cast. Furthermore, there are many tricks you can pull with "common household items" to create the illusion of darkness without making a room pitch black.

When using light to create effect, start by setting up the room. Get your scene arranged the way you want it. Now you need to find the right level of light. Avoid high wattages and white light. Multicolored light bulbs have the broadest effect. By arranging multicolored light bulbs in different parts of the room, you can create shadowy areas and still have well-lit "white light" areas where the colors intersect. If you have track lighting, recessed multi-colored bulbs work very well. If you can't get multicolored bulbs, cloth draped over lights work just as well (but avoid putting cloth in direct contact with hot bulbs). The key is contrast from low wattage bulbs. Keeping enough low lights to contrast with one another results in plenty of light to see by and plenty of shadows to hide in. Play around with different combinations to determine what works best for your mood and scene.

Regular lamps aren't the only things you can use to illuminate a room. If you're doing a club scene, a strobe light works well. Believe it or not, blinking Christmas tree lights also help to create a nightclub atmosphere. Candles, electric or real, also help with certain scenes. However, we recommend that you avoid using real candles if you plan to have a lot of players. If you do use real candles, keep a fire extinguisher handy in case of accidents. If you have a fireplace, it can be helpful in creating certain moods. If you don't want to build an actual fire, a small recessed lamp behind some wood can provide a soft, permeating glow.

If you keep your wattage low, avoid direct white light, and experiment with your color schemes, you should be able to find the right combination to create the proper atmosphere for your story.

Props

"Where does he get those wonderful toys?"
—The Joker, *Batman*

After you've got a story, players, a place to play and even selected a cool soundtrack to accompany the game, something else is still needed to bring the story to life. This is the point at which props come in. Props for a story don't need to be grandiose or expensive. Most props can be found in your own home or your grandparents' attic.

In most forms of theatre, props play an extensive role. In fact, in modern movies, props can at times overwhelm the viewer, sometimes detracting from the film. In this game, props should be kept relatively simple and should not attract more attention than the story itself. Only a few touches are needed to help a player's imagination fill in the blanks. Since this is a storytelling game, imagination is of the utmost importance. This is not to say that you should be sparing with props. If you have the available materials, go wild. Just make sure that the props are not the focus of the story. The spotlight should always remain on the characters, not on what surrounds them.

General Props

General props are items that can help you further a story by giving players something that they can physically examine. The Storyteller should be wary of how often physical props are used and what impact they have on the story. If they are allowed to dominate a story, players may begin to rely on them rather than interacting with one another. Be sure to inform players when props will be used in a story. Otherwise, they are likely to disregard an important clue, considering it just another feature of the place you're playing in.

Many items can be used as general props to help enhance your story. Books, jewelry, documents and pieces of artwork are a few examples. These props can be used to actually give information, or they can merely give insight into the character of the person possessing the prop. Sometimes an item has to be represented by an item card, as in the case of weapons. Also, a card may be discreetly attached to an item, giving more information to a player who inspects the item.

Different props can have different applications. A ring might merely be a character's memento, a reminder of days past, but those past events might be important to the story and the ring can serve as a clue to that importance. Alternatively, the ring could belong to a murder victim, perhaps dropped or misplaced. Someone examining the ring with the Discipline of Spirit Touch could learn much from the prop. Books can be used to indicate the owner's interests, or can conceal hidden documents or letters. A vial of blood can even be concealed somewhere in the playing area, perhaps somewhere as obvious as the refrigerator. The container, containing some sort of red liquid (not real blood), can have a note attached to it revealing what the contents are and exactly how much is present. (This is particularly important when representing the number of Blood Traits in the vial).

Some props that add ambiance to a story are a little more obvious than the ones discussed above. A letter of invitation to a party or other event, giving players some hint of what is to come, advances the story and makes events seem real. Serving players red liquids can add a nice touch. Tomato juice works well.

Creative and effective usage of general props can make a story more interesting for everyone. The important thing is to stay focused and avoid overloading yourself with them. If you come up with an idea for a prop, but are unable to implement it, don't panic— your story can stand on its own. After all, people, not things, make a story.

Personal Props

Personal props, like costumes, are used by players to help distinguish them as their characters. These props can be particularly useful for Narrator characters, especially when Narrators must often change from character to character.

Many different items can be used to help portray a character. Cloaks, jackets, scarves, hats, canes and jewelry are only a few of the accessories that can give a character a distinctive look. You may want to provide certain items to players to aid them in this manner, especially if players are uncertain of the characters they are playing. For example, if you plan a story involving an anarch gang, you may supply players with matching bandanas to identify them as gang members.

Many personal props can be found right in your own home. Searching through the attics of relatives can reveal old clothing and jewelry. Costume jewelry works best; real jewels can be far too valuable to lend out for a game. Should all else fail, second-hand stores can be great places to pick up a few last-minute props at an affordable price. All manner of clothing, including hats, canes and costume jewelry, can be acquired at such emporiums.

In many stories, not much is needed by way of personal props. Sometimes, only a cane or piece of jewelry can make a character. The most important thing to remember is to have fun with props, avoiding dangerous ones.

Safety

Safety is an important consideration. **The Masquerade's** code of conduct should be reviewed at the start of every story, no matter how experienced players are. It should be enforced with draconian vigilance.

Some props can be potentially dangerous and cannot be allowed. For instance, all weapons must be represented by item cards. The use of real or artificial weapons in Mind's **Eye Theatre** is simply too dangerous.

Besides weapons, other props can be potential hazards. Lit candles should only be used with extreme care. Remember that there are a fair number of people moving about the area, so candles are best placed in inaccessible, or at least out-of-the-way, places, where it's unlikely that anyone will come in contact with them.

Finally, if the area chosen for your story is unfamiliar to you, it's best that you examine it thoroughly for any potential hazards. If you come across a potential hazard, declare that area off-limits for the game, rope it off or choose another game site.

Make-Up

"Just paint your face and shadows smile,
Slipping me away from you."
— The Cure, "Burn"

After you've assembled the props for a character, only a few final touches are needed to complete the masquerade. Make-up can help to complete the transformation from human to vampire. You needn't be a professional make-up artist to apply it. Make-up supplies are available year round at theatre supply and costume shops.

To give yourself a pale vampiric complexion, a very light base of clown white should be sufficient. Be sparing; only a slight amount is needed to significantly lighten your features. You should powder your face immediately after applying the make-up to keep it from smearing. If make-up is unavailable, an application of powder alone can suffice in a pinch.

For a Nosferatu character, liquid latex can be used to create hideous features. Though not as readily available as white grease paint, it is still available at most theatre supply shops. Liquid latex takes a little more skill to apply properly, but with a little care and patience, great results can be obtained. For instructions on application, books on make-up artistry can be found at your local book store or library. You may also discover other ideas for creating a vampiric look while perusing such books.

No vampire is complete without fangs. Fangs of all different varieties can be found at costume shops. The only problem with fangs is that they tend to impair speaking, which a fundamental part of the game. The types that work best, if you intend to wear them for the entire story, are fitted caps that slide directly over incisors. These are attached with a temporary adhesive.

Makeshift fangs can even be created with drinking straws. One end of the straw is clipped off to allow it to fit snugly over the tooth, while the other end is cut in a V shape that hangs down over the incisor.

Cheap Tricks

These are tricks you can use involving props to make the story a little more interesting for players and help progress the plot. Cheap tricks with props can draw players further into the story while making the experience more "real".

If the story is a murder mystery, spots of blood can be placed on the floor, perhaps showing how the body was moved after the murder. The spots can be made of pieces of cut red felt laid on the floor. If one of the players notices them, they can serve as a valuable clue, or you can simply use a lot of them for special effects.

A jacket can be provided to one of the players as a personal prop for his character. Unbeknownst to him, you have placed an item card in the inner pocket of the jacket. If he thinks to look there, the item is his to use. This item could be any number of things: a vial of blood, a weapon or perhaps an important clue. Whatever the item, it should be something that would reasonably be in that character's possession.

If a computer is available at the game site, computer disks can be used as props, with important information stored on them. If you have the talent, actually write a program with a puzzle in it that players must crack before getting any information. Of course, the same thing can be accomplished by resolving a Simple Test using a character's Computer Ability, but presenting players with a puzzle is much more fun. Audio tape can be used in a similar fashion, such as when a cryptic message is left on an answering machine. In addition, a book can have a post-it note on the inside cover ("See Narrator for information."). The lucky player may discover that the copy of Macbeth she was perusing is actually a book of ancient Tremere rituals, or maybe the private memoirs of a Methuselah.

Staying Focused

At times your story may drift away from its original plot, or players may become lost. They may become too wrapped up in their own subplots or may be unable to unravel a puzzle. When this happens, you need something to bring the story back on course.

Having a few extra props available can be helpful when the story goes off on a tangent. Many of the prop ideas already suggested can be used to reorient players. For example, an answering machine audio tape with an important message can renew characters' interest in their original goal. Documents containing important information are another option, allowing characters a new avenue in pursuit of their original goal.

Chapter Seven: Scripting

"Let me show you the world in my eyes
I'll take you to the highest mountain
To the depths of the deepest sea
We won't need a map, believe me."
— Depeche Mode, "World in My Eyes"

This chapter provides information intended to help guide you in preparing your own stories. A story is not something that can simply be thrown together. It is a series of events that are linked by several common factors, such as theme, mood and plot. For a story to succeed, it must be thoroughly planned, carefully laid out and skillfully executed.

Creating Stories

Story creation can be as simple or as detailed as you want. The more effort you put into preparing a story, the smoother it runs when its executed. There is no small amount of satisfaction to be gained from writing a successful and appreciated story.

Inspiration

"I used to travel in the shadows and I never found the nerve to try to walk up to you."
— The Smithereens, "A Girl Like You"

Finding the right combination of stimuli to ignite creative thought can be difficult. For some of us, creativity comes naturally. For others, it's more difficult to bring creative aspects of personality to the fore. However, this is exactly what you must do in order to create a good story. Creativity is not generally taught in school. In fact, it's often discouraged. Rediscovering your childhood enthusiasm is one way to find a wellspring of imagination.

Inspiration can come from any source. Magazines, movies, books, theatre, television, friends, family... you get the picture. The challenge is to take what you see and change it into something all your own. Inspiration can be, quite literally, any stimulus that ignites the process of creative thought. Hence, inspiration is very often as dependent on what's without as on what's within. What sends one person's mind racing may bore someone else. You must find the things that inspire you (if you don't already know) and associate with them in order to ignite your creative fires.

Theme

"I'll show you a place
High on a desert plane
Where the streets have no name."
— U2, "Where the Streets Have No Name"

The theme of a story often conveys an idea or emotion. Every story needs a theme— it's what holds all the parts together. By choosing a theme, you define the heart and soul of your story. However, a theme is more than the simple moral of an Aesop's fable. It's the tangible embodiment of the story's purpose and meaning. Theme helps to lay the groundwork for all the portions of the story. Without theme, a story's mood, plot and elements are mere window dressing.

A story's theme is never something you announce to players. It's something you leave buried in the story to be discovered later. The best themes are subtle rather than overt and poetic rather than analytical. A theme should never have the feel of a prepackaged lesson.

From an intellectual standpoint, the purpose of a story is the exploration of a theme. The things we learn from a story are usually aspects of its theme. Not all stories have relevant themes, but stories that are more than just "adventures" do. A theme is simply a tool to help you create a story with more depth, pathos and poignancy. If you don't place a great burden on the theme, it will usually work for you.

When you are trying to create a theme for a story, ask yourself what the story is really about. What lesson does it teach? What's the point? Theme is usually expressed as a question that is never actually answered (at least not directly), but asked over and over in many different ways. Players are expected to find their own answers. A theme can be practically anything from "What is evil?" to "Why do we want what we can't have?" The following are some common topics for themes:

• **Revenge** — Revenge usually seems to lead to tragedy. Why does revenge not always work? What compels us to even the score? What happens after we get revenge?

• **Romance** — Why do we love? Why should we love? Who should we love? Is love weakness, or is it strength? What does love provide? How are love and lust different? Do we need love?

• **Chaos** — Why do things always fall apart? Is there any such thing as true security? Can you trust in anything? What are the constants in life? Does tranquillity really exist? What is reality?

• **Betrayal** — Who can you trust? Why do you need to trust anyone? What happens if you trust no one and nothing? Can you trust too much? Why do we betray friends? Does greed lead to betrayal, or is it envy?

• **Rebellion** — Does the dynamic always win over the static? Is established order always doomed to fall? Does revolt ever lead to real change? Is society always in rebellion?

• **Morality** — Are ethics useful or necessary? Why be "good"? Why not be "bad"? What is conventional morality? How can it be improved? Is perfect morality possible? Are there any absolute and immutable rules?

A story begins to take form from themes like these. A story does not be limited to a single theme. It is far more challenging and enjoyable for players to have several different themes to contend with. You should choose and place your themes with care, because a story is only as good as the themes that fuel it.

Mood

"How much more black could it be? And the answer is none. None more black."

—Derrick Smalls, "This is Spinal Tap"

Mood is perhaps the most elusive part of a story's creation. The feelings engendered by mood help make The Masquerade so unique. Mood places players in the right frame of mind from the very beginning. It's what projects Gothic-Punk flavor. Mood should permeate every aspect of the story, giving each hallway and every shadowy corner the same distinctive feel and taste.

The moods of a story can vary widely. In fact, given the many subtleties of human emotion, a story's mood can have a nearly infinite number of permutations. Moods can range from angry to festive, from brooding to hopeful, or anywhere in between or beyond. In short, you can draw the mood of your story from anything in the wide range of human emotions.

The mood of a story is not something to be advertised. It should be felt. Players should sense the mood in a story's title. They should feel the mood in their backgrounds. They should experience the mood in the ambiance of the game site. They should recognize the mood in the unfolding plots. It should never be blatant or announced. You should never have to tell the players the mood you intend; it should be sensed and not considered. If players seem to be straying from your mood, let them, as long as they're having a good time. Always remember that the story exists for the players' enjoyment.

The following are some examples of different moods:

• **Anger** — Everything and everyone in the story is angry. Tensions run high and Kindred are ready to lash out. The anger can have a source, or you can make it more ephemeral (and thus more suspenseful).

• **Celebration** — Everyone is in a positive frame of mind; it's time to party. Excitement is in the air and players should feel ready to kick back and have fun. No one should feel like they have to watch what they do; there should be no penalties for taking chances.

• **Brooding** — The mood is dark and ominous. You want to make players feel reflective and a little pensive. You can bring past actions back to haunt characters. This is a very difficult mood to capture, but can lead to intense interactions between characters if used properly.

• **Hope** — Characters have the opportunity to turn things around. This opportunity should not be a guarantee, only a chance.

• **Apprehension** — Something bad is on the horizon and everyone is worried. It should not be an immediate threat, more an unknown factor. The situation should be mysterious enough to pique the characters' curiosity, making them uneasy and concerned.

Plot

"I'm only hangin' on, to watch you go down…
My love."

— U2, "You're So Cruel"

A story's plot is its progression of events. Plot not only involves the machinations of the powers that be, but the machinations of the characters as they pursue their own goals in the story. Plots are essential to the successful progression of the story. They serve as a beginning to, and a guide during, the story.

A story can have any number of plots (see "Story Style", below, for more details on this). These plots should all be wound together with skill and care before the actual game begins. The trick is to have all the pieces of a plot already written in the characters' briefings so they can read about their own respective parts of the overall plot at the game's beginning. Together, the characters' backgrounds compose the main plot, and by pursuing their own parts of the plot, characters progress the plot as a whole.

For example, Kassandra is a Gangrel playing in a story. The theme for one of Kassandra's subplots is revenge. Years ago, one of her progeny was brutally slain by an older vampire. Kassandra was not powerful enough to seek retribution at the time, but now, years later, she has the opportunity to do so. The player's background on Kassandra and her list of contacts should explain who this older vampire is and should explain the general circumstances (as Kassandra would know them) concerning her progeny's demise. This information contains all the necessary details the player needs to develop and explore this subplot. Kassandra knows who the older vampire is, what he did, why she is angry about the murder, and maybe something about the older Kindred's weaknesses or enemies. It's up to Kassandra to decide exactly how she goes about seeking revenge, but you have set the wheels in motion.

When Kassandra's plot coincides with goals that other characters are pursuing, an overall plot evolves. With a degree of skill, this can help build the main plot and theme of a story.

During a story, it's often helpful to keep a schedule of events. This is a pre-planned sequence of events (usually initiated by outside forces) that's going to occur regardless of the characters' actions. Typically, characters played by Narrators keep the schedule on track. It is also helpful to integrate occasional Narrator characters into the story to assist the progression of the plot (or plots). These tactics should be used sparingly; otherwise players may grow dependent upon interaction with Narrators instead of with each other. However, occasional Narrator intervention can add a new level of unpredictability and excitement to a story.

Elements of a Story

*"I got the ways and means
to New Orleans,
I'm going down by the river
where it's warm and green.
I'm gonna have a drink, and walk around.
I've got a lot to think about…"*
— Concrete Blond, "Bloodletting"

The elements of a story are best defined by its components or stages. It is often helpful to think of plot elements in terms of tense (past, present and future). In terms of story structure, these elements are the addressed in the opening, climax and resolution. At the beginning of the story, characters reflect on events of their past that have brought them to the story. The story's climax is where the story's plot (or plots) are exposed and dealt with by some or all of the characters. Finally, there's the resolution, where the story comes to a close and story hooks for future stories can be laid.

Opening

The opening can be any point from which you choose to begin your story. It can be a gradual, gentle start (the characters awake, each in their separate havens) or a dramatic one (the prince calls a Blood Hunt).

At the beginning of a story, each character should have a written synopsis of recent events that are common knowledge. Each player should also have a background of recent personal events. Players should begin with a list of contacts (other characters in the game and how they know them).

The synopses of common knowledge and recent personal events should be brief explanations of the situation at hand. They should be precise and intriguing. These synopses should be the first media through which players get a feel for the story's mood. The synopses should also hint at the story's main theme. You may even wish to foreshadow the plot, but that depends on your personal style.

Climax

When the main plot is on the verge of conclusion, the story is considered at its climax. This usually happens when characters have discovered all they need to know to solve whatever problem faces them and are on the verge of resolving the story. The tension is usually at its highest point at this time. If the opening was staged carefully, and the players are cooperative and imaginative, the climax can be reached with little additional effort on the part of Narrators. However, even the best of plans can be mislaid, or perhaps the Storyteller and Narrators prefer to take a more active role in the progression of your story's plot. Either way, there are times when a Narrator's intervention is warranted. The climax should be the high point of the story, something the players should always anticipate and work toward. However, this element should never be rushed. It's a matter of timing.

Resolution

The story's resolution is where all (or most) of the pieces come together. The resolution should be used as a means of winding the excitement down while cultivating an interest in future stories. Players should always end a story feeling as though they have accomplished something. They do not have to uncover the big picture; merely knowing they've found another piece of the puzzle is often enough. In **Mind's Eye Theatre**, players often enjoy gathering for a group wrap-up session after a game. Unlike roleplaying games, players of **The Masquerade** rarely see all of the action that takes place— they get wrapped up in their own ends, not the group's. During wrap-up sessions, many players look forward to learning more about "the big picture." At the wrap-up, players share their version of the story and, in so doing, give other players an opportunity to see more of the game they just took part in.

Story Considerations

There are several factors that must be taken into consideration before you can begin scripting a story. The scale, number of players and general character types are all important elements that must be kept in mind. If you have a great idea for a plot involving the primogen of a city, it won't work if the players are set on playing anarchs. Likewise, a plot involving a whole gang might not be easy if you only have a few players. These problems can easily be overcome by making slight alterations to your original story idea. For example, suppose your original story involved the murder of a member of the primogen, with the players as the elders of the city trying to determine who the murderer was. If your players are set on playing anarchs, the story can easily be changed to involve an anarch gang whose leader has just been murdered, with the players as gang members. You would still have the same basic concepts, but the setting would be changed.

Scale

The first consideration you have in writing a story is the number of players participating in it. Though the number of players does not usually limit you to the type of story you tell, it does dictate the approach you take. Although we have written these rules for groups of five to 15 players, you can easily run games with many more. In fact, one of our playtest sessions at a convention had more than 300 players.

Adding players is easy; you simply set them in opposition to each other. You make them antagonists to each other. With a few players, the story revolves around a single coterie of characters (the players). The Storyteller and the Narrators fill in as all the other characters involved.

Different-sized games each have their own needs and problems. Narrator characters tend to play a larger role in stories with a small number of players, filling in the gaps. Games with larger groups of players can be more complex in terms of scale. Having a lot of Cast Members enables you to tell a story involving more than one faction. Players can play both anarch and loyal Camarilla characters, or perhaps even members of the Sabbat. Fewer Narrator characters are needed in a large game, as trusted players can be assigned antagonist roles. However, such large-scale games carry a greater risk for open conflict, often degenerating the story into a slugfest. The larger the game is, the more is required to keep players in line.

Enforcement of the Masquerade can be a very useful Narrator tool if events get out of hand. Make one of the players the prince and let her keep everyone else in line. The ultimate burden, however, is on you. Remember, the number of players does not really limit the story you can tell, only the way you tell it.

Scope

The scope of your story is a very important consideration. Whether the story involves a massive plot to awaken the Antediluvians or a scheme to befriend a reclusive Nosferatu is a matter of scope. Scope boils down to what's won or lost. Scope can be limited by the number of players in the game. You shouldn't always have stories with huge scope; players grow bored with always "saving the world." Likewise, you should not keep the Cast from getting involved in potentially earth-shattering stories. Balance is the key.

Cast

Another factor to take into consideration is the type of characters Cast Members portray. The best way to determine this is to ask them. A story usually works best if players are enacting characters they are comfortable with, although it can occasionally be interesting to cast players in roles different from what they're used to playing. This variation in casting should only be done if you think it would be enjoyable for all the players.

An important consideration is whether you are giving players pre-made characters, with complete backgrounds, Attributes and Disciplines, or if players are allowed to make their own characters. Sometimes the guidelines lie somewhere in-between. Obviously, the easiest of these options is to use pre-made characters. This allows you to customize your story to the characters, tying them to one another to make for a more intriguing plot. The problem with this is that Cast Members are sometimes disappointed with the characters they get. This can detract from everyone's enjoyment.

There are several compromises that can be made if using pre-generated characters. You can ask Cast Members exactly what type of characters they want to play. The characters can then be made to suit the players and tailored to work into your story. If you must hand out "pre-gen" characters, you might allow some alteration of those characters. For example, you can let players choose their own Attribute Traits and Disciplines. Perhaps some minor alterations can even be made to the characters' backgrounds, assuming changes do not affect the overall course of the game.

If you are running a chronicle, and not just a single story, it's suggested that players be allowed to create their own characters. You can still lay some general guidelines, stipulating that characters must be anarchs or loyal members of the Camarilla, or you can request certain character concepts (see "Character Concepts", below). You may also choose to restrict certain clans or even Disciplines, depending on the nature of your story or chronicle. Weaving such player-devised characters into an already written story can be difficult, but not impossible. The easiest way to do so is to closely monitor the creation of characters, guiding players in their effort, seeing that characters fit story and chronicle parameters. If this is not possible, alterations to the story or chronicle may be necessary.

Story Style

Style is the method you use in constructing your story. It describes how the subplots tie in with the main plot and how characters interact with the environment you have chosen. Style is the thread from which your story is woven. Without style, a story has no cohesive form and might become boring for players. You need to develop and hone your style so as to be able to craft a finely tuned story, with many layers and intricacies for players to explore.

Main Plot

The main plot is the root of a story, and any other lesser plots will grow from the main plot. The main plot is what brings characters together, unifying their attention. The main plot of a story should be all-encompassing, in that all characters should be affected by it in at least a minor fashion. The main plot should illuminate every other aspect of the story. Not all of them need be touched by it directly, but each character should be aware of the main plot at least on some peripheral level.

The main plot is often the most obvious part of the story. It should have a rather blatant goal that characters seek to obtain. They might be attempting to reach this goal as a group or compete against one another. An example of such competition is the election of a new prince. There are probably several different candidates for the position, with other characters backing the one they deem the most worthy. This is an example of both cooperation and competition. However, all characters are certainly involved in the resulting power struggle.

Subplots

In most novels and movies, subplots are just filler material. They are essential to Mind's Eye Theatre. Subplots keep characters busy and carry them from moment to moment. They are the stories that are woven around the characters. A story gives players ample opportunities to explore subplots, and due to the unique nature of this sort of game, subplots can be taken as far as the players want to take them.

Each character should be involved in as many subplots as possible. A subplot can be any personal goal a character is trying to accomplish. Subplots should be crafted so as to intermingle with one another, so that characters become embroiled in a web of intrigue.

The possibilities for subplots are nearly endless. Some examples are a Malkavian wanting to get a ring back from an old lover, a Brujah needing cash to pay off a blackmailer, or a traitor who is being hunted. More than one character should be tied into the same subplot; you need interaction to make it work. Subplots should be linked as often as possible. The blackmailer may be the traitor, and he may be the one with the Malkavian's ring.

The more layers of intrigue in a story, the more players enjoy untangling them. Indeed, if your setting is intricate enough, you may find players developing subplots of their own, adding to the confusion. This should be encouraged, because it helps the story grow and gives it a life of its own.

A subplot can sometimes be almost as large in scope as the main plot, the difference being that it is not necessary for everyone to be involved. However, you should take care that the subplot does not override the main plot.

Character Relations

Hans plays with Lotte, Lotte plays with Jane
Jane plays with Willie, Willie is happy again
Sukie plays with Leo, Sacha plays with Britt
Adolf builds a bonfire, Enrico plays with it
　　— Peter Gabriel, "Games Without Frontiers"

Character interaction is a part of every story and every chronicle. Intricate character interaction is essential to a story. That is not to say that all characters will get along harmoniously— character strife is usually much more interesting. However, making sure that characters relate to one another requires a bit of planning on your part. Here are three ways to keep players interacting with one another.

Rumors

"I love the fact that the tricks themselves are a rip-off, a lie within a lie within a lie."
　　— Penn Jillette, "Penn & Teller's Cruel Tricks for Dear Friends"

Each character should know a few rumors. Rumors can often be tied to different subplots, initiating those subplots. For example, a character may have a goal of achieving Golconda. If he hears a rumor that an elder (another player) in the city has recently achieved that state, the two characters are tied together— some sort of interaction is assured. Players may also develop their own goals and subplots through rumors that you introduce. Rumors help stimulate player interaction as players try to find out the tidbits of knowledge others possess. Rumors can lead to a great deal of interaction as characters barter for knowledge.

Secrets

"It's no secret that a friend is someone who lets you help
It's no secret that a liar won't believe anyone else
They say a secret is something you tell another person
So I'm telling you… child."
—U2, "The Fly"

Everybody has secrets. Some are minor, while others, if made known, could change a character's life. The point is, everyone has something they want to hide. The more a character has to hide, the more he has to lose. Optimally, everyone should have something he or she needs to hide from other characters. Conversely, each character should be able to offer a few hints and clues as to what other characters are hiding. Try giving different characters insights to others' puzzles. Such partial knowledge gives players impetus to interact among themselves. Characters are encouraged to trade others' secrets while desperately guarding their own. This type of interaction can be quite lively and usually leads to small clusters of players engaged in hushed whispers.

Connections

"I got a name and I got a number,
I got a line on you."
　　— Genesis, "Just a Job to Do"

It is often helpful for players to have a few established ties between their characters and others in the game, even before the game begins. Contacts can be allies, enemies or simply acquaintances. These links between characters are referred to as "connections", and they may or may not tie into characters' Influence and Status traits.

A connection can exist between any two characters and can vary in importance from minor to all-encompassing. For example, two characters can begin the game already Blood Bound to one another, or they might be feuding elders capable of destroying the city. Connections are a good way to give players a sense of involvement right from the start. Connections provide players with people they can interact with right away. Connections also give Narrators a means by which to anticipate the direction a story might take. Setting two characters up as old friends and giving each of them a piece of the same puzzle ensures that the puzzle gets solved quickly. On the other hand, giving the same information to two characters who are enemies can make for some complex interaction before the puzzle is solved. How you set things up depends on how quickly you want the problem resolved.

Multiple Goals

"I came here to do two things: kick ass and chew bubblegum… and I'm all out of bubblegum."

— Roddy Piper, *They Live*

Each of possesses a multitude of goals and ambitions. Many of them conflict, and we have to choose between them. For instance, you might want to go to the movies on the same day you want to visit a friend. Multiple goals complicate matters, and while in real life that can be bothersome, in this game it only adds to the excitement. The more complicated you can make things, the better.

Complications such as multiple goals give characters depth and keep players busy. A player with several goals is usually occupied throughout the course of a story and is rarely bored. Indeed, if players with multiple goals achieve even one of those goals, they probably leave the story with a sense of accomplishment.

We're don't suggest that you overwhelm players with a staggering amount of goals. You should establish a balance. It may take a few stories before you discover the right balance. Don't worry, it's like fine tuning the reception on your stereo. Just be patient, keep trying and you'll eventually get it right.

Story Archetypes

"A long time ago, in a galaxy far, far away…"

— Star Wars

Just as a character has a Nature and Demeanor (called archetypes) that define who he is, a story can also have an archetype, which helps define it. A story's archetype is the framework, or skeleton, of the story. Story archetypes are classic story molds that have been used since the dawn of storytelling that continue to be used today. Story archetypes can be inspiration for the events of a plot, and inspiration for theme and mood as well.

The following list of story archetypes is by no means complete, but it provides examples that will hopefully kick your imagination into gear. The best stories have one main archetype but contain elements of others. Such a combination makes for a more complex and well-rounded story.

Auction

"Master of the house
Keeper of the zoo
Ready to relieve 'em
of a sou, or two."

— Thenardier, "Les Miserables"

One of the Kindred in the city, or perhaps even a mortal, has something of value to auction. This could be anything: a rare artifact, a scroll, turf, influence, a ritual, a nightclub or perhaps a secure haven. An auction of this nature might not be for money, but it could perhaps be for favors, promises of information, blood or another item of equal value. A fair number of Kindred in the city may compete in the auction, each trying to outbid the others.

The setting for this type of story is most likely the residence of the auctioneer. This adapts easily to a **Mind's Eye** setting, as it can be reproduced in the living room of your own home. You should make several other rooms available to allow bidders the opportunity to discuss matters alone, thus creating more opportunities for intrigue.

Each of the characters can come to the auction armed with a number of different things to offer. Some may have their own nefarious plans and choose to blackmail the auctioneer or otherwise intimidate her. Some may decide to pool their resources, to make the best bid. Others may choose the route of eliminating the competition.

There is plenty of opportunity for intrigue in an auction story as each of the characters maneuvers to get a better position than the others. The course that such a story takes depends on whether the story takes place as a one-shot, or as part of an ongoing chronicle. If it is part of a chronicle, players are much less likely to take drastic measures, such as out-and-out murder. Blackmail and intimidation may still be prevalent, though, depending on the nature of the group.

One important consideration in an auction story is who plays the role of auctioneer. Is it one of the players, or is it a Narrator? Again, this usually depends on whether the game is a one-shot or part of a chronicle. If it is a one-shot, a player best fills the role. This makes for a greater level of intrigue since players are able to interact with one another in a more direct fashion. In such a story, Narrators may be able to sit back and watch the action unfold, only intervening if there is a rule dispute or some other trivial matter. Or a Narrator may wish to intrude, playing a non-Cast character to add a twist to the story. Perhaps the character is a late arrival to the bidding war.

If an auction story occurs in an ongoing chronicle, the role of the auctioneer may be best played by a Narrator. If one of the players is interested in playing a different character for an evening, however, the auctioneer makes a good rotating character. In either case, the auctioneer assumes an air of mystery. The players cannot be certain of her motives.

Conspiracy

"If things are done that the enemy would be ashamed to do, there is an advantage."

— The Book of Lord Shang

In a story of conspiracy, characters are embroiled in a plot to overthrow or at least undermine a figure or organization in power. The classic example is a plot to overthrow the prince. Cast Members can be involved in the story from either side, although it's best if they're in a battle of wits against each another.

A conspiracy often starts as a subplot. Even if you intend a conspiracy to be the main plot, it works best if at first it doesn't appear to be. For example, the story may at first seem to involve a simple power struggle. The prince of the city is gone, for whatever reason, leaving a vacuum. Several capable Kindred rise to the challenge and declare themselves prince. The primogen of the city decree that they will choose the new Prince. All of the candidates agree, and so the decision is up to the vote of the primogen. No one is aware that one of the candidates is actually a plant of the anarch characters. Once in power, the plant intends to wreak havoc in the city, bringing it under the control of the characters. Now it's up to the characters to discredit the other candidates. This could be further complicated to deepen the conspiracy. The anarch prince, could, in fact, not be an anarch at all, but an Archon, long undercover. Once elected to prince, he plans to lead the anarchs into an elaborate trap to destroy them, ridding the city of its anarchs once and for all.

Power Struggle

"There can be only one!"

—Highlander

In this type of story, a position of power within Kindred society has become available and everyone is vying for it. The players are members of the different power groups, each trying to get their representative into the position of authority. One or more of the players can even play the individuals vying for power.

There are many possibilities for this type of story. The contested position could be anything from a Justicar to prince of a city to an anarch gang leader. The reason behind the position's opening can help set the mood for the story. Has the prince been assassinated? Is the Justicar retiring in mid-term for mysterious reasons? Has the anarch leader switched sides and joined the Camarilla, or, worse still, the Sabbat?

Contenders may have to pass certain tests or qualifications before they are eligible for the position. These tests can be very different depending on the nature of the position. An anarch gang probably has physical requirements, whereas the Camarilla probably tests the social skills of a contestant. For example, someone contesting for leadership of an anarch gang might have to perform some extraordinary physical feat, such as winning a fight single-handedly against several opposing gang members, or escaping from a burning building. The final test may even involve facing off against a rival contestant. By contrast, the Camarilla counterpart may face Social Challenges. Leaders within the Camarilla, with the exception of prince, are often chosen by vote. This requires a contender to convince others that he is right for the position.

Those who support a contender have very important roles as well, for without supporters, a contender stands no chance of victory. Sometimes the victor in a confrontation is decided by sheer weight of supporters. Supporters wage the war in the streets, trying to convert one another to their cause. This may be achieved through open violence, more subtle means of blackmail or other treachery.

Each contestant in a power struggle should have a fatal flaw that can be used to bring him down. There may be rumors floating around about a contestant, but none may be based on truth. Many of these secrets and rumors can be damaging, however, and enough discrediting evidence fabricated or uncovered could spell doom for a contestant. A contestant's secrets should be carefully buried in the character's background, and should have to be pieced together before the whole picture is developed.

An interesting twist on a power struggle, if you have enough players, involves a mortal election for mayor, governor or even President. In this type of story, different Kindred factions attempt to influence the outcome. Due to dealing in such close proximity with mortals, great care has to be taken to maintain the Masquerade. Physical violence is out of the question, although political intrigue and deceit are rampant.

Golconda

*"I can only say, there we have been:
but I cannot say where.
And I cannot say, how long,
for that is to place it in time."*

— T.S. Eliot, "Burnt Norton"

Usually an individual seeks Golconda, but it's conceivable that a small group of Kindred can band together for the same purpose. Such a story revolves around the tragedy of being a vampire. Perhaps characters are searching to regain their humanity.

Quests for Golconda require heavy Narrator intervention, and as such, probably work best as goals pursued over several stories in a chronicle. Characters have to be very close to have such a unified, personal goal. Characters may be neonates who knew each other as mortals and have decided upon this united path. They may have chosen to travel together because they know their journey will be a long and arduous one, a quest that some may not complete. They hope, however, that their friendship can hold them together.

The quest for Golconda should never offer an easy path. This is not a story you should force upon characters; they should choose it for themselves. The greatest challenge of a Golconda quest is facing and overcoming the Beast Within. This dilemma can be staged by confronting characters with various moral questions, forcing them to make choices. In the end, most characters probably fail, although perhaps one of them might succeed. Success should arise only after some extraordinary soul-searching, searching that should be felt by both player and character.

Mystery

"Elementary, my dear Watson."
—Sherlock Holmes (stage and film version)

Events have occurred that have the city's Kindred baffled. Perhaps a Kindred or prominent mortal citizen has been murdered, perhaps there have been break-ins at several havens, or perhaps there have been mysterious sightings. Generally any story in which perpetrator and motive is unclear makes for a mystery. Characters must discover who or what is behind the unusual occurrences.

Players must solve the mystery by interacting with Narrator characters, who offer different clues and other information. Props are ideal for such a story, serving as physical clues. Such props are items that players can physically examine to learn more about the mystery. If you are particularly industrious, you can even recreate a crime scene that players can explore. The scene can be complete with physical evidence and perhaps even eyewitnesses played by Narrators.

Another option is to have one of the players pose as the perpetrator, the others trying to determine who among them the perpetrator is. This makes for a classic "whodunit." Each of the characters in this type of story should have a motive for the crime. Each of the characters should begin the story knowing only certain facts about the others. The combination of any physical evidence and characters' interaction should eventually lead players to a conclusion about the guilty party. Placing information is the key here. If players know too much, the story could be over before it's begun. You must be careful how you place information; characters should not be able to draw conclusions until many different clues can be pieced together. You may even wait to introduce a vital piece of information until later in the story to maintain suspense.

An additional factor to consider is why the culprit sticks around. There are several possibilities. Perhaps he wishes to frame someone else for the crime. This requires him to stick around to ensure the frame is successful. The crime could have been committed in the haven of an elder, and he may decree that it must be solved before anyone can leave, denying the culprit an escape. The elder may even place limitations, such as demanding that the crime must be solved before dawn or all will be destroyed.

Choosing the method of telling a mystery story— with an outsider or player as perpetrator— can be affected by the context of the story, such as whether the story is told as a one-shot or as part of

a chronicle. An outsider as perpetrator is generally appropriate if the story takes place as part of a chronicle. This allows players to work together as a team to solve the mystery. A character as perpetrator is appropriate as a one-shot. Making one of the characters the criminal offers an opportunity for inter-player interaction, which can be the means for a great story. Even in a chronicle, it's possible that a player may not mind having her character become the villain. Of course, you should make it very clear that she probably won't be able to play her character again. Indeed, the character may not even survive.

Rebellion

"If there is oppression from above
there will be disruption from below."
　　—Chun Ch'an

A powerful group, usually anarchs, has grown restless and decides to openly confront its oppressors. The players can be in either faction, or both, trying to settle the dispute before it escalates into full-scale conflict, or are trying to inflame it even further.

This type of story can tie in easily with a conspiracy story. Players can be on both sides, each vying for power. The ultimate goal of this story is probably the determination of whether the city descends into rebellion. Playing out an actual revolt doesn't make for a very good story because of the logistics involved. However, segments of the rebellion can easily be made into stories, using many of the story archetypes listed here. These stories can be told as a series of one-shots, or even as part of a chronicle where players represent opposite factions.

An actual rebellion story can take many forms. It can involve a meeting between anarchs and the Camarilla in which the anarchs try to seize power they feel is owed them. This can be further complicated by assassination attempts or other subterfuge. An anarch leader can even be blackmailing the prince into giving him power.

Rescue

"Aren't you a little short for a stormtrooper?"
　　— Princess Leia, *Star Wars*

A compatriot of the characters has been captured, and the heroes have to attempt a rescue. This avenue relies heavily on Narrator characters, unless players can enact both sides of the story with one side as the captors and the other side as the rescuers.

In order to set the mood of the story, the motivations of the captors must be known. The captors' motives often tie this story in with another of the story archetypes. The capture can be an act of revenge or an act of sheer terrorism. It may be that one of the lovers in a love triangle (see "Romance") has chosen to take matters into her own hands. The kidnapper in this type of story is usually considered the antagonist.

The setting of a rescue is vital. There needs to be a degree of separation between captors and rescuers so that both sides can make plans. This type of story doesn't need to end in brutal conflict, although you should be prepared for it. It is possible, in fact preferable, that players negotiate their differences. In a story where players are on both sides, this negotiation probably becomes an important part of the story. Tracking down the villain to his lair can also be an essential part, especially if a Narrator is playing the abductor. This hunt can be accomplished through the placement of clues, similar to those of a mystery story. In fact, the beginning part of a rescue may have many aspects of a mystery, requiring investigation of the abductor.

The rescue story is ideal for those who enjoy combat. The climax of such a story is likely to see characters pitted against each other in an out-and-out bloodbath. If you don't want to see your characters rend each other limb from limb, this probably isn't the story for you.

Revenge

"Re-Re-Re-Revenge!"
　　—Michael Palin, *A Fish Called Wanda*

In this story archetype, one character seeks revenge on another for past transgressions. Both sides of the story can be enacted by players, or one of them can be a Narrator character. Revenge often involves making the target's life as difficult as possible by constantly throwing various obstacles in his path. This may take any form, from framing the individual for a crime to attempting out-and-out murder.

The motive for revenge is an important part of the story. Is the transgression real or imagined? If it is imagined, what caused the person to feel slighted? Perhaps it is merely a figment of imagination, or maybe the object of revenge has been set up. The web of intrigue can become very complex in a story of this type. Exactly who is getting revenge? Imagine if a Toreador in a city had been slighted by another Toreador because he was not invited to a particularly extravagant party. He is angered, but can take no direct action because the other Toreador is his elder. He therefore contrives a situation in which his elder offends another elder, who can strike back, giving the original character revenge by proxy.

A story of this type may work best as a subplot within a larger story. A revenge subplot can add a significant amount of tension, which may be lacking in a larger story. Revenge is something that can easily be worked into an existing story should things be dragging. You may even find spontaneous revenge plots developing between characters.

Romance

"My life would be right
If only you knew
I'd come back tomorrow
To be with you…"

— Information Society, "Tomorrow"

Romance is a very common theme in vampire lore. It is often a motivating factor for Cainites, as they are easily swept away by their passions. Romance works best as a subplot for a **Mind's Eye** story, but can easily become the main plot, especially if the group is small. You should be very careful when casting players in a romance plot, as it is easy to put someone in an uncomfortable situation. It's usually best to place players already romantically involved in lead roles, but if your players are capable of it, more excitement arises if the leads are not involved. Players already involved know each other too well and may bypass any emotional obstacles you throw in their path.

A romance story can take place between Kindred, or, as often happens in literature, between a vampire and a mortal. For such a story to be interesting, there must be some conflict involved with the romance. The love can be forbidden. Perhaps the prince of the city feels that relationships between mortals and Kindred pose a threat to the Masquerade. The tale can be one of unrequited love. This is most appropriate for characters of Clan Toreador. The sight of her beau's face might make her go mad with passion, yet he spurns all her advances. A love triangle can make for an intrigue-filled story, as two people compete for the affections of another. A doomed or tragic love affair is another option. When a mortal learns that her lover is a hideous beast, a vampire, she may no longer bear to be with him. Yet she may be torn by her emotions, for she still feels love for him. These are only a few examples of the romantic stories you can tell. Countless others exist.

Rewards and Punishments

"You made your bed, now lie in it."

— *someone's mother*

Throughout the progress of a story, characters must make decisions. Some may be good, others not. The purpose of this section is to explore the results of both types of decisions. This is not to say that these are the only two extremes. A character's actions can have an impact on many different levels. What you need to do, however, is make it worthwhile for characters to strive for one extreme while making it detrimental to continue choosing the other.

Rewards and penalties work well to help players profit from their foresight and learn from their mistakes. Rewards should be granted and penalties imposed at the conclusion of a story. These should be worked into your chronicle. For example, if players interacted well and their characters made good decisions throughout the story, grant them a boon from the prince. This rewards characters for their efforts as well as serves them in future stories. However, if characters really screwed up (perhaps they broke the Masquerade), have them end the story (or begin the next) by suffering the prince's wrath. The prince's wrath can lead to another story in and of itself.

Rewards

- Boon from the prince or an elder
- Permission to sire progeny (given by the prince)
- Rare or magical item (use this one sparingly)
- Vial of potent vitæ
- Valuable information
- New contact
- Improved Status
- Characters are owed a favor by an anarch gang
- Opportunity to learn a new or rare Discipline
- Exclusive hunting territory
- Improved resources
- Additional retainer
- New ally

Punishments

- Loss of Status or Influence
- Curtailed hunting grounds
- Blood chalice (characters are made to drink the blood of many elders, coming one step closer to a Blood Bond with all of them)
- Forced to do service (a mission of some sort for an elder)
- Blood Hunt
- Final Death (again, use this one sparingly, if at all)
- Lost resources
- Lost ally or contact
- New enemy: elder, prince, anarch gang, hunter, Lupine
- New Derangement

Finally, remember that rewards and punishments should always be given as a direct result of characters' actions. A reward or punishment should always be pertinent to the story and the characters' actions. In short, characters should reap what they sow.

Chapter Eight: Narration

"In your head is the answer
let it guide you along
let your heart be the anchor
and the beat of your own song."
—Rush, "Something for Nothing"

Now that you have written a story, you need to make it work in a live game. Narrating a story is an art akin to juggling; you have to keep up with all story threads, play judge and make sure that none of the players get bored— you'll be juggling quite a few of them. Narration requires a lot of work and planning and usually leaves you exhausted. You, however, have a ringside seat to the story and can watch it unfold in its entirety. Because your control of the story is loose (tight control denies player freedom), you may be surprised by how the story twists and changes in the hands of your players. If you do your job well, you will be rewarded with the players' thanks.

Of course, with the great rewards of storytelling comes a great deal of responsibility. You have to initiate and guide the story and present it in an entertaining manner. You, above all people involved, can destroy the story. Even a very good story can be ruined if it's not presented well. If a few required player handouts are missing, or if players have no idea where the game is taking place, you have failed. It is very important that you prepare every aspect of that story as far ahead of time as possible. If you try to prepare an entire game at the last minute, you'll be stressed out by the time the game begins. The game will suffer heavily from your exhaustion.

Veteran roleplaying gamemasters should take note that running a live game is very different from running old-style roleplaying games. You can no longer sit down an hour before play commences and dream up a quick plot. If you try to do this, your story will have lots of holes. If you change your setting in mid-story, you need to represent the change in some way so players realize where they are without having to ask. Prepare everything in advance or suffer the folly of sloth.

The main rule to remember when preparing your story is "show, don't tell." You have to present your story so players can make their own impressions of the environment without your impressions being forced on them. Live games work because players can take the lead based on information they discover themselves. If you have not fleshed out your story enough— if you have to tell players what's going on— you might as well be playing a tabletop roleplaying game.

To be a Storyteller, you need to work magic. You have to create the illusion that your players are vampires, living by night and preying on humankind and each other. Fortunately for you, players probably cooperate in every way to help you maintain the illusion, but it's up to you to direct their attention from the game-like aspects of roleplaying.

How to Host a Game

"Thorough preparation makes its own luck."

—Joy Poyer

Once you have created your story, you need to cast it. Your story may require that certain key players be present for the evening. You need to make sure that players necessary to the plot are going to show. Make a list of two or three players who are willing to help you narrate the game and serve as backup players. Call your key protagonists and antagonists the night before the game to make sure they will be present. In a game with as many as a dozen people, odds are that one or two will fail to show.

When you are preparing to stage a story, remember that you are playing host to dozen or so guests. Plan the event as you would a party. You can even send out written invitations corresponding to the theme. Like any party, you need to make sure your guests are comfortable, that they have drinks and perhaps food, and that they are entertained. As food and decorations cost money, ask your players for help. They can bring drinks and munchies or donate money to help cover costs.

Running an entire chronicle can be exhausting unless you pace yourself. Expect to spend a minimum of an hour per player writing the story and setting everything up. Expect to actually play a story bi-monthly or even monthly. Trying to run a weekly game is very taxing and may result in the eventual death of your chronicle. Don't make your games frequent and tedious, but rare and spectacular.

Storyteller Focus

"Carefully study the well-being of your men, and do not overtax them. Concentrate your energy and hoard your strength. Keep your army continually on the move, and devise unfathomable plans."

—Sun Tzu, *The Art of War*

As a Storyteller, your focus should always be on keeping the game running as smoothly as possible. To ensure that the game doesn't get out of hand, make sure you have enough Narrators. These Narrators usually assume the roles of elder vampires or antagonists. They also serve to answer players' questions and resolve the majority of inter-player disputes. Your arbitration should only be required in the most extreme circumstances.

You should also concentrate on keeping the story dynamic. Always keep your players guessing. Have small subplots ready that you can thrust into the game should it become static. Perhaps a Sabbat recruiter shows up on the scene, or a nosy police investigator arrives and starts questioning characters about their nocturnal activities. If you notice players milling about or ignoring each other, assume the role of an elder vampire and introduce them. If players seem lost, gather them together for a Conclave to discuss the various intrigues of the night. Give players something to occupy themselves with and they will be content.

Concentrate on where players stand in terms of resolving the plot or solving the mystery you have given them. If they are struggling, drop a few hints and spread a few rumors, then watch your vampires scramble to discover new information. If they are too close to solving the mystery, throw in a red herring or create a new scene on the fly. Improvisation is a potent art, and Storytellers who learn to use it are well-rewarded.

If you are playing in public, you must serve as a buffer between the authorities of the real world and the potential mayhem players can create. Discretion is the better part of valor. Educate players on responsible playing and do not hesitate to hand out rewards or punishments as the need arises.

Preparation is essential to running a successful story. The greater the preparation, the less you have to worry about maintaining focus. A well-prepared game frees you to enjoy your creation and interact with players, while a poorly prepared game leaves you scrambling to maintain control. When you maintain focus on story elements, the surroundings and your players, you need not fear the results of any game session.

Pre-Game Tasks

"Nothing makes a person more productive than the last minute."

—Unknown

There are several things you need to do to set up and run a game of **The Masquerade**. The following is a checklist which may help you prepare a game, presented as a real-life example of a timetable used to narrate a 12-player game.

Most of these things need to be accomplished, but the schedule is subject to other considerations. If you are running a larger game, printing out your final handouts should be accomplished prior to day of the game. Working with a partner or two can help with pre-game tasks, as one partner can prepare the environment while the other prepares the player handouts.

This story is designed by two Storyteller/Narrators, Frank and Sandi. It is an example of how much work can go into a story, as this particular one relies heavily on props and special effects.

• **T minus 2 weeks** — Frank advertises the game to his circle of friends through calls and messages. He creates a guest list from the replies he receives and decides that he can, with the help of his girlfriend Sandi, manage to narrate the game with no additional help. A good ratio is one Narrator for every seven players, although this can vary depending on the scenario and experience of the players.

Frank and Sandi sit down and go over the entire story and player handouts, making revisions. The process of revising the story continues right up to the evening preceding the game. Final copies of player handouts are easy to produce, as they're stored on computer.

Frank creates a list of all the props needed for the game. Sandi locates and constructs all the props and stores them safely. Because the setting of the game is an occult auction—requiring many stage items—two boxes are needed to store all the props. Frank spends much of his time putting finishing touches on lighting and sound systems to create the effect of a thunderstorm in the background.

• **T minus 2 days** — Sandi makes a grocery list for the game and picks up food and drinks to feed a dozen people for the evening. Frank and Sandi clean up the townhouse, clearing away any potentially dangerous items from the play area.

• **T minus 1 day** — Sandi prints the final versions of all player handouts. Frank sorts the handouts into manila envelopes for each player so the material can be handed out quickly once players arrive.

Sandi checks the props against the list to make sure everything is finished.

Frank calls all the players to make sure everyone can make it. One player has forgotten and another is ill. Frank is able to replace the one player, resorting to a list of standbys.

• **T minus 2 to 4 hours** — Sandi prepares the food and drinks and lays out the props in their proper places. Frank does a final test on the lighting system and finds a bug.

• **T minus 1 hour** — Frank and Sandi go over the plot one last time to make sure both have a good idea of events taking place during the story. Frank makes his best guesses at things that might go wrong and suggests ways to respond to them. This preplanning allows both Narrators to share the work of resolving plot problems.

• **Game time** — As players arrive they are each given their envelopes and sent into a spare room to read through the material. After players finish reading, they are led into the main room to begin play, with the help of Sandi's narration. Frank stays in the spare room to handle lingering questions.

• **T + 4 hours** — After the game is over, everyone sits down to discuss how it went. Frank and Sandi award packs of Pez candies to the best players.

Character Creation

"Let us make a man — someone like ourselves,
to be the master of all life upon earth and
in the skies and in the seas."
— Genesis 1:26

It is your role as Storyteller (aided by Narrators) to guide players through the character generation process. After your players arrive for the game session, you need to introduce them to the basic premise of the game, as well as describing the rule systems. Your main goal should be to make story contribution as easy as possible for players. If players are beginners, show them the basics, but let them discover the intricacies of the game on their own.

Start by laying out any briefing sheets you want to use on the table and invite players to look them over. You can pass out character cards at the same time. Give the players a minute to look everything over and ask questions. If players can refer to the briefings and their character cards while they listen to your explanations, they'll better understand how things work.

After everyone understands what's going on, go through the character creation process step by step with the players. The other Narrators can help with any questions.

It's likely that you have certain roles in the story that you need filled. Your story probably has requirements, in terms of characters and setting, that must be understood by all concerned. Even if you don't have specific requirements, you probably have a general idea of the types of characters you need. These roles should be described only in terms of concept (and perhaps clan); allow the players decide who plays whom. Disputes can be resolved with a test.

Introducing Your Story

"Welcome back, my friends, to the show that never ends.
We're so glad you could attend, come inside, come inside."
— ELP, "Carn Evil #9, First Impression"

When players begin to arrive, you need to give them information. You need to tell them what's happened since the last story (if anything) and should provide goals and motivations for the upcoming evening. Prepare as much information as you can in written form for players to read as they arrive. Here are some handouts that we provide (or you can create) to facilitate your story's introduction.

• **Character Cards** — You need to have enough of these for all your players. It's wise to have spare cards on hand, since players, who have their own characters, may forget their cards.

• **Timetable** — (For Narrators only) This sheet contains a chronological list of all events that take place. Timetable sheets are useful for planning complex stories. Events listed might be, "10:00 PM — prince and entourage enter." Make sure each Narrators has her own copy and go through the events on the handout during your Narrator briefing.

• **Background Briefing** — This is a one-pager that you can create to provide a short background for the important Kindred of your chronicle. You should include any important events that have occurred, rumors that are circulating throughout the city and important things that have happened in previous games. A new player should be able to pick up this handout and immediately have an idea of what is going on in the city. The handout can mention things like what city the chronicle takes place in and the name of the prince and important Kindred who are likely to make an appearance. Make several copies of this document and give one to each player, or leave several out in the open for players to take.

Example Briefing Sheet

The Justicar for Clan Ventrue has made an abrupt decision. He's retiring, leaving the Camarilla for reasons unknown. The problem is, he's only four years into his 13 year term. An emergency Conclave is being called to select a new Justicar. Baltimore is hardly the best choice for a Conclave, but that's just the site that the departing Justicar has decreed. Tensions rise with the arrival of the Inner Circle. The breath of the Sabbat is hot upon the city's neck. As the prince and his brood struggle to maintain control, and many factions are struggling to make themselves heard.

• **Character Briefing** — While the background briefing contains information all Kindred in the city know, the character briefing describes events that pertain to a specific character. A separate page should be prepared for each character. If you have a small group, you can provide this information orally. This briefing should describe the important events that have happened to each character since the last story. Include a few events that have nothing to do with the current story to give your chronicle a more richly woven texture. Toss in a few red herrings for good measure. After the description of events, list some of the goals the character might like to pursue during the story (but don't force any on a character). You may find that as players become used to acting out stories in **Mind's Eye Theatre,** you no longer need to list players' goals. Experienced players can design their own schemes. Novice players often appreciate the advice, though.

The last section of each character briefing sheet should list what the character knows of other Kindred's activities. Provide at least three rumors or clues for each character, making up whatever important or nonessential details you feel flesh out the story. If this is the first game in your chronicle, you may provide several rumors and clues to give players something tangible to pursue. With later stories, rumors and clues virtually create themselves. Each Cainite should have an entry about each of the other characters, even if the entry says the character knows nothing about the other Kindred.

Perhaps the best way to present all the background and character material to players is to arrange an area away from the main playing space. Set up a few tables, chairs and pencils. As players wander in, lead them to this area to create their characters and read the various briefing sheets. When a player is finished, she may enter the main room to begin the story. The idea is to keep all reminders that you're playing a game away from the storytelling space. Players should assume their characters as they move from the introduction area, instead of trying to read material and interact in character.

Guiding Players

"... take him by the hands. Make him understand.
The world on you depends, our life will never end."
— The Doors, "Riders on the Storm"

As your players begin to play out the story, it's possible that they may be unsure of themselves. New players in particular need some sort of guidance to help them learn the rules and get used to acting out their characters' actions. Step into a minor character of your story and engage a new player in a minor challenge to get her used to the rules. The challenge system works well in play, but most people do not immediately understand it until they actually defend themselves in a challenge. Try to let new players win your challenge, as it builds their confidence, and confidence is sorely needed when newcomers play in the same game as more experienced players.

Sometimes Cast Members also need help with their goals. A story that leans heavily toward investigation may frustrate players who miss one or two vital clues. Eventually, some players may come over to you asking for help. Unless it is a rules question, or you have to clarify some point that a character should know, you might not want to give information away too easily at first. If a player receives immediate assistance from a Storyteller or Narrator, you introduce an omnipresent being into the game. Players may become dependent on you.

Instead of giving direct answers to player questions, encourage players to figure things out for themselves. Later, if a player really does need help, have another Narrator, in the guise of a minor character, assist the player. If another Narrator is not available, you can approach the player and offer aid through your own character (although having another Narrator do it involves a touch of finesse). Pull your assistance off cleanly and the player will never know you have responded to his plea.

You can also use antagonists and protagonists to provide information, asking an experienced player to help out. Suppose a member of the Sabbat is at a party looking for his contact in the city, and has not found anyone who answers to the proper code phrase: *"Blood brings death."* If the Sabbat asks you, as Storyteller, for help because he needs to begin plotting with his contact, tell him to keep looking. You can then trot over to the Sabbat's contact and wonder out loud why the wild looking guy in the purple shirt keeps rambling about blood and death. Hopefully, the contact will soon talk to the Sabbat member. If the characters still don't pick up on their connection, have another Narrator, playing a minor character, introduce the two. Remember, if the success of your story requires that certain events happen, don't let it be known that events are being staged intentionally. It takes some of the spontaneity out of the game.

You also need to invent things to do for players who seem bored with the game. These players have usually accomplished or hopelessly failed their goals or can't find the motivation to pursue a difficult goal. Your best option is to get a bored player involved in another plot, or to make up a customized plot on the spot. If your character mentions a lead to a powerful item that others are looking for, the player may spend time following that lead. Alternatively, giving the bored player a clue that someone else has missed allows you to kill two birds with one stone. It's a good idea to have a library of new plots on hand that you can drop into your chronicle as needed.

Remember to be vigilant for bored players during your first few games; first-time players might not come back if they're bored all evening long. If you don't keep the players busy with plots, their characters may start killing and feeding from each other just for something to do. At this point, the game quickly degenerates into a free-for-all. You'll probably find that players stay busy as your chronicle progresses because they spend more time involved in the plots of other players.

Interacting with Cast Members

Your key to interacting with Cast Members is the minor character known as an extra. An extra can be a pre-generated character already woven into the story, or a character created on the spur of the moment to fix a problem. You rarely need to create a character card for your extra; a basic concept is usually enough.

Each character you introduce needs to have an easily identifiable mark so players can recognize which minor character you are playing. A wearable prop, such as a hat, coat, scarf, bandana or amulet is usually enough. A distinct speech pattern, like an accent, is at least as useful. Remember that the mark needs to be something that you can put on and take off quickly, since you may end up having to switch between several minor characters in an evening's story.

Your extra(s) should be enjoyable to play. During the middle of a story, you may find that you and the Narrators have little to do. You then have a chance to play your bit parts just for fun. Go a little wild. Try to provide some comic relief.

There are certain Narrator characters that are particularly useful when telling stories:

The Socialite

A socially active character is very useful for pulling Cast Members into a story. While not all extras need to be sociable, you should plan on having one or two available during your first few stories. Some characters may not know each other and may shy away from interacting outside their circle of friends. You need someone to hook up with people, introducing characters to each other and quickly moving on to other conversations. A fun example of a socialite is a Malkavian who is bright and cheery, but has an unusual hang-up about names: he introduces everyone by the wrong name. By the time players have reintroduced themselves with their correct character names, the Malkavian has wandered over to another group. Dress your socialite in a flashy item of clothing, like a top hat or opera cape.

The Elder

You typically need a powerful extra to provide a symbol of authority. One character needs to be powerful enough to direct major plot twists, to order protagonists around and enforce the Traditions. This character helps you deal with emergencies and rewrites, and can initiate new goals for bored players. So that players can easily distinguish this extra, have him bear some symbol of power, like a cane or a large, noticeable ring.

The Informant

You need someone who has access to information, so you can provide helpful clues to players who get stuck. This character can be a standard contact for several players. The informant should be dressed in dark or nondescript clothes. Find an old woolen coat at a thrift store.

The Bully

You need someone who is strong and sufficiently taunting to goad and dare players into performing dangerous actions. Occasionally, players are hesitant to do certain things and you need a strong, imposing extra to prod them into acting. Outfit the bully in a leather or jean jacket.

Player Questions

"And you may ask yourself, 'My God!
What have I done?'"

    — Talking Heads, "Letting the Days Go By"

Aside from having a way to deal with players within the context of the story, you need to handle players' questions outside the story. During the first half hour of a game, it's a good idea to keep a Narrator "out of game" to answer any questions players might have. When players step out of character to ask questions, you don't want them in the main playing area. Set the "outside" Narrator up in another room. The most important thing to remember when interacting with players is to never remind them they are playing a game; addressing a Narrator as a Narrator does just that.

You may occasionally need to impart information that a mortal or vampire can not offer. You have to provide such information as discreetly as possible without distracting players from their characters. If your plot involves a large amount of investigation, you can assign a Narrator the sole job of providing information that can be discovered. This Narrator is responsible for telling players the results of searching a room, or tells what happens to characters when they drink drugged blood.

If you want to be stylish about offering game information to players, you can prepare notes for Narrators to hand to players who discover things. You can also put notes in closed envelopes where clues might be found. You can write requirements on the outside an envelope, requirements that must be met before the player may look at the clue within. For example, you might introduce an occult book which describes a new Tremere ritual. There might be an envelope inside which says, "Do not open unless you have an Occult Ability Trait." The envelope contains a description of the ritual. By using a note, you present information non-verbally, preserving the illusion of the story.

One thing you want to avoid when dealing with players is letting them overuse Narrators. Players may try to use Narrators as messengers, to summon other characters, or to handle uses of Aura Perception so that the character using the Discipline can remain unknown. If a player asks for such favors too often, Narrators can simply refuse their help. They're busy enough managing the game, and they can get bogged down performing players' tasks. Narrators should only serve as players if you have the luxury of a Narrator for every four or five players.

Working with Narrators

As a Storyteller, you can't do everything yourself. It's not possible. No matter how good a Storyteller you are, you're going to need the help of Narrators (unless, perhaps, you have only five or six players). If you try to run the whole story, you will quickly become overwhelmed. It's best to delegate tasks and let your Narrators make judgment calls.

Ideally, you, as Storyteller, should not have to deal with players very much (unless you establish yourself as a Narrator as well as Storyteller). You should wander around and observe to make sure the story is proceeding well. Players should learn to go to Narrators with their questions. A player should refer to you only if a Narrator has no idea how to handle a question.

To ensure that Narrators understand what's going to happen in the story, you should meet with them early in the evening. If no one but you knows what's going on, Narrators aren't much use. You should assign tasks to Narrators at this time. For example, you can ask a Narrator to provide a clue to a character, but let the Narrator work out how and when it's delivered.

During the story, you need to send Narrators on various "missions." These might involve overseeing a major battle or staying near a central character. Suppose a Lupine has entered the city carrying a talisman that can repel vampires. A Narrator needs to stay near the Lupine to enforce the effects of the totem.

Narrators need to keep you informed of their rulings and of story events. Avoid reversing a decision that a Narrator has made. Doing so makes Narrators seem indecisive and leads players to doubt them. If you want to run a large game, you are going to need assistants, and you have to learn to communicate with them effectively.

Pacing the Story

More often than not, a story does not run according to schedule. It either drags late into the night or Cast Members work too quickly and become bored with their accomplishments. It's during times like these that you need to reach into your bag of tricks and adjust the pace of the story.

Dealing with stories that are running too long is, thankfully, relatively simple. It's easy to push on the accelerator. You can start by doling out clues and information through character contacts and new props. One of the simplest tools you can have in your repertoire is a number of characters to throw into the adventure. Simply introduce a character who has the tools to help solve the problem, but for a price.

As an example, suppose your story requires that a protagonist discovers a vial of blood, aiding in a final confrontation with a Ventrue elder. If, by the end of the evening, the player has not found the vial, you can introduce a Tremere lackey who is looking for the vial as well. The Tremere can "find" the vial, then sell it to the protagonist or require some other favor for it.

You should have enough spare props on hand for Narrators to assume bit parts, like this one, without confusing players. If you can manage different voices or accents when playing these "new" characters, all the better.

Prolonging play time is a little more tricky than reducing it. Prolonging play time means prolonging the story, but if the story is complete, you have to make up new events in the spot. However, instead of creating an entirely new plot, you might be able to extend the "finished" story by going on past its logical conclusion. If the protagonists have already figured out who assassinated the Toreador primogen, have them present their case to the prince. There might be some sort of trial, followed by a confrontation with the killer. Extending stories works very well if you have a group of Narrators who are flexible, creative and who like to work "on the run."

If you foresee the story ending early, there are ways of prolonging it by distracting players. Essentially, you introduce subplots in order to pull characters off the beaten path. If you have a chance, work out one or two subplots for every story. Some tried-and-true subplots include:

• **Witch-Hunters** — Hunters have tracked a Kindred to the players' current location. Have an available Narrator or two play mortals who are trying to trick a character into breaking the Masquerade. A hunter turned loose in a group of vampires can delay the game for quite some time. You might also have the hunter be a wizard of some kind, with goals all her own. When the vampires finally catch the hunter, they have to deal with the moral dilemmas involved in disposing of her.

• **Innocent Bystanders** — Sometimes mortals wander in just in time to witness some event which breaks the Masquerade. Street gang members or mortal party-crashers can appear at any point during the evening. Characters may bully or dominate the mortals and send them away after a few minutes. However, you can then have the mortals' friends show up, wondering what happened to the others.

• **Police Raid** — A great way to screw things up, possibly for a reason that has nothing to do with the story, is the arrival of police. There might be reports of suspicious activity that a pair of police are investigating. A riot team may be called out to deal with reports of fighting.

• **Sabbat Attack** — A Sabbat strike force seeks to violently recruit several Kindred. This subplot almost inevitably leads to a big fight. Try to make the Sabbat just powerful enough that players can force them to escape. You don't want the Sabbat to win and drag several characters away, you just want to distract players for a while.

• **Haunting** — Perhaps the locale where the game takes place is haunted and a ghost appears. Maybe a mortal died in the locale. Or maybe a companion of one of the protagonists appears to warn him of some impending danger.

Try not to overuse any of these devices for prolonging a story. The best way to slow players down is to present them with something new. Invent a bizarre new magical item or a Kindred who displays unusual powers. One of the more unusual tricks to use while improvising is to create a set of events with no obvious explanation. Then listen to the explanations your players propose and choose one to be the case, or base your explanation on the theory you like best. While this tactic may seem cheesy, some absolutely amazing stories can be developed this way.

Rescue 911

"Shut her down Scotty, She's sucking Mud…"

—error message from a TRS-80 Model II computer

In **Mind's Eye Theatre**, the Storyteller and Narrators have only limited control over what occurs in the story. While you can often predict human behavior to know where a story might lead, things never work out as planned. Players have a tendency to ignore old goals, creating new goals without a second thought. While such situations can be disconcerting, it's not always a bad thing.

Unforeseen plot turns are, in fact, what **Mind's Eye Theatre** is all about. No other game is so open or free. No other game is so full of possibilities and surprises. No other game lets players be as creative or have as much control. The trick is to use what the players give you, instead of fighting with them.

If players generate new plots, you can continue them in the next story, providing you with new material upon which to build. If you let players run with what they come up with, your story may go on for some time. While the story may go off on a tangent, headed toward no foreseeable conclusion, you can usually apply finesse to work things out. The hardest part is knowing when to say "no" and when to stop destructive subplots in their tracks. The rule of thumb is, if a new direction adds depth to the story, entertains people and doesn't get in the way, let it run its course. As with all things, though, people can go too far. The following are some signs indicating that events might be getting out of control:

- Characters begin attacking everything that moves for no obvious reason.

- There is more than one unexpected character "death" during a game.

- A key antagonist is killed, disabled, captured or otherwise prevented from becoming a key figure in the story.

- Important items or clues are destroyed, discarded or stolen.

- A very serious breach of the Masquerade is committed.

Try to avoid halting the story altogether. Work within the story to put things right. Once a player puts a plan into motion, you can add elements to his plan which cause it to fail. Only when things look bleak, and you have tried in vain to fix story problems, should you introduce the *Deus Ex Machina* ending. *Deus Ex Machina* is a literary term which translates to "god out of the machine." It means you are taking charge by using a mechanism to insert an overwhelmingly powerful plot change. Here are some examples of what can happen:

- The prince shows up with his entourage and preserves the Masquerade by use of force. If several Kindred have died, the prince is likely to send a group of followers to clean up the mess, punishing guilty parties. This is a really good choice for dealing with a small group of players who get out of hand, as you show players the consequences of breaking the Masquerade. If you are severe enough, it won't happen again.

• Announce that sunrise is imminent. Normally, the game takes place in real time, but you can play a bit with time and break the game up by changing the flow of time. This kills the game quickly, and should only be used when you need time to reconstruct the plot.

• The building catches fire. When things start to break down, some character may destroy something that catches the building on fire. Another option is having a hunter or lone arsonist be responsible for the fire.

• Simply stop the story, allowing it to be continued at a later time. This is a pretty ugly solution, but if you can't think of anything else, you can rewrite the story. You can then pick up where you left off at the end of the last session.

Sometimes you may want to bring an immediate end to the game, to give yourself time to plan the next story. If the story ends prematurely, apply some of the prolongation tips described above. Ultimately, it's advised that you avoid *Deus Ex Machina* tactics. They should be your last recourse in a story gone wild.

Pre-Packaged Stories

You can save a lot of time and energy with a pre-packaged story. These stories are detailed and provide an arsenal of handouts for the game, as well as ideas for how to handle events when the plot goes awry. These stories also have the advantage of being playtested, with plot holes and continuity problems worked out— a luxury you might not have with your own stories.

Of course, with a published story, you are not able to tailor it as much to your characters and players as you could your own story. If possible, get characters involved that match the concepts recommended for the story. You may also have to change antagonists and some plot elements to merge the story seamlessly into the tapestry of your chronicle. If a pre-made story just doesn't suit your chronicle, you can at least lift ideas and subplots from it, integrating them into your own stories. It's not an easy task to modify a pre-packaged story, but it's often a lot easier than writing your own from scratch.

Laying Down the Law

"He couldn't walk very far. I cut off his leg and his arms and his head. I'm gonna do the same to you."

— Rutger Hauer, "The Hitcher"

It's your responsibility to ensure that players are not a hazard to others, including people who are not involved in the game. It is mandatory that the normal rules of social interaction be strictly adhered to. Most players will probably work with you in this regard. However, from time to time, there are those who prove disruptive to other players and the environment where the game is being played.

Many times this disruption occurs by accident. However, there may be instances when players get out of hand on purpose. If such a situation presents itself, it's not considered bad taste to remove the offender from your game. It is, after all, your game and your creation. The integrity of your game should be preserved for the enjoyment of other players. The integrity of the game should also be upheld in the minds of those who do not play or understand **Mind's Eye Theatre**.

Resolving Arguments

"I'm really, really sorry. I apologize unreservedly. I offer a complete retraction. The Impartation was totally without basis in fact and was in no way a fair comment."

— John Cleese, A Fish Called Wanda

As Storyteller, and to a lesser degree as a Narrator, you have final word in any dispute that may arise between players. It is your responsibility to maintain peace between players to insure the smooth flow of the story and its enjoyment by all.

Players should be given the opportunity to speak their minds on a situation in which they disagree. While it is suggested that you listen to a player's grievances, remember that your decision is final and must be adhered to by all concerned. It's best to combine an understanding ear and a firm hand. Keep your wits about you and your players will respect you for it. If a player's problems prove a disruption to the story, they may have to be put on hold and dealt with after the night's session.

Breaking the Rules

"The world is your exercise book, the pages on which you do your sums. It is not reality, although you can express reality there if you wish. You are also free to write nonsense, or lies, or to tear the pages."

— Richard Bach, "Illusions"

The rules are yours to use and abuse as you see fit. The novelist Richard Bach once said, *"Argue for your limitations, and sure enough, they're yours."* Do not limit yourself to this set of rules. Your concept of the way **The Masquerade** should be played may change constantly. Bend or break the rules to your liking. The rules serve the story; the story does not serve the rules. If you come upon a situation that isn't covered by the rules, don't panic— improvise. Improvising rules involves applying common sense to a situation. Don't be afraid of going against the grain in such cases. By playing this game, you are exploring a new frontier in roleplaying. It is your duty to test the limits of **Mind's Eye Theatre**.

Tradition of the Masquerade

"You had something to hide
Should have hidden it, shouldn't you?
Now you're not satisfied
With what you're being put through.
It's time to pay the price
For not listening to advice
　　—Depeche Mode, "The Policy of Truth"

The Masquerade is the first and most sacred of the Camarilla's Traditions. It is the tradition mandating that the existence of vampires be kept secret from the mortal world. Breaking the Masquerade is considered the most heinous crime a vampire can commit. Even the most violent Brujah anarch thinks twice before breaking the Masquerade. As a Storyteller or Narrator, you need to be constantly vigilant of this consideration. You also need to be prepared to present your players with the consequences of breaking the Masquerade.

Importance of the Masquerade

It is only through the preservation of the Masquerade that knowledge of vampires is kept from the mortal populace. In the modern age, with its mass media, if the existence of vampires was made known, vampire society would be shaken to its very foundations. Panic would ensue, feeding would become nearly impossible and every vampire would have to live in fear for her existence. The vast amount of resources available to modern man would put the continued existence of vampires in great jeopardy.

The Masquerade can be a very useful tool for the Storyteller and Narrator. Fear of breaking the Masquerade can be used to keep characters in check and to keep the game from getting out of hand. A Narrator character who is a powerful Archon or Justicar, and determined to punish transgressions, should keep characters in line. Indeed, if your Cast has a tendency toward combat, setting the game in a public place can discourage open conflict, forcing players to use more subtle methods of interaction. After all, no vampire character wants to be photographed or, worse still, filmed while using Wolf's Claws or Celerity.

Enforcing the Masquerade

The Masquerade is self-enforcing. Revealing one's true nature to a mortal is risks destruction; the wrath of elders is of secondary importance. Maintaining the secret of his existence is second nature to a vampire.

Yet despite the appalling risk, there are those who ignore the Masquerade. Perhaps they enjoy the terror that they inflict in those to whom they reveal themselves. Perhaps they delight in the irreverence of defying the Traditions. Perhaps they're just careless. Whatever the reason, there must always be consequences to breaking the Masquerade, whether it be the retribution of the prince or actions taken by mortals who are made aware of vampires.

Enforcement of the Masquerade is a fundamental part of being a Storyteller and Narrator. Players must always be reminded that their actions have consequences. This is not to say that you should pull them aside and remind them in the middle of a story. Rather, make them aware of their transgressions by introducing new elements to the story. If the Masquerade is dangerously near to being broken, you can play the part of an emissary of the prince, or a character's sire, warning that if events continue, the character will certainly be punished. You can also act out the reactions of any bystanders, should there be an obvious use of vampiric powers. If the Masquerade is repeatedly breached, a character can be forced into Blood Bond with the prince or another elder, to ensure obedience. Or a hunter can learn of the vampire and begin stalking him, introducing a whole new plot line. The hunter can be played as a Narrator character or by another player, depending on the nature of the chronicle.

Overall, the Masquerade can be very useful to both the Narrator and Storyteller. Not only does it give you a method of keeping players in line, but it opens up story possibilities.

Chapter Nine: Chronicle

"Life is pain; anyone who tells you differently is selling you something."
— "The Princess Bride"

If characters are the lifeblood of **Mind's Eye Theatre**, then the chronicle is the body they sustain. Although **The Masquerade** can be used and enjoyed as a series of loosely connected stories, such games often lack a sense of continuity and offer little opportunity for character development. In a chronicle— an ongoing series of stories— not only do characters reside in a familiar environment, but one that evolves as they interact with it. Developing and maintaining a chronicle is a satisfying task, but it requires continuous effort and dedication on the behalf of you and your Narrators. This chapter assists you in this task, explaining the elements involved in creating, evolving and maintaining a dynamic chronicle.

Setting the Stage

The first element to consider in chronicle construction is the atmosphere you desire. The two aspects of atmosphere are mood and theme. Each is a fundamental ingredient in the alchemy of a chronicle. Although mood and theme have already been discussed in terms of story, and some ideas previously presented apply here, mood and theme for a chronicle involves other aspects.

Mood

Mood is the underlying emotional sentiment of a chronicle. It should be powerful and moving, yet subtle. Mood is like an ocean wave. It starts out gentle and rolling, but as it reaches the shore, it can crest to an enormous size. Consider a few of the following moods:

• **Surreal** — The world is a dreamy, shifting place where reality twists along like some immense Moëbius strip. The players are at a crossroads of nightmare and fantasy.

• **Mysterious** — Secrets abound at ever turn. Nothing is ever as it seems. No truth ever resists close examination, and with every discovery, more questions arise. Only with cunning perception and diligent observation do even the smallest enigmas unravel.

• **Defilement** — An indelible stain of darkness and evil pollutes the world. The few things that are pure are soon soiled and dragged down like everything else.

• **Madness** — Sanity is a lie and chaos is king. The only logic that exists is a warped and twisted parody of sanity. Players can either embrace this madness or fight it and possibly be consumed by it.

• **Excitement** — A nonstop rollercoaster ride where no one ever gets a chance to slow down. Never let up with the action. There are no stops.

Theme

An effective chronicle theme should permeate all aspects of the characters' lives. Consider the theme of rebellion. The players' characters are relatively young Kindred rebelling against the brutal hierarchy of their elders. To drive the point home, you should paint the world in terms of rebellion: rebellion of mortal youths against authority; rebellion of the third world against the first; rebellion of the dynamic against the static. Try to incorporate imagery or analogies. You can allude to civil wars and coups both current and historical. An appearance or allusion to the works and persons of famous revolutions is a good idea.

Themes can emerge as seemingly inconsequential encounters or as the major focus of a chronicle. Avoid overemphasizing theme, however. Overemphasis makes related events expected and predictable rather than haunting and prophetic. See the "Theme" section of the Scripting Chapter for ideas on story themes that can be applied to chronicles.

Setting

The setting is the stage upon which the drama of a chronicle is played. Setting is composed of environment and locale. Environment describes the overall scheme of the world. The environment of **The Masquerade** involves vampire sects, the Traditions, clans and vampire origin myths. **Book of the Damned** details many setting backgrounds. However, your chronicle doesn't have to follow that book's example. On the contrary, differences, whether relatively minor and cosmetic or major and widespread, can make your chronicle all the more unique and enjoyable. A myriad of potential alternatives are available. It's your reality— do with it what you will.

Locale, or the physical point where you choose to place your chronicle, is the next step toward chronicle creation. The easiest choice for chronicle setting is the very city in which you and your players live. During your games, you can visit and utilize parts of the city in which your stories take place. It's also a good bet that your players are familiar enough with their setting to incorporate all sorts of firsthand knowledge into their play.

If you don't think your home town would do as your chronicle's locale, or simply don't want to use your actual location, there's a whole world out there. Bookstores, libraries and tourist bureaus can provide you with enough detailed information to set a chronicle in almost any city. This sort of research is also helpful if your players move around a great deal in the chronicle. Using foreign locales takes a bit more imagination, but if you're playing this game, you're probably not running low in that department anyway.

When it comes down to it, who says your chronicle must be set in the modern day? Although we suggest other times only for experienced players and Storytellers, a number of historical eras provide excellent settings for chronicles. Some unique vampire settings include:

- **Imperial Rome** — A culture of dazzling splendor and shocking perversity. A Kindred could find even his unique needs and practices common, if not a trifle blasé.
- **Middle Ages/Inquisition** — A dark time for the guilty and innocent alike. Evil's servants walk among men, but this time humanity knows evil's name. The hunt is on, and Kindred are the prey.
- **Renaissance Europe** — The world has entered an age of enlightenment and reason. Humanity is casting aside the mantle of superstition and myth that reigned throughout the Middle Ages. What is the place of Kindred, who were the subject of many old superstitions and myths, in this new age?
- **The Industrial Revolution** — Humanity has begun to apply its mechanical toys to every aspect of life. The cities swell as humans migrate to them to man factories and workshops. Do the Kindred suffer or benefit from the dizzying changes taking place?
- **The Roaring '20s** — Reckless abandon, rampant crime and decadence at every turn. A wild and exciting time to be alive. Probably not a bad time to be undead, either.

Players might also enjoy witnessing and participating in historical events they are familiar with. Besides, this allows you an opportunity to explain how the Kindred have influenced all manner of events throughout history, while providing a rich foundation for chronicles set at later times. Once again, ample research and a working knowledge of the time period prove invaluable to a successful "elsewhen" chronicle.

Creating the City

The city is the locus of your chronicle. It is where vampires feed and hide, and it is where they are trapped. You need to present your city in a realistic and consistent manner so that players believe in it. The setting must live and breathe for players and, until it does, characters cannot come to be. The city is where your stories take place — the more interesting and exotic it seems, the more your stories come to life. With each story you run, define the city a little more, but don't give away everything at once.

As the chronicle progresses, add details of geography, custom and plot. Build the city bit by bit at whatever pace you choose. The mortal half of the city is fairly easy to establish. Though the setting of **The Masquerade** is Gothic-Punk, much of it is identical to the world we know. However, the city isn't quite the one you live in. It's fictional. You may want to change a few details here and there to suit the mood of your game.

Creating the vampire aspect of the city is more difficult. You need to decide how the city's vampire power structure functions and who controls it. The prince is likely to be the single most important individual in a city, but that is not always the case. The prince might

be the actual ruler, or he could simply be a figurehead with some elder manipulating things from the shadows. Intrigue among the Kindred is often ferocious, so decide how vampires in your city relate. How many different sides are there? Why are they opposed to one another? Members of various clans can be antagonistic, or the classic elder-anarch conflict can be the major source of division. Are there Methuselahs behind the scenes, manipulating the various sides, or are most Kindred slaves to only their own passions?

You need to decide what coteries are in opposition to the group or individual who controls the city, and which groups support the status quo. How do the Kindred of the city interact with mortal rulers? Are the police becoming suspicious, or do ruling Kindred control mortal authorities? Some cities, especially smaller ones, might suffer from very few or no conflicts between Kindred. But how interesting is that? Don't make your city one of those peaceful, boring ones. Fill it with enough intrigue and inequity to inspire a hundred stories, or at least plan future strife to devastate the peaceful city you create now.

Last but not least, you should make sure the design of the city meshes well with the motif of your overall chronicle. If the chronicle is going to be about corruption, the city ought to be corrupt as well, both in its mortal and vampiric aspects.

Casting the Parts

The body of your chronicle lies bare before you, and you must now breathe life into it. Of course, the life of a vampire chronicle is conflict. What powers lie at the center of action and reaction in the city? Generally, very old Kindred, locked in seemingly endless struggle, provide the initial source of conflict. Their schemes and manipulations filter down a procession of vampires, each with his or her own hopes and desires.

Ancient Vampires

It is probably easiest to begin at the top of the hierarchy and work your way down. Perhaps a couple of fourth or fifth generation Kindred occupy the primary positions in your chronicle. However, employ these characters sparingly. At these high levels of power, participants are few. Their goals are pervasive and easily orchestrated when weaker Kindred are puppets. The exact opposite is true of the goals and efforts of the characters. Goals tend to be small and attainable on the short-term, but fathoming the natures, goals, identities and even existence of more venerable vampires is nearly impossible. Obviously, the eldest vampires in the city are parts that Narrators should play. And when Narrators do play these parts, you can utilize the full potential of such powerful vampires. Only with time may the mighty be supplanted by particularly ambitious and energetic characters.

Ancient Kindred have untold centuries, even millennia of experiences behind them. Treat them appropriately. When developing ancient elders, ask yourself these questions: Where did they come from? What was their mortal life like? Who Embraced them? What are their hopes, dreams and fears? What sorts of tactics and schemes do they employ? And what plans do they have for the future, both theirs and others'?

Now, what sort of conflict is worthy of such venerable creatures? When deciding this, make sure the conflict is stable enough to endure for some time, but not so static that no shift in power ever occurs. The best way to achieve such balance is to make sure each side of the conflict is reasonably equal (usually several weak allies must unite to confront a powerful one). As for the nature of the conflict itself, consider the following:

• **Rivals** — Two Kindred, possibly Methuselahs, are engaged in a shadow war against one another, with the city as their battlefield and their lessers as their armies.

• **Wolf Pack** —A small group of Kindred, say fifth generation, strive to bring down an even more ancient Cainite, possibly their sire. This unholy alliance could quickly sour if the aggressors also seek their elder's blood for diablerie.

• **Survival of the Fittest** — An apparently unknown lord of the city hones his unwitting legions of undead, to pit them against a real or imagined threat.

• **The Sleeper** — Deep in the arms of torpor lies a Kindred of immense power, perhaps an Antediluvian. For now, she slumbers peacefully, but who knows when she will awaken? For that matter, what she will do when she does?

Elder Vampires

Beneath the ancient vampires of the city are the elder Kindred. While not the near omnipotent beings their "ancestors" are, elders nonetheless possess impressive power and influence. Generally, there is one elder Kindred for each faction (groups based on clan or politics) in the city. Larger or more powerful factions may have even more elders, but one usually holds dominance over the others. These factions provide an excellent means to organize the city's vampires and draw neat battle lines.

Elders have weathered the test of centuries and most are highly ambitious. They, more than any other group of Kindred, are in a precarious position. On one side are the Methuselahs and Antediluvians who seek to or already control the elders. On the other side are young rebellious Kindred who seek to bring the elders' carefully laid plans crashing to the ground, or worse still, seek to slay elders and inherit their power. How do these rightfully paranoid Kindred deal with this war on two fronts? Their choices depend as much on their personalities as on the nature of the threats they face. Some elders surround themselves with loyal servants. Others hone their personal powers and depend only

on themselves. Some band together with their peers for mutual protection, or ally themselves with more powerful Kindred. To create realistic and dynamic elders, you should assign them positions of importance in the city. Some positions include:

• Prince
• Prince's lieutenants
• Clan lieutenants
• Spy/Traitor
• Clan elder
• Crime boss
• Political puppeteer
• Justicar
• Wealthy elite
• Inconnu agent
• Archons
• Business tycoon
• Artistic gentry
• Sabbat pack leader

Elder roles can be assigned to either Narrators or very experienced players (as long as they understand what they're getting into).

Kindred Peasantry

Dwelling in a restless mass beneath the ancients and elders are the ancillæ, neonates and childer. These Kindred are generally far weaker than their elders, but make up for their shortcomings by sheer number and vitality. This group is also the most diverse of the Kindred. They range from rebellious anarchs to BMW-driving yuppies. The majority of characters belong to this group of Kindred.

Many of the Kindred from this level of undead hierarchy band together in small groups called coteries. "Young" Kindred might be motivated to work together because they are acquaintances. Most, however, have more powerful motivations to work together. Some motivations include:

• **Revenge** — This group of Kindred shares a desire to make someone or something pay for a wrong done them. Once their revenge is achieved, if possible, members of the group probably go their separate ways. Many, however, remain together, realizing the benefits of companionship or simply to defend against reprisals.

• **Shared Threat** — These Kindred are hounded by the same danger and seek better odds of survival as a group. There are many threats that can face young Kindred, including zealous and experienced hunters, vengeful elders, enraged Lupines and even other lowly Kindred.

• **Nomads** — The life of the wanderer means freedom and no fixed responsibilities. It also means new dangers at every turn, with no one but fellow coterie members to rely on. Still, the open road is the only life for some people. If the characters do not form a coterie of nomads, a similar coterie can move in and out of the chronicle on an irregular basis.

• **Runaways** — This is a twist on the Nomad motive, in which wanderlust is the least of the coterie's worries. Something in the characters' past forces them to live on the run. This reason can be shared by all the members of the group, or each can have her own reason for running.

• **Street Gang** — Members of this coterie are tied by bonds of the street as well as by those of age and blood. Characters can be drug dealers, gun runners, racketeers or even guardians who strive to keep the streets free of crime. Most commonly, these gangs are anarchs who favor a lifestyle that embodies their disdain for authority and the establishment, both Kindred and kine.

• **Bands** — Characters' desire to express themselves through music forms the bond between members of this coterie. Members find themselves gifted with powers that make them among the world's greatest performers, but the anonymity demanded by the Masquerade is put in jeopardy. Variants on this motive can include a theatre troupe or street performers.

• **Outlaws** — Members of this coterie have chosen to utilize their supernatural powers to pursue a life of crime. It's hard to think of any crime that a human could commit that a Kindred couldn't do better. Jewel or art thief, corporate raider, credit fraud and computer hacking all involve a certain flair and romance that Kindred might find alluring. For those of a simpler bent, strong-arm robbery, burglary and safe cracking (quite literally) are viable options.

Feel free to combine these and other motives to unite and inspire your "young" characters. Allow a coterie to change its motives when appropriate. For example, a coterie with a Shared Threat could turn on its tormentor and become driven by Revenge.

Kindred Interaction

With so many groups and factions of Kindred acting within the same city, the place is rife with intrigue. To reflect all these layers of duplicity, you must layer the intrigue of your chronicle. One way to accomplish this is with secret or desperate alliances, competitive interests, strange bedfellows and ever-changing fronts and oppositions. As far as many Kindred are concerned, it's fine to work with others as long as needs are served, and when they no longer are, it's acceptable to move on. You should strive to make these interactions as realistic as possible. Everyone has an ulterior motive or something to gain. The world of vampires is less than kind to the altruistic soul.

Pay particularly close attention to inter-clan and primogen politics. The interrelations of a Camarilla-controlled city can be quite complex. Determine which clans support the current prince and primogen, and which clans are allied and opposed. A web diagram showing these relationships is useful, both to you and your players (an example of such a diagram is provided later in this book).

One phenomenon of intrigue that originated with the elders is the existence of sects and organizations. The largest of these are the Camarilla and Sabbat. These organizations claim to support two violently opposed policies on the way vampires should act towards the rest of the world. Another theory claims that these factions exist for the benefit of the ancient Inconnu. By using these factions, it's argued, the Inconnu present a unified front against their foes, or will use such organizations for cover when the trumpets of Gehenna sound.

The characters' place in the scheme of Kindred politics requires careful consideration on your part. What sort of influence do you want characters to have on the evolution of your chronicle? Consider the role they play. Do they shake the foundations of the Camarilla or are they a footnote in Kindred history? Are the characters saviors, destroyers or nothing at all?

To start, determine who sired the characters and why. They may have been created by a single vampire, or by several different vampires. The Embrace is the characters' birth into the World of Darkness and, like mortal birth, has a great deal of influence on who characters follow (just as mortal children usually follow their parents). Perhaps the characters' creation was an accident or embarrassment to their sire(s). Perhaps the sire has decided to kill, ignore or chase off his unwanted childer. If the characters were intentionally created, what plans does their sire have for them? Do the sire's enemies know about his childer? Do enemies try to use the new Kindred against the sire?

Depending on the motivation players have chosen, decide where the characters stand in the chronicle. Who knows them, who do they know and just how did they meet? Have they already made allies or enemies of any of the city's personalities or coteries? Do they have any allies or enemies outside their coterie? If so, how do these relationships influence the characters' relationships with their peers? Deciding where characters stand in the chronicle is important because dropping characters cold, so to speak, into a setting only serves to alienate them. Early connections serve to draw characters into the web of intrigue you have woven.

Coteries

A coterie is a group of characters with enough shared motivation and background to work together toward a common goal. There is usually one character who is the leader (such as an elder among her progeny, retainers and ghouls), though this is not always the case.

In games of over 15 participants, dividing players into different coteries is essential. Even if you have a small group of players, it can be very helpful to design your city in terms of coteries. Coteries divide players' characters and Narrator characters, and facilitate adding more players at another time; new players can join an existing group or form their own. Several coteries working together and against each other also establishes immediate layers of intrigue and politics. When you design your chronicle you can treat each coterie as a separate unit.

Though members of coteries are often tightly bound to one another, it's always fun to plant the seeds of dissent among them. Two characters can vie for leadership positions or they can simply hate one another; a character can be looking for a way out of the coterie or a character can be a spy. Some examples of coteries include:

• **Anarchs** — Seeking only survival, at least at first, these Kindred are banded together for mutual protection.

• **Ancillæ** — These Kindred band together to gain power and status in the regimented caste system of Kindred society.

• **Primogen** — Those that help rule the city must work together to ensure that their rule goes unquestioned.

• **Prince** — The prince and his retainers are the lords of the city... or so they think. They also enforce the Traditions and keep the anarchs in line.

• **Sabbat** — A Sabbat pack is very close-knit. They sneak into the city to scout and spy on the Camarilla, sometimes posing as anarchs.

• **Inconnu** — These ancient vampires seek nothing more than continued survival. However, with Diabolists seeking their rich vitæ, survival is often difficult.

• **Clans** — Members of the same clan can band together. This can be for protection or to gain an advantage over rival clans.

Look at the above chart as an example on how you can illustrate the character relationships of a coterie. When running your first story, use this type of chart to plan out the characters' attitudes toward each other. These sentiments should be translated to and illustrated on players' briefing sheets. Later, when your chronicle is in full swing, you can use this chart to keep track of inter-character relationships as they change and develop.

You can also use a similar chart to map out the interrelationships of all Kindred in the city. You can create a massive wall chart with every character on it, or simply treat each coterie as a character and demonstrate how they interact.

Place each character or coterie's name in one of the open shapes. Along the arrows between each shape write down a word or two that best describes the way the characters or coteries feel about each other. Use simple words such as Trust, Tolerance, Love, Hate, Respect and Blood Bond.

Intrigue

Intrigue is a vital ingredient of your chronicle. For people to play out intrigue, they need to be drawn into it. Power is often a lure. This power needs to be immediate and real. It needs to be visible and obtainable. It needs to be given out only occasionally to inspire characters to pursue it, but not so often that opportunities are passed on.

Dark secrets can help inspire intrigue, but this reason alone is not enough. Props and quests are also good. Rewards, of course, need to be given regularly (money, possessions and, occasionally, magic). In the end, the chance to seize power is the true lure into intrigue.

Ambition

Many characters eventually want to assume positions of power in the city. In some games, this is just another aspect of the self-generating plots players contrive on their own. In other games, you may plan the characters' search for power from the beginning. In either case, you need to learn what long-term goals your players want to accomplish in the chronicle. You can then tailor an occasional session to these goals, but don't give the players everything they want. Some may covet powerful positions in the Camarilla, such as clan elder, primogen or perhaps even princehood. Others may seek the ever-elusive state of Golconda or answers to the nature and origin of the Kindred. Both goals are power in one form or another, both over others and over one's self.

More than a few players don't know or admit what they want in the long-term, or may not desire power. Don't worry, they'll set their sights on something in time, especially if tempted by the likes of elders and the Sabbat. Practice stringing players along. Keep a carrot dangling before them. After all, you've got to offer something to keep characters coming back for more.

LODIN'S BROODS

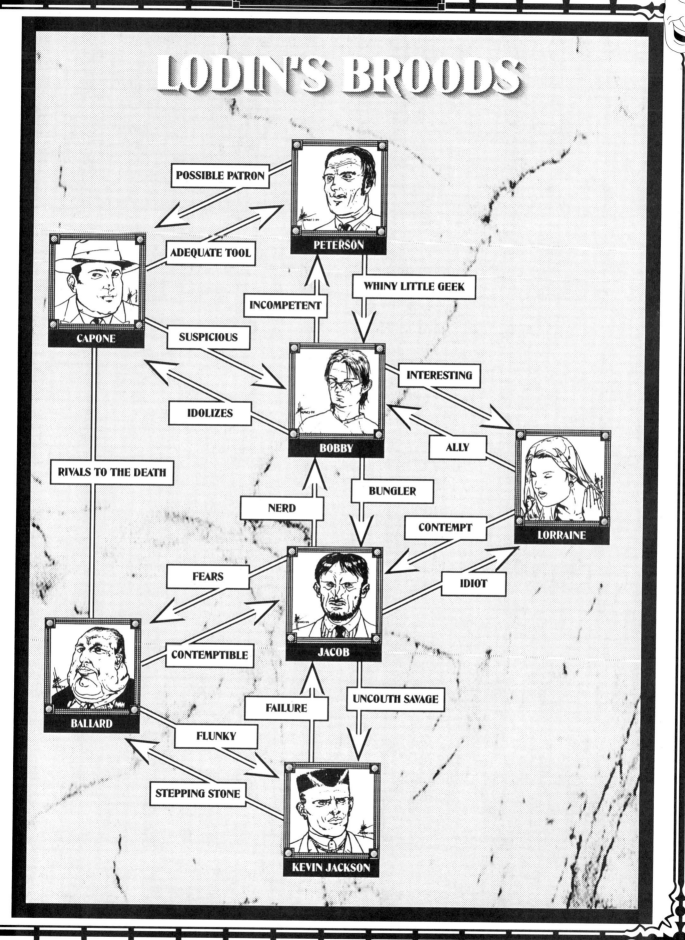

POSSIBLE PATRON

ADEQUATE TOOL

PETERSON

WHINY LITTLE GEEK

INCOMPETENT

CAPONE

SUSPICIOUS

INTERESTING

IDOLIZES

BOBBY

ALLY

RIVALS TO THE DEATH

NERD

BUNGLER

CONTEMPT

LORRAINE

FEARS

IDIOT

CONTEMPTIBLE

JACOB

BALLARD

FAILURE

UNCOUTH SAVAGE

FLUNKY

STEPPING STONE

KEVIN JACKSON

The Price of Power

"You know your place in the sky,
you hold your course
And your aim
And each in your season
Returns and returns
And is always the same.
And if you fall
As Lucifer fell:
You Fall
In flame."
— Javert, "Les Miserables"

In most chronicles, it's likely that one or more characters are in a position of power. Indeed, some might be elders. If this is the case, the players need to know exactly what their responsibilities and advantages are. In general, any players in the role of elder should be experienced enough to assist you as a Narrator. As elder characters can have tremendous impact on lesser characters and the story as a whole, players should know what the ramifications of their actions are and must take them into consideration. Only experience in play develops this insight. The following section lists the various positions elders can hold, and discusses the advantages and responsibilities of those roles.

Prince

"Once there was a man who decided he knew everything
Once there was a book he threw in my face
Once there was an angry mob that marched
Up and down the street
Don't ya know they all called my name
What do they want from me?"
— Oingo Boingo, "Fill the Void"

The prince is not usually a true dictator, although in some instances can be. In general, the prince is the one who maintains order in the city. The influence of Kindred in a city can usually be gagged by the power of the city's prince. If the prince of a city is very strong, it stands to reason that elders of the city are powerful as well— a prince is rarely more powerful than her supporters. Generally, there is a balance of power between a prince and the elders. The prince should be powerful enough to maintain control of the city, while the elders, if joined together, should have the power to remove her should she get out of line.

The prince's biggest obligation is maintaining the Traditions, particularly the Masquerade. In terms of privileges, the prince sets the limit on the number of Kindred that may exist in the city, extends feeding privileges and extends the right to sire progeny. The prince is also the final arbitrator in any dispute between Kindred. Here's a precise list of the prince's powers:

- **Right to Progeny** — The prince is the only one who may sire progeny. No others have this right unless the prince grants it to them.

- **Mastery over Domain** — The prince's word is law over any Kindred who enters her domain. Traditionally, newcomers must present themselves to the prince. Failure to do so is invites severe punishment.

- **Freedom to Feed** — The prince may limit feeding (in the interests of protecting the Masquerade) if she desires. These limitations usually control when and where the Kindred of the city may feed. Those who disobey may be punished for breaking the Masquerade. The prince, of course, faces no such restrictions.

- **Power over Enemies** — The prince has the power to call a Blood Hunt—a sanctioned persecution. This costs the prince two temporary Status Traits, but will cause the subject to lose half of her Status within the city. She may also dole out punishments to those who defy the Traditions.

Even with the great privileges the prince possesses, she must still be careful how she applies her power. Her power stems primarily from her supporters, and if they revolt, the prince is powerless. It is therefore in the prince's best interests to ensure the contentment of her supporters, especially the powerful or ones with broad influence. Ensuring contentment does not necessarily mean losing power, though. The prince must be a consummate manipulator, constantly playing one faction of elders against another. Even the anarchs must be kept content to some degree, for a full anarch revolt can spell doom for even the most powerful prince.

Should you need to cast someone in the role of prince, give careful consideration to the individual you assign the role. It should be a person who can handle a great deal of responsibility, and someone you can trust to help guide the story.

Primogen

The primogen of a city is a group of elders who "advise" the prince. Generally, the eldest members of each of the seven clans in a given city has a seat on the primogen, though in many cases, members of each clan nominate a candidate who is then approved by the current primogen. Collectively, these Kindred are considered the most powerful vampires in the city. It is even possible that an individual member may be more powerful than the prince, but is not inclined to that position for whatever reasons. The primogen usually act as city clan leaders, organizing clan meetings and affairs.

As with the prince, primogen roles should be assigned with care, unless, of course, all the players are primogen for the purpose of the story. Any player who is assigned a primogen character should be experienced enough to act as a Narrator. Those on the primogen are generally granted special privileges by the prince. In addition, there are several advantages that naturally come with the position:

• **Choice of Domain** — The primogen of the city are usually given first choice of hunting grounds. This is, of course, subject to the prince's approval. Any disputes over domain are arbitrated by the prince.

• **Grants of Influence** — Primogen are not only allowed to gather as much influence as they can, but may actually be granted it by the prince or by those seeking favors.

• **Clan Influence** — A member of the primogen who represents his clan generally wields a great deal of power in that clan. He is often considered clan leader in that city.

• **The Prince's Ear** — Those on the primogen have the opportunity to directly influence the prince. Many Kindred use this advantage to further their own objectives while feigning to further other goals.

Justicar

Justicars are the only Kindred with true authority over all of the Camarilla, princes included. Justicars have supreme power to make judgments involving transgressions against the Traditions. There are no official guidelines concerning punishment; it's at the Justicar's discretion, and their decisions are often harsh. A Justicar is supposed to hold a Conclave to pass judgment, but over time, Justicars grow in power. Some no longer feel the need to hold councils, meting out justice as desired.

The judgment of a Justicar may only be challenged by another Justicar. A Conclave is then called, wherein the Justicars come together to resolve the dispute. Judgment is usually put to a vote before the Assembly.

As with the prince and primogen, you must be extremely careful when assigning a Justicar as a character. A Justicar wields an incredible amount of power. You must be cautious lest the player abuse his power. Generally, a Justicar is best assigned as a Narrator character.

Justicars face many challenges, so are granted much in the way of privileges:

• **Judgment** — A Justicar is considered the ultimate authority in matters concerning breaches of the Traditions. Punishment is determined solely by the Justicar.

• **Summon Conclave** — All Justicars have the right to call a Conclave whenever they wish. Conclaves may be called to pass judgment on one who has broken a tradition or to solve some other problem, such as a prince accused of abusing her power.

• **Right to Progeny** — A Justicar may create a number of progeny deemed reasonable to serve him as Archons for the duration of his term.

• **Freedom of Movement** — Justicars are not restricted in where they may travel. No prince may ban or banish a Justicar from her city, nor must the Justicar present himself to the prince upon arrival in her city.

Archon

A Justicar often has a coterie of vampires, often his progeny, who enforce his will and report breaches of the Traditions. These assistants are called Archons. Archons are always willingly Blood Bound to their Justicar, though they need not be from his clan. Archons do not wield as much power as a Justicar, but are widely respected for the connections they have.

Archons can make very useful Narrator characters and can keep players in line when they are in danger of breaching the Masquerade. In fact, if Kindred in a city are notorious for defying the Traditions, a busy Justicar might assign an Archon to reside permanently in the city as a reminder of the Justicar's power.

Archons essentially have the same power as other elders (below), but have more Status; their word is taken before any other elder's, and even the prince is wise to heed an Archon (though she still has the power to challenge an Archon).

Elder

There comes a time in a vampire's existence when there are few who are more powerful than he. It's at that point that a vampire is considered an elder. Even once they have attained physical power, many elders seek social power in the form of status (a social dominance that the game term, Status, can reflect), perhaps becoming prince or Justicar. Others, however, are content to use their status to do what they will, remaining free from the responsibilities that come with positions of authority. This status and freedom confers certain privileges to elders. Here are some sample elder privileges:

• **Authority** — Greater status gives an elder authority over those of lesser status. This is even more so within one's own clan.

• **Positions of Power** — Status gives one the opportunity to attain positions of power, such as the primogen or even princehood.

• **Progeny** — Those of great status are more likely to be successful in petitioning the prince to sire progeny.

• **Deference** — Neonates and ancillæ are expected to defer to an elder in any matter, whether it involves choosing the best table at a restaurant or selecting a prime vessel.

There is growing unrest among "younger" Kindred who feel that status among vampires is awarded based on age, not proof of worthiness. Most would change their minds, however, when directly confronted by "old" elders.

Chronicle Dynamics

The key to a successful chronicle is a constant and uninterrupted flow of action. In the real world, events never stop occurring, and everyone, in one way or another, gets dragged into life's chaos. Your chronicle should have the same power. All characters should be drawn into the events around them. Every character should be doing something. Those in conflict may bide their time and pause to marshal their forces, but the tension never recedes. The illusion of tension and chaos can be accomplished by artfully deploying a few tricks, like these:

• **Overlapping** — Stories have no clear cut beginning or end, but flow into each other. If your group is large enough, two or more stories can run simultaneously.

• **Transitions** — Cues to new stories should be distributed in the process of normal play. Don't make a grand affair when you begin a new story. Each story involves what seems to be the next logical course of action for characters. It's also a good idea to hint at several different stories at once. This way, characters are allowed as great a measure of free will as possible.

• **Nuances** — Not every interaction between Narrators and characters has to relate directly to the story. Characters can meet people or become involved in events that are simply part of everyday life. Included in this vein are red herrings, which purposefully distract characters from truly significant events. Red herrings are fun because you can reintroduce them later, sometimes as legitimate story concerns.

• **Mystery Figures** — This is a catch-all for recurring figures from the past. They can be archenemies, haunting spirits or mysterious benefactors. These friends or foes display a remarkable ability to survive destruction, slip away at the last moment or simply appear at the most unexpected of times and places. Don't overuse this device, however, for it can ruin your chronicle's credibility.

• **Crossovers** — Another advantage to having more than one story in progress at the same time is that they can intersect with each other. This tactic really promotes interaction when one or both groups, pursuing separate goals, discover something that can benefit the other.

• **Multiple Goals** — Each character has a separate motive which, if made known, can lead to conflict as characters argue over what course to take. Perhaps characters have discovered a valuable mystical artifact. If they've received many offers for it, who, if anyone, do they turn it over to? In Greek mythology, Paris got into a lot of trouble with a golden apple when put into a similar position. Chances are the characters will get in trouble too.

• **Unfinished Business** — Whoever said a story has to be played to completion the first time around? After abandoning a goal, or believing their goal achieved when it really is not, characters can return to that goal in a later story. Maybe they learn the vampire they destroyed was not actually the murderer the characters thought he was. Who was the real killer, and how do the characters atone for their grievous error?

Trouble in all Shapes and Sizes

There are dozens of things in a story that can go wrong. This is particularly true of a chronicle. With the added level of complexity that comes with a chronicle, problems with continuity, advancement, numerous players, constant change and background plots are inevitable. A few of the more common chronicle problems, and how to deal with them, are detailed below:

• **Problem Players** — This problem is probably one of the most delicate and potentially disastrous you can face. For one reason or another, one or more players are disrupting the story and ruining everyone's good time. This can be the result of many things: cheating, rule quotation ("rules lawyering"), personal vendettas or improper behavior.

Once you detect a problem, your first action should be to approach the players privately and explain what they are doing and why you don't like it. At that point, most people attempt to change their ways... and that's that. Unfortunately, some are prone to backsliding or just don't take the problem seriously, disregarding your warning. The next step to consider is some sort of penalty. Temporary suspension from the chronicle is usually effective. If players continue to make trouble, you may have to perform the distasteful task of barring them entirely from your chronicle.

• **Favoritism** — There is often a tendency to give friends special treatment. Be vigilant to this habit in all those who run and play the game, including yourself. If the problem does arise, try to remember that this is just a form of entertainment; no one can reasonably hold you responsible for a character's loss. If the problem continues, try to isolate problem individuals from encounters where favoritism might occur. As a final option, remove the offender from any position in which she can dispense favors.

• **Grudge** — In this situation an individual is treated unfairly for some reason that is not related to her character's nature or actions. Such is often the case with players who are not fond of each other in the real world. Handle it in a manner similar to favoritism problems.

• **Stagnation** — Even the most imaginative Storyteller occasionally runs out of ideas. Perhaps you're running the game too often to give yourself time to create new and original stories. If this is the case, consider spacing sessions further apart to provide yourself more planning time. Another solution is to take on more Storytellers or Narrators to give the chronicle a greater creative base to draw on. A plot coordination council of some sort is almost essential to running large-scale chronicles.

• **Logistics** — Problems with supplies and locations are bound to arise. If this is the case, be sure to communicate with everybody involved in the game. Players are often able to help procure a setting, props, incidental supplies and all manner of other needs.

• **Getting the News Out** — Sometimes you just don't have enough people to play the type of chronicle you've planned. This is more often a case of poor advertising than genuine lack of bodies. Consider posting notices on electronic bulletin boards or your local university network, in game and hobby stores, at conventions, at gaming organizations, with theatre or drama groups, on college campuses and anywhere else you think imaginative people with a taste for the original might frequent.

Maintenance and Record Keeping

It's a simple fact that the longer a chronicle runs, the more complex it becomes. The increased size of some chronicles only amplifies this fact. Developing a method and the habit of keeping records is essential.

The easiest part of the chronicle to keep records on is characters' statistics. Having a master copy of each character card has several advantages. Someone is bound to lose his character card and may need a replacement. Without a good memory or a master copy, this can pose a problem, especially with advanced characters. Storyteller records of characters

also discourage unscrupulous players from altering their characters. Furthermore, you can make use of character information when designing new stories. And it's a good idea to update your master copies after each story, given changes arising from experience, rewards and penalties.

A journal of events from each session proves equally invaluable, helping you understand changes the chronicle undergoes. You can then apply these changes to new stories. Ideally, you, the Narrators and players should all file some sort of informal report after each story. Records from everyone can keep you appraised of all events and let you in on players' individual intentions. To encourage players to provide this information accurately, consider making reports mandatory or award experience only after you receive them. Make it clear that these reports are confidential and will not be used to "screw players over."

Advancement and Balance

The greatest reward for some players is the sheer joy of playing. However, many players prefer to see their characters improve in status and power. Both needs must be satisfied.

Players who enjoy the story for its own sake are easy to please. In fact, they often please themselves by pursuing the goals their characters desire, which are often interpreted by the players themselves.

Pleasing accomplishment seekers is a little more difficult. Allow characters chances to improve their station in the chronicle, if it's within the scope of things. When characters make achievements, their players are happy. However, to keep players happy without their characters achieving massive power, be prepared to take characters down a peg or two, or allow other characters to do so for you. Besides creating revenge motives, such attacks fire players' desire to achieve more.

Experience points, which players spend to improve their characters, are one form of reward, but there are others that are just as satisfying. Gaining the favor and support of other Kindred can be more rewarding than any Discipline. Furthermore, there are numerous positions of power that experience points can't buy, but ambition and tenacity can.

Even in well-planned chronicles, players may reach a point where they are bored and discontented with their place in the story. A player in this position actually has a couple of options. Starting a new character, only playing the old one from time to time, helps players see if they still have what it takes to see a character survive. As a Storyteller, make sure the player doesn't use this option to accumulate power for both his characters. Bringing in an old character's "relative" and allowing interaction between the siblings can mean trouble as they "work together." The easiest way to discourage this is to deny any direct ties between old and new characters. Another option to is to take the "advanced" character as a Narrator or Storyteller character. The character's experience with your chronicle and game as a whole can be used as a resource by lesser characters (i.e., other characters seek help from the experienced character), and the older character can be the means for future stories.

Advancing in the Story

Characters grow stronger and more powerful in game terms by acquiring more Traits and Disciplines. However, **The Masquerade** is about storytelling, not crunching numbers (or hoarding Traits). Thus, you probably want to account for characters' improvements in terms of the story. After all, a character just doesn't walk down the street and acquire a new Discipline just because his experience points were cashed in. The new Discipline should be accounted for in the story. Is the character taught the power by another Kindred? Does the character reach a transitional point in unlife which leads to the development of new powers? Do recently aroused instincts inspire new powers? In the end, it's up to the players, but you should encourage them to account for their characters' changes and improvements in the story.

End Notes

As a Storyteller or Narrator, you have accepted a sizable responsibility and workload. You're to be applauded. Without people like you, games like this one would not be possible. Congratulations and gratitude are in order. Hopefully, the sight of players enjoying themselves is reward for your effort. But remember, for many new players, you are the first impression they have, not only of **The Masquerade**, but of live storytelling in general. Their opinions about this and similar forms of entertainment are determined by you. Try not to let your power go to your head. You'll make mistakes— be big enough to admit them. You'll need help—don't be too proud to accept it. Following your example, players will also strive to make the game a fun one.

Chapter Ten: Adjudication

"Suave… He's just so… suave."
— Dennis Hopper, "Blue Velvet"

As a Storyteller and Narrator, one of your most difficult tasks is adjudicating the rules. When two players have a dispute, you're the one responsible for settling it. In order to do this well, you need to intuitively understand how the challenge system works.

Challenges

When two players meet in the course of a story, they may become involved in some sort of conflict that cannot be settled through roleplaying. Players often have specific goals for their characters, and rather than roleplaying a situation that they know would be detrimental to their goals, they naturally want to offer resistance so that they can continue following their motives. This kind of situation requires a method by which to determine the outcome. When all other interaction comes to an end and a dominant figure cannot be determined, a challenge is declared.

A challenge can be called to resolve almost any confrontation, but this should be a last resort. If extraordinary vampire powers are put to use, a challenge may not occur: the target sometimes relents before the superior power presented before him. A challenge only occurs if the target resists. A challenge may also be called when someone wants to find out a particular bit of information or wants to exact his will over another's. As with extraordinary powers, scenes involving information gathering, seduction or just plain intimidation should be acted out before going to the extreme of a challenge.

There are many ways to avoid a challenge. Straight-up acting offers people the chance to practice their "poker face" while telling lies and persuading opponents to reconsider their actions. The mere comment "you really don't want to do that" can strike terror in the hearts of many, such as when a Malkavian says it and laughs heartily. However, there comes a time when even bluffing doesn't work and players must resolve their conflicts through rules.

Appropriate Traits

Challenges do not usually require your involvement as a Storyteller or Narrator. This is especially true when players are experienced. However, there is some room for interpretation in the challenge rules. If two players get particularly stubborn, they may need your assistance.

For instance, players can usually only bid Traits that sensibly apply to a situation. The basic rule is that a challenge must use either Physical, Social or Mental Traits. Only Traits from the correct category can be used in the challenge. Even then, not all Traits in a category are valid. Brawny is useful when punching someone, but it's hard to justify how it can help when wielding a gun. For quickness of play, you can decree that all Traits of the same category apply, but for more realistic play, such as with experienced players, you can decree that only truly applicable Traits apply (applicable Traits are usually determined by the contestants of a challenge).

To toss another wrench into the works, there are some circumstances where traits of different Attribute categories may be appropriate. Say, for example, that two players are debating. Their applicable Social *and* Mental Traits might apply. Again, both parties must agree which Traits apply.

Intervention

It's very common for players to have questions about the rules. Unfortunately, it's almost as common for them to argue about the rules. This is where you come in. We don't encourage players to call for a Narrator, because no character interaction takes place when players step out of character. It's best if players can work out their problems in the context of the story. It's even better if a Narrator can resolve their problem while playing a character herself.

If you or your Narrators are busy, you can encourage players to ask their peers to make rule judgments. Allow them to call another player to serve as mediator in their challenge. Of course, all players must remain in character. It's best to call upon the mediation services of an experienced player. In terms of the story, have players call upon another player who has a character of earlier generation. This elder figure has authority over the two characters, and his player is probably familiar with the game (as previously suggested, it's best to assign elder roles to experienced players). If players repeatedly call upon the mediation services of an elder, the characters may eventually accrue a debt to the elder— he can demand prestation for helping— which should encourage players to resolve any future rule disputes themselves.

Multi-Player Challenges

When three or more players decide to enter a challenge, they will usually need the assistance of a Narrator. These large challenges can get rather confusing and can be drawn out by player arguments and indecisiveness. Your job is to remain level-headed and to work the challenge out as quickly as possible.

The first thing you need to do is decide who is challenging whom. This is usually obvious, but when it's not, you need a quick way to work things out. Simply have everyone involved count to three at the same time. On three, each player points at the individual he is challenging.

The first challenge that must be resolved involves the person who has the most people pointing at him. Determine what the appropriate category of Traits would be— Physical, Social or Mental. Each player pointing at the defender must bid one appropriate Trait. This group must also choose a leader. The defender must then bid as many Traits as there are people opposing him. If he does not have enough Traits to do so, he automatically loses the challenge. If he does have enough Traits, a test is performed between the defender and the chosen leader of the attackers. The rest of the challenge continues as normal, although any comparison of Traits or overbidding may only be done by the group leader.

If the defender wins the test, he is unharmed, but he can choose to affect one member of the attacking group. Usually, as in the case of a combat, this would mean inflicting one wound. Additionally, all Traits bid by the attackers are lost. If the attackers win, they may inflict one wound, and the defender loses all the Traits he had risked.

After the first challenge is concluded, go on to the next one. Continue the process until each character who has declared an action has been the target of a challenge or has donated Traits.

A few clarifications should be made regarding bystanders. People directly involved in a group action (those who point at a group target) who are not the lead challenger do not *have* to donate a Trait to the lead challenger or the target. The player may leave the group action and get involved somewhere else. However, the player can only attempt to get involved in one other action, or does nothing while other characters act around him. So, if a player moves from one group action to another, and is not the lead challenger there either, he may not move on again. He must donate a Trait to someone in the new group action or do nothing at all.

If the roaming player is confronted by someone else outside any group actions, he can be challenged directly.

Acting Out Combat

One of the most difficult questions to answer is what to do about the outcome of combat. Typically, players react in a manner appropriate to the outcome of each combat challenge. For example, if a character is hurt by another, the player of the target may choose to yell out in pain after the challenge. This probably attracts the attention of the victim's comrades. Then another action may be taken by the victim to counterattack. A good rule of thumb is to allow one verbal and one physical reaction to the outcome of each combat challenge. Each combatant, after a combat challenge is resolved, can call out once and decide on another single course of action. The next course of action for both is often determined by one character's plan to continue attacking. The thing to remember is that combat attracts unwanted attention. Calling out and counterattacking, thereby using both actions to call attention to the struggle, is often a defender's best defense.

Progress in Time

In **The Masquerade**, time is assumed to pass in the game as it does on the clock. Time is time, and it doesn't stop or fast-forward on command. With a few minor exceptions for powers such as Celerity, time marches ever onward. However, there are a few rules about time that are worth noting.

The "three second" rule is a combat rule that states that a person is considered surprised if she does not react to a Physical Challenge within three seconds. Surprised people are at the mercy of their attackers. Chapter Four explains the rules for surprise in detail.

Rules of time usually involve powers such as Thaumaturgy, Celerity, Rapidity and Fleetness. Such powers often have time limits measured by actual watches or clocks. If a character spends 15 minutes performing a Thaumaturgic ritual, the player must spend 15 minutes undisturbed in one place. For powers that work with seconds, players must count the seconds aloud. This is a signal that other players must remain frozen (as in the case of Celerity and related powers)

As a Storyteller or Narrator, you always have the right to call for a time-out, but you should rarely do so. A time-out stops all activity among those players who can hear you, giving you time to resolve a particularly sticky situation. Time-outs, however, ruin the flow of the story. It is far better to take contestants into a side room and talk to them there rather than stop everyone else from roleplaying.

Advice on How to Judge

Typically, there is no right or wrong way to judge Mind's Eye confrontations. Using your head and thinking logically enables you to answer most questions as they arise. Players can actually be good at resolving conflicts among themselves.

The only thing you should really be concerned with is keeping the storyline interesting so that players aren't tempted to kill other characters just for the thrill of it. Nonetheless, there are situations you may encounter that may try your patience. Persevere through it all and you will be rewarded with a good time for everyone.

Breaking the Rules

At some point during the game, you may wish to break the rules to keep the story rolling. This is perfectly acceptable, as long as you don't do it all the time. Doing so makes players dependent on you. Try to resolve problems based on the logic of the story, particularly if the "official" rules call for a resolution that doesn't exactly make sense in the context of the story. Don't be afraid to break the rules. As long as the game is fun, players probably don't care that you've disregarded the letter of the law. The spirit of the game is more important.

Game Tools

Although **The Masquerade** is primarily about storytelling and roleplaying, there are elements of stories that must be addressed in terms of rules. For instance, how do you handle magical items or animals in the game? This section offers details and insights into how to manage events, characters and items in terms of rules. If you partake of several different games of The Masquerade, acting as player, Storyteller and Narrator, try to keep your knowledge of the following information to yourself. Announcing the specific Traits of an animal only ruins everyone else's fun. And even though you have inside information, try to behave as if you don't when acting as a player; try to make yourself as ignorant as your character.

Artifacts and Inventions

Occasionally, a vampire may create an artifact, an invention, or a magical or scientific device to use in the story. These devices sometimes have strange abilities, and sometimes they have none at all; they're just really old. When you use these items as a focus for your stories, they can figure prominently even if they're never seen. The Maltese Falcon is a good example of this type of item, in that it drives the central theme of the movie, but is hardly ever seen. Everybody wants it, but nobody is sure what it is. Be careful not to use these too often in your stories. Your players may become bogged down in the acquisition of material things.

Use your imagination when making up artifacts and inventions, but be careful that you limit their use. As with weapons, you must not design them to be a crutch for your Cast. Live interaction is the name of the game. Make some of them fairly innocuous, like a gold statuette of Caine, sculpted by a Malkavian in the 13th century. One or two devices could be powerful, with Disciplines all their own, but

may require the blood of an Ancient vampire to work. Let your imagination run free.

If players want to introduce artifacts or inventions, you have to judge their impact on the game. Decide whether the item could become a crutch or interfere with roleplaying. Also decide if the item will unravel your story. If you fear that an item is causing trouble, tone down its capabilities or disallow its use.

The following are some magic items that can be introduced to your games, either as story hooks or tools utilized by characters. Magic items should be represented by cards or props that you create.

The Tortuous Glass

This magical mirror was designed by a particularly sadistic Tremere to torture a few vain Toreadors. The possessor of the mirror must sacrifice a Blood Trait to it each day to fuel its powers. The Trait can be the possessor's or a victim's. (Blood must be poured into a small funnel hidden in the scrollwork at the top of the mirror.)

When the mirror has been fed with blood, it alters the images of vampires who look into it (mortals looking into the mirror appear normal). Vampires can be made to look horrific or cast no reflection at all. The mirror also duplicates all the current Mental Traits that the blood donor has at the time of feeding. If a vampire looking into the mirror fails a Static Mental Challenge against all the Traits invested into the mirror, the vampire gains a Derangement. The Derangement usually involves a response to a horrific appearance (Nosferatu are therefore immune to the effect). The Mental Traits invested in the mirror fade at the next sunrise; they are not lost if the mirror loses a Mental Challenge with an onlooker.

The mirror is virtually unbreakable and has spent years hanging on dungeon walls as a means of torture for vampiric prisoners. Some believe that the legend of vampires casting no reflection may have originated with this item.

No one knows if humans can manipulate the mirror. If they could, it would be a great boon to many vampire hunters.

Toecuffs of Cold Iron

These punitive devices are designed to go on the toes of magic-using creatures. They dampen the magical energy of such creatures by "grounding" them. They are therefore highly effective against Tremere. Many Tremere accused of breaking the Masquerade have been punished this way. Unfortunately, there are few sets left today; few have had the proper rituals spoken over them.

When a Tremere has these properly attached to his toes, he must make a successful Static Mental Challenge against five Traits before even attempting to perform any ritual. If the Mental Challenge fails, all Traits bid are lost for the duration of the story. However, if the Mental Challenge succeeds, the Tremere retains his Traits and may proceed with the intended ritual.

In terms of the game, rubber bands can be wrapped around the player's individual toes, or around all the toes of each foot. The player is then left to enact travel with such a burden. Removing the toecuffs is difficult and requires someone with the Security Ability to even think about trying it. The attempt then requires a successful Static Mental or Physical Challenge, whichever is appropriate to the means used to remove the cuffs. The Storyteller is left to determine the static difficulty of removing the cuffs so that players don't become complacent, expecting the same difficulty each time. If application of the Security Ability to remove the cuffs fails, the Tremere might lose his toes!

Blood Amulet

These magical items were created during some time of strife in the distant past. There are amulets for each clan. An amulet endows the wearer with one basic clan Discipline, and a single Trait that may be applied to any single challenge— Physical, Social or Mental— every night. A vampire must be of the same clan as the amulet for the Discipline and Trait to function. Indeed, if a member of a different clan wears an amulet and tries to activate the amulet's Discipline or its "free" Trait, the wearer automatically suffers one injury and the Discipline or Trait fails to activate. More than one amulet can be worn at the same time (provided amulet and wearer are of the same clan), but if the wearer naturally possesses an amulet's Discipline, the item is of little value. The extra Trait still serves the wearer, though.

To use an amulet's "free" trait, the wearer must present the jewel to the challenge's opponent. However, if an opponent in any other challenge suspects the wearer has an amulet and is gaining power from it, that opponent may present the amulet as a Negative Trait against the wearer. The wearer is penalized a Trait in the current challenge. It's therefore best for an amulet's wearer to keep the item hidden until needed.

The Discipline invested in an amulet can be sensed as soon as the item is put on.

When Worlds Collide

"A man's got to know his limitations."
— Dirty Harry Callahan

In Mind's Eye Theatre, people who work against the players' characters are called antagonists. Sometimes players themselves assume the roles of antagonists, facing off against other players. For the most part, though, antagonists are played by Narrators. Chapter Five of this book details the different hierarchies of vampires, indicating their advantages, responsibilities and motivations. This section details different kinds of opponents in game terms.

Indeed, you should refer to this section if players get bored, or if they think their characters are too tough for most opponents. Paranoia, sleepless days and even outright terror strike characters when you mention enemies like Lupines, Methuselahs or ghosts.

Antediluveans and Methuselahs

Antediluveans and Methuselahs are ancient Kindred of third or fourth generation. They have existed for thousands of years— no one is sure exactly how long. It's said that they wield god-like powers, and a drop of their blood is supposed to grant immense power. It is also said that these ancients only gain nourishment from the blood of other Kindred.

Methuselahs are the more likely of these two ancients to involve themselves in the affairs of lesser Kindred, but they stay out of the spotlight. They use their lessers to wage wars upon each other. Under no circumstances should it be possible for characters to capture or harm a Methuselah, at least not without great effort by at least ten characters. Even then, the task should be extremely difficult.

Antediluveans are the more powerful of the two groups. It's said that they sleep within the earth, awaiting Gehenna (the time of destruction). On this night, they are supposed to rise to drink the blood of lesser Kindred. This is the only blood that sustains them, and after eons in the soil, they will be hungry indeed.

Elders

Elders are very old vampires who do not directly rule the city, but still maintain a great deal of influence over it and its lesser Kindred. Elders typically have 10 primary, eight secondary, and six tertiary Attribute Traits. An Elder also has five to 10 Disciplines (including intermediate and advanced ones). As they are very experienced, elders have a considerable number of Abilities, generally 15 to 20. Elders also have a great deal of Influence over mortal society and have many servants, retainers and even some progeny to draw upon. The number of Attribute traits indicated on the "Generation Table" in Chapter XX is the starting number an elder has by generation. More experienced elders clearly have more, as reflected by the numbers given above.

The Prince

The prince is usually the single most influential and powerful Kindred in the city... at least as far as she knows. The actual power any given prince wields varies from one city to the next, usually depending on the support and ambition of the various elders. The prince's power also depends on the strength of the anarch faction.

A prince can have 15 primary Attribute Traits, 11 secondary Traits, and eight tertiary Traits. A prince usually has 10 to 13 Disciplines, 20 to 25 Abilities and extensive Influence in mortal and Kindred society. Again, Blood and Willpower Traits are a direct reflection of the prince's generation.

Lupines

Lupines, or werewolves, inhabit the countryside surrounding many cities. They are numerous, and on occasion, they venture into cities to hunt their mortal enemies, vampires. Vampires are, Lupines believe, part of a great, corruptive mystical energy they call the Wyrm. The Wyrm is seen as responsible for the entropy that grips our planet, and it is werewolves' sworn duty as defenders of the world to stop it. Perhaps there is some truth to Lupine mythology— maybe within the legend of the Wyrm there is a clue as to the genesis of vampires.

Lupines are fearsome creatures. They usually concentrate on Physical Attribute traits. They cannot have vampiric Disciplines, but are considered to have Fortitude, Celerity, Wolf's Claws and Potence. Typical Lupines have 14 Physical Traits, nine Social Traits and five Mental Traits. Lupines are exceedingly dangerous. More exacting details on Lupines are included in **Mind's Eye Theatre: The Apocalypse**.

Mummies

Mummies have their origins in ancient Egypt. Each one has received the Spell of Life, an ancient Egyptian ritual that renders the recipient immortal. Of all the individuals inhabiting this dark world, mummies are the only ones who experience the continuous cycle of life and death. They are therefore true immortals and are rarely extinguished.

Mummies rarely involve themselves in the affairs of others, although there is a distinct faction among them that works against the Followers of Set. Indeed, their origins can be found in Set's dark history. When a mummy does involve herself in Kindred affairs, it is often for personal reasons. Most mummies are aware of the existence of Kindred and are aware of their various strengths and weaknesses. A mummy's typical role is manipulative rather than confrontational. However, their knowledge of Kindred weaknesses and their centuries-old skills make them deadly adversaries.

Mummies have access to various potions and amulets (many of which can grant them additional traits). A mummy begins with at least eight primary, six secondary and four tertiary Attribute traits. Bear in mind that because of their immortality, it is entirely possible for mummies to have considerably more Traits than the number listed here. Also remember that there are less than 50 mummies believed to be left in the world. Mummies can come from any profession in ancient Egypt and therefore vary widely in Abilities. They have at least eight different Abilities. Some mummies even have magical powers at their disposal.

Humans

Humans present an interesting challenge in **The Masquerade**. They are the one encounter that players have on a constant basis. Characters need humans to feed, and a Narrator should be able to make up human characters on the spot.

Humans normally have the same number of Attribute Traits as 13th generation vampires. They also have the same number of Abilities. They may not learn vampiric Disciplines, though; human beings are not of the supernatural, so they usually have no supernatural powers.

There is one power that humans may have, however— Faith. Faith is found only in those with an extreme conviction in a Higher Being. Faith acts as a powerful repellent to vampires. If a human character presents his Faith (in a religious display in which some religious symbol is presented), vampires present must make a Mental Challenge against the human to remain in his presence. The action is resolved as a multi-player encounter if there is more than one vampire present, the vampire must win the challenge to remain present. Otherwise, she will flee the human's presence and cannot confront him again for a full two hours. Even then, the vampire must win another Mental Challenge. Expenditure of a Willpower Trait allows a vampire to remain in the Faithful's presence, but if the human continues to demonstrate his Faith, successive Willpower Traits must be spent to remain.

If the human with Faith loses a Mental Challenge to keep vampires away, he loses the Mental Traits bid (as a reflection of his spiritual exhaustion). The power of Faith itself is not lost; it is merely rendered ineffective once all Mental Traits are lost.

Faith is a power left to the Storyteller or Narrator to assign. Remember, very few humans have Faith, so grant this one sparingly.

Ghouls

Ghouls are the human servants of Kindred. They are created by allowing a mortal to drink of Kindred blood. After drinking vampire blood, a human temporarily ceases aging and acquires some of the abilities of vampires. Ghouls make excellent retainers, for once a ghoul drinks his master's blood three times, he is Blood Bound. If more than a month passes without the opportunity to feed, a ghoul becomes mortal once again and the Blood Bond fades (Blood Bond does not have the powerful hold over mortals that it does over vampires). If a ghoul has been sustained past his mortal life span, but is abandoned, he ages very quickly. Many vampires create ghouls as servants to protect them during daylight hours.

Ghouls can be enacted by players or Narrators. They make intriguing characters for players. Granted, ghouls do not have the sheer power of vampires, but do have certain advantages. For instance, they can move about freely in sunlight and do not need blood to sustain themselves.

Many interesting subplots, or even main plots, can be woven around ghoul characters. Perhaps a vampire promises that the ghoul who serves her best will be Embraced after completing a certain task. This can make for a rivalry between two or more ghouls, as each strives to best serve the mistress. Maybe a ghoul is dissatisfied with his master and seeks a new one, or his master has met Final Death and the ghoul must find a new one before the month is up.

As Narrator characters, ghouls can be used as low-level messengers of powerful individuals. Or, if the setting is the dwelling of a powerful Kindred, such as the prince, Narrators can play the parts of ghouls in the service of that vampire. Such roles allow Narrators to mingle without seeming out of place. They can step out of character only when needed to settle a rule dispute. Such characters can also be used to help advance the plot, spreading rumors and other tidbits of information to visiting Kindred.

As a human, a ghoul has the same number of Attribute Traits and Abilities as a 13th generation vampire. All ghouls begin with the vampiric Discipline of Potence, and some have even come to learn a few other Disciplines that their Regnants possess. Most Ghouls have one Blood Trait, although some have more. A very few exceptional ghouls may have one Willpower Trait.

Wraiths

Wraiths are restless souls who haunt the living. For one reason or another, a wraith has been kept from its final rest and roams the mortal realm. Wraiths can be of any disposition: Benevolent, vindictive, malicious— regardless of the motivations and emotions that sustain them, they are very passionate creatures. They can be summoned and commanded to perform a task or can be "indigenous" to a locale. Wraiths have incredible sensory abilities and are normally invisible to all but the spirit sensitive and those with Auspex. Wraiths make excellent spies.

A typical motive for a Wraith is revenge. This is, however, by no means a wraith's only plot option. A wraith is rarely free to simply roam around. If one is not summoned, it is probably tied to a certain location, event or person. Sometimes wraiths are bound to a certain goal or purpose.

Mages

Mages are practitioners of arcane lore. They are humans of great power, and most Kindred avoid them whenever possible. However, a few Kindred have been known to ally with mages, occasionally forming friendships. Some mages hate the Tremere with a vengeance, branding them traitors and extinguishing them whenever their paths cross. Mages practice their own form of the masquerade, keeping out of sight of mortals and most Kindred.

Mages can add a new depth to a story, but should generally be used only as Narrator characters. A mage can be a useful contact should a character seek an item of mystical nature. It is possible that a mage could request a service of some sort in exchange for an item. Such contact with mages can lead to a whole series of new stories. A mage could even be a Kindred's patron, offering rituals or enchanted objects in exchange for things the vampire can attain, like the blood of an elder vampire or werewolf teeth.

Mage characters have several Attribute Traits and Abilities. Mental Traits are primary. They also have access to forms of magic not available to vampires, in addition to Thaumaturgy. A mage often has one or more Willpower Traits; one must be strong-willed to wield magic.

Faeries

Sometimes the Garou encounter beings that have never been fully explained. A variety of beings draw upon the power of magic to cross into this plane of existence from a realm called "Arcadia." Perhaps they are attracted to magic and magical places like moths to a flame. For the purposes of Mind's Eye Theater, we shall refer to them as faeries.

Faeries exist in a magical realm. Arcadia, the Otherworld, Hy-Brasil, Tir-na'nogth— regardless of the name used for this realm, it is the place where the fey are all-powerful. Their forays into this world are but accidental intrusions. It is usually on days of special magical import, such as Samhain— the day that gates between the worlds are weakened— that faeries enter the mortal world. Some Garou, particularly the Fianna, have a sort of kinship with the fey, and may even at times call on faeries or the kin of the faeries for aid. As with all dealings with faeries, there is always a price.

Faeries prefer to not be seen in our world. They use a variety of natural Obfuscation powers. Faeries generally have high intelligence (Mental Traits are primary). Faeries also have their own form of magic, which no Kindred or werewolf has ever learned. Few things are known to harm faeries, but there is legend that cold iron may drive them back to their own realm. Knowledge of faeries is limited to legend, however. The secrets of their world remain to be seen.

Sabbat

The Sabbat is the enemy sect of the Camarilla. They believe the Camarilla is just a pawn of the Antediluvians, who will consume the blood of all childer upon their awakening at the time of Gehenna. The Sabbat have made it their primary goal to destroy the Camarilla. They accomplish this by any means possible.

The Sabbat are very different from the vampires of the Camarilla in that they no longer see themselves as human in any way. They think it foolish to attempt to hold onto humanity, instead searching for a higher morality. Many of the Camarilla perceive Sabbat ways as evil, for the Sabbat view mortals as lesser beasts to be used as the vampires' needs require.

The most probable option for a Sabbat character in a story is that of a spy observing the Camarilla. What this spy is attempting is dictated by your story. In an ongoing chronicle, a spy might not reveal herself until after several stories have been told, if even then. Generally, a Sabbat spy's goals are to learn of weaknesses within the hierarchy of the Camarilla. A spy might even sabotage the plans of elders whenever possible and create friction among the clans, leaving the city open for a Sabbat takeover.

As a Narrator character, a member of the Sabbat can seek to subvert one or more of the characters, offering them bribes or gifts. Such offerings might be particularly tempting to a character who has been unwillingly Blood Bound, as the Sabbat supposedly possess a ritual for breaking the Bond. Beware, though, for once a character joins the Sabbat, he is theirs forever.

It's also possible that you may want to tell an entire story from the Sabbat's perspective. Such a story would have a very different feel to it than the usual Camarilla story. Combat would be emphasized, with a higher risk of character mortality.

Sabbat characters should be made exactly as other vampire characters, though some of the Sabbat clans possess unique Disciplines.

Other Rules

So what now? You've looked over this book and understand the game's systems. What more is there?

There's a lot more, my friend. Limits to the rules are not limits to your imagination. While all the systems described in this game are good guidelines, there is a lot more you can add.

Not every adjective in the English language is listed under Attribute Traits. Any single word that describes a quality can conceivably be used as an adjective in this game. If there is an appropriate word for a situation, use it. As a Storyteller or Narrator, your powers are limitless. The point is to create fun for you and your players.

If you want to create new Disciplines or Abilities, do it. If you want to experiment by creating new rules, do it. Nothing is prohibited; everything is permitted. You may wish to use the techniques of flashback to describe past events more fully to your players. You may wish to set your world in the distant past or future. Whatever you do, have fun doing it.

The following sections are additional rules that you can apply to the game, but only as needed and as you please.

Cards

Included in this book is a sheet of card templates. On it are cards that represent weapons, animals and prestation.

Weapon cards depict the weapon possessed and list all positive and Negative Traits attributed to the weapon. These cards need to be held when the weapon is produced. Some weapons, like swords, rifles and shotguns, are impossible to conceal without a trench coat and should be carried for public display at all times. Other cards can be kept hidden away until the weapon is drawn.

Animal cards indicate all the positive and Negative Traits of the animal in question (as listed below). Such cards are carried if a character has an animal companion. Others are given to those with the Nature of the Beast Discipline to indicate Traits received from the animal spirit contacted.

Prestation cards are blank, with space left for players to write in favors held over other characters. Favors are measured in Social Traits, usually ranging from one to five. These traits can be used from story to story until the favor owed is paid off. The name of the dupe— the one who owes the favor— should be written on the card.

More cards will be released in future Masquerade supplements.

Spirit Combat

Psychically projecting individuals can readily see each other as long as their line of sight is not impaired by physical world structures or creatures, or supernatural barriers. Such projecting characters may also communicate freely with one another. Only purely Mental and Social Disciplines, such as Aura Perception, Telepathy and Entrancement, may be used against one another (see the Psychic Projection Discipline in the Chapter Three for full details on the power).

A far more common form of confrontation among Psychically Projecting characters, however, is a mental duel. In this scenario, the combatants lash out at each other's psyches with either ego or intellect. Eventually, one falters and is driven back to his physical body. Alternatively, combatants may draw on their corporeal resources in a last ditch effort. The price of defeat for an individual who expends these last reserves, however, is death.

In game terms, characters in a psychic contest of wills perform contests much as physical combatants do, except they may only employ Mental and Social Traits. The two match wills and presence to overwhelm each other. The first one to yield in a challenge or expend all of his Mental or Social Traits is banished from the astral plane, back to his earthly body. Thus, if you ever relent in a contest of wills, you are immediately driven out of the astral plane, but if you continue struggling, you have a chance to remain there and drive your opponent out. A Kindred who loses or relents in this contest of will or Presence may not project her spirit from her body again until *all* Mental and Social Traits are regained. (It doesn't matter what Traits were lost in the astral plane, all Mental and Social Traits must be restored).

Those who refuse to be driven from the astral plane when the above rules demand may draw on the Physical Traits of their bodies for power (although Physical Disciplines cannot be used). In this way, a combatant may continue to fight, but not without a cost. Any Physical Traits spent and lost in astral plane contests are lost *permanently*. If a combatant expends the last of his Physical Traits, he perishes and his spirit dissipates. Even if a combatant uses Physical Traits in the astral plane and remains there (drives his opponent out), any Physical Traits bid and lost are still lost *permanently*.

Status Traits can be used in astral battles, but only if applicable to the situation. If combatants are fighting to the physical and spiritual death, one's respect within the Camarilla doesn't have much effect on an opponent.

Animals

The following are the Traits possessed by different animals that might be encountered in a story. Their traits can be bid in contests against Kindred (note that some new traits are introduced to reflect the unique natures of these animals). Each animal also has its own "Derangement". Animal Derangements are the natural tendencies of beasts, indicating how animals behave and in what kinds of situations they lose control (or "frenzy").

The Storyteller or a Narrator is free to alter the health levels of animals as compared to Kindred; a bear might have to be injured twice before being wounded, whereas a small rat might be killed after being injured only once. Furthermore, in dishing out damage, a bear might cause two health "levels" of damage for every blow, whereas a small rat might have to bite twice to reduce a vampire by one health "level."

• **Owl** — Insightful, Knowledgeable, Reflective, Discerning
Derangement: Must avoid well-lit areas

• **Wolf** — Ferocious, Tenacious, Cunning
Derangement: Deferment; will not act against the first individual who defeats it in any Physical contest

• **Bat** — Quick, Quick, Quick
Derangement: Must avoid well-lit areas

• **Rat** — Nimble, Resilient, Cunning
Derangement: Agoraphobic; fear and therefore avoidance of open spaces

• **Bear** — Stalwart, Resilient, Relentless, Intimidating
Derangement: Short-tempered; becomes enraged if injured

• **Eagle** — Vigilant, Vigilant, Dignified
Derangement: Claustrophobic; fear of enclosed spaces

• **Tiger** — Dexterous, Dexterous, Ferocious, Surefooted
Derangement: Solitary; seeks to be solitary and avoids others

• **Stallion** — Tireless, Robust, Surefooted, Brawny
Derangement: Reckless; wild with abandon

Because of their unique natures, animals often exist outside **The Masquerade's** rules. For instance, their Derangements are often different from those of Kindred. The Storyteller and Narrators are given wide latitude when playing animal characters, and they are free to bend the rules whenever an animal's nature is best represented by doing so. Narrators should also pay close attention to characters with the Nature of the Beast Discipline, ensuring that animal qualities are roleplayed satisfactorily.

Conversion Rules

Vampire is the tabletop storytelling game played in the same setting as **The Masquerade**. Because the rule systems of these two games are as different as petals and thorns, it might seem impossible to transport a character from one game to the other. But, because both are designed with the same priorities, conversion from one to the other is surprisingly easy.

Guidelines for converting a character created using the **Vampire** rules are presented here in five steps. These five steps parallel the steps of **Masquerade** character creation. Only the powers described in the main **Vampire** rulebook are covered here, but with an understanding of the conversion process and a little extrapolation, you should be able to convert all the powers available in other **Vampire** supplements.

Of course, if any of the conversion procedures do not properly convey your **Vampire** character in **Masquerade** terms, feel free to alter your **Masquerade** equivalent as required. A perfect duplicate, only under a different game system, might not be possible without some fudging of the following "rules".

Step One: Inspiration

This is the easiest step of the five. Static **Vampire** character information such as name, Demeanor, Nature, clan and generation transfers directly to **The Masquerade**. Both games share the same world and the same background.

The **Vampire** character's personality can be forced into one of **The Masquerade** character concepts, but it doesn't need to be. In essence, the converted character's personality need not change at all.

Step Two: Attributes

The adjective Trait system of **The Masquerade** corresponds to the point system for Attributes in **Vampire**. In **Vampire**, starting characters are allowed to distribute seven points to their primary Attribute category, five to their secondary and three to their tertiary. They also receive three initial points in each Attribute category, with one allocated to each subcategory. With the exception of these initial three points, the **Masquerade** character gets as many Attribute Traits as the **Vampire** character has Attribute points. So add up all the dots the **Vampire** character has in each Attribute category and subtract three from each— the resulting figure is the number of Traits the **Masquerade** character has in each Attribute category.

Now you have to choose exactly which Traits you have. **The Masquerade's** adjective Trait system describes characters with more diversity and precision than does **Vampire**. Because of **Vampire's** less than perfect match, you have to apply some creativity, deciding how your **Vampire** character's identity translates into adjectives.

Masquerade Trait categories— Physical, Social and Mental— can be subdivided into the same Attribute subcategories used in **Vampire**. For example, Physical Traits can be classified as Strength, Dexterity, Stamina and miscellaneous statistics. To keep the general trend of Attributes for the converted character, pick the same number of Traits (minus one) as points in the **Vampire** Attribute subcategories. (For example, if the original **Vampire** character has four points of Dexterity, choose Graceful, Lithe and Dexterous Traits, since these are related to Dexterity. The fourth Trait is lost because it is owed to a **Vampire** free point.)

Feel free to play with the number of **Vampire** Attributes you have so you can choose some miscellaneous Traits, too. Here is an informal breakdown of **Vampire's** Attributes in terms of **The Masquerade's** Traits:

Physical

Strength — Brawny, Wiry, Ferocious, Stalwart, Tough

Dexterity — Dexterous, Nimble, Graceful, Lithe

Stamina — Resilient, Tireless, Robust, Rugged, Enduring

Miscellaneous — Energetic, Tenacious, Athletic, Vigorous, Steady

Social

Charisma — Charming, Genial, Eloquent, Dignified, Charismatic

Manipulation — Empathetic, Commanding, Ingratiating, Persuasive, Beguiling

Appearance — Alluring, Magnetic, Seductive, Elegant, Gorgeous

Miscellaneous — Diplomatic, Expressive, Witty, Intimidating, Friendly

Mental

Perception — Insightful, Vigilant, Discerning, Attentive, Observant

Intelligence — Cunning, Knowledgeable, Reflective, Rational

Wits — Intuitive, Alert, Clever, Shrewd, Wily

Miscellaneous — Disciplined, Dedicated, Patient, Creative, Determined, Wise

Vampire's Virtues convert into three **Masquerade** traits. Conscience converts into the Social Trait of Compassionate. Self-Control converts into the Mental Trait of Calm. Courage converts into the Physical Trait of Stalwart. However, the **Masquerade** character only receives these traits if the **Vampire** character has a score of five in the Virtues.

René looks at her **Vampire** character sheet, which holds information on a character named Linda. She counts six dots in Physical, 12 dots in Social, and nine dots in Mental Attributes. She subtracts three in each and ends up with three Physical, nine Social, and six Mental traits for her converted **Masquerade** character. Now she has to choose what Traits are appropriate.

For Physical, she chooses Graceful, Resilient and Energetic, all of which reflect qualities of her **Vampire** character. The Traits are also chosen in roughly the same point distribution of her **Vampire** character's Attributes.

For Social Attributes, she picks Alluring twice and Seductive once. She selects two Empathetic Traits because of her **Vampire** character's high empathy, a Persuasive Trait, and a Beguiling Trait because of her **Vampire** character's high Subterfuge. She rounds this out with two Charming Traits (stemming from her **Vampire** character's high charisma).

For Mental Traits, she chooses Insightful, Observant, Cunning, Wily, Intuitive and Determined.

Step Three: Advantages

Masquerade Abilities are not rated by points. Otherwise, they serve the same purpose as their **Vampire** counterparts. Just take an Ability for each talent, skill or knowledge the **Vampire** character has of level three or more. Not all **Vampire's** talents, skills and knowledges exist in **The Masquerade**. You can create new **Masquerade** Abilities or choose ones that are close to **Vampire** talents, skills and knowledges.

René's converted character has Politics, Subterfuge, Animal Ken, Drive, Bureaucracy, Investigation and Law as **Masquerade** Abilities.

Disciplines in **The Masquerade** do not have point ratings as they do in **Vampire**. Instead, **The Masquerade** rates Disciplines in terms of relative power. If a **Vampire** character has a level three Discipline, the **Masquerade** character receives all equal and lesser Disciplines. You might decide to limit Disciplines that can be taken to clan allowances, or might just let the converted character have whatever Disciplines relate to the **Vampire** Disciplines the character has. (Discipline prerequisites may also be ignored, or imposed to limit what Disciplines the translated character can have.) Here is a chart to help you transfer **Vampire** Disciplines over to **Masquerade** Disciplines:

Vampire Discipline	Level Possessed	Masquerade Discipline
Animalism	• to ••	The Beast Within
	•••	The Beckoning
	••••	Song of Serenity
	•••••	Embrace of the Beast
Auspex	•	Heightened Senses
	••	Aura Perception
	•••	Spirit's Touch
	••••	Telepathy
	•••••	Physical Projection
Celerity	•	Alacrity
	•• to •••	Swiftness
	••••	Rapidity
	•••••	Fleetness
Dominate	•	Command
	••	Forgetful Mind
	•••	Mesmerism
	••••	Conditioning
	•••••	Possession
Fortitude	• to ••	Endurance
	•••	Mettle
	••••	Resilience
	•••••	Aegis
Obfuscate	• to ••	Unseen Presence
	•••	Mask of a Thousand Faces
	••••	Cloak the Gathering
	•••••	Soul Mask
Potence	•	Prowess
	•• to •••	Might
	••••	Vigor
	•••••	Puissance
Presence	•	Dread Gaze
	•• to •••	Entrancement
	••••	Summon
	•••••	Majesty
Protean	• to ••	Wolf's Claws
	•••	Earth Meld
	••••	Shadow of the Beast
	•••••	Form of Mist
Thaumaturgy	•	Blood Mastery
	••	Inquisition of Captive Vitae
	•••	Theft of Vitae
	••••	Potency of the Blood
	•••••	Cauldron of Blood

Rene's character has an Auspex of three which will give her Heightened Senses, Aura Perception and Spirit's Touch.

Influence Traits in **The Masquerade** can be equated based on the Background of the **Vampire** character. **Vampire** has an actual Background quality of Influence, but this quality is only a reflection of **The Masquerade's** Influence Trait; many factors make up **The Masquerade's** Influence Trait. Choose three **Masquerade** Influence Traits that reflect the **Vampire** character's Background. If the **Vampire** character has a lot of clout, more Influence Traits can be taken.

Step Four: Last Touches

Characters in **The Masquerade** only have three Blood Traits. Characters in **Vampire** can have several Blood Points. After conversion, a character simply has three Blood Traits, and that's all there is to it, unless he is of lower than 13th generation (see the "Generation Table").

Characters in Vampire often have more than one point (the equivalent of a Trait) of Willpower. Since **Masquerade** characters usually only have one Willpower Trait, excess Willpower points can be translated into Mental traits that reflect on the **Masquerade** character's strength of mind. **Vampire's** Willpower points can be translated into Mental Traits like Disciplined, Dedicated and Determined. However, these "extra" Mental Traits replace any Mental Traits that the **Masquerade** character has already been assigned, above. Otherwise, a **Vampire** character with several Willpower points would create a **Masquerade** character with immense mental faculties.

If the **Vampire** character is lower than 13th generation, he has more than one Willpower Trait when translated. This means the character has one less Mental Trait to take as a reflection of mental fortitude. Of course, this isn't a penalty by any means, as you do get more than one Willpower Trait.

Vampire characters have weaknesses according to clan. The Humanity of **Vampire** characters is also reflected by points, while **The Masquerade's** Humanity is reflected by Beast Traits. Low Humanity can be reflected by taking an additional Beast Trait.

Choose Derangements that reflect the Vampire character's personality. If any mental quirks possessed by the **Vampire** character cannot be equated to **Masquerade** Derangements, make up new Derangements.

There are no freebie points in **The Masquerade**. The closest things are Negative Traits, which allow for the application of more positive Traits. As freebie points in **Vampire** are already taken into account in the translation of the character, freebie points themselves do not have to be accounted for here.

However, if the **Vampire** character has a zero or one in any Attribute, that might represent a Negative Trait for the **Masquerade** character. Choose any Negative Trait that seems appropriate and add a positive Trait to counterbalance it. We recommend you do this no more than five times. Furthermore, if the **Vampire** character has any low Virtues—a score of one or zero—choose Negative Traits to reflect this. If the **Vampire** character has a low Conscience, take a Negative Social Trait, such as Callous. If the **Vampire** character has a low Courage, take a Negative Physical Trait, such as Cowardly. If the **Vampire** character has a low Self-Control, take a Negative Mental Trait, such as Violent.

Also, take Submissive as a Negative Mental Trait if the **Vampire** character has less than two points of Willpower.

Here is an informal breakdown of Negative Traits:

Physical

Strength — Puny, Flabby

Dexterity — Lame, Clumsy

Stamina — Delicate, Sickly, Decrepit

Miscellaneous — Lethargic, Docile, Cowardly

Social

Charisma — Obnoxious, Dull, Callous, Condescending

Manipulation — Naive, Tactless

Appearance — Repugnant, Bestial

Miscellaneous — Untrustworthy, Shy

Mental

Perception — Oblivious, Shortsighted

Intelligence — Ignorant, Forgetful

Wits — Gullible, Witless

Miscellaneous — Predictable, Impatient, Submissive, Violent

Step Five: Spark of Life

Give the converted character a number of Status Traits appropriate to the **Vampire** character's Background. There is a Status score in **Vampire**, but **The Masquerade's** Status Traits are a reflection of many aspects. Thus, **The Masquerade** character's Status traits may be based on the **Vampire** character's Status score, or on any other qualities of the **Vampire** character's authority or clout.

Rene's converted character receives her Malkavian Derangement of Catatonic (a new one) and Regression, and takes two Status traits. She's done.

THE MASQUERADE

Player Name: _____

Character Name: _____

Chronicle: _____

Physical Traits

Social Traits

Mental Traits

Disciplines

Status

Abilities

Concept

Coterie: _____
Demeanor: _____
Experience: _____

Clan: _____
Nature: _____
Haven: _____

Backgrounds

Influence

Health

☥ **Bruised** — One Trait penalty to initiating challenges.

☥ **Wounded** — Lose all ties. If your opponent has more traits than you do, he may also make an additional test.

☥ **Incapacitated** — Out of play for ten minutes—must heal at least one wound level before you can move or challenge.

☥ **Torpor** — Out of play until revived by the blood of a vampire at least three generations lower than yourself.

Blood Pool: ○○○○○○○○○○ □□□□□□ □□□□ □□□

Willpower: ○○○○○○○○○○ □□□□□

Blood Trait

Blood Trait

Blood Trait

Blood Trait

Blood Trait

Blood Trait

Blood Trait

Blood Trait

Blood Trait

Blood Trait

Blood Trait

Blood Trait

Blood Trait

Blood Trait

Blood Trait

Blood Trait

Character Name _____

Character Name _____

Character Name _____

Character Name _____

Character Name _____

Character Name _____

Character Name _____

Character Name _____

Character Name _____

Character Name _____

Character Name _____

Character Name _____

Character Name _____

Character Name _____

Character Name _____

Character Name _____

Status Trait _____

Status Trait _____

Status Trait _____

Status Trait _____

Status Trait _____

Status Trait _____

Status Trait _____

Status Trait _____

Status Trait _____

Status Trait _____

Status Trait _____

Status Trait _____

Status Trait _____

Status Trait _____

Status Trait _____

Status Trait _____

Character Name ____

Character Name ____

Character Name ____

Character Name ____

Character Name ____

Character Name ____

Character Name ____

Character Name ____

Character Name ____

Character Name ____

Character Name ____

Character Name ____

Character Name ____

Character Name ____

Character Name ____

Character Name ____

OBLIVION

live action for the dead
winter 1996

Beauty. Passion. Horror.

Expanded.

Hardcover.

More hopeful.

More terrifying.

Completely rewritten.

Art from George Pratt.

Original fiction from Rick Hautala.

More interaction with the physical World of Darkness.

The same attention to content and aesthetics that made

Mage: The Ascension's Second Edition outsell **Vampire: The Masquerade.**

Wraith: The Oblivion, Second Edition
Eternity Is Under New Management

WORLD OF